GIRL OUT OF SIGHT

HELEN MATTHEWS

CHAPTER ONE

Odeta is learning English, but she hasn't told Kreshnik. She'll keep it secret from him until they arrive in London. He'll be so surprised.

As daylight evaporates, she waits, nursing the bubble of excitement that lodges in her chest whenever she thinks of him. Fidgeting on a wooden kitchen chair, she thumbs through her textbook and glances at the door. It's a chilly evening, but she's opened the window to neutralise the smell of the lamb stew they'd eaten for dinner. Her mother had wanted to invite Kreshnik to eat with them, but Odeta made an excuse.

It's not that she's ashamed of her family. Her grandparents were peasant farmers, toiling in fields seized from local landowners in Enver Hoxher's agricultural reforms. But in recent years, her father (who owns the village shop) has prospered.

Odeta worries about her parents' manners. She doesn't want Kreshnik to see her dad lighting up one of his disgusting cigars and belching out smoke while he shovels chunks of meat into his gob. She's afraid her mother might decide to set down her fork and scoop up food from her plate with a chunk of bread. When her mother eats with her hands, she seems not to notice rivulets of tomato gravy dribbling down her chin. So Odeta had told Kreshnik to come after dinner, to drink sugary coffee and a glass of *raki* with her father.

The book she is using to learn English is about the daily life of a stiff British family. She'd spotted it in a box of cheap novels at the market, and was attracted by the cover picture of a box-shaped house with windows on each side of the front door and a garden with grass and flowers. The page she's reading has a coloured sketch of a woman and a boy sitting at a table. Their conversation is so stilted. She tries reading it out loud to see if it will make more sense:

"Good morning, Dick," said Mother.

"Good morning, Mother. Where is the dog, Nip?"

"Nip is in the garden. He is playing."

She flicks back to the first page. An ink stamp inside the cover reads *Woodgate School Library*. It's dated 1959, and a thick black line has been drawn diagonally across the flysheet. So the book is meant for young children – and it's older than her mother. Working hard to make sense of it, she leans forward and props her chin in her hand, and her dark hair swishes across the book as she turns the pages.

The scrape of a footstep on the back step, followed by a sharp tap on the kitchen door, makes her jump. Odeta hides her book under a corner of the embroidered tablecloth. She's on her feet, her heart is thumping, and her high heels tap-tapping as she crosses the flagstone floor to open the door. For the two years since her father took her out of school to help him in the shop, her days have been measured out in scoops of tedium. Soon she'll turn eighteen. She'd always thought nothing interesting would ever happen to her, but then Kreshnik came into her life and everything changed.

"Greetings, Odeta," he says, handing her a single rose. It's dusky red, and a thorn pricks her hand as she takes it from him. He's carrying a much larger bouquet, and she guesses this is for her mother. In the twilight his face appears monochrome and she can't quite make out his expression, but as he steps inside she sees he is smiling. She exhales and her whole body relaxes. She's wearing her highest heels, but she has to tip her head back to smile up into his face and mumble thanks for the rose.

"Come." She holds out her hand and draws him inside, her fingers tingling at his touch. "My father is waiting for you."

She leads him along the narrow passage. They pass the locked door that opens into the shop where strings of onions and garlic hang from the rafters. And there are carcasses in there too: two of them in the cold store room, freshly-slaughtered and waiting for her father to carve them into chops and joints. On those days, blood and offal will stain the straw-covered floor and the smell of flesh will mingle with the scent of cinnamon pastries.

Shopkeepers in the surrounding villages have set up business in their front rooms, so their families must now retreat to the kitchen as their only living space. Odeta's father's vision was bolder. He built his shop on the front of the house: a concrete extension with small windows, as ugly as the thousands of Cold War bunkers that still litter the Albanian countryside. He's never bothered to render the walls, which are made of concrete blocks sandwiched unevenly together, but at least he's preserved the sitting room as a place for the family to congregate.

Kreshnik slips his phone into his pocket as Odeta pushes open the door and ushers him inside. Her parents have switched on the central electric light, as well as the table lamp with its olive-green fringed shade. Her father conserves electricity more closely than a miser guards his gold stash. They have made this great sacrifice to welcome Kreshnik.

Her father levers his bulky frame out of his chair and strides across the room.

"Welcome," he says, greeting the visitor with a solid handshake and a slap on the back. "I am Idriz Lazami, and this is my wife, Besarta."

"Kreshnik." His name occupies the room. Odeta doesn't know his family name. He seems to have no time for old-fashioned formality; it must be his city ways.

She tries to view the familiar sitting room through her guest's eyes. The upholstered armchairs are lumpy, but the chairbacks are draped with starched linen covers, and the wooden furniture glows with a mellow patina from years of polishing. On the mantelpiece are family photos: her grandmother, stern-faced in a long black skirt and white apron; her parents' wedding day; her brothers in neat school uniforms and short trousers.

Her mother blushes as she accepts the flowers, and her father pours clear liquid from a decanter into a tumbler, filling it almost to the brim. Kreshnik takes the glass and sips, while Odeta's father drains his own smaller glass and slams it down on the table with a shout of "Ha!" The men begin a round of toasts – to good health, to happy families, to beautiful Albanian daughters. Idriz doesn't offer his wife or daughter a drink. Odeta places her rose on the mantelpiece and sits down; Besarta remains standing, cradling her bouquet.

Evidently alerted by the rumble of laughter and the clink of glasses, her young brothers, Leon and Afrim, tumble into the room. They scuffle on the carpet, grappling with each other like puppies in exaggerated play-fight, until Idriz gives them a stern look and they spring apart and stand to attention. Besarta scolds them and gives their backsides a light slap. She hands the flowers to Leon and sends him off with instructions to put them in water.

Kreshnik sets down his glass, clears his throat and glances at Odeta. She nods, and he gives her a warm smile that sets her heart racing. It's time for him to broach the subject he's come to discuss. She fiddles with the pearl-and-gold bracelet Kreshnik gave her, and shivers. It isn't cold, but she notices a pattern of goosebumps running along her arms like embroidery stitching. She should have warned her parents. Perhaps they think he's come on a mission to ask for her hand in marriage. She flicks back her long black hair, letting it tumble down behind her shoulders, then juts out her chin and straightens her spine. She's no old-fashioned country girl waiting for a chance to marry, settle down in her village and turn into a brood mare. Perhaps one day in the future she'll want that, but now she's restless. She's been toiling in the shop for too long, and she's still only seventeen. It's time to get out and see the world.

Kreshnik takes a gold-plated cigarette case out of his pocket and offers it to her father, who sniffs suspiciously. The cigarettes are unfamiliar: the tipped variety. He takes one and Kreshnik lights it for him. Her father puffs, and Kreshnik begins.

"For two years I've been living in England," he says. "My cousins own a workshop in London, making sample garments for the fashion industry."

"How long have they lived there?"

"Ten years. My cousin and his wife will help me find work opportunities for Odeta."

"But Odeta doesn't sew." Her father frowns, and his bushy eyebrows knit together.

She glares at him, humiliated. Everyone's eyes are still on Kreshnik. A cold draught whips across the room as ten-year-old Leon sneaks back in and squats down on the floor next to his brother.

Kreshnik shakes his head and laughs. "She wouldn't need to sew. My cousins are looking for models. Fashion models to feature in their clothing catalogues. Girls with a fresh look and style are always in demand."

Odeta doesn't look up as he says these words, but feels her cheeks turning scarlet.

"Odeta has that elusive something," he tells them. "Exotic cheekbones, moonshine eyes and a shy smile. She could be the face of the future."

Idriz gawps at her, and then turns back to Kreshnik. Her father's cheeks are glowing, ruddy under the harsh electric light. Is he going to criticise her appearance? Destroy the fragile confidence Kreshnik has given her?

Then Kreshnik plays his ace card. He tells Idriz how much she could earn each month.

The older man's Adam's apple begins to quiver, his jaw slackens, his mouth drops open, and a bead of saliva stretches across from his lower lip to his chin. She can tell his businessman instincts have taken over. Usually his head is full of numbers that don't add up to much.

Besarta gets to her feet, and her full skirt makes a swishing noise as she crosses the room and places her hand on Kreshnik's arm. She fingers the sleeve of his jacket, and the softness of the cloth seems to tell her all she needs to know. "Go well, my Odeta," she harrumphs, making the sign of the cross on her upper chest. "Remember your old parents and your brothers. Many mouths to feed in this family."

Odeta squirms in her chair and looks down at the floor. Her brothers are sprawling on their stomachs, digging their elbows into the carpet and propping their chins up on their hands. They've been listening to every word, goggle-eyed. Leon nudges his brother in the ribs. Afrim topples closer to the floor and buries his giggles in the hearthrug.

A frisson of fear travels up Odeta's spine and tickles her neck. She feels the weight of family expectations descend on her slim shoulders. What if she doesn't get modelling work straight away? Perhaps she'll work in a shop, like she does at home?

The air in the room smells of stale cigarette smoke. Her parents look at Odeta, exchange glances, and sit with dreamy stares and slim smiles on their faces. Even fidgety Afrim stays still.

Kreshnik gets slowly to his feet and prepares to leave. He looks down on them all from his considerable height.

"Ponder on it for a few days," he says. "Then we'll speak again."

He bows his head to show respect to her parents, then swivels sideways and flashes Odeta a quick smile. She senses his eyes lingering on her, scorching her, making her burn up inside. Like the day he took those photographs...

She shivers again. Best not to think about those pictures.

CHAPTER TWO

The sickly aroma of over-ripe fruit wafts up from a box of plums on the table outside the shop. Odeta picks out a couple of squashed ones sprouting grey mildew moustaches, and with a deft aim pitches them under the thorny hedge that runs along the boundary of their property. A cloud of dust billows up as they hit the ground.

The sun has dipped below the horizon and the sky is a pinkish-orange; it's time to shut up the shop. She's still wearing her work apron, soiled with earth after a day spent shovelling potatoes out of sacks into customers' baskets. They had few fresh vegetables in the shop today; only some tomatoes and wilting salad. The customers weren't happy, but even if there had been vegetables they couldn't have afforded them. Three people asked for credit, and her father backed away into the storeroom, leaving her to deal with them as usual. He knows Odeta is more hard-headed, less connected to the old days and unmoved by sob-stories.

She picks up the wooden box and tucks it under her arm, wincing as a splinter snags her forearm. Back inside the shop she removes her dusty apron, folds it and places it under the counter. Her father is up at the school watching her brothers play an early evening football match; her mother is away visiting her sick sister in the next village and won't return until tomorrow. Odeta will have to make supper for her father and brothers.

She goes back outside and unfastens the hooks that hold the blue-painted shutters flush against the front wall of the shop, letting them swing free. How many times has she done this over the last two years, and how many more days to come? The tedium of opening and closing the shop; the strain of dragging sacks of vegetables into position; the boredom of standing all day behind the counter. But perhaps it won't be for much longer? Soon she will escape with Kreshnik to England.

Her father built the shop on shallow foundations, and the walls have gradually nestled deeper into the earth. The shutters no longer line up with the windows, and she has to force them into the alcove before she can draw the iron bar across and padlock it. She breathes heavily, and lets out a mild curse as she leans her full weight against them and pushes.

The light pressure of a hand descends on her shoulder. "Here, let me help."

She spins round. "Kreshnik!" Her face breaks into a smile, but her heart is racing. Thank goodness she's taken off her grimy apron.

She gratefully steps aside and lets him take over. He has height and strength, but he doesn't approach the task with brute force. He stands back, examines the angle of slippage, slides his hand beneath one shutter and lifts it above the level of the sill. She watches him ease the shutters into place, making it look effortless.

"Thank you."

He nods. There's not a mark on his white short-sleeved

shirt, and the tempo of his breathing is unaltered. "I have something to show you. Can we go inside and have coffee?"

She hesitates. Her mother wouldn't like her to invite a man inside the house when no one else is there, but Besarta doesn't know that she has already been alone with Kreshnik on several occasions at his uncle's house. Somehow, inviting him into her family home seems different. Taboo. It's not as if they're engaged. Her parents haven't yet said if she can go to England. Her mother is probably discussing it with her aunt this very day.

"Go around to the back door," she says, disappearing into the shop to lock the door from the inside. She decides not to take Kreshnik through the shop because she hasn't closed the cold store. She doesn't want him to see the stains on the floor and the fragments of bone left behind from her father's butchery session. It's her job to clear those up. Later, she will don her earth-stained apron, pour soapy water from a bucket across the floor and sweep it towards the hole in the wall that leads to an outside drain. When the floor of the cold store is dry, she'll scatter fresh straw on top of the old.

She glances at her reflection in the shop window, wishing Kreshnik wouldn't turn up without warning. She doesn't feel at all glamorous, but in the dingy glass she can see her eyes are sparkling. Did he mean it when he said they shone like the moon? Her hair smells clean, but it's a mess. She doesn't have a comb so it'll have to do. She can hear the back door rattling and quickens her pace to reach the kitchen. Although the back door isn't locked, it sticks when she tries to pull it open. That's strange, because there's been no recent rain to cause the wood to buckle and swell. For a fleeting moment, she senses the house is trying to protect her from something. But from what? Damage to her reputation? Huh! She laughs. She's not superstitious. Or scared.

"Parents not around?" Kreshnik asks, placing a fat brown envelope on the kitchen table.

She shakes her head.

"Good." Kreshnik grasps her around the waist and pulls her towards him, pressing her so close that she can feel his ribs and every contour of his body. He rests his chin on top of her head, trapping her face against his upper chest. Other men she knows reek of tobacco and sweat, but Kreshnik smells of pine forests. It's clean and pleasant, but she's suffocating and twists her head sideways to gulp in some air. Kreshnik takes hold of a hank of her hair from near the crown and winds it around his fingers. He eases her head back so she stares up into his face. She tries to read his expression. Is it desire, or could it be love? He bends and covers her mouth with his, kissing her until her lips part and he can push his tongue between them. When he finally lets her go, her head is whirling and she puts out her hand to grasp a chair-back for support.

"Coffee," he says. It sounds more like an order than a question.

She nods and fills the kettle, then takes the metal pot and scrapes out the coffee grounds left over from breakfast.

Kreshnik sits at the table, one hand resting on the splodged oilskin tablecloth. With an index finger, he slits open the envelope and draws out a swatch of paperwork. A slim booklet, with the double-headed eagle crest on the cover, tumbles out onto the table. He picks it up and examines it, flicking through the pages. Odeta is curious, but she busies herself with making the coffee and pretends she's not watching. He dangles the notebook between his thumb and forefinger, waving it in front of her, whipping it away until he seems to tire of teasing and hands it to her.

"Your passport," he says, flipping it open at the photo page.

The solemn face of a young dark-haired woman, eyes open slightly wider than usual, stares out at her.

"That's me!"

He nods, smiling and showing off two rows of ivory-white, even teeth. No one in Albania has teeth that good.

"You took the photograph of me on that day?"

"I did."

"Let me see." She reaches out to take the passport from his hand. On the stove, the kettle hisses and the kitchen clouds with steam. She ignores it, leafs through the pages and begins to read.

"It says here *Marije Kaleci. Born 1995.* That's not me."

He shrugs. "It's the best I could do."

"But I don't understand. That's my picture but some other girl's name."

"Listen, Odeta." His voice is steely. "A passport costs over seven thousand lek. Do you have that money?"

She thinks of the daily takings in the shop, and the meagre pocket money her father hands her each week. "No."

"Then why not use a secondhand one?"

Is he telling her the truth? She doesn't know about such things. He flicks through the sheaf of documents and pulls out one at a time to show to her. There's Marije's birth certificate and other information about her.

"You'll need to study these papers and remember Marije's personal details. Do you think you can do that?"

She nods, and pulls a strand of her long hair across her face so he can't see her confusion. "But why do I need to know those things about Marije?"

"This passport isn't all you need, Odeta. Marije's passport was issued before passports stored biometric data in a microchip. Even for a short tourist visit to England, we Albanians need a visa. I've filled in the online form and made an appointment for you next Tuesday in Tirana. You'll have to provide your fingerprints, too."

Her thoughts are all jumbled up: fingerprints, visa. Her head is full of noise, and she wants to press her hands over her ears to block it and figure out why it feels that something isn't quite right. Does she want to go to England with Kreshnik? Yes, of course she does, but it's all so confusing.

"So why go to all this trouble? If I need to get a visa, why can't I have my own passport in my own name?" She glances around the kitchen, drawing strength from familiar objects: a blue bowl with a crusting from the morning's breakfast, or the cracked teapot no one ever uses because they don't drink tea.

"Don't you trust me, Odeta?" he asks. "Do you want to ask your father to spend so much money?"

No, she wouldn't want that. He'd be sure to use it as a reason to stop her going to England. Her shoulders droop, and the kettle yells ever louder. She gets to her feet and attends to it. A thought occurs to her. "What about Marije? Won't she be needing her passport?"

"You're full of questions, my pretty one." He taps his forefinger against the side of his nose. "We're going to England soon and we're going to be together. Let's celebrate that. And as for Marije – no. She won't be needing it."

CHAPTER THREE

Odeta and her mother rise in the grey light of dawn to start baking. After a week of waiting, her father finally gave his consent. Tomorrow she leaves for London. She would have chosen to spend the day quietly at home, but her father has invited family and neighbours for a celebration.

"Why did Dad ask so many?"

"He wants them to join in wishing you God-speed." Besarta dons her apron and ties the strings in a limp bow. "Daughter, I hoped to give you something for London," her lip quivers, "but this party – so expensive."

Odeta understands. Her mother must have raided the meagre savings she keeps in a glazed pot on the mantelpiece to buy food for their guests. Where else could she get money? She has no bank account and no access to the store's takings. Idriz expects his wife to cater for the family's needs with left-over vegetables and gone-off meat from the shop. Every Friday he hands her a small bundle of folded notes, clutching them so tightly she practically has to tug the money out of his fist.

"Don't worry." Odeta pats her mother's hand. "When I find work in London I will send money home to you."

Idriz has closed the shop for the whole day – something that's never happened before. Disgruntled customers turn up outside; some have travelled down from hillside villages. When they read the *Closed* sign pasted onto the shutters, they rattle the door-handle or tramp round to the rear of the building and rap on the glass pane of the kitchen door.

Odeta sighs and opens it. "We're closed all day," she says. The customers must be able to smell the home baking – chocolate and honey – and she can understand their frustration. If they need milk, or eggs, or anything in a tin or packet, Odeta fetches it from the shop. But she won't serve meat or vegetables, and she won't open the shop door.

By the time Idriz descends, unshaven and grouchy, the kitchen table is dusted with a fine layer of flour. Racks of baked goods are piling up – sweet and savoury fusing together. The boys sprint into the kitchen, yawning and rubbing sleep from their eyes. Besarta shoos them away, but Odeta suggests they help out.

"Look, Afrim, fetch that folding table and put it outside the back door." She turns to Leon. "You can be shopkeeper. Here's a pot for the money. Afrim can be your runner and fetch things from the shop. Afrim, take your time. Don't bump into Mum."

Afrim weaves around Besarta as she bends to open the oven.

Odeta balances on a chair, lifts down glasses one by one from a high shelf, and polishes them with a cloth until they sparkle. Her mother takes a tray of small cakes out of the oven, but they are blackened around the edges. "Bad omen," she whispers, her cheeks sinking into the hollows where a trainee dentist extracted too many molars. Once she was beautiful, but it's hard to see that now.

"No, Ma," Odeta comforts her. She knows her mother is already mourning the forthcoming departure of her eldest child. She takes a sharp knife and pares off the burnt bits. "See – no one could tell." Besarta takes Odeta's hand and squeezes it, but her eyes are still sad.

Leon and Afrim shut up the makeshift shop and carry kitchen chairs with their woven rush seats through into the sitting room. Eight-year-old Afrim can carry two at a time, upended with the legs waving in the air. But his brother, two years older, can only manage one and has to pause to rest halfway along the hall. When he was five, a lung infection kept Leon in hospital for two months. He defied the doctors' predictions by making a recovery, but he'll never grow as strong and active as his brother.

Idriz stops his sons from taking the last chair, settles down heavily on it and lights up a cigarette. He demands coffee, and Odeta pours it for him.

"Come here, daughter, and talk to me." His voice sounds plaintive, but she shakes her head. She's finished polishing the glasses, so she starts buffing up the silver plates they use on special occasions.

"No, Pa. Too much to do."

He talks to her anyway. The usual monologue about his hopes and dreams; about everything he's sacrificed for his children. She's heard it before, but this time he's moved the script on to musing about her future and what she must do for the family. *Lah lah lah*, she sings in her head to block out his words.

The first guests roll up at midday.

"Greetings, Brother," says Idriz. Uncle Ervin nods as he dabs at his forehead with a grubby handkerchief.

"You came by furgon, then?" The shared passenger minibus will have dropped them some distance away, and Ervin's wife Maria is red-faced and wheezy from the half-hour walk. She plonks a wicker basket, covered with a red checked cloth, down on the kitchen floor. Odeta guesses it contains eggs, as if they didn't have enough from their own hens and in the shop. Everyone edges round it.

Uncle Ervin is five years younger than Idriz, but his eldest daughter is already married, heavily pregnant with her first child and cannot travel. Idriz is sitting on the only chair left in the kitchen, so Maria parks her sturdy buttocks on the edge of the table, knocking a salver onto the floor. Ervin leans against the wall to take the weight off his feet.

"Besarta, bring coffee for my brother."

She hovers, uncertain. "Give that to me, Mother." Odeta takes the tray from her hands. Besarta makes coffee.

Soon the house is thronged with people. Odeta wanders around, offering homemade snacks to distant relatives she hasn't seen since her childhood and people she recognises as customers from the shop. Today everyone wants to kiss her cheek or pat her on the back. Perhaps they hope some of her good fortune will rub off on them.

Idriz is pouring out glasses of wine and *raki*, measuring each one – a measly two fingers. Odeta guesses he doesn't trust his guests to help themselves. He knows all about shrinkage. It's too easy for someone's backpack or coat pocket to swallow up a bottle of *raki*.

Besarta bustles from room to room, replenishing snacks. When someone detains her long enough to chat, she grips her crucifix and waggles it towards Heaven. During her childhood, religion was officially stamped out in Albania; churches were turned into cinemas or community halls, and she was starved of this means of expression. Now that things have changed she embraces it in all its forms – the ceremony, the comfort, the language. She's always giving thanks to God for something or other. Today it's her eldest child, her golden daughter. "So proud," she murmurs. Odeta knows she's blessed; most families don't value their daughters half as much.

To please her parents, she's changed into traditional clothes: a long black skirt and a white blouse with an embroidered yoke. She feels like a freak. The blouse is high-necked and fastens right up to her throat. It's chokingly tight, so she's undone the three top buttons.

Kreshnik has been invited to the party, but he's not arrived yet. With every new arrival, Odeta's heart skips a beat. She overhears a cousin remarking to her father that no one around here seems to know this man, Kreshnik, or his family.

"We live in modern times," Idriz replies, knocking back another glass of *raki* and wiping the back of his hand across his mouth. "These young men from the city – they travel. They understand the world. They know how to make money."

"Yet many of our own young men from the village have worked in London."

"Pah!" Idriz is not impressed. "But what do they do? They don't speak the language! I hear they work at hand car wash." He clears his throat and spits a gob of phlegm, but he's in his own sitting room, not in the street, so he catches it in his hand and wipes it on his trousers. Odeta is used to her father's habits, but wishes he was not so coarse.

"So where does their money come from?" The cousin is persistent in his questioning.

Idriz shakes his head. "That English money buys good value over here. I hear they wash cars seven days a week."

The room is crammed with people, and smells of cheese and sweat. Odeta opens a window. She collects up some half-eaten snacks from the table, noticing the polished wood is marked with rings where guests have set down their glasses. As she carries plates along the corridor towards the kitchen, Uncle Ervin approaches. She steps to one side to let him pass, but he puts a chubby hand on her arm and stops to talk to her. They are about the same height, but her uncle doesn't look at her face. He's staring at her breasts.

"Odeta, niece," he begins. His voice is gruff. "Take care."

"Of course, Uncle. I always take care."

"You are sure about your young man?"

She sizzles with annoyance. "He's not my young man, Uncle." What has her father been saying? If Kreshnik turns up and finds her father telling everyone they are engaged, what would he say? "I like him, but – he's just a friend. Helping me to go to London to start a career. That's all." Every time she spins this story she thinks of his kisses, and wishes she knew his true feelings for her. Perhaps in the city kisses don't mean so much. Of course, she wants to be with Kreshnik – not here in this village, but strolling hand-in-hand with him through London, Rome or New York.

Her uncle's hair is grizzled brown, and the stubble on his chin is grey. His face has a smudged look, as if a child sketched it then took an eraser and rubbed part of him out. In the narrow corridor, she feels his body press up against hers and smells *raki* on his breath. She takes a step away, but he catches hold of her wrist, drawing her closer. It's as if he is looking deep inside her and decoding details of her relationship with Kreshnik that her parents would never in a million years suspect.

"Men may say one thing but act another," he says. "He's travelled abroad, this Kreshnik. He will know foreign women. Who can say what his plans towards you may be?"

Odeta shivers. Whether it's the awkward proximity of her uncle's body or the impact of his words, she couldn't say. She tenses and stares at the floor. "I have to go and help my mother," she says, easing away from his clutch.

In the kitchen, she stands at the sink rinsing *raki* glasses and drying them with a cloth. Uncle Ervin's words won't leave her mind. His questions have jolted her back to the day, several months ago, when she first met Kreshnik.

———

She was alone in the shop, perched on a stool behind the counter, reading a magazine. It was a hot afternoon, the quiet time of day. There'd been no customers since lunchtime. Flies were buzzing over the sheep's cheese and she swatted them with her magazine. The sound of a car made her look up. It wasn't the usual phut-phut engine but more of a purr. Peering into the sunshine she saw the dark silhouette of a tall man get out of a Mercedes and stride towards the shop's entrance. She watched him duck his head to enter under the low lintel. Once inside, he straightened his back and brushed dust off his left sleeve.

"Can I help you?"

"Cigarettes?" He looked at her with an expression she couldn't decipher. She was used to men staring at her, their eyes holding many kinds of expressions – some lustful, others mournful like a puppy. There was something about this man's gaze that reminded her of the studied concentration of farmers at the market sizing up livestock. He seemed to be performing some kind of calculation; she could almost see the figures running behind his eyes.

Don't be foolish, Odeta she told herself.

"Just this kind." She placed a pack on the counter. "And tobacco."

"You don't have imported?" His eyes drilled into her and she flinched.

"These are from Greece."

"Men from your village don't go to Europe much, then?"

"They do – but..."

Yes, they did, and they brought back cigarettes and premium alcohol, but they sold it privately to friends. Why would they trade it through the shop when they could sell on the black market and take all the profit themselves?

"I'll take these." He held out some notes. Calmly she took them. He offered his upturned palm for the change but she placed it on the counter. She couldn't risk letting her fingers touch his.

"Anything else?"

He lingered, seeming in no hurry to leave. "Tell me about yourself. You finished high school?"

She flushed. "Left early. I didn't graduate. My father needed me to work in the shop."

Indeed he did. With Odeta running the shop, Idriz could spend his own days drinking coffee with other men at the café in the square. Sometimes he sat outside under the trees watching the village go about its business. He would chew on his unlit pipe, taking it out of his mouth only when someone stopped to chat and offered him a cigarette. Twice a week he would drive his old van up into the hills, rattling over the potholed roads, calling in on farmers to collect their produce and drink their new season plum *raki*, puttering home in time for dinner.

The shop bell clanged again, and an old man entered, wearing a flat cap and tweed jacket. He stomped up to the counter and shouldered the stranger aside with the jealous territorialism of the elderly. Odeta felt a prickle of alarm. The stranger would be sure to leave now. She didn't want him to go.

But the stranger didn't leave. He strolled away from the counter and looked around the shop with his hands clasped behind his back. She watched him, over the head of the old man, as he peered at undecipherable labels on tins of vegetables. He bent down and scooped up a handful of herbs from an open sack as the scent of rosemary filled the air.

She served the old man quickly, side-stepping his

conversational gambits, never taking her eyes off the stranger. When the old man hobbled out, the stranger held the door open for him.

"Good afternoon," he said and shut the door briskly, almost trapping the old man's jacket.

Odeta giggled, and the stranger grinned back.

"Have you visited the capital?"

"Tirana? Not since I was a child. I used to go there for gymnastics competitions – you know."

But he seemed not to hear her, and his questions headed in another direction. "Any relatives in Tirana?"

She wrinkled her brow. "A few, I think. We don't see them much."

"How about these families...?" He reeled off a list of names she didn't recognise. "Do you know them?"

She shook her head. "I don't think so."

Using his fingernail, he slit the cellophane wrapper of the cigarette packet, peeled it off and crumpled it in his hand. She noticed his fingernails were white and clean.

"You want one?"

She shook her head. "You must go outside to smoke."

Idriz permitted smoking in every room in his house. He himself smoked in the kitchen, the bedroom and even when using the toilet, but he drew the line at smoking in the shop. She gestured to a narrow strip of decking that formed the shop porch. Two chairs, one rusty metal and one wooden, stood on either side of the doorway. The decking creaked as he sat down. Odeta leaned against one of the posts that supported the porch, balancing on one foot, and watched him light his cigarette.

"Won't you sit down?"

She shook her head, but he leaned forward and drew the metal chair closer. "Please." He patted the seat, dislodging flecks of peeling paint. She sat, straight-backed but perching on the edge, while he puffed on his cigarette and appraised her through curls of smoke. "You said you took part in gymnastics competitions?"

So he had been listening.

She nodded. "From age seven, gymnastics was my life." Would it be immodest to tell him she won every junior competition she entered? "My coach thought I might one day compete for my country." Her shoulders drooped. "But it was not to be. I had a fall from the balance beam."

Her broken ankle had mended, of course. No one else noticed that even now she sometimes walked with a limp when the pain was bad. She always covered it with a smile.

"I'm sorry," he said, his face softening. He began to talk about himself. She'd already guessed he was educated, but it didn't sound as if he'd finished his studies either. Instead he'd joined the exodus of young Albanian men travelling first to Greece, then Italy. "My name is Kreshnik. For some years I have been in London," he said. "Working for my cousins."

"What do they do?"

"Clothing business. But London is a special city   you should go. All the world is there. So many rich people." He spoke of rock concerts in Hyde Park, and mixing with celebrities. "You have heard of Princes William and Harry?"

"I think so." Her eyes grew wider as she lapped up his stories, but if he was in the fashion business, perhaps he really did know everyone.

By the time he climbed back into his car and started the engine, she'd agreed to meet him at the café in town on her day off.

CHAPTER FOUR

The party is waning along with the daylight. Neighbours slip away, their shadows lingering on the walls. Family members from the next village are considering their options. Someone has a car and offers to take four passengers; five or six if they sit on laps. There's a flurry of decision-making. Should they leave now, or walk to the main road for the furgon? But will it come? Maybe not.

Odeta is in the kitchen making more coffee. Still no sign of Kreshnik, but the kitchen door swings open and her best friend, Ariana, bounces in.

"You've come!" Odeta exclaims, rushing to hug her, and they shed a few tears. It's been so long since they've spent any time together. Ariana works long hours on her family's smallholding, and even today her parents couldn't spare her to come to the party until after she'd locked the hens up for the night. This is not the future the girls had dreamed of when they were at school.

"Here, I've brought you something." Ariana hands her a small box tied with a blue ribbon.

"So exciting!" Odeta opens it and takes out a pendant on a silver chain. "A St Christopher! Thank you."

"You like it? St Christopher's the patron saint of travellers. I thought he would keep you safe."

"I love it. I'll wear it always." She fastens it around her neck and kisses Ariana on the cheek.

Abandoning the coffee-making, they sneak upstairs to her cubbyhole of a bedroom. Since they last met, Ariana has cut her hair short and dyed it platinum blonde.

"Look at you – so cool, like a rock chick."

"I know." She tousles it with her fingers. "But roots are coming through – look. I must bleach it again."

Suddenly, Odeta can't wait to get out of the frumpy black skirt and ridiculous blouse. She feels such a peasant, trussed up in traditional costume. She tugs at the skirt's zip, almost ripping it in her haste, then strips down to her underwear, wriggles into tight denims and pulls on the stretchy top she's selected for her journey tomorrow.

"That's better." She exhales and flops down on the bed beside Ariana, the only place to sit. As well as the bed there's a chest of drawers, a shelf and a mirror, but only room for one person to stand on the floor at a time.

"Now, tell me all your news."

As she begins, Odeta realises how few details she has about the trip. "We'll be staying with Kreshnik's cousin and his wife. He thinks there's a job for me in their business, but I have to tell the immigration people that the visit is a holiday."

And, on top of all this, she has to remember that she's not Odeta, but Marije. She shakes her head. "It's complicated."

Ariana pokes her in the ribs with her elbow and gives a slow grin. "Tell me about him – Kreshnik. What's he like?"

Odeta opens her mouth to speak, but her mind goes blank. "He's different. But so exciting to be with. I often wonder what he sees in me." He's a puzzle she needs to solve but keeps putting aside to grapple with later.

"And you're in love with him?"

"I think so. I must be."

"So, are you and Kreshnik – you know – doing it?"

A blush appears on Odeta's cheeks and warmth spreads from her face to her neck. Slowly she nods her head as she remembers the first time.

It was a fortnight after he first came into the shop. They'd met a few times for coffee, but now she had a whole day off and he was taking her to his uncle's farmhouse high in the mountains. Kreshnik drove his Mercedes fast along the snaking road, and although she was wearing her seatbelt the sharp movement buffeted her. She braced her back against the seat and stretched out one arm to hold the dashboard.

"Don't do that," he said. "If I stop suddenly you might break your wrist."

She took long, slow breaths and didn't look down as the car climbed higher until the road petered out and turned into a track made of packed earth and stones. Showers of grit spurted up and rained back down on the car. The parched ground stirred up dust clouds that settled on the windscreen. Kreshnik's windscreen-washer bottle ran dry, and he stopped to pour in water from his drinking bottle. They'd been travelling in silence, but now Kreshnik slid a CD into the player and the car was filled with a blast of music, jerky and dissonant.

"What's that?"

"It's rap. Jay-Z," he said, taking both hands off the steering wheel to drum on it with his fists. "Good, eh?"

She nodded, keeping her head straight but swivelling her

eyes to study him without him noticing. His hooked nose, more prominent in profile, was softened by his dark, wavy hair. She couldn't see his expression, but his lips curved in a slight grin. Compared to the boys she knew, he was so sophisticated. He hadn't told her his age, but she guessed he was at least twenty-five. What would they talk about? Would he think her very dull?

They turned in between two high stone pillars, redundant with no gate to support, and crunched along a driveway. Ahead of them was a farmhouse encircled by a yard with dried mud and loose stones. Off to one side was a chicken coop, where the corpses of two hens lay side by side near the fence, the rest of the flock evidenced only by a few clumps of mangled feathers.

Kreshnik parked the car close to the door and reached into the glove compartment for a bunch of keys.

"Can I help?" she asked, as he began unloading the boot. He shook his head and lifted out a wooden crate larger than the ones filled with apples they had in the shop. She could make out the shape of a bottle, and something else – some sort of equipment.

He put the crate down on the step, unlocked the front door and beckoned her inside. The air was stagnant and dusty, with long-dead flowers in a vase on the windowsill, whilst the kitchen shelves were empty of food but crammed full of glasses and crockery. The rust-seamed door of an old fridge hung open on flimsy hinges. Kreshnik set down the crate on the table and began to unpack, lifting out two bottles and a camera, while she stared out of the kitchen window to a field beyond the yard. Two goats, with dried mud clinging to their matted coats, pressed up against the wire fence.

"Where is your uncle?"

Kreshnik shrugged. "Must be away. Probably in London. He's the father of my cousins who have the fashion business."

"But who looks after the goats?" She'd never seen such mournful expressions on the faces of living creatures.

"Who knows?" He took the bottle of wine out of the crate and poured some out into a tumbler for her. She sipped it, holding it in her mouth and waiting for the sour flavour to pass before swallowing.

"Come. Bring your drink and I'll show you around." He led her into a sitting room with a chimney and a large open grate. The floor was made of packed earth, but two rows of glazed tiles had recently been laid in the area surrounding the fireplace. A carved wooden mantelpiece was propped against the wall, waiting to be fixed into position.

"Cool, yeah? Cousins brought it from London."

The dark polished mahogany seemed out of place in this simple farmhouse. Dotted around the room there were easy chairs like they had at home, and some metal furniture that looked as though it had been designed by a child. Along the opposite wall, under the window, was a maroon velvet sofa with its back missing. One end was low, and the other rolled up in the shape of a scroll.

"Is that seat broken?" she asked.

Kreshnik smiled. "It's called a *chaise longue*. Comfy. Try it."

What a strange word. She giggled as he took her hand and led her across to the long sofa thingy. He sat down first and patted the space next to him. The seat was springy and comfortable, but there was nothing to lean against, so she sat stiffly, with her back straight and her feet planted on the floor. From his pocket, Kreshnik produced a small bag with a flowery design and a zip along the top and handed it to her.

"What's that?"

"A present. Open it and see."

She unzipped it. It was full of make-up: foreign brands she'd never heard of, but one name was familiar; it spelled luxury. *Chanel.*

"Wow!" she exclaimed taking out the lipstick and checking the colour – bright red.

"Thank you, Kreshnik." She aimed a kiss towards him, but he was getting to his feet. He disappeared into the kitchen, returning with the bottle and a mirror.

"Use that to make yourself up," he said, topping up her glass. "I want to take some pictures of you."

She was wearing a trace of pink lipstick, but her eyelashes and brows were naturally black and glossy so she never used eye make-up. Solemnly, she laid everything out on a side table and experimented with a black tube, shaped like a pencil, drawing a thin line on the back of her hand. Squinting into the mirror she outlined her eyes, but her hand shook and it went fuzzy around her lower lashes. She tried sweeping it up at the outer corners of her eyes, pleased with the oriental look. She plastered a layer of red lipstick on top of the pink and practised smiling, admiring the white luminosity of her teeth.

Kreshnik was busy assembling a tripod and setting up his camera.

"What do you think?"

He looked at her, pursed his lips and wrinkled his brow. "Here, let me." He strolled across and took the make-up bag out of her hand. Using a tissue, he scrubbed away the black line she'd drawn around her eyes. "You look like a panda," he said, with a grin.

She felt a spike of anger but held it tight inside her, waiting to see how he wanted her to look. First, he squeezed some beige foundation out of a tube and whisked it over her face with his fingertips. In the two weeks they'd known each other, he'd kissed her and she'd felt the touch of his hand fleetingly. As his fingers skimmed across her skin, a sensation sparked inside her making it hard to breathe. Using bronze powder he highlighted her cheekbones, his face so close to hers she could smell his minty breath.

"Open your eyes wide," he said, and layered mascara onto her lashes. Finally, he shaped and darkened her eyebrows with a soft pencil and handed her the mirror.

She gasped. Her face was alluring – perhaps beautiful. Catching her breath, she turned to Kreshnik, inviting his admiration. His eyes were blank and detached. A terrible idea struck her. She remembered school friends gossiping about men who were interested in clothes and make-up, men who chose not to be with a woman and made relationships with other men. Perhaps Kreshnik was gay? The excitement that had been fizzing inside her drained away.

But before the idea took root in her mind, Kreshnik dispelled it. Leaning forward, he grasped her shoulders, pulled her towards him and kissed her on the mouth, pressing his lips against hers for so long that she felt breathless. She clung to him, as if drowning but not wanting to save herself. His hand slid under her t-shirt and he began to undress her.

"Stop," she said, as her clothes slid to the floor. She tried to push him away, but strength had drained from her. While her voice said no, her body whispered 'yes'.

He shushed her, stroked her hair, nuzzled her neck, and murmured in her ear, "You're so beautiful, Odeta."

She trembled as he made love to her. Heat and soreness seared her body. She tried not to whimper. When he stopped, she lay very still, her mouth dry, her lips swollen, her body cold. Kreshnik fetched a woollen rug and wrapped it round her, stroking her forehead with soft fingertips. Gradually her body and her breathing settled, but she couldn't lift her head to meet his eyes.

"More wine?" he asked, his expression soft, his mouth curving into a smile.

"Can I have coffee?" It might stop her head spinning.

He nodded and went out to the kitchen. The rough wool rug chafed her naked skin, but she pulled it tighter and shifted on the *chaise longue* trying to find a comfortable position. What a useless piece of furniture. As her body relaxed, her head buzzed with a strange sensation, excited yet scared. This must be what falling in love is like.

Kreshnik returned, a cup of coffee in one hand, a glass in the other, and the wine bottle wedged under his arm. He handed her the coffee and she shifted along to make space for him to sit next to her, but he seemed to have forgotten she was there. He poured himself a glass of wine and returned to setting up his camera.

"What are you doing?" she asked, a sulky edge to her voice. Surely she deserved his full attention?

He smiled and held a finger to his lips. "Look at me. Don't move." He whipped out his smartphone, pointed it at her, clicked a few shots and crossed the room to show her the pictures on the screen. She almost didn't recognise herself; the fresh-faced girl had been replaced by a sophisticated stranger with sultry eyes and glowing face, her body invisible, cocooned beneath the rug. Kreshnik perched on the edge of the sofa, put his arm around her and kissed her, peeling the blanket away with his free hand and stroking her breast. Then he sat back and took another shot with his phone.

"Hey!" She flinched and covered herself with the blanket. Kreshnik laughed and yanked it off, leaving her exposed and naked. Draping it around his shoulders like a cloak, he tramped back to his tripod, and before she registered what was going on he was clicking away from behind the camera.

"Stop," she called out, folding her arms over her breasts and crossing her legs. She groped around on the floor for her clothes as panic knotted inside her stomach. "What are you doing?"

"Hey, darling. Don't be shy." He walked back over to her and whispered a kiss on her bare shoulder. "You look beautiful. Your pictures will be wonderful."

"But why?"

"It's for London, for the modelling job – I told you. Cousins will need to see your body shape, your measurements." Gently, he lifted her legs up onto the *chaise longue* and arranged her so she was lying with her back propped against the raised end.

"Bend your right knee and put your other leg like so." He angled one leg and left the other lying stretched out along the rubbed velvet. "That's right." He picked up the cup and offered it to her. The coffee tasted bitter. Her throat tightened and she couldn't swallow, but he'd called her *darling* and her body tingled at his touch, too limp to resist.

"Now put your arms like this." He uncoiled her crossed arms, stretched them above her head and fastened her fingers loosely together, hooked over the back of the sofa.

Then he was back at his camera and shooting again. "Turn this way – now that way. Move your head to the left, look at me, put one hand on your belly, slide your feet to the ground, let your hair fall around your face, now look straight into the lens."

The room grew warm, and the air smelt of stale dust. Feeling awkward and ashamed, she concentrated hard on the red and blue design of the tiles in front of the grate. It was not a traditional Albanian pattern, and it didn't look Greek either. In one corner of the room was a brown, shrivelled plant: a weeping fig that had wept so hard most of its leaves had dropped in a sad pile on the floor.

Her body moved like a mechanical doll responding to Kreshnik's instructions. He was her first lover, this was her first time. She tried to recapture the thrill that surged through her when he touched her. Why was he taking photographs instead of caressing her? Perhaps he did this with other women? She felt blood singing in her cheeks, her breathing was shallow, and her heart tapped out an uneven rhythm.

Did he see her as a lover? But if she wasn't that, what was she?

Ariana touches her on the arm, still waiting for an answer to her question. Odeta shakes herself back to the present, covers her mouth with her hand and whispers, "Yes. We have been sleeping together." The truth is out and she can't take the words back. She squeezes Ariana's arm. "You won't tell my mother, will you? Or yours? Promise!"

"Of course not." Ariana knits her fingers together and twists them around so the last of the light glints on a thin gold ring with a prominent red stone. Odeta's been so obsessed with her own life she hasn't even noticed her friend has news too.

"Ari," she exclaims, pointing at the ring. "You have something to tell me?"

Ariana looks up, her lips sealed in a tight smile, not showing her teeth. "I've been seeing someone too." She extends her hand for Odeta to examine the ring. The cut of the stone is rough to her touch, and Odeta can see it's not a genuine ruby. Is it even real gold? It's hard to tell.

"That's wonderful." Odeta leans to kiss her friend's cheek.

"It's Sami," Ariana says in a flat voice.

"The Sami who went to high school with us? Always forgot his lunch and nicked food from everyone else?"

Ariana nods. "That's him. I guess I'm lucky to have found him. Not many guys left around."

Odeta nods. It's true. Few of the boys they'd known at

school had stayed in the district. Most went to Tirana to look for work, others had left the country. "Life's not fair, is it? We girls get stuck here slaving for the whole family while the boys swan off abroad."

"Not you," Ariana points out, her eyes gleaming with reflected excitement. "You're escaping."

They sit in silence, contemplating their lives. At school, they had shared their hopes and dreams and plotted out their futures. Now they are living in that future – and so far, it's not delivering.

"I envy you, Odeta. I wish I could come to London with you."

"Me too." She squeezes Ariana's hand. While they've been chatting, darkness has fallen. There's electric light in the bedroom, but Odeta is trained not to switch it on. She hears muffled voices and spurts of laughter floating up from the party downstairs. Surely everyone will leave soon?

White light blanches the ceiling: car headlights. Instinctively she knows it's Kreshnik, and her breathing accelerates. Ariana kneels up on the bed, slides the mirror and family photographs along the sill, and peers out of the window. "Is it him?" she whispers. "Come on, let's go down."

They scramble to their feet and make their way down the narrow stairs, edging past Afrim and Leon who are on their way up, escaping from handing round of plates of food and having their arms pinched by old ladies with cackling voices. Odeta gives Afrim a quick hug as he passes. He grins at her as he squirms out of her grasp. She's going to miss her brothers.

Odeta and Ariana enter the sitting room and join the small knot of remaining guests. A crimson-faced man, one of her father's drinking cronies, is snoring in an armchair, his chest puffing out and falling in time with his grunts. A loud exhalation jolts his head forward. He seems sure to wake, but he doesn't, and lounges back, his throat vibrating. She and Ariana stand, side by side with arms linked, facing the door when Kreshnik enters with Idriz.

The room glows in the soft green lamplight. A row of candles flickers on the mantelpiece. Everyone stops talking and stares at Kreshnik as he strides across the room towards Odeta. She feels them watching, and lifts her head towards the magnetic pull of his eyes. Is he going to kiss her in front of all the family? She holds her breath, and the assembled guests also seem to be collectively holding their breath, waiting and watching. Uncle Ervin raises his camera, points it in her direction and prepares to shoot.

Kreshnik stands facing her and gazes, for a nanosecond, deep into her eyes, then he twists his head to one side, takes her hand and shakes it formally, like a stranger. The crowd exhales with an audible sigh. The spell is broken.

CHAPTER FIVE

There's an inn in the village, but no one has stayed there for years. On the ground floor is a restaurant where no one ever eats, and a bar where men of the village congregate to drink, tell stories and play cards. The innkeeper has been invited to Odeta's party. She hardly knows him; he's another of Idriz's mates.

"Can you find this man, Kreshnik, a bed for the night?" she overhears her father ask.

Oh, please let him say yes.

The innkeeper demurs. "Is late to ask my wife to get out from bed and change sheets. I do not know if electricity is working in guest rooms."

"Come, my friend. Do this for me." Idriz claps him on the back, and the innkeeper looks at him with sheepish eyes and grudgingly agrees.

"Follow." The innkeeper signals to Kreshnik. The night sky is tar-black and moonless. Kreshnik bids her a solemn goodnight and gives a little bow to the stragglers as he takes his leave. During his brief stay he's managed to sink five glasses of *raki*, yet he looks and sounds sober. When she introduced him to Ariana she watched his eyes wander over her friend's face and figure, and felt a stab of jealousy. But Kreshnik didn't talk to her for long. He re-joined Idriz and the men yammering in a corner.

"I will leave the car here," he announces, pointing to his Mercedes parked outside the shop, and trails behind the innkeeper, who has a torch that lights their route to the hotel on the square.

As the door closes behind them, the stress of the day drains from Odeta's body. She was afraid her father would invite Kreshnik to stay with them, but where would he sleep? The thought of bumping into him in their primitive family bathroom makes her blush.

Odeta rushes around the house gathering up empty plates and glasses. She and Besarta stand side by side at the old stone sink washing the dishes, a ritual they've repeated every day since she was seven years old. She can't remember her father ever carrying a dirty plate to the sink, or lifting a cloth to dry a cup. Odeta doesn't care. Time with her mother is precious, and Besarta tells her stories about her own childhood and how she was raised on her parents' farm when Albania was still a closed country, cut off from the outside world.

"Once we travelled to Saranda in the south," says Besarta. "From there we looked across the sapphire water to Corfu. So close – I thought of swimming there, but of course I could not swim. Anyway, it was too dangerous. Border guards used to take pot shots at people who tried to swim across."

"I don't believe you!" Odeta's eyes widen and a shiver creeps up her spine.

"It's true. Except they had to account for all the bullets used. So often, they would give chase in their boats and drown the fugitives instead of shooting them."

Besarta's laugh plumps out the grooves and hollows that give her face its sunken look. "How my sister and I longed to travel abroad, but in those days ordinary Albanians weren't allowed to leave the country. Now that dream is coming true for you."

"You say everything changed after the Communists fell, so why was our education so bad? Why didn't I learn to speak English at school?"

Besarta shrugs. "The school said they taught you English. Why didn't you pay attention?"

Her mother's rebuke stings. Odeta remembers those lessons. It's true there were English classes, but they were taught by teachers who struggled to write a grammatical sentence in English. None of them had ever travelled abroad. It didn't help that there were few books in English at school. That, at least, has changed. Leon and Afrim have already learned more English than she ever did, but when she was their age all she really cared about was gymnastics.

Besarta takes the drying-up cloth out of Odeta's hands and gives her a hug. Growing up she remembers more smacks than kisses, but she's never doubted her mother's love. She hugs Besarta back, and when they draw apart she notices a tear glinting in the corner of her mother's eye.

"It's nothing." Besarta wipes it away. "I'm so proud of you. Glad you have this chance. Now – go and make yourself ready. You've done enough here."

Her mother is right. She still has to pack. Preparations for the party took all her energy, but it's a long journey to Tirana, and Kreshnik wants to set off at six the next morning. She goes upstairs, peering into the boys' room on her way past. Her brothers are fast asleep, their breathing musical and steady. They have a bed each, but tonight both are sleeping in Leon's bed, Afrim twined around his brother like ivy on an oak. Afrim's abandoned school bag lies on the floor, and amongst its spilled contents she spots an English dictionary, tiny enough to slip into a pocket. *He'll need it.* She turns to leave, but the voice in her head whispers, *You need it more.* She bends and picks it up, closing the door softly so as not to wake them.

In her own room, she shuts the door and snaps on the light. She hopes her father won't notice, but she can't pack properly in the dark. She pulls the battered suitcase out from under her bed. The dust makes her sneeze. She takes a cloth and gives the case a wipe. It's hard to believe no one has used this case since her mother married and left her family home. When they travelled to Tirana for gymnastics competitions she and her mother went by furgon, but Besarta couldn't manage the suitcase so they crammed everything into a blue and white woven sack with handles. To this day, she remembers the humiliation of standing with her laundry bag alongside competitors from the city with their Nike backpacks.

She opens the suitcase and finds it full of linen: hand-embroidered pillowcases and sheets of fine Egyptian cotton. Her mother once told her how, in the weeks leading up to her marriage to Idriz, her grandmother sat up night after night sewing pillowcases and making filigree lace inserts. They use the lace antimacassars on the armchairs in their living room, but the embroidered bed linen has been forgotten and turned yellow along the folds. Odeta lifts it out and piles it on top of the chest of drawers.

In the bottom of the case she bundles shoes and three books. She opens a drawer and takes out underwear, curling her mouth with disgust at her high-waisted knickers – the sort a schoolgirl would wear. She crumples them into balls and stuffs them inside her shoes. In London, when she's working, she'll buy everything new. She has three pairs of trousers, made locally and cut in the same manly design, and two pairs of imported jeans, bought secondhand from a market. The labels say *Levi;*

they have narrow legs and cling to her body, emphasising her slim shape. Two sweaters, two blouses, one dress, one mini-skirt and three t-shirts; one with the name of a rock band Ariana brought back from a trip to Macedonia. It's so faded that she can no longer read the band's name. She adds some toiletries from the Greek range they stock in the shop, along with the make-up bag Kreshnik gave her, and her packing is complete.

She lies on her bed and scrunches her eyes shut. Every time she feels a wave of sleep rolling towards her, her head fills with things she must remember and drags her back to reciting Marije Kaleci's biography. An instinct makes her get out of bed to rummage in the suitcase, sliding her hand to the bottom layer and feeling around between shoes until she finds what she's looking for: the childish English reading book and the pocket dictionary she stole from Afrim. She pulls both books out from under the layer of sweaters and repacks them in her handbag.

CHAPTER SIX

Odeta sleeps for only three hours. Yawning, she slides her feet out from under the bedcovers and lowers them onto the cold floor. She opens the blinds. Kreshnik's silver Mercedes is still at the front of the shop where he left it last night. Then she notices a movement in the driver's seat. He's there already, waiting.

Panic constricts her chest. Sounds float up from downstairs – her mother is bustling around in the kitchen, but she doubts her father or brothers will be stirring.

In the cramped bathroom, she squints into the mirror, pinching her cheeks to coax some colour. A smear of pink lipstick brightens her complexion, but only slightly.

Her case is heavy. She lifts it and starts to drag it down the stairs, bump, bump, one stair at a time. Leon appears from nowhere. "Let me!"

She smiles. "It's too heavy." But Afrim helps, and between the two of them they hold it aloft like pall bearers and carry it down, puffing.

Surprisingly, her father is up, sitting in the kitchen, unshaven and bleary. He's wearing a vest but no shirt, and his trousers are hitched up with braces. As the clock strikes six, Kreshnik appears at the back door and joins them for coffee.

"Eat something, Odeta," her mother hisses at her, but she shakes her head. She can't swallow, and her stomach feels sour. She takes a few sips of water.

Her parents and brothers form a solemn-faced line by the door and shake Kreshnik's hand. Her father pecks her cheek and picks up her heavy suitcase, but Kreshnik takes it from him and strides on ahead to the car. Besarta wipes away a tear and presses a few crumpled banknotes into her hand. Odeta kisses her mother's rough cheek. She knows, though Besarta does not, that Albanian money will be of no use to her in London.

If she tries to kiss her brothers, they will squirm away. "Bring us back stuff," says Leon.

"Yeah, Xbox," says Afrim.

She laughs and ruffles his hair, landing a kiss on top of his head. Perhaps he'll be taller than her when she comes back. When will that be? Kreshnik has been vague about how long they are staying in London. She feels her fingers trembling as she gives the boys a final hug.

She climbs into the front passenger seat, clutching her handbag as her family regroups on the shop porch, ready to wave. Kreshnik starts the engine and the car glides forward down the hill. She swivels round, and a drowning sensation engulfs her. She keeps her eyes fixed on the place where her family stands, until their figures are obscured by a cloud of dust billowing in the car's wake.

The airport is modern and full of shiny high-tech equipment, but it's still a surly place. Odeta watches travellers milling around, jostling trolleys. They must be the most impatient breed on earth. Kreshnik leads her towards a queue where she can check in her suitcase. She's brimming with questions and tries to get his attention, but he seems twitchy and won't catch her eye. The queue edges forward. They are next in the queue to be called to the counter when Kreshnik glances down at her case and appears to notice the luggage label: *Odeta Lazami*, handwritten in jaunty green felt-tip. He frowns and beckons the next passenger to overtake them, then takes a penknife from his pocket, bends down and slices off the *Odeta Lazami* label.

"Why did you do that?" she asks, but she knows.

"You are Marije Kaleci, not Odeta anything," he hisses. His face looks chalky, and there's a bead of sweat on his forehead. Perhaps he's feeling ill.

They approach the desk, and she arranges her face in a smile as she answers questions. "Did you pack the case yourself? Did anyone give you anything to bring? Do you have any sharp items?"

"Your penknife," she whispers to Kreshnik, who unzips a pocket of her suitcase and slips it inside. That's when she notices that he has only hand baggage.

"You don't have luggage?" she asks, as they turn away from the counter.

He shrugs. "I have things at my cousins' place."

"What's it like, their place? Will we be staying there?"

"It's not far from the airport. Near a canal. A place called Uxbridge..." He clamps his palm over his mouth and won't say more.

The airport lighting is harsh, and her high-heeled shoes pinch her feet. She makes a detour to the Ladies and joins a queue of women and young children, snaking out of the washroom door and onto the concourse. Customers leaving the toilets seem angry and are yelling abuse at the attendant, who shouts back, "There's no water. What do you expect me to do?"

When it's finally Odeta's turn, she understands what the fuss is about. The toilet bowl is blocked, and the stench is overwhelming. There's no running water in the hand basins either. She rubs neat liquid soap on her hands and scrubs it off with a tissue, but her hands feel sticky and clammy.

Kreshnik is waiting near Passport Control. "We'll go through."

With a jittering heart, she flips Marije's passport open at the photo page and takes a step towards a kiosk staffed by a female official, who is spending a long time with each passenger. Kreshnik puts a hand on her arm and hauls her back. "That one's too slow," he whispers. "And too thorough."

At the adjacent booth, a plump male official barely lifts his eyes to look at travellers' faces or documents before nodding them through. As the man waves them on, Odeta notices a glance flicker between him and Kreshnik.

"Do you know that man?"

Kreshnik shakes his head. He's checking the departure board and scrutinising the list of flights. "Shit," he exclaims. "Look at that delay!"

It's true. This board is showing different information from the one in the check-in hall.

"All the flights are delayed," she says. A message flashes up on an overhead screen:

Due to technical problems flights may be disrupted.

She finds a seat, but Kreshnik stands, foot-tapping. After a while he paces across to the window, making a circuit past the café and the Duty-Free shop and back.

"Coffee?"

She nods. He strolls over to the buffet and brings her drink in a paper cup, so flimsy it scalds her hand. The coffee tastes bitter and stale, as if it was brewed yesterday. They sit side by side, but there's a gulf of awkwardness between them. She tries to draw him back to her. "Tell me more about your cousins?"

He leans towards her, his shoulder sloping down to meet hers, and whispers, "Have you memorised Marije's story?"

Her eyes spark with anger and her dark hair spills loose from its clip. "This is crazy." She raises her voice. "A stupid game. I'm not Marije, I'm Odeta." A man sitting opposite lifts his eyes from his smartphone and gives her a curious look.

Kreshnik's face hardens. "I'm not joking." He pulls the papers with Marije's potted life-history out of her bag. "The British immigration people will ask you questions. You need to know the answers."

"I do know them."

"Where were you born, Marije?"

She scowls. "In Tirana."

"And what is your occupation?"

Marije's paperwork says she's a nurse, but to annoy him she says, "Shop worker."

With a grim expression, he folds his arms and twists his head away. She blinks back a tear. Why is he acting like this? This isn't the Kreshnik who buys her gifts and acts respectfully towards her father. Now she's lost his attention and she wants it back. She paws at his hand. "Kreshnik, I'm sorry. I'll get it right, I promise. Tell me about Marije. Is she in England? Will I meet her?"

He softens, puts his arm around her and pulls her head to lean against his shoulder. "You're tired, Odeta. Close your eyes and rest."

The familiar tang of his aftershave soothes her. She drifts off, imagining they are lying curled together in a pine forest, until a flight announcement, crackly and indistinct, wakes her.

"Did you hear that?" Kreshnik holds up his hand with the palm towards her. He strolls over to check the departure board listings. She can read it from her seat: their flight is still delayed – but only by one hour.

As she watches, Kreshnik pulls out his phone and makes a call. He's too far away for her to hear his words, but he curves his hand around the mouthpiece like a clamshell. Standing very straight, with his jacket draped around his shoulders, he's the tallest man in the crowd and the best-looking – and he's with her. She feels a warm glow. She'll play along with the Marije Kaleci charade, stop antagonising him, and things will go back to the way they were. She smiles at him as he settles back on the seat beside her, seeming mellow and resigned to the wait. They chat about London, English food, and terrible weather. The hour slides by.

Their flight is called, and they board and buckle up their seatbelts. There's a whoosh, her head bumps against the seat back, the plane rumbles along the runway and they're airborne. She never thought she would get the chance to fly, and now she's here. What bliss. There's a hollow clank: a sound like failing machinery. She sits bolt upright in her seat, stifling a scream, and grips Kreshnik's hand. "What's that?"

He grins and squeezes her hand. "Undercarriage. Wheels folding up."

"Oosh," she sighs, and her body flops back against the seat.

Cabin crew scurry along the aisles offering drinks and food. A blonde woman with a heavily-powdered face and bright red lipstick presents her with a tray of sandwiches, a yoghurt and slices of fruit: elegant food, delicately presented. The sort of food Dick and his mother eat in her English textbook. Is this how she'll eat in England? A cellophane envelope contains cutlery and tiny sachets of salt and pepper.

"Look at this, Kreshnik." She wants to share her delight, but he's waving his meal tray away and asking for Scotch and coffee. The flight attendant hands him a plastic beaker with ice, but he leaves the ice cubes in the cup and swigs the whisky straight from the miniature bottle. He grins at her and she melts with happiness, but before long he presses the *Call* button and orders another, giving the stewardess his special smile.

What does she expect from Kreshnik, after all? When he's moody and off-hand she's miserable, but it's not as if he's ever promised they would get married one day. He hasn't asked her father, and he hasn't told her he loves her. Or not in so many words. But whenever they were alone together, they made love. Sometimes they went back to his uncle's deserted farmhouse, but on days when she could only snatch a short break from the shop, he would pick her up in his car, drive up into the hills and pull off onto a roadside lay-by. He would turn off the engine and they would climb into the back seat, where he kept a thick blanket. After the first time, it didn't hurt so much if she stopped tensing her muscles and relaxed. Afterwards she felt light-headed and happy. How could she help falling in love with him?

Deciphering his feelings was another matter. "Good," he said to her on one occasion. "You're getting the hang of it. Next time make some noise. Moan and shout out a bit."

Kreshnik takes a glossy magazine from the seat pocket and flicks through it. He's finished his third Scotch, and asks for another. "See that," he says, grinning and pointing along the aisle at two cabin crew speaking in hushed voices. "They're discussing whether to let me have another drink. You don't think I've drunk too much, do you?" He takes hold of her hand.

She shakes her head. "What are you reading?"

He slides the magazine towards her.

"It's a business travel magazine. Look here." He shows her pages of men's fashion, pointing out designer watches and hand-stitched shoes, and translates the prices into lek for her. She gasps.

"You see, people in England can earn that sort of money." He peels back his shirt cuff and shows her his watch. "It's a fake. Next time I'm getting this one." He jabs his index finger at an advert in the magazine featuring a photo of an actor she recognises from the film *Titanic*. The plane tilts, and the magazine slides off his lap onto the floor.

"We're falling," she whispers.

"That's the nose, pointing down. We're coming in to land." He leans over and refastens her seatbelt, his hand lingering on the contours of her body. She closes her eyes and purses her mouth. Perhaps he'll kiss her. She's parched with longing for his touch, but soon the drought will end. Perhaps tonight at his cousin's house in London.

Standing in the queue for immigration, she reaches for Kreshnik's hand and squeezes it. The queue edges towards the booths where uniformed officials sit in judgement on new arrivals. She looks around at the other passengers; some are yogic in their stillness, others fretful or twitchy. Children whine and cling to their mothers. As they get closer to the sign saying *UK Border*, she counts how long it takes for each person to be processed. A woman in a yellow and black batik dress, wearing flip-flops and no coat, seems to have taken up residence at one of the booths. More officials are called. Four of them cluster round and examine the woman's passport.

"Will it take so long for us?" she whispers to Kreshnik. "I only know enough about Marije to fill two minutes."

He seems to find this amusing. "We'll sail through, don't worry." Kreshnik crosses the line painted on the floor and approaches the booth. He's right. In less than two minutes he's through, and the immigration official signals that she's next.

She hands over her passport and landing card. The man is

wearing a turban and has kind eyes. "Now, Marije ..." He looks at her passport and smiles. "Just a few questions about your visit to the United Kingdom."

Her rehearsals pay off. Answers glide off her tongue, word-perfect. "What is the purpose of your visit?"

"A holiday. Visiting friends."

"And where will you be staying in the United Kingdom?"

She recites the address that Kreshnik has told her to give. Funny, it doesn't mention Uxbridge. Never mind. Blinking, she emerges on the other side of the barrier with a stamp for three months in Marije's passport.

Kreshnik is waiting for her. "Well done." He holds out his hand. She slips her own warm hand inside his, but he shakes it away and says brusquely, "No, woman. The passport. Give it to me."

She blinks as she hands the passport over. "Where now?"

"Now we fetch the baggage."

Odeta trails behind him up an escalator and into a vast hall of pounding conveyor belts. She watches, open-mouthed, as bags tumble out of a hole covered with flyscreen-style flaps onto a carousel, then travel round in a solemn circle. People step up to the conveyor belt and drag their cases off.

"Don't they get stolen?"

"Not often. Who would want yours?"

She blushes. The catch of her scuffed brown case had refused to close, and her father tied an old leather belt around its middle to stop it springing open. Other people's cases are fuchsia-pink and sky-blue, or rucksacks with secret wheels.

"Look – here it comes," she calls, but Kreshnik's mobile phone is ringing and he's walking away to answer it.

She sidles up to the conveyor, grabs the handle and tries to lift her case off. The force of the moving belt drags her forward. She treads on an old man's foot and he glares at her. A younger man sees her struggling. "This yours?" he asks with a smile, and lifts it off for her.

Flustered, she can't think of the English word for *Thanks*, so she smiles and nods. Kreshnik pops up at her side, inserting himself between her and the helpful man, forcing him to back away.

"I'll take it." His voice is stern as he lifts her case onto a wheeled trolley. She smiles, but his face has slipped back to its stern expression, lips drawn in a tight line.

What's wrong with him? Is the strain of travelling making him grouchy? Or is it her? Has she annoyed him in some way? She trails behind him through the Green channel, where yawning officials show not a scrap of interest. A flustered young African is unpacking his suitcase under the scrutiny of three customs officers and stares around, panic-stricken, but Kreshnik won't let her linger. He hurries her towards the exit and the doors slide open to let them through.

It feels like walking onto a film set. Chaos, colour and a scrum of people lining up behind a long barrier: young children hopping up and down, old people bent over walking sticks; dark-skinned people, girls with flame-red hair, men with shaved heads, women in burkas. And there is noise: a cacophony of languages spoken very fast. Everyone is pointing or waving. Some men stand aloof in sober jackets, holding up signs with exotic-sounding names like *Smith* and *Tipalingam*. New arrivals scour faces in the crowd and run forward, squealing with joy to embrace husbands, mothers, girlfriends. Beyond them is a row of cafés. Everything looks shiny and efficient – there's sure to be running water in the toilets here. There's a buzz in the air; everyone around her seems to be happy, glad to have arrived in England.

The atmosphere lifts Odeta's mood too. "Where are we going?"

"Someone should be here to meet us."

"Your cousin and wife?"

Kreshnik peers along the line of faces and pushes the trolley ahead of him with one hand. "Wait here. By that pillar." He leaves her with the luggage trolley. She smells the strong aroma of coffee, and on the far side of the concourse she notices a brightly-lit café with a display of cakes.

Kreshnik strides through the hall, swiping at his phone and punching in a number. He's no longer the tallest man in the crowd. There are black guys and blond Nordics who are practically giants, but still he stands out. He stops in the middle of the concourse, engrossed in his phone call and blocking a thoroughfare so couples have to break apart and pass either side of him.

Odeta notices a thickset man, wearing a leather jacket, step down from one of the café stools and stand for a moment staring out into the crush of people. This man, too, is holding a mobile phone pressed against the side of his head as he scans the crowd and seems to single out Kreshnik. His eyes narrow and his face sags into a scowl. Now the two men are striding purposefully towards each other, slipping their phones back into their pockets.

They halt an arm's length apart; they don't shake hands and show no pleasure in the act of recognition. It can't be the cousin; perhaps it's some driver. The stranger thrusts a hand inside his jacket pocket and draws out an envelope. Odeta can't quite see, but it looks like a letter: a very thick one. He hands it to Kreshnik, who accepts it with a nod. He doesn't open it but holds it in his hand. The two men turn and look in her direction, Kreshnik gesturing with his thumb. He must be discussing her with the fat man. She blushes as they amble towards her, Kreshnik keeping pace with the dumpy stranger without looking at him. When they reach her they stand very close. It's an odd sensation, like being enclosed by a copse of trees: Kreshnik a lofty willow, the other man a stubby spreading bush. She tests out a smile of welcome on the stranger.

"This man, Tomas, will take you to your accommodation," says Kreshnik. He fiddles with the envelope he's holding, folds it in half and pushes it into his pocket.

"But you're coming too?" Her voice stutters and rises, turning her statement into a question.

He shakes his head and examines his shoes.

"I don't understand." Her heart is hammering as she stares at Tomas's tight leather jacket, noticing how the zipper gapes open to a point midway down his chest. Its vast, jagged teeth remind her of Afrim's toy dinosaur. She winces as a hand clamps onto her arm above the elbow. The fat man has hold of her. In her bewilderment, nausea constricts her throat.

"Get off." She jabs her elbow backwards, but she can't shake off his grip. "Kreshnik, make him let go of me."

But Kreshnik is fidgeting with his cuff. He takes out a cigarette and positions it between his index and middle fingers but doesn't light it. The other man, Tomas, peels his lips back in a grin exposing two front teeth, chipped into triangles. He spits a wad of chewing gum into his free hand and drops it on the floor.

"Kreshnik," she pleads, grabbing hold of his sleeve and tugging. She feels dizzy, and her eyes flit around without focusing. "What's going on? Stop being so weird." Passers-by pause to stare, but they clearly don't understand Albanian.

"Shush," he says, raising a finger to his lips. He leans towards her, clears his throat and speaks rapidly. "Now listen, Odeta. Be a good girl and go with Tomas. Do as he says and everything will be fine. There's nothing to worry about. I have business to attend to, I'll be away for a while. When I get back we'll be together. Okay?"

She stares into his face, and notices his eyes are shuttered against her. His forehead is shiny, he looks pale, and he's breathing heavily. Is he ill?

"I don't want to go with him." She claws at his arm, her voice dry and cracking. "Let me come with you. I won't be any trouble."

Kreshnik takes a step away from her. His expression is grim, but he looks at her with a deep sadness. He does love her – she's sure of it now – but why does he look so unhappy? Something has happened here in London; some business must have gone horribly wrong.

She lunges tearfully towards him, reaching for his arm but grasping thin air as he steps back again. She loses her footing and stumbles. Tomas still has hold of her arm. He pulls her back to her feet, and in that moment of distraction Kreshnik slips away. She sees him striding towards a sign marked *Exit*.

"No," she wails. "Come back."

People turn and stare at her, but they clearly don't want to get involved. Her heart is smashing against her ribcage as she watches Kreshnik's figure grow smaller and smaller until it's a tiny speck. And then he's gone.

CHAPTER SEVEN

Odeta fights a wave of panic as Kreshnik fades from view. Where is he going? When will she see him? On her left wrist is the pearl and gold bracelet he gave her. She rolls it between her index finger and thumb, solid and real – it must mean something. This can't be happening.

Tomas is still gripping her arm. She's in a foreign country, lost and alone, yet all around her people are carrying on with their normal business. Not everyone is in a tearing hurry; some are walking at a leisurely pace wheeling cases behind them. Others are joshing with their mates. Ordinary families are pushing loaded trolleys. Women scuttle to catch up with children intent on skipping away from them. A smiling sun-tanned couple, wearing matching stripy tops and white anoraks, are approaching.

The woman glances at Odeta and stares, as if she detects something amiss. Odeta tries to make eye contact to blink out a signal, but Tomas seems to notice and shifts his grip from her arm to her wrist. He pulls her towards him and holds her in a clinch as if they're a couple, embracing after a long separation. His fingernails dig into her wrist. He's not a tall man, and over his shoulder she locks eyes with the woman in the white anorak and moves her lips in a silent plea. The woman's face flickers with unease, and she whispers something to her husband. He glances at Odeta over his horn-rimmed spectacles, then looks away, linking his arm through his wife's and hurrying her on. The woman swivels her head and looks back over her shoulder mouthing a word that looks like *Sorry*. Then she's gone.

All around her, crowds of people surge towards the exit where Kreshnik disappeared, towards their everyday lives. She scans the passing faces, but no one will catch her eye.

"Come on, get moving," Tomas hisses, nudging her forward with his hip.

Her chest is tight with fear. "Where? I won't go with you."

"You heard what he said. I'm taking you to your accommodation."

"Then let go of my arm." She tries to hold her ground, but he's strong, and half-drags, half-slides her towards the exit. He's slung his right arm around her so they look like a couple, entwined, to give the illusion that she's moving forward of her own accord. They pass car hire offices, a bureau de change, a news-stand with racks of papers and magazines, and a fridge full of water bottles, and there are hordes of people everywhere. She tries to shout for help, but something's happened to her voice. When she tries to speak, her words are diluted and float soundlessly away on the air.

They reach a high glass door that opens automatically, and a blast of chill from the outside smacks against her face. A young man wearing a fluorescent yellow jacket and a hat that could be part of a uniform is standing guard, watching people arrive and depart. This could be her chance.

"*Më ndihmoni!*" she shouts in the direction of the officer, but her plea for help is faint and feeble. He turns around and seems about to take a step towards her, then his handset crackles to life. He answers it with a seamless reflex, turns on his heel and strides off in the opposite direction.

"Shut up." Tomas propels her out of the door and across a road towards a car park.

Fear is a taste. It's cold metal in her mouth and reflux in her throat. It chokes her, robbing her of ability to act. Asking for help in Albanian is pointless; no one will understand. She dredges her memory for some English words. *May I go and play with Nip, Mother? Do you want a cake?* Useless.

Still gripping her arm, Tomas rambles on, talking to himself. Is he trying to muffle any sound she might make? No. It's a monologue; he seems to be giving himself instructions: *Get ticket, Level Two Parking, Blue.* They stop at a machine in a deserted lobby, where he fumbles in his pocket for change and feeds coins into a slot. The machine swallows them.

"Let me go! You're hurting me."

He tightens his grip and drags her with him. Now he's navigating between rows of parked cars, flashy models she's never seen before, heading for the furthest corner.

In that corner is a blue van, streaked with dirt. There's a dent in the back door and a seam of rust around the wheel arches. She reads the letters and numbers on the registration plate and tries to remember them; it feels as if it might be important. Tomas opens the rear door of the van and nudges her towards it. Can he mean to shove her inside like some animal? She braces her feet against the edge of the kerb. His fleshy torso rams against her back, and beneath the blubber she feels taut muscle. He pushes harder; she resists. Suddenly he stops, takes a step back and looks up. Odeta follows the line of his eyes. Overhead, the red light of a security camera is winking at them.

"Get in the front," he hisses in Albanian, escorting her round to the open passenger door.

"I won't."

A knee jabs against her back, and meaty hands lift and push her into the seat. He slams the door shut behind her. Desperately she pumps the handle, but it won't budge. He's walking around behind the van and will soon reach the driver's door. He climbs in and leans across to fasten her seat belt. She smells alcohol and garlic on his breath.

"Get off me!"

Why is he still leaning across her? Hasn't he already fixed the belt? But he's bending down to fumble underneath the seat, and pulls out another strap. He stretches it across her lap and into another buckle with a combination lock. It clicks into place, and she's caught up in a contraption of straps like a strait-jacket.

He starts the engine, follows signs to the exit and slides a ticket into a slot. A barrier lifts. There's no human operator, but she notices another camera mounted on a gantry above the entrance pointing at the van. She raises her arms and waves towards it, thumping her fist on the windscreen. The van advances through the barrier out of sight of the camera's blinking eye, and Tomas casually leans over and punches her in the stomach. Pain is sudden, strong and intense. It winds her. She whimpers, and her upper body sags and folds towards her lap.

When she's able to lift her head, rubbing her sore stomach, she notices the van is turning away from blue signs saying *Motorway* and following a side road that seems to be part of the airport complex. They drive alongside high wire fences enclosing shabby buildings, runways and row upon row of cars. Never in her life has she seen so many cars. She tries to memorise what the roads look like, and make sense of where they are. In the bottom of her handbag is the mobile phone Kreshnik gave her so he could contact her to set up their secret meetings. Last night she was so tired she forgot to charge it, but she has brought the charger with her. As soon as they arrive somewhere with electricity she will charge up her phone and call for help.

Odeta has seen films and knows bad things can happen to women, but until now she always thought those things only happened in America, to women with long blonde hair and too much make-up. She's never heard of anything bad happening to an Albanian girl, but how many Albanian women does she know who've travelled abroad anywhere other than Greece? None.

And what about Marije Kaleci, whispers a voice inside her head. *What's happened to her?*

They've left the airport complex and are driving along a road with rows of houses on each side, bunched close together with no space between. The only way of telling where one house ends and the next begins is that some of the walls are painted different colours: white, yellow, beige, and even a blue one, but they all look grimy – not at all like the house where Dick and his mother from her English reading book live. The sky is the colour of a filthy dishrag, and people are plodding along the pavement wearing anoraks with the hoods up and carrying umbrellas.

Tomas signals and turns in through high gates to an area with long low buildings made of red brick. The buildings are dark, with rows of white lines painted to show where cars should park. Tomas ignores the parking spaces and drives around behind one of the buildings, stopping next to a rusting metal container, higher than his van and overflowing with rubbish. He stops the van and gets out.

"What are you doing? Where is this place?" Her heart hammers as she gazes out at the expanse of concrete, bricks and tarmac. Is he going to leave her here? Everything is hard, gritty and deserted.

"Nosy, aren't you?" He walks round to the front of the van,

bends down and tugs at something. She can feel the van rocking as he pulls until the thing comes away in his hand. It's a sticker with a number and letters on it. He crumples the fake number plate into a ball, tosses it onto the driver's seat and does the same with the sticker on the back of the van.

When he climbs back into his seat he's talkative. One minute he's smashing his fist into her stomach, the next he's chatting to her in Albanian as if they were old acquaintances. Her head is aching. It feels as though it might explode, but she forces herself to listen.

"Those cameras at the airport," he says. "They recognise number plates. But they won't find this one, because we've never been there."

Odeta nods. Her teeth are chattering and she's shivering beneath her cotton jacket. There's no heating in the van, and she didn't expect it would be so cold here.

"Where are we going?" she asks.

"You'll see. You want the radio?" He doesn't wait for her shrug, but presses a switch, and music surges from the speakers and jangles against her aching head.

They drive on, and Tomas follows the blue road signs onto the widest road she's ever seen. There are three or four lanes of cars going in the same direction as them, while on the opposite carriageway a procession of traffic has come to a dead stop. Odeta tries to read the signs but they flash past in a blur before she can spell out the letters in her head. The road narrows and starts to climb; it seems to have turned into a bridge. They reach almost to the top of the incline, slow down and take the exit marked *Kew, North and South Circular*. They drive inside a kind of open tunnel underneath the legs of the road they've just left, and join the end of a queue.

"Bloody traffic. Worse than Tirana."

She ignores him.

"Answer when I speak to you, Marije."

"I'm Odeta."

"You're Marije. Not that you'll ever replace her." He sniffs and draws the back of his hand across his nostrils.

"You mean Marije Kaleci, don't you?"

"Listen, don't fucking ask questions." He thumps his hand down hard on the steering wheel, just catching the horn so it emits a short blast. The driver of a silver car in front sticks his arm out of the side window and holds up two fingers.

There are houses everywhere. Sometimes the monotony of the chain of houses is broken up by a small parade of shops: brightly-painted, with their windows illuminated and stuffed full of goods for sale. How her father would love this place, if only he was here. Her fear and anger are drowned out by a wave of homesickness.

The streets are lit with white or orange lights on high poles. So much wasted electricity. How do the people in this country afford the cost?

Why is she thinking these thoughts when she's stuck in this van with crazy Tomas? She must focus, but her eyelids droop and she leans back and dozes. After a while she snaps awake as the van judders over humps in the road. Potholes. Just like Albania. As they turn a corner she catches sight of a street sign: *Joplin Street*. It's not a name she's ever heard. She repeats it to herself – Joplin Street. It seems important to remember.

Tomas pulls the van off the road and parks in front of a house with number thirty-eight on the black door and metal bars over the front windows. Can this be the home of Kreshnik's cousins? A flight of stone steps leads up to the front door. He switches off the engine, and the grinding sound is replaced by the hum of passing traffic. In the distance a siren wails.

"Don't make a noise," Tomas warns, unfastening the lock attached to her seat belt and opening the van door. It's a long way down to the ground, but agility is in Odeta's DNA; she springs from the cab and lands lightly. Tomas hustles her up stone steps, keeping one hand pressed against the small of her back. In the other hand he holds a bunch of keys, sorts through them and undoes three separate locks. They step into a hallway. On the right-hand side of the door is a sitting room, with purple curtains drawn across the bay window and a gigantic television screen showing a football match. A skinny man is lounging on a sofa with his feet up on a low table. There's a hole in his left sock, and his big toe is sticking through. Odeta takes a step into the room but Tomas hustles her on past. The thin man gets up and strolls out into the hall. She's sick of being manhandled.

"Are you Kreshnik's cousin?" she asks in Albanian. If he is, he'll help her. What were his cousins' names? He never told her. The man's face is stippled with acne, and his eyes, set off-centre, are as dark and beady as a crow's. He ignores her question.

"Is that the new Marije?" he asks.

Tomas nods, his face creasing in a frown.

"Good as the other one?"

Tomas's hands seem to rise of their own accord and his fingers curl into fists. "Shut it. Don't talk about Marije."

Through the fog of exhaustion and confusion, Odeta cranes her ears to make sense of this. The skinny man is measuring her up with his eyes. She won't put up with this. Circling her arm, she raises her elbow towards her shoulder. Stabbing it backwards in a powerful arc, she frees herself from the grip of Tomas's chubby fingers.

He laughs. "Strong and stupid, hey?"

She tenses her diaphragm, waiting for the blow that doesn't come.

"I'm not staying here. I'm leaving now." She swivels on her heel and heads towards the front door.

"Not so fast, madam." Tomas puts his arm around her back,

slotting it beneath her armpits and lifting her off her feet. Now he's dragging her along the corridor towards an open door, through which she can see burnt pans and smell grease. But before they reach the kitchen, he turns left and kicks open a wooden door with his foot. In the gloom, she can just make out an uneven staircase leading down to a basement and the smell of something organic: plants or leaf mould.

"Where are you taking me?" The tang of fear is back in her mouth. She tastes blood; she's bitten her own tongue.

"Your room's down there." He snaps on a light and points down the flight of stairs.

"I'm not going down there." She grips onto the door post, digging her fingers into the flaking paintwork. "Help me!" Desperately, she looks around for the skinny man. He's disappeared back to the television room.

"So, am I gonna have to kick you down those stairs?" he asks. "Break a few bones, I'd guess."

She scans his fleshy face, tiny eyes with dilated pupils that are intensely black and empty. Defeated, she steadies herself with one hand against the wall and walks unaided down the basement stairs. Tomas follows. She can hear his grunting breath close behind her.

"Where is my room?" She's standing in a long narrow corridor with three doors. He opens a door directly ahead and hustles her inside. The room has a hard floor and a rectangle of carpet that stops some distance from the walls. It smells of damp and earth.

She shivers. Something about the room makes her think of a grave, even though it's not entirely subterranean. For a basement, the ceiling is surprisingly lofty, perhaps two metres above her head. A narrow rectangle of window sits high up the wall just below the ceiling, while a single bulb emits a weak light that gradually grows stronger like magic and illuminates the room. She doesn't like what she sees: a double bed with a metal frame, covered with a sheet, and a frayed blanket folded over one end. The sheet is stained with patches of yellow and brown.

"This is dirty," she says, pointing to the sheet.

Tomas ignores her. "Notice where everything is," he says. "Look carefully." He points out a washbasin fixed to the far wall. There is liquid soap, a thin hand towel, and above the sink a mirror with a crack running diagonally across it. He bends down and ferrets beneath the bedstead, drawing out a pink china bowl with a handle.

"Yuck," says Odeta. It's a chamberpot, like something peasants in her country would use. She wrinkles her nose with disgust, but Tomas isn't looking at her. While she was glaring at the chamberpot, he's strolled around behind her and is standing in the doorway.

"This place is filthy. I'm not staying here." She spins round, but he's already stepped outside, with a guttural rumble of laughter, and closed the door behind him. She hears a key turning in the lock, followed by the snap of a switch, and the room plunges into blackness. Panic grips her throat and presses on her windpipe. She gulps short pulsing in-breaths through her mouth. As her eyes become accustomed to the gloom she sees outline shapes of furniture but no detail. Sliding one foot ahead of the other she crosses towards the door until she reaches the wall. She places the flat of her hand on the wall and gropes around the perimeter of the room. There's no light switch.

CHAPTER EIGHT

Odeta crouches on the floor and sobs. Her throat aches, and the lining of her nostrils feels thick and swollen. Why is she in this horrible place? Where is Kreshnik? When will he come and take her away? She fumbles in her sleeve for a tissue but doesn't find one. At home, in Albania, darkness never troubled her. There are no streetlights in her village, but the moon and stars pepper the sky with a friendly glow. Here, in this alien room, her imagination sketches new terrors. She fixes her eyes on the strip of window high up near the ceiling, too narrow for a kitten to squeeze through, and waits for dawn to roll in.

At last, pinkish light suffuses the sky, and she can breathe again.

There's a dark shape lying on the floor: her blue shoulder bag, its contents spilled everywhere. But where is her suitcase? Kreshnik placed it on a trolley and wheeled it through Customs, but after Tomas appeared there's a void in her memory. Tomas didn't put it in the van, so perhaps it will be found at the airport and someone will look for her. Her heart canters, until she remembers Kreshnik snipping off her name tag. Odeta Lazami, the girl she used to be, never travelled to England.

Her tears have dried, leaving a damp chill through her body. Robotically, she collects and sorts the contents of her bag. The English book and dictionary are there, but where is her passport? The smiling immigration man in the turban handed it back to her and wished her a pleasant stay. And then? She gave it to Kreshnik. *Stupid, stupid.* All thoughts become roads leading back to Kreshnik. But he'll finish his business and be here soon. He can't know how she's being treated.

Brush, comb, make-up, purse containing some euros and the lek her mother gave her, though Kreshnik told her these would be no use because in England they use pounds. And something else: her mobile phone. She trembles as she cradles it in her hand. The battery's sure to be flat, but the charger must be here somewhere. Her fingers find it before her eyes do, snagged up in the bag's cheap lining. She attaches it to her phone and searches for an electric socket and finds one near the skirting, but the plug-in end of her charger won't fit into the holes. She examines it, realising it has two pins, but this socket has three and they don't line up. Perhaps if she prises the prongs wider apart it will fit. Sitting on the floor she inserts her hairbrush handle in between the two prongs and presses.

A draught drifts across the room, and she looks up and sees the skinny guy from the sitting room standing in the doorway.

"I shouldn't bother." His legs, in tight jeans, are thinner than a teenage girl's. An unlit cigarette dangles from his mouth. He takes it out and holds it between his fingers while he draws his lips back into a grin, exposing black and white teeth with gaps like pieces on a chessboard. He's holding a bowl of grey-brown slop and offers it to her, dipping his head in a mock bow.

Odeta stands up and faces him, twisting the charger flex in her hand. She's slim, and shorter than average height, but next to this wasted man she feels muscular and powerful. "I must phone my parents," she says. "Immediately."

The man places the bowl of slop down on the floor and shunts it to one side with his foot. He takes two paces towards her and holds out his hand. "Gimme."

"No." She clutches the phone, with charger attached, against her chest. He lunges and grabs it, tugging on the wire. But she won't let go, so he drags it out through her closed fist, scraping her palm.

"Give it back!" She dives at him, pummelling his chest with her fists. He flinches, stumbles and kicks the bowl over. Lumpy liquid splashes over the rim and onto the floor.

He straightens up and taunts her, dangling the mobile and charger in front of her face. Behind him, through the open door, she can see the corridor and the uncarpeted stairs leading upwards. Gymnastics training made her flexible and swift on her feet. She sidesteps him and bolts through the door, filling her lungs with oxygen and sprinting up the stairs towards the light.

She's halfway up before he catches her. He dives forward, and as his hand closes around her ankle she stumbles and the whole weight of her body collapses forward onto her hands. Pain shoots through her left wrist. Bracing herself, she kicks back towards his face and searches for a handhold, but there's nothing to grip. As he drags her back down by her feet she feels every stair tread grinding against her ribs. Her body screams out in pain, but she seals her lips and scowls. He pulls her to her feet and she notices he has a scar, the colour of raw meat, running across one cheek, partly concealed by his pitted complexion. His side-set eyes bulge as he stares at her. "Kreshnik was wrong," he says. "You're no beauty."

Drawing back his hand, he slaps her across the face. The

force of the blow sends her brain bouncing inside her skull. She's shaking with shock and pain.

He pushes her back inside the room and picks up the bowl from the floor. "Maybe tomorrow, you'll eat," he says. "Maybe not."

When Odeta next opens her eyes the room swims in front of her like a grey ocean. She's out of her depth, drowning. Her face is hot and swollen, her jaw throbs, and with a stab of foreboding she tests the left side of her mouth – first with her tongue, then with a gently prodding finger. As she suspected, one of her teeth worked loose when he hit her. She thinks of her mother's sunken face, with its decayed and missing teeth, and feels a wave of panic, but she's distracted by an agonising pain in her gut. She gropes underneath the bed and drags out the chipped pink chamber pot. Feelings of shame will have to wait.

Her urine is the colour of the apple juice they sell in the shop, but it doesn't smell too bad. As she carries the pot across to the sink to tip the contents away, she steps on something. "Ouch!" More pain. She bends to pick it up – her charger, but her mobile's no longer attached. Stephan must have taken it. He's broken her last link to the world outside this room.

The water in one tap is warm, but she chooses cold and splashes it on her face. She can guess the position of the bruise without looking in the cracked mirror. The thin towel smells cheesy, so she pats her face dry with her sleeve and stumbles back towards the bed.

Morning has arrived, daubing miserable shadowy light on the walls. The door opens a few centimetres, and an unseen hand slides in a plate of dry bread, leaving it on the floor. Does he expect her to scramble for crusts like a dog?

"Let me out of here," she yells, pounding on the mattress with her fists.

There's a brief laugh, then the door rattles shut. This time he leaves the light on so she can stare at the blank walls, floor and ceiling. Her stomach gurgles, so she picks up the plate and chews a dry crust. Fear lurks in every corner, but she's brave. She's not scared of walking along a street in the dark, she knows how to wring a chicken's neck, she understands the ways of the countryside – but nothing has prepared her for this. She doesn't know how to be in this room.

CHAPTER NINE

Time is passing. Miserly grey days slip from Odeta's grasp as she struggles through the terrors of each ink-black night. She guesses this is her third day, because food arrives only in the morning: soup or porridge with stale bread. Once the skinny man brought her coffee, waiting wordlessly in the doorway as she gulped it down.

She's sitting on the bed leaning her back against the wall, her head propped against a pillow. Her eyes are unfocused, but her ears are on full alert. She's learned to recognise who is approaching from the timbre of the footsteps on the stairs: the clink of a steel-capped boot means it's Tomas; a squeaky trainer signals the skinny man who brings her food. The approaching footsteps are heavy: Tomas.

The door bangs open. He's holding a towel draped over his arm, and is carrying a drawstring bag. He examines the bruise on her cheek, tracing its outline with a finger. "Bloody Stephan, ignorant bastard." He hands her the bag containing soap, deodorant and make-up.

"Get ready," he says. "Time you started work."

Work! Odeta's heart hammers. Yes, work – she'd like to. "In a shop?" she ventures. "At home I work in my father's shop."

Tomas laughs so hard that the fleshy folds of skin on his face swell, and his eyes sink like currants in a lump of dough. "Not in a shop. You'll be working from home."

Odeta stares back at him. What's so funny?

"Ha ha. Bad English joke. Working from home, shirking from home. You will start by working from home. After that, we'll see."

He ushers her to the sink and presents her with the folded towel as if it were a precious gift. "Wash yourself and cover that bruise with this." He indicates a tube of liquid foundation.

The drawstring bag also contains some foil packets, plus black mascara, eyeliner, and lipstick. The lipstick is blunt and used.

"This isn't mine."

He shrugs. "It's all there is. Make yourself look good." He's gone again, slamming the door behind him.

Odeta washes herself, standing on each leg in turn and swinging the opposite foot up into the basin. She examines the rubbed pink skin on her hips and belly from when Stephan dragged her down the stairs. She dabs water on the grazes, but they aren't deep. The make-up is several shades too light for her skin tone and makes her face ghostly pale. Beneath it, the bruise mutates from angry purple to pale blue.

Tomas returns, carrying a bundle of bed linen and a shopping bag. She watches him unpack the contents. First he takes out a glass vase with a screw-on lid, containing a clear liquid. He unscrews it and arranges, not flowers, but some long sticks. Gradually, a floral scent creeps out of the bottle and spreads across the room, cloaking the damp earth smell with the aroma of a rose garden. From somewhere out in the corridor he fetches a stepladder, positions it in the centre of the room and stands on it, reaching above his head to change the harsh white light bulb for a soft pink one.

"Smoke and mirrors," he announces. Odeta doesn't see smoke, and the mirror above the basin is still cracked. Yet the room looks and smells different, as if a thin veil has been draped across it, concealing its squalor.

She changes the bedlinen. It's wrinkled and creased, but smells of fresh soap – cleaner than her own stale t-shirt. She sniffs her armpit, wrinkling her nose at the sour vinegary smell. "Where is my suitcase? My clothes?" she asks.

He spreads his hands wide in a careless gesture. "Later."

As she smooths down the creased sheet with her palm, she wonders about the work they want her to do. Could it be something to do with modelling? Perhaps they will bring clothes from Kreshnik's cousins' factory for her to wear, and take more photographs? She lets this idea occupy her mind, because lurking behind it is another more frightening thought. At least she won't be in this place for long. When Kreshnik finishes his other business in London he will come to fetch her, and Tomas will have to answer to him for the brutal way she's been treated.

She sits on the bed and hugs her knees, drawing them up close to her chin. She doesn't cry – no more tears will come. She waits.

The unnamed thing she's been dreading arrives. Escorted by Tomas, he advances into the room, his stinky breath filling the cramped space. He's dark-skinned, with grey hair and bushy eyebrows, and more hairs sprout from his nose and curl inside the V-neckline of his shirt. He's talking to Tomas in an unfamiliar language – maybe Arabic. Tomas appears not to understand, and answers "Yes" or "No" in English, then leaves, closing the door behind him. For once she doesn't hear the key turn in the lock, and files this snippet of information away in her mind.

The elderly man gapes at her, eating her up with his eyes. He crosses the room to the sink and washes himself; first his hands and face, then he removes his jacket and shirt and washes his torso, mumbling some kind of incantation under his breath. Her mouth is parched and her throat aches. He turns back towards her and crosses the room, leering. Without speaking, he pounces, pushes her down on the bed and slumps on top of her. Beneath the crush of his body she can feel his unsteady heartbeat.

"Don't hurt me," she whispers in Albanian.

The old man babbles a reply in Arabic, unleashing a belch of aniseed. He rolls up her t-shirt and grabs her left breast. Before she can react, he clamps his mouth onto her nipple.

English words come to her now, a whole shower of them. "No – get off me," she screams, jabbing his chest with her elbow. He swears at her – an English word she's heard from Kreshnik – and showers her with spittle. Lifting her knees, bit by bit she levers his body away from her. His heartbeat stutters, but he won't give up; he jerks and thrusts, but he's lost his erection. Hoisting himself up, he glares at her with hate-filled eyes and utters another round of expletives. She backs away. His face grows scarlet, he gasps for air and his body folds in a fit of coughing. Recovering, he crosses to the basin and spits. He runs water into his hands and scoops it into his mouth, picks up his jacket and stalks towards the door, pausing to shake drops of water from his hands over her.

The door bangs behind him, but the lock doesn't click. She sneaks into the corridor and watches him stomp up the stairs, listening to his voice boom in the hallway above and Tomas shouting back, raising the tempo. It sounds as if the old man is trailing Tomas from room to room and protesting, the pitch of his voice sliding up the scale from basso profundo to falsetto.

Odeta rearranges her clothes and leans against the corridor

wall, cooling her flushed face against the whitewashed brickwork. Heart pounding, she turns away from the stairs and tiptoes along the passage. Could there be another door? It's dimly lit by a single plug-in nightlight, but at the far end of the passage daylight is struggling in through another half-buried window, high up the wall like the one in her room. Something brushes across her face. She catches her breath, but it's only a spider dangling on a thread.

"Go home, little spider," she whispers, gently scooping the creature into her palm and stringing it back up on its web.

There's another door opposite, and she tries the handle. It's locked, but from inside a female voice calls out in strongly-accented English, "Who's there?"

Her heart quickens. "Odeta. Who are you?"

The voice switches from English to Albanian. "I'm Elira. Unlock my door."

Another Albanian woman in this place. Relief surges through Odeta as she hunts around for a key, reaching up and feeling along the ledge on top of the door. "There's no key. Do you know where it is?"

"All keys are upstairs. In a locked box near the front door."

"But why are the doors locked?" whispers Odeta.

"Because of her."

"Her?"

Elira's reply is drowned out by a commotion from above. The ceiling vibrates to the tramp of footsteps, and Tomas's shouting gets louder until it drowns out the old man's voice. Eventually the front door slams, shaking the fabric of the building. Odeta moves away from Elira's door and peers up the cellar stairs. The footsteps are moving closer. A switch snaps on and light streams into the corridor. She blinks as Tomas reaches the last step.

She crosses her arms and faces him, jutting out her chin.

"That old man..." she begins, "attacked me." One look at Tomas's livid face silences her. He grabs her arm and forces her back inside the room. As she tries to resist, he knocks her off balance and raises his hand. She lifts her arm to shield her face; seconds later his blow lands on her upper arm.

"You fucking bitch," he bellows. "Didn't play ball. Wanted his money back."

Mutely, she rubs her stinging left arm and stares at his scowling face, pupils black and dilated so the irises are barely visible.

"Didn't Kreshnik teach you anything?" He slaps her again and she stumbles against the bed, raising both arms in front of her to ward off further blows. Peering through her fingers she sees his stubby fingers playing with his tight belt, his stomach bulging above his trousers. And suddenly – oh God – he's not wearing trousers.

"Gonna have to teach you myself." As he lunges at her, blood sings in her ears and she screams with terror and rage. Tomas presses his meaty hand over her mouth, and she struggles to remember how to breathe.

CHAPTER TEN

"Was that a scream?" Kate Davison asks her husband Nick. It's three weeks since they moved into their new home at thirty-six Joplin Street. By day the road outside rumbles with traffic, but from mid-evening, street sounds are muted with only occasional sirens ripping through the silence. Since supper they've been sitting side by side on the sofa – both working, but locked in separate universes, eyes focused on parallel laptop screens.

"Give me a minute, darling!" Nick grunts, shifting position and circling his hunched shoulders without raising his eyes to look at her.

"Did you hear what I said?"

"I did. Probably next door's television."

Kate lifts her eyebrows a fraction and sighs. Snapping her computer shut, she slides it off her lap, stands up and strolls across to the bay window. She grasps a handful of one of the maroon silk curtains and tweaks it aside. The much-loved curtains came from their old flat, but Joplin Street has loftier ceilings and they now dangle an undignified half-metre above the floor. Stepping into the bay, she peers out across their front garden towards the phosphorescent glow of a street lamp. Across the road is a leafy park, locked at dusk, but that doesn't deter youths from clambering over the metal gates with skateboards tucked under their arms. The street is deserted, with no further sound of shouts or screams.

"Where are you going?" calls Nick, as Kate leaves the room, steps along the hall and opens the front door.

"Just taking a quick look outside," she calls. "Won't be a minute."

"Honestly, Kate!" With the echo of Nick's words drumming in her ears, she crosses the road and stands close to the park's wire fence, peering through at the ivy-clad trunks of a copse of trees. The night air holds a leaden dampness, through which no sound permeates. It's hard to see past the trees to the grassy area beyond. Feeling foolish, she turns and walks fifty metres to the padlocked gates, from where a gravel path, lined by flowerbeds, winds towards the children's play area. There's no one in sight. She retraces her steps until she's back opposite her own house and looking across at the comforting glow of yellow light from her sitting room. By contrast to this beacon of warmth, her neighbours' properties look gloomy. Number thirty-four is in darkness, but there's a hint of light from behind the curtains of number thirty-eight, where a blue transit van is crammed into an off-street parking space.

She crosses the road, closing her front door softly so as not to wake their ten-year-old son Ben.

"All quiet." She flops back down on the battered leather sofa next to Nick.

He smiles and nods. "Told you." As he reaches across to stroke her hand, she notices a new streak of silver in his dark hair. It suits him. Nick's infectious grin and boyish charm lingered well into his thirties, but now his brow is scored with lines. His expression is thoughtful, but his mood can be unpredictable.

"Give me two more minutes. Last couple of slides to polish up for tomorrow."

Kate glances over at his screen. It's awash with pie-charts in lurid shades of yellow and magenta. "Can I help you? Proofread or something?"

He shakes his head, so she reaches for her own laptop but diverts her hand to conceal a yawn. After spending all day tethered to a screen, it would be nice – just occasionally – if Nick could make time for a chat in the evening.

"We've been here three weeks and haven't met a single neighbour," says Kate.

"Can't say I'm bothered."

"Why don't we invite people round for Christmas drinks?"

"Christmas – don't remind me!"

"You still have sixty shopping days. Don't panic."

This will be their first Christmas in their new home; she must make it special. She shifts her feet and waits. No response from Nick. She sighs. "I'll just pop up and check on Ben."

"Uh-huh." He's not listening.

Kate slips off her shoes and pads up the uncarpeted stairs. A pool of yellow light seeps from under Ben's bedroom door. Perhaps he dropped off to sleep with his lamp on. She should have checked on him earlier; he's not used to the new house yet. Softly, she turns the handle and edges the door open.

But Ben isn't asleep. He's not even in bed, but sprawled on his stomach on top of his Crystal Palace football club duvet cover, fiddling with his iPad. He lifts his head, his fair hair sticking up like straw, blinks his pale blue eyes unseeingly, and turns straight back to his game.

Anger constricts Kate's throat. She clenches her fists and digs her fingernails into her palms. This isn't the first time.

"Give that to me, Ben." She holds out her hand. Her face is a mask of fury, but Ben won't notice. He struggles to read faces or decode emotions.

"No." Ben scowls, shoves the tablet under his pillow and sits on top of it. She's so close to losing it with him, and counts to ten under her breath. "It's eleven o'clock, Ben. School tomorrow. I'm confiscating it."

She peels back the pillow and grabs the tablet. Why did she ever agree to let Nick buy it for him?

Now it's Ben's turn to erupt. He jerks his body back and bangs his headboard repeatedly against the wall. "Bollocks," he shouts – a word she's certain has never been spoken in their house.

"That's enough. Go to sleep." She snaps off his bedside lamp, and the room thickens into darkness. Ben flings himself face-down on his pillow, emitting fake sobs.

As Kate turns and walks towards the door, he shouts, "I hate you. You're a bad mother." It's the kind of clumsy insult a much younger child might use, but still the words have the power to sting.

Kate trudges down the stairs, the iPad a dead weight in her hands. She glances at the frozen screen: bright shapes against a stark landscape. A face and message pop up in one corner of the screen:

> Where u go?

Who has Ben been chatting to? He doesn't have friends. She has a vision of row upon row of faceless children, alone in their bedrooms, all around the world, reaching out to strangers.

She pushes open the sitting room door. "Nick, we have to do something about this." She hands him the tablet, tapping the screen with her forefinger. "Look at that."

Nick glances at the screen and laughs. "He's playing *Minecraft*. What's the problem?"

"Online with some stranger. See – doesn't that name sound Russian? Might not even be a child. Could be anyone."

"Do we have to discuss it now?" Nick's eyes are bloodshot, and his shoulders drooping with exhaustion.

"Don't you care about our son?" she begins, but lacking energy for a fight. "Okay. I give up. Laptop wins again."

"Don't talk to me as if I'm playing bloody computer games, Kate." He checks his watch and sighs. "I have to deliver this presentation ten hours from now."

She knows the unremitting demands of international finance mean long hours and loss of family time. This is the sacrifice Nick's made, changing career from Maths teacher to an analyst in the City. He did it to earn a higher salary so they could move from their poky flat to this house.

In her heart Kate knows she's being unfair. But still smarting from her fight with Ben, she snaps, "You don't get it, do you? I'm off to bed."

"Wait!" He gets to his feet and puts his arms around her, pulling her close. "Look, darling. I know you're worried. We'll have a proper talk about it tomorrow."

"Promise?" She manages a faint smile and leans in towards the reassurance of his goodnight kiss. He pulls her close and they stand, briefly united, in the centre of their warm sitting room with its lofty ceiling and ornate cornices.

In contrast, the chill in her bedroom is arctic. She'd left the window open to drive out the whiff of damp neglect that clings to the fabric of the building, empty for a year before they bought it. Resuscitating it will mean a slow meander from room to room, treating patches of damp, polishing wooden floors, pinning up makeshift curtains until the house bends to her will.

She'll wait out the winter gloom and choose the final colour palette when spring sunshine arrives.

The window judders in its frame as she forces it shut. That frayed sash cord will need replacing: another expensive job. Light from her bedroom filters down on the jungle of brambles and junk that is next door's back garden. Tonight there's a mangy urban fox sniffing at the contents of an overturned dustbin. Gross! Next door must be flat shares or bedsits, where no one cares enough to maintain the outside space. As she draws the curtain, she notices something else: coils of barbed wire along the top of the garden wall. Is that even legal? She's also noticed grilles on the front windows – a common sight in some parts of London, but surely not in this modest area. Whoever lives in the fortress next door must have an irrational fear of break-ins.

CHAPTER ELEVEN

Long after Tomas has gone, Odeta lies prone and shaking on the bed. If she raises her head, dizziness explodes inside her skull and she flops back down onto the grey pillow. She blanks her mind and thinks about dying. Digging deep into her memory she searches for a prayer from her haphazard experience of religion. Although her mother has recently turned to God, she's not sure if her family is Orthodox or Catholic. When her parents were brought up, religion was banned in Albania. Once, when playing with old dolls at her grandmother's house, she found a crucifix stashed away in the toy chest. She showed it to her grandma, who seemed edgy but agreed she could keep it. The next day she took it into school to show her teacher, and nothing bad happened. Picturing that crucifix now – yellow-gold studded with tiny rubies – she wishes she had its solid comfort to hold in her hand. She touches the silver chain at her throat. Ariana's St Christopher is still there, but it hasn't been much help.

Her parents will surely be worrying. She promised to phone as soon as she arrived, but will they think she's so wrapped up in her new life she can't take the time to ring them? Grief wells up inside her. Even if her parents became worried and tried to look for her, how would they find her? She knows there's no record of Odeta Lazami ever having entered England. She hoists her limp body up, crosses to the basin and washes every part of her skin that's been in contact with Tomas. In the mirror, her eyes look pink and her skin is raw and as shiny as a peeled onion. She dabs her face dry with the towel.

What time is it? She's lost track. Darkness shrouds the slit of window; it must be late. Perhaps if she closes her eyes, sleep will come.

The silence is ruptured by footsteps. It's him, Tomas. Speechless, she shudders and hugs the towel to her, but he doesn't even glance at her.

"Your next punter."

A young man with pale skin and greasy blond hair sidles into the room.

"Don't forget what I told you." Tomas wags his finger at her as he leaves.

Her jaw drops open. It can't be more than an hour since he raped her. Was she expected to do this all over again? Words of a prayer come to her now: *Ati ynë që je në qiell, u shënjtëroftë emri yt.* She remembers the Lord's Prayer and mumbles it under her breath, gripping hold of the washbasin for support.

The young man is wearing a denim jacket over paint-spattered overalls, but he must have finished work hours ago because his breath reeks of beer. He speaks to her in what sounds like English, but his accent is rough and she can't understand him.

"Help me," she pleads, hoping he'll understand her poor English. He frowns, sits on the edge of the bed and beckons her to join him. She doesn't move.

He sighs, crosses the room, unfastens her fingers from the sink and leads her towards the bed. "Come, Marije," he says, propelling her with a hand on the back of her waist and pulling her down to sit beside him. He lifts her left arm and inspects it, running his fingers over her veins.

"What are you doing?" she asks in Albanian.

"Uh?" He doesn't understand her either. Next, he scrutinises her right arm, seems satisfied, and nods. From his pocket, he takes a small silver foil packet containing one of the things Kreshnik used when they made love, though he didn't always bother.

The man undresses and indicates she should do the same, but Odeta doesn't move. Listlessly, she watches him prepare himself and roll the condom on. He isn't angry, but he's here for a reason and he's going to get it. "Come here." He's firm, but not rough; polite and very persistent. She cries out when he thrusts into her and judders his way to a climax. Within seconds, he's back on his feet, tugging off the condom, and wiping himself on the sheet. She watches him fastening his belt, and begs for help in a jumble of Albanian and English.

He scratches his head. "What you saying?" He laughs as if they've shared a joke, and pulls on his denim jacket. At the door he turns, and says in English that even she can understand, "I'll come and see you again, Marije."

A promise or a threat? He kisses his own fingertips and flicks the phantom kiss in her direction.

CHAPTER TWELVE

Nick's late home again. It's almost nine o'clock when the glass panel in the front door rattles and his footsteps pound along the hall.

"Hi." His smile is tentative, as if uncertain of his welcome. He pauses in the kitchen doorway and leans against the frame.

"Expect you're starving?" Kate turns to relight the gas and stir the pan on the hob. He shuffles off his shoes, leaving them stranded in no man's land, and advances into the kitchen. He drapes his jacket over the back of a chair and sits down at the table.

"Smells good."

Kate peers into the pan. The burnt edges and viscous coating weren't there when she and Ben ate earlier, in tense silence. Ben hasn't forgiven her for kidnapping his iPad and holding it hostage in a drawer.

"My presentation went okay," says Nick.

"Good." Kate spoons a portion of cassoulet onto a plate. "Fancy a beer?"

"Please." Nick's expression brightens as he picks up his fork and spears a chunk of sausage.

Kate takes the chair opposite him, sipping her white wine in silence until Nick finishes eating, breaks off a piece of baguette and wipes the last of the gravy from his plate.

"Delicious. Thanks."

"Right – can we talk about Ben now?"

A shadow creeps across Nick's face, but he nods and leans towards her.

"I made an appointment to see his teacher after school today."

"Mrs Gibson?"

"Yes. Five minutes was all she could spare. Nothing's changed."

"How do you mean? His school work's fine – she told us at parents' evening."

"But he has no friends, Nick. He spends all his break times alone."

"Did Mrs Gibson say he was being bullied?" Nick's brow creases, and Kate has a glimpse of how he'll look twenty years from now, when he's turned into his father.

"Not exactly. She said he doesn't seem to notice that the others exclude him. All Ben ever wants to do at break time is stay in the classroom and use the computer."

"Well, if that's what he enjoys, where's the harm?" Nick swallows the last of his beer straight from the bottle. "I was nerdy at his age. Trainspotter. Sat all day on the station platform writing down engine numbers and swapping them with my mates."

"That's the difference. You had mates. Ben can't make friends." She feels hot tears pricking the back of her eyes.

Nick pushes his plate away. His fingers tap restlessly on the table top waiting for her to continue.

"When I was growing up in Abercwmmer, all the village

kids played together outside. I don't remember anyone being excluded. And we had so much freedom to roam."

"Times have changed, Kate. We live in London – not in the middle of nowhere in Wales. Besides, we moved to this house because it's opposite the park. Ben can go there to play."

Kate sighs. Why must he insist on misunderstanding her? "Look, he needs to make friends, and it's up to us to help him. We need to get out and meet other families. But first, we have to liberate him from his Xbox and Internet addiction."

"How do you mean, addiction?"

"Remember that small handheld game console he had?"

"Think so. Nintendo, wasn't it?"

"I don't know." Kate shrugs – brand names mean little to her. "Ever wonder what happened to it?" Not waiting for Nick to answer, she continues. "I tried to take it off him. He'd been playing on it for hours and wouldn't come for his supper. He flew into a rage – chucked it down on the floor and stamped on it."

"Why didn't you tell me?"

"You were moving jobs and had enough on your mind. But now he's just as bad with the tablet. Still fuming at me for taking it off him last night."

She takes a deep breath. "We have to wean him off technology, but we can't expect him to do it on his own. So, why don't we all give up tablets and the Internet at home, say, for a year?"

Nick's lower jaw sags. "Tell me this is a joke."

Kate talks faster, her eyes gleaming with excitement. "Six months, then. It would do us all good. You work long enough hours. No need to be wired up to the office all evening."

Beads of sweat appear on Nick's forehead. His face reddens, and he undoes a button of his shirt.

"I could write about our experience as a family living without technology. Maybe get a commission for a whole series..." *Take it more slowly, Kate,* she tells herself. *Give him time to get used to the idea.* Too late – she's gone too far.

"So, you want to turn our lives into some kind of social experiment?" Nick retorts. "How far back d'you want us to go? Stone Age?"

"You're not listening. This is for Ben. And us."

He grimaces, transferring his irritation to his chair and pushing it back with an angry scraping sound. "Mind if I go and check a few things on the computer in the study – or are you expecting me to stop using the Internet right now?" He edges towards the door. "Ouch!" He stubs his toe on one of the shoes he abandoned in the doorway.

Next morning Kate wakes early, puts on her trainers and creeps out of the house. The sky is leaden, and a spike of frost pierces the autumnal damp as she crosses the road to the park and joins the early morning runners. She smiles at people as they jog past. Most are wired up to earpieces or checking Fitbits, too focused to respond, but she wins an occasional nod, raising her hopes of making friends in this new neighbourhood.

She returns home energised. Nick's mood has lightened too.

"I'll drop Ben at school," he offers.

"Won't that make you late?"

"I was logged on and working till midnight. They owe me."

"Imagine having no Internet at home. When you've already put in a ten-hour day, you ought to forget work when you leave the office."

"I'm afraid you're too late – that ship has sailed. Soon

working from home will be the new normal." A rueful smile tells her that her old Nick, with his sardonic wit and zest for life, isn't lost.

"Look, I'm not saying we have to do this for ever. It's for our son's sake."

But Nick's already left the kitchen and is ushering Ben out of the front door towards the car.

Without changing out of her running gear, Kate heads straight to her desk. If she can secure a commission and a decent fee for her planned series of articles, it might nudge Nick in the right direction. Money's been tight since their move.

She dials her editor, expecting Veronica's personal assistant to answer and give her the 'She's in conference' brush-off. When she first started working freelance it was liberating, but living inside her own head all day is lonely; trapped on an endless carousel of pitching ideas, generating copy and worrying that each commission will be her last.

A glossy voice comes on the line – Veronica herself. "Kate. Good to hear from you. Aren't we expecting your *Gender Politics* piece today?"

Veronica is adept at making journalists achieve the impossible. "We have a new assignment," she'll say. "And you're just the person to write it." And Kate finds herself agreeing: "Forty-eight hours? Of course, Veronica."

Today she grasps the initiative. "Sure. My article's ready. I was hoping to come in and deliver by hand, and run a new idea for a possible series past you."

In the ten-second pause that follows Kate visualises Veronica concocting excuses, but instead she says, "Fine. I'm free at two-thirty, see you then." Her line goes dead.

It's ten-fifteen – too early to catch the train into town, but perhaps Ceri will be free to meet for a coffee. She taps out a message, wondering if this will be the last WhatsApp she ever sends. Within seconds Ceri pings a reply:

> Great. Meet you at 1.00. Usual place.

Despite the weak October sunshine, the kitchen feels chilly. She's frugal with the central heating, letting it click off after Ben and Nick leave in the morning; who knows what the bills will be in this new house? She's wearing a shapeless Arran sweater and drapes a rug over her legs like an old lady. Last winter, when they were still in their old flat, she tried typing with gloves on, but they made her fingers fat and clumsy, so she cut the toes off an old pair of socks to cover her hands, leaving her fingers free to skate over the keys.

She thinks about how to pitch her series about a family living for a year, unshackled from technology. Not having Nick and Ben on board is a stumbling block, but it will be worth it if it brings her son out of his shell. She wants him playing outdoors with friends, devouring an actual book instead of snacking on YouTube junk.

When it's time to get ready she changes into beige trousers, black jacket and suede ankle boots, and teases her bobbed hair into a shape that looks vaguely styled. Her right shoulder droops in anticipation of a heavy bag, until she remembers she's not taking her laptop, and the sense of freedom makes her laugh. She slips a USB stick and a notebook into her handbag. That's all.

Closing the front door behind her, she pauses on the step and inhales the odour of Joplin Street: a whiff of diesel and a lungful of dust. Her house is Edwardian, semi-detached, with a slab of front garden. Over decades the houses have shifted with the wealth and pretentions of their owners. Some are smart family homes; others are carved up into bedsits, identified by multiple dustbins.

A young woman, wearing a headscarf and propping a baby on her hip, emerges from number thirty-four, the house that's attached like a Siamese twin to Kate's right wall. Kate calls out a greeting. The woman gives her a blank stare, but the baby's solemn face ripples into a grin.

She turns left towards the station and strolls past number thirty-eight, the only detached house in the street. It dates from an earlier architectural period, probably Victorian. No doubt, when it was originally built, it stood in larger grounds. Her own house and neighbouring properties were probably built on what was once number thirty-eight's garden.

Plane trees line the pavement, pruned by the local Council into lollipop shapes, their leaves tumbling to clog the gutters. Fallen leaves also conceal what lies beneath: as she reaches the corner, she treads in dog mess. She stops to scrape her boot on the kerb, but the brown gunge proves hard to dislodge. Scuffing through a pile of crunchy leaves she glances back at the downstairs windows of number thirty-eight, wondering again why they have metal grilles fixed to the outside of the windows. The front door too is studded with mortice locks, while black paint is peeling off, exposing bottle-green underneath. She stands on one leg and takes off her boot to check it, but the mark on the suede still has a whiff of dog poo. She'll have to go back home and change. As she retraces her steps, the transit van, with the ghost of a utility company's logo visible beneath its coat of blue spray paint, begins to reverse.

"Hey," yells a voice.

She's in the driver's blind spot. Kate jumps aside and the van misses her by centimetres. She glares at the driver, who has swung the van round and halted with two wheels on the pavement waiting for a gap in the traffic. His eyes are hidden behind dark glasses, his face is dark with stubble, and he has fleshy, bulldog folds around his neck. Noticing Kate watching him, he whips off his shades and ogles her with tiny, sneering eyes. She will remember those opaque eyes long after the rest of his face has faded to a blur.

CHAPTER THIRTEEN

Odeta sniffs her t-shirt; it smells of unpasteurised goat's cheese. She rinses out her underwear but there's no heater in the room to dry it. The temperature feels as low as her father's cold store, and she huddles, shivering, beneath the tattered blanket.

Later that day Tomas brings new clothes. Not the sort she'd wear at home: black fake-leather trousers (a poor fit); a plunging sequin top; a black padded bra. In Albania, if you wore clothes like that they'd call you a prostitute.

As he lays the clothes out on the bed, she notices he is carrying something else: a kind of pouch. He opens it, takes out a syringe and comes towards her.

Her heart hammers. "No!" She retreats to the far side of the room and wedges herself into a narrow space between the washbasin and the corner. "Take it away."

Tomas guffaws – everything seems to amuse him, especially inflicting pain. "Stay still. Expensive stuff, this. Don't wanna waste it." He grabs her upper arm, slips a belt around it and tugs it tight so she can see blue veins rippling beneath the surface of her skin.

"Stop. Get off!" She hits out at him with her free hand, but he grabs it, pins it against the wall and traps it under his weight. He forces her fingers into a fist and jabs the syringe directly into a vein.

Odeta imagines poison seeping into her body, circulating round her network of veins and onwards to attack her heart and her brain. Hyperventilating, she clings to the basin, forcing her body to stay upright while Tomas watches her from the doorway. Gradually, a feeling of euphoria erupts inside her skull. Gravity drags her to the floor where she sits for what seems like hours, wired and stunned, until the warmth leaches away like an outgoing tide. Now she's cold and rigid, gripped with nausea. She vomits all over the floor.

When she opens her eyes, she's lying on the bed, her head dangling over the side. The floor has been cleaned, but the bed looks filthy; little black specks coalesce to form new shapes like smudged ink. She blinks and they're gone.

Much later she wakes again, her thoughts muffled, and pain jabbing above one eye. From outside she hears her brother, Leon, calling to her in his high-pitched voice: "Odeta, stop working. Come out and play with us." She replies: "Yes, darling. I'll be there." If the boys are playing outside it must be summer. Why is she always working? She wipes her hands on her apron, pulls it off and walks towards the shop door; she turns the handle and finds it locked. Her father never locks the door during opening hours; he won't want to miss a customer – Leon must be playing a trick on her. She rattles the handle, pushes and kicks against the door. Why won't it open? She panics. Her brothers are waiting for her, she must get outside.

"Leon! Afrim!" She hammers on the door with her balled-up fists, giving it a sharp kick. There's a loud cracking sound and a splinter of wood breaks away from the door.

Someone is shouting. Footsteps thud outside in the corridor, and a harsh voice, definitely not Leon's, calls out, "What the fuck?"

Someone has cleaned up the vomit from the floor, but the room is airless and the smell lingers. Head throbbing, she watches Tomas inspect the crack in the door. She has no memory of kicking it, but it's on the inside, so it must have been her. Eyes smouldering with hatred, she waits for him to beat her for damaging the door, but he shrugs.

"You are going out," he says.

"Out?" Her heart leaps and she starts trembling.

"Out to work." His raisin eyes gleam in his sallow face. "Get dressed."

He stands by the open door and watches her splash her face with water. She pulls on her jeans, stiff with dirt and sweat.

"Not those. The other things." He points at the bundle of clothes he left earlier, and potters out into the corridor while she changes. She hears the scrape of a key turning in the door opposite.

The vinyl trousers smell like sick and make her legs sweaty, and the sequin top must have been made for a woman with a huge bust. She tugs it down at the back to try to raise the gaping neckline a little, and tucks it into the trousers.

"You ready, bitch?"

She goes out into the corridor just as Tomas opens the door opposite, and a blonde woman emerges.

"Elira?" she whispers tentatively. The woman looks her up and down and nods. She's not a natural blonde, and her olive skin tone is disguised by a layer of pale make-up, but it's Elira's china doll eyes that make Odeta inhale sharply: expressionless yet not dead, the kind of eyes that seem never to have lived.

The two women follow Tomas up the stairs and along the hall with its claret-red wallpaper, patterned with gold Grecian urns. Odeta trails her fingers along the wall, the raised urn motifs feel fuzzy beneath her fingers.

"Where are we going?" Odeta whispers to Elira as they wait for Tomas to unlock the front door.

"You'll see."

The front door swings open. "Wait there," Tomas hisses, and jogs down the front steps.

The sky is the colour of smoke: dull and flecked with wisps of cloud, but the sudden rush of daylight stings Odeta's eyes and makes them water. After living in darkness and weak strained light for so long, she has to close her eyes and ease them open slowly. Obediently, she waits on the top step, craning her neck to see beyond the van across the road to a space filled with brown and orange trees and green grass.

She taps Elira's arm. "What's that?"

Elira hovers in the porch, lighting a cigarette, while Tomas backs the van up so the rear doors are against the steps. "It's a park."

"A park." Odeta's legs quiver as the muscles come back to life. If she ran down these steps and sprinted across to the park she could disappear among those trees. But it's too late. Tomas has already opened the rear doors and they butt up against the porch pillars, forming a holding pen and blocking her view of the street and the house next door. He flaps his arms to usher the two women inside, knocking the cigarette out of Elira's hand and stamping on it. She shrugs and climbs into the van like an obedient dog. Odeta hangs back, soaking up the damp greyness of outside.

"Get in the van." Tomas manhandles her as if she were a sack of potatoes; her father would treat his vegetables with more respect. The van floor is heaped with tools and old tyres. Pushing them aside, she squats down on a greasy tartan rug.

"Don't get your clothes dirty," warns Elira, as Tomas grinds the gears.

"Who will care?"

"They like us to be clean."

"Who are 'they'?" The van drives over a speed bump, throwing Odeta up against Elira who lets out a shriek. Tomas swivels round and glares.

Elira puts a finger to her lips. "Shh. Later."

The van pelts along, sometimes lurching forward, sometimes screeching to a halt. The women are buffeted and flung around; there's no window, and Odeta's head is pounding. Elira hangs on to a strap fixed to one side of the van, but there's no handhold on Odeta's side. She watches Elira, whose dead eyes stare from under the curtain of bleached hair.

At last the van jolts to a halt, and Tomas opens the rear doors. They are in the back courtyard of a row of buildings. Rain is spilling out of gutters and plopping onto the pavement and dustbins.

Elira clambers out without speaking and walks across to a metal fire-escape that zigzags up the rear of a brick building. Every window is shuttered, but specks of light seep through the slats. In her dingy basement, Odeta has dreamed of light; she hates grey and loves colours. She remembered when her father called them all into the sitting room and produced the new green lampshade with a fringed trim. Solemnly he placed it over the stiffened white paper shade that was there before, and they all "Oohed" and "Aahed" as the room transformed from harsh whiteness to a shady olive grove.

She plods behind Elira up the metal stairs to first-floor level, where she pushes open a heavy fire-door. They trek along a white corridor, then Elira tweaks a curtain aside and they enter what looks like a doctor's reception area. Behind a desk sits a woman wearing a white coat, which looks out of place against her red lipstick and candyfloss hair. She greets Elira with a smile and a hug and asks, "Who's this?" jabbing a thumb in Odeta's direction. She's not Albanian, but her accent suggests she's not English either.

"Dunno," says Elira. "Maybe Marije, maybe Odeta."

The woman puts on thin tortoiseshell glasses and squints at a pad on her desk that looks like a register of names.

"Marije. I have the name Marije here." She places a tick beside it.

Odeta's pulse quickens – perhaps this place is a doctor's office. Her experience of doctors' surgeries is limited. After she fell from the balance beam during a gymnastics display, she was sent with her mother to the hospital in Tirana. They had no car and no money for a taxi. She'd clung to her mother's arm and hobbled through the streets half-fainting from the pain. When they got to the hospital the waiting area was packed and the doors had been closed so they had to join a queue in the street outside and wait for hours. When she finally saw a doctor, he told her she shouldn't have walked to the hospital or put weight on her injured leg. He said it would affect the way the bones knitted back together. He was right – she never took part in a gymnastics competition again.

There's no sign of any medical equipment in this cramped reception area, but why else would Tomas send her here? Elira's no help; she seems to have lost the power of speech. Her eyes are glassy, and underneath the make-up her skin looks sore and flaky, like a plant left too long without sunlight and water.

"When will I see doctor?" she asks in Albanian.

"Uh?" The woman doesn't understand her. Tentatively Odeta slides one strap of her top off her shoulder, turns sideways and taps her forefinger at the stigmata of Tomas's last assault: a purple bruise snaking down her back like an ugly tattoo. The woman wrinkles her brow. "You'll keep that hidden if you know what's good for you."

She's speaking English. Odeta turns to Elira. "I don't understand?"

"You'll see for yourself – bruises turn some of the punters on."

The older woman grins, revealing a mouth crammed with brown stained teeth. Does everyone in Britain have foul teeth? Even the worst dentist in Albania couldn't wreak this much havoc. She tests her own loose tooth with her tongue – it's rocky, but still clinging on.

A buzzing sound drills into the room and Odeta flinches, looking round for a bee. The fluffy-haired woman peers at a blurred black and white screen and presses a button to activate a door.

"Go through to the lounge, girls," she orders, flapping her hands to shoo them away. Elira opens a door and beckons Odeta to follow her into an adjoining room where three young girls are staring at a television screen. Dressed in microscopic skirts and skimpy tops, with slim curvy figures, they look stunning, until Odeta blinks and refocuses. The room smells of cheap perfume, and one of the girls has lank greasy hair. But she's not that clean herself. A bath or a shower were luxuries to be savoured at home, but here they are beyond rationing. Non-existent.

Her eyes are drawn to a coat rack, fixed to the wall just beside the door, where she sees a row of crisp white cotton overalls. She lifts one down from its peg, noticing the neat buttons and an embroidered logo above the right-hand breast pocket. Doubtfully, she grapples with the mismatch between the overalls and the young women; they don't look old enough to be medically qualified. She goes and sits beside Elira and asks, "What happens now?"

"Now we wait. Soon it will get busy. Then it will be our turn."

"Our turn to see the doctor?"

"God – you are most ignorant, girl." Elira picks up a glossy magazine and flicks through it, pretending to read but peering at Odeta over the top of her magazine. She hisses, "Do you think we come here for medical checks or beauty treatments? We are the sex trade."

Her words slam into Odeta like a punch, and her whole body stiffens. Trembling, she jerks her head up to look at the television, mounted on a bracket high up on the wall. It's showing a chat show with a live audience; the presenter's words are gobbledy-gook punctuated with nervous laughter from the audience. But none of the other girls seems to be watching the programme; she can tell that some of them are slyly watching her.

It's hard to breathe through the fug of stale perfume. She walks across to the window, pulls aside the brown velvet curtain and peers down into the street below. Life is going on: couples stroll by holding hands; a group of girls and young men meander along, laughing and calling out to one another, before turning into a doorway opposite. In a window Odeta notices a parrot in a cage, and reads the sign: *Golden Dragon Chinese Restaurant.*

She tries to open the window but it won't budge. Although they climbed only one storey of the metal fire escape, they seem to be two levels above the pavement. There's a sign fixed to the wall below the window she's looking out through, she can see its reflection backwards in the darkened window opposite.

"It says *Beauty Spa.*"

Startled, Odeta spins around. She didn't notice the girl with dark hair, ironed straight, coming to stand beside her at the window.

"It used to say *Sauna and Massage*," the girl continues, in halting English, "until police began clampdown in this area."

"Please speak slower," says Odeta. *Police* she knows, and *sauna*. "What is 'clampdown'?"

The girl looks at her oddly. "I see you are new to this work. *Sauna and Massage* was like code name for brothel," she explains. "There was a plan to clean up this area, drive out sex workers. Salons were raided and closed down."

"But this one stayed?"

The girl nods, her lips drawn together in a tight line. "Owners of this place received tip-off. In one week, they changed everything. Wait till you see treatment rooms. Full of skincare products and lotions." She pauses for breath. "I'm Cassie, by the way."

"Odet....no, Marije." After all, what's the point?

"Did Louella tell you about fire drill?"

"Fire? No." She thinks about being trapped two storeys up, and shudders.

Cassie giggles. "When alarm sounds, it doesn't mean there's a fire. It's warning of a police raid. And then..." She strolls across to the neat row of white jackets and lifts one off its hook. "We all must run in here and put on a jacket." She slips her arms into the sleeves, digs her hand into the pocket and pulls out a name badge, which she fastens onto the breast pocket, just below the embroidered logo. Gathering up her long straight hair in one hand she twists it around and fixes it in a neat bun with hairgrips from the pocket.

"So now I am beautician. Magic – see." She gives a theatrical twirl.

Odeta's head is spinning. She understands, but it makes no sense and she can't find words to frame her questions.

"Cheer up. Nearly Christmas," says Cassie. "Starts early here. So people spend more money in shops."

"How do you know that?"

Cassie points down at the street. "Trees in windows, lights in the shops and streets. Haven't you noticed?"

Odeta shakes her head as Cassie points out a shop window, fringed with fairy lights, twinkling in blue, red and white. Next to it is a café with a gold artificial Christmas tree outside on the pavement and showers of shooting stars painted in glitter on the window. All along the street, ropes of lights are swinging from high lampposts. Everywhere is festooned with light. How could she not have noticed?

The door swings open; they turn away from the window as the fluffy blonde receptionist enters. "Marije," she calls. Odeta gapes; the name doesn't connect. She turns back to the window, captivated by the glittering lights.

"That's you, isn't it?" Cassie elbows her in the ribs. Still she doesn't move.

The older woman stalks across the room and tweaks her arm. "Yes, you. Marije. New girl." Her voice is harsh with irritation as she pulls Odeta away from the window. More manhandling. She wants to scream.

"Your first client."

Odeta's skin prickles with heat. Under the watching eyes of the other girls, she juts out her chin and follows the woman along a corridor to another room, another cell, where another man is waiting.

CHAPTER FOURTEEN

Kate rides the up-escalator from the bowels of the London Underground, reading the freebie newspaper over the shoulder of the man in front. Outside the station she turns left down a side road. Not far along is an old-fashioned sandwich bar. Peering through its steamed-up window, beyond the ready-filled rolls piled up under a Perspex cover, she sees Ceri is already inside, waiting for her.

"Hi!" Ceri flicks back her long blonde hair as she slides down from her high stool and greets Kate with a kiss on both cheeks. "Don't know why you still insist on meeting in this dump. There's a Starbucks on the corner."

Kate laughs. "You know I've renounced large corporates. Besides, this is our tradition. The place we always met when we came to London as students."

"After we escaped from Abercwmmer," adds Ceri, who has lost all trace of a Welsh accent.

"Don't you sometimes miss it, though? The innocence of our childhoods?"

"Never." Ceri extracts a bank card from a choice of a dozen lined up in her wallet. They join the queue at the counter, and in full hearing of the other customers she quips, "That's why Nick always says *You can take the girl out of the village but you can't take the village out of the girl.*"

Kate stiffens. Nick means it affectionately, but on Ceri's lips it sounds like a criticism. "It's just that I wish Ben's childhood could be more like ours."

"It didn't end well, though, did it? Not for Rhys."

Suddenly breathless, Kate's chest tightens. "I'll find us a table." She leaves the queue, chooses a seat and sinks down onto it.

"Two skinny lattes, please." Ceri places their order and makes hand signals across the hubbub of voices and roar of steam, to ask if she wants anything to eat. Kate shakes her head.

After Ceri returns to work, Kate takes out her spiral-bound notebook, with its jaunty blue and cerise swirly cover, and jots a few notes. She pats her jacket pocket, feels the USB stick and rolled-up plastic wallet containing her article, then sets off for her meeting.

She pushes the revolving door and enters a hushed marble reception hall. Publishers, designers and other creatives share space in this building. Self-consciously, she announces herself to the receptionist, who points to a visitors' seating area next to an ornamental pond where Koi carp swim aimlessly. She watches the fish, counting seven, including a black one, while she waits to be summoned. When the call comes, she takes the lift to the seventh floor and Terrie, Veronica's personal assistant, ushers her into an office gleaming with minimalism. On Veronica's desk, a Mac in duck-egg blue stands shoulder to shoulder with a tablet, but apart from a few copies of the magazine, fanned out on a coffee table, paper might never have been invented.

"Kate – lovely to see you," Veronica coos, smoothing an invisible crease from her sleeve. Her trio of bracelets jingles as she lifts her wrist for a limp handshake. "It's been a while."

And could that be because Kate's invitations to the past two Christmas parties have been mysteriously lost in the post? For five years she's been churning out articles to fill the pages of *Women First*, but her contact with Veronica and the section editors has been mainly by email. Often they don't even acknowledge receipt, and she has to prod them: *Was that article okay? Can you send me a purchase order number so I can invoice?*

Veronica must have read her mind. "We'll be sending out invites for our Christmas party very soon," she breathes. "This year we're taking over a whole floor of the Design Museum. Do hope you'll join us." Her smile is wide, yet barely ripples the surface of her face. She must have had work done.

Kate lays the yellow memory stick down on the desk.

Veronica flinches, visibly. "Err, what's that?"

"My article on Gender Politics."

Veronica reaches out a manicured fingernail and flicks it across the desk towards her. "Virus-checked?"

Kate nods.

"Hmm. Best be sure." She presses an intercom button on her phone. "Terrie." Her assistant materialises, smiling and upbeat. "Get the IT helpdesk to virus-check this for me, please."

"Transcript?" she asks, wagging her finger in the air. Kate extracts the plastic folder. It looks a tad crumpled.

Veronica squints at the cover page. "I see you've used Verdana font: sans serif. Our latest guidelines say..."

Kate lets her ramble on about why the magazine is turning back to using Times New Roman. It's not a font she's personally keen on. It gives an old-fashioned look and feel to the printed page, but that could be good news for the series of articles she's come here to pitch. Aware her slot in Veronica's diary won't exceed fifteen minutes – any moment now, Terrie will breeze in and call time – she takes a deep breath and begins.

"I'd like you to consider an idea for a series of articles about a family living without the Internet." Rapidly she outlines her proposal. "My working title is *Life Offline*."

Veronica swivels her chair sideways and stretches her legs out in front of her, one dainty shoe dangling from her pedicured toe. As she twirls her ankle, she gives the impression of thinking deeply. "I'm not sure about that idea, Kate. *Women First* is at the forefront of what's happening now. Our readers thrive on technology. Appreciate the benefits Apps bring to their lives. Why would they want to turn back the clock?"

"You've run articles about wartime baking."

"Maybe – but that's retro. Baking is so now."

Veronica's face says it all. Why would anyone in their right mind want to opt out of online existence? Shopping delivered to the door, theatre tickets and weekend breaks clicked on a whim, entertaining friends with Instagram pics and Facebook posts.

"People want to stay in touch, Kate. You know what I'm saying? Live technology, love technology. And I can't have writers who won't deliver their copy by email."

"It'll come to you typed. I'll send it on a memory stick."

"But why should we go through all that faff? Honestly, Kate."

"If I'm going to write about an Internet-free life and forging links with my local community, I have to live those values. Interact with people face-to-face." She knows she's rambling. What's happened to fluent Kate, the wordsmith?

Veronica peers at her watch and stands up. Perfume wafts around her, not quite strong enough to conceal the stale whiff of a lapsed non-smoker. She crosses the room and holds the door open as Kate gets slowly to her feet, her hopes evaporating like fine drizzle. If she can't negotiate a deal with Veronica, how will she convince Nick that technology addiction is stunting Ben's childhood?

"Write it and I'll take a look," Veronica says, with a crisp handshake. "But I can't offer a commission or promise to publish. I don't think your concept is right for our readers."

CHAPTER FIFTEEN

Tomas brings a toolbox to repair the split Odeta kicked in the door. Despite a vertical crack running across one panel, the lock has held firm. She watches him work, chewing her fingernails. Not that there's much left to bite. She's nibbled them down to the quick.

In the corridor behind Tomas, a shadow glides along the wall. The shadow stops and its outline quivers. Her pulse quickens. It can't be Elira – Tomas left her behind at the Beauty Spa when he turned up and dragged her away. "Come, Marije. Time for working at home."

The shadow shifts again, and she sees it's attached to a sort of man-child – not very tall – wearing tracksuit bottoms and a too-tight t-shirt that strains across a wobbly belly. If the man's body is an odd shape, his face has the moon-like eyes of a young calf. Odeta has seen animals being slaughtered. Sheep are the worst (they seem to have antennae for danger and their eyes are huge with terror), but calves are trusting to the very end, their expression turning to bewilderment only in the instant the knife falls. This man's eyes have that same haunted puzzlement.

Although the strange man is making no sound, Tomas must

have sensed his presence. He puts down the tube of filler and turns around. The man flinches and tries to scurry away, but Tomas gets up from his kneeling position and grabs hold of him. "Want to see her, do you, Geoffrey?" He positions his thick body behind the strange man. Tomas isn't tall, but he towers over this stranger. Clamping his vice-like hands on the shorter man's shoulders, he propels him forward into Odeta's room.

"There – take a good look." He jabs a finger at Odeta, who stands up, clutching a blanket around her shoulders. She can see the man is trembling – if she had any compassion left, she might feel some for him. The man's head lolls, as if he has trouble supporting it on his neck, but it could just be the puppet-master way Tomas is holding him. A sliver of pink tongue protrudes from the corner of his mouth, and Odeta prays he doesn't open it so she won't have to see his teeth. The man mumbles, shuffles and stares down at the floor.

With a hooting laugh, Tomas shoves the man in the back so he staggers towards Odeta. His ungainly body bumps up against her and bounces off. She can't step back (the bed's in the way), so she shifts sideways, and Tomas's next push shunts the man onto the bed. He slumps forward, covering his face with his hands, and groans.

Surely this man can't be a client?

"Like what you see?" mocks Tomas, grabbing a hank of the man's hair and twisting his head round to look in her direction. "Your type, is she?"

The man he called Geoffrey shakes his head. His eyes flare with panic, and his mouth opens and closes like a fish.

"Better push off then, Geoffrey." Tomas yanks him up from his sprawl on the bed, spins him round and slaps him on the bottom. Geoffrey shambles off, gathering speed as he scuttles out of the door and up the basement stairs. Odeta can still hear his laboured breathing after he disappears from view.

"Who...?" she begins.

Tomas opens his mouth, as if, for once, to acknowledge her existence with a reply, but changes his mind, shrugs and turns to survey the patch-up job he's done on the door. He's squirted some white stuff into the crack and nailed a wooden baton alongside the lock. The result is a tacky bodge-up, but he reviews his handiwork with pride, as if he were an actual carpenter. The short stint of manual work seems to have calmed his temper. "Stephan will bring you food," he says, as he shuts the door.

He's left the syringe lying on a side table. Looking at it makes her eyes burn. She wants to stamp on it and destroy it, but that would spark his fury and another beating. She looks for a place to hide it, but apart from under the mattress there's nowhere. She's felt along every inch of wall, counted every brick, stood on tiptoe on the bed and reached her hands towards the high-up, half-buried window, too narrow for an adult to squeeze through. Even a tiny body like hers: abused, starved, and shrinking by the day.

<h1 style="text-align:center">CHAPTER SIXTEEN</h1>

It's that time on a Friday evening when conversation swells from chatter into a din, and laughter ripples around the room. No one, except Kate, notices the supper plates, smeared with gravy and couscous, waiting to be stacked up and cleared. She closes her eyes and blocks them out.

A warm shape nudges her lower leg. She bends down, scoops up Oscar the cat, and settles him in her lap, his coat prickling with static electricity. Kate's thoughts wander to the battle she had getting Ben to bed before their guests arrived. He used to go willingly, happy to play on his iPad without his parents checking up on him, but now she's taken it away. Stroking Oscar calms her frazzled nerves. She glances at the folk clustered around her table. These people are her closest friends, so why does she feel so cut off from them and their conversation?

"That was delicious, Kate."

She swivels her head towards the sound of her name. Lisa is asking for the recipe. She nods. She'll get it later.

"Look at this." Ceri leans over and dangles her latest smartphone in front of Kate's face.

"Very – err – nice," says Kate. The sleek silver technology holds no interest for her.

"No, I mean this website." Ceri taps her lilac-polished fingernail on the screen. "A new online magazine for women like us. I thought you could write for it."

Kate takes the phone from Ceri and peers at the tiny screen. The publications she writes for all have websites, but still manage to keep their magazines on the newsagents' shelves. Online magazines, especially start-ups, mean downward pressure on pay rates, enticing writers with the message: *We can't pay contributors at the moment, but we'll give you a complimentary one-year subscription.* A free subscription won't pay the supermarket bill, as Ceri should know.

"Women like us." Kate echoes Ceri's words, glancing at her friends and wondering if they still have anything in common.

"Yeah." Lisa twists a lock of blonde hair around her finger. "Knocking on the door of forty with hair way past our shoulders. I don't care. I'm not cutting mine."

Charlotte laughs. "Me neither. And I'll be fending off the wrinkles with Botox."

Kate conceals a yawn. She doesn't care about ageing, and she's not that interested in hair. Hers is a sort of chestnut bob that she shampoos in the shower every morning and towels dry, and in five minutes she's ready to go. Has Friday evening conversation sunk this low? What happened to the days when they used to sit around the supper table in girl/boy/girl/boy order – split away from their other halves – to talk about culture, politics and world events?

Down at the male end of the table, Ceri's husband, Dan, crowbars his way into the conversation. "London property's still booming, guys. We're making forty sales a month. Valuations up, viewings through the roof. It's mental!" He turns to Franco, who's sitting on his left. "Take Bramley Avenue, where you and Charlotte live, Franco. How much d'you think?"

"No idea, mate," says Franco. Dark patches of sweat have spread from the armpits of his lilac shirt matching the dark stubble on his chin. "I leave those calculations to you. Next place I buy will be back home in Perugia, if – I mean when – I make partner."

Kate glances across at Nick, who still seems exhausted and short-tempered. How he hates working in the City. She shivers thinking of the sacrifice he made giving up Maths teaching, which he loved. Back then he was just as tired, but more comfortable in his skin.

Nick rouses himself and leans towards Josh. "Meant to tell you – there are new IT jobs coming up at my place soon."

Josh blinks, his dark eyelashes twitching like an insect's wings. "I thought you'd outsourced everything to India?"

"Yeah, but they screwed the contract price down too hard. We analysts get a shit service, and it's impacting business, so they're setting up a small in-house team and bringing the work back to the UK. I'll send you the link."

"Cheers, mate." Josh is the geeky one, clever and serious. Lisa had nagged him to leave a secure job and follow the money into IT contracting, but lately it's been more famine than feast.

"Bloody IT taking over the world," yawns Franco, draining his glass of red. "Some idiots are predicting lawyers will be next. Computers taking over from professionals? Not in my lifetime."

Kate knows about this topic. She's been covering it for one of her magazines, and her research has spooked her. Will there be any jobs left for our children?

"I've heard that sales and admin jobs are at risk," she says, cautiously. "But surely not law – all those years of study."

"Nah, that's rubbish," says Dan. "Sales jobs will never go. People buy from people."

Kate's not so sure. She stands up, her chair scraping on the wooden floor, and everyone hands their plates along like a game of Pass the Parcel. Kate stacks and carries them into the kitchen. She finds the recipe printout for Lisa, and dabs a smudge of gravy off one corner with damp kitchen roll.

Cheese next, or dessert? She can't decide, and the chilly kitchen, with its black granite worktops and stainless steel appliances, doesn't speak to her at all. *This kitchen isn't me*, she thinks. Before they moved in she'd tried to convince Nick they should change it to a farmhouse style filled with mellow antique pine. Too dated, he'd argued. It would decrease the value of the house. Since he went to work in the City, everything has been a commodity to him.

She coaxes the Brie from its wrapping. It oozes onto the cheeseboard and she carries it in. The dining room is layered with noise: vintage Springsteen, clinking glasses, and loud guffaws as the men share a dodgy joke. Kate hovers on the sliproad of the conversation waiting to filter into a gap, but already Nick is fidgeting. She pings him a warning glance, but he ducks it and gets to his feet. The other men fix their eyes on him, expectantly.

"Great supper, darling. We're just popping into the study, okay?" He ruffles her hair on his way past. She shrugs away, and a lock of her hair gets trapped between his fingers.

"Nick – you promised." She glares at him as the four men troop out to get their fix of online gaming, now a feature of Friday evenings.

"Top-up, anyone?" Kate offers the wine bottle round.

Charlotte shakes her head, "I'm driving."

"Mineral water for me," says Lisa, reaching past the cheeseboard for the green bottle and helping herself.

"Oh, here's the recipe you wanted." Kate hands it across.

Lisa yawns and drops the printed sheet on the table without giving it a glance. "Could you email me a copy?"

The central heating timer clicks off. Soon the room will cool, draughts will seep down the chimney and the air will smell of damp soot. Kate turns down the music and they chat lethargically, waiting for the men to be ready to leave.

Ceri swipes the screen of her mobile, scrolling through Instagram and Facebook, checking for evidence of life happening elsewhere. Holding her attention is getting harder, and Kate feels a surge of loneliness for the friend she's known since the age of two.

Somewhere in the room a mobile beeps. Ceri scrambles to check her screen, but her face clouds with disappointment. "Not mine," she shrugs. "Maybe yours, Kate?"

"Doubt it." Why would she bring her phone to the table? She swivels round and fishes it out of the fruit bowl, where it's buried beneath a satsuma. The text is for her, and it's from Nick:

> Any more coffee going?

"Right, that's it! He's not getting away with this!" She slams down her cup and strides out of the dining room, across the hall and into the study. The guys are crouching around the screen like Neanderthals, clutching controllers and jamming buttons. They gawp at her as she storms across to the electric socket, grabs hold of the main cable and yanks it out. The screen wobbles on its pedestal and topples forward.

"What the hell?" Nick stretches out his arms to save it while Kate scrabbles in the desk drawer and finds a pair of scissors. She whips it out and snips off the plugs from the disconnected TV and Xbox. The four men watch, slack-jawed, as she dives underneath the desk, scissors poised for further attack, the rough carpet scratching her knees.

Josh mobilises first. "Kate, some of those wires are live. Watch out."

"Don't try this at home," quips Dan.

Everything in the study is plugged into a single adaptor: a giant hydra sprouting cables. One by one Kate disconnects them and decapitates their plugs with her scissors until Nick bends down and grabs hold of her arm, wrenching it up behind her back. Pain jolts through her as he hauls her out from under the desk. The light on the processor flickers and dies; the infernal hum of printers and hubs – that buzzing in the ears no one notices until it stops – falls silent. The room holds its breath.

"You bi..." Nick hisses, stopping himself before saying the word. He wrests the scissors away from her, his expression raw, his face gleaming with perspiration. The women leave the dining room and congregate in the study doorway, but no one speaks.

Josh gets to his feet. "Time we were off." He signals to Lisa, who collects everyone's coats and hands them out. They head for the door, fastening buttons.

Only Dan and Ceri linger voyeuristically. At last, Ceri has found some real-life action more gripping than staring at her phone.

"What was that all about?" she hisses in Dan's ear.

"Slasher movie?" he whispers, grinning at her, before adopting a solemn expression and turning to Nick. "Anything we can do, mate?"

Nick glares at them and they put on their coats and slip away, slamming the front door.

"Right. What the hell's going on?" Nick shouts. He's still gripping her arm, and gives her a rough shake so her head judders forward and whips back.

"Let go of me." She pulls away from him and he doesn't resist. She feels drained, as if recovering from a long illness. This wasn't meant to happen, but when she tries to say sorry the words won't come. She forces herself to meet his eyes. "Right, I've warned you. Now perhaps you'll realise I'm serious about giving it up."

"Giving up what?"

"The Internet. Technology, all of it. I'm banning it from this house."

Nick gapes. The blood rinses from his face and his eyes bulge. "I work my butt off all week. Don't tell me what I can do in my own house!"

He drops the scissors into the desk drawer, slams it shut, and without turning his back on her reaches behind the curtain and feels along the windowsill to the place where he tries to hide his special bottle of single malt. There's a tumbler on his desk, and he splashes a hefty measure on top of whatever's in there already. As he lifts the glass to his mouth, his hand is shaking.

Folding her arms, Kate watches him across the invisible barricade that has sprung up between them. She swallows hard, but the lump in her throat won't shift.

———————————

CHAPTER SEVENTEEN

Every day three or more strangers come to Odeta's room. Once, she counted eight men in a single day. Sometimes they ask her to do things to them – disgusting things – but she doesn't always understand what they're asking. Sometimes it's perverted things involving peeing, and she feels worse than an animal. But when they want to do things to her it's even worse.

One day a man turns up with a battery-operated toothbrush. She's never seen such a thing before, and looks at it, puzzled. He switches it on and demonstrates, showing his teeth and running the brush over them. It whirrs away, harmless as a child's toy. He stops miming and grins, showing off bright white teeth in a creased leather face, then walks across to the sink and runs the brush under the tap. Okay. She gets it now, but she hopes he doesn't expect her to clean her teeth with the same brush.

What he does try to do is far worse than she imagined.

"Get off," she yells, grabbing the hand he's using to steer the toothbrush and levering his wrist back to a right angle. The handle breaks off and the buzzing stops. Cradling it in his hand, the man stares, baffled – he's not the brightest candle on the cake, and his mouth crumples into a childlike pout. He spits abuse and flounces out, guarding the severed stem of his toothbrush like a precious orchid.

Odeta's next client is plump as a turkey, and wearing a pinstripe suit with a buttoned-up waistcoat. He snaps open his case and she glimpses a slim computer, about the size of a small picture frame. For one wild moment, she thinks about stealing it. She could stow it under her mattress, in the place where she's hidden a newspaper and a few banknotes that fluttered from a client's pocket while he was getting dressed.

"Put this on, pretty one," says the plump man, holding up a costume that might fit a ten-year-old. There's a white shirt with a stiff collar, a striped tie – no wider than a ribbon – and a skirt that hardly covers her backside. She sighs as she wriggles into the ill-fitting garments. The man produces elastic hair bands, parts her hair and yanks it up into two bunches either side of her face. He clicks a few settings on his computer and props it up on the side table.

"You're going to be a film star," he says. "Smile!"

She glowers, and he waggles his podgy finger in her face. "You've been a very bad girl, my dear. I'm going to have to punish you."

She can tell from his accent and from his clothes that he's posh. This one must be English, but he speaks in the simple language someone might use with a child. She understands individual words, but not what he wants her to do. He pushes her forward over the bed, so she swivels her neck to see what he's up to. He's grinning inanely in the direction of his computer, as if recording a film. With a flick of his wrist he lifts the skirt and spanks her bare backside till it smarts.

She shoves the heel of her hand into her mouth and bites on it, steeling herself against the stinging pain. After a while he stops spanking and presses himself up against her, but then he deflates, seeming content with what has passed between them.

He clears his throat and straightens his clothes. The red braces holding up his trousers have slid off his shoulders; he pulls them up and they ping into place. "You're a beautiful young thing, Marije," he tells her, easing her hair out of the elastic bands and stroking it flat. "Pure as the driven snow."

He snaps his computer shut and slides it back into his case. "Keep the clothes."

"Why I must keep?" she asks. English words are coming to her now: words she didn't think she knew.

"You can wear them again. I'll be back to see you soon."

"Too small," she says, plucking at the ridiculous skirt with her thumb and index finger.

"No – age twelve. Just right."

"Age is eighteen," she says, jabbing her index finger at the centre of her chest. When she entered this room she was seventeen, but on one unmarked day in the November of her imprisonment, the calendar pitched her forward to her eighteenth birthday and beyond.

His face sags, but he's still beaming at her. Could this be her chance? She rifles through the rag bag of English words she's picked up from the other girls at the salon and from television. Words are stacking up in her brain, waiting to come to her defence. She's learnt that *Help me* doesn't get a good reaction. When she says that, men panic.

"Please," she says.

He cocks a matted eyebrow and looks at her properly, his eyes misty like an ancient dog. A slack-mouthed smile lifts his jowls.

"Yes?"

"Name Odeta."

"Not Marije?"

"No," she shakes her head. "Men keep me here." She takes her time to sound out the words, but she can't stop her tongue straying towards the word *Help*. She tries to say *Help me to get away*, but it comes out as "Hellmeya".

He's confused. He exhales, puffs out his cheeks and turns towards the door. She stretches out her hand, places it on his arm and grips tightly, letting her eyes continue the conversation.

He's rattled now. He tightens the knot of his tie and pulls it too hard so his Adam's apple wobbles in his fleshy neck. How can he breathe with so much loose skin? Doesn't it suffocate him? He doesn't look kindly any more, but she links her arm firmly through his and accompanies him out through the door.

Halfway up the stairs her heart is hammering; if she sticks tight to his side, can Tomas stop her walking out of the front door? Perhaps this old man will stand up to him and protect her?

Three steps from the top she has her answer. Dragging his arm free of her grasp, he swats her away as if she were a mere insect. As she stumbles on the stairs, he dodges in front of her and runs, slamming the door so the heavy lock activates automatically behind him.

CHAPTER EIGHTEEN

Friday comes again, and the milk in the fridge has gone off. Nick pours some onto his cereal, wrinkles his nose and makes a sour face. He examines the container and glares across the table at Kate. It's a pose he's adopted all week – ever since she vandalised their Internet connection and he suspended a question mark over her sanity. As far as Nick's concerned, the jury's not even out on her conduct. He's already judged and condemned her.

"Perhaps you think we shouldn't have a fridge in our home any more?" He jabs his forefinger at the expiry date on the carton.

I know, I know. She half-closes her eyes to blot out his frown. All week she's been working on her *Life Offline* article for Veronica, and basic chores (like stocking the fridge) have slipped. Her working title for the first piece is *Cutting the Cord:* a metaphor for taking the plunge and giving up technology. She's not yet sure if she dares to describe how she kicked off the experiment by snipping their Internet router cable.

With Nick still furious, she faces a weekend of glacial

silence. "I'm going home to Wales," she announces, though the idea has only just occurred to her. "I'll take Ben with me."

"Suit yourself." Nick shrugs and stands up, abandoning his spoon in the bowl of milky sludge.

"I'm staying with Dad," chimes Ben. "There's nothing to do at Nana's." What he means is: they have a dodgy Wi-Fi signal, too weak for playing games. He shovels Golden Grahams into his mouth, oblivious to the age of the milk. Kate unscrews the plastic cap and sniffs; it smells fine to her.

"Go to Wales with your mother." Nick gulps the last of his coffee, pulls on his coat and heads out of the door without saying goodbye.

"Don't forget to feed Oscar," she calls to his departing back.

Ben explodes into angry tears. She studies his face covertly. Is he genuinely upset? Ben's not normally sensitive to atmosphere or other people's feelings; he prefers to stay locked in his tight bubble. Ben's teachers want to refer him for assessment, but Kate has refused. She doesn't want her son labelled whilst there are still things they can try to help with his social skills. Not yet.

Before they moved to Joplin Street they lived closer to Ben's school, and she used to walk him there in the mornings and strike up conversations with other mothers. Being freelance, she needs to work every hour of the school day to meet deadlines, so she had to turn down invitations to coffee and rush home and get on with her writing. Still, she passed the initial screening by the school gate mums' mafia, and was admitted to the outer reaches of their universe.

Problems began when Ben's classmates started to celebrate their birthdays. She would arrive in the playground to find envelopes being passed furtively between parents' hands, or popped inside a child's schoolbag. "Be sure to show that to Mummy when you get home." One day, Clarissa handed out a sheaf of envelopes, then approached Kate and muttered, "So sorry. Ben wasn't on Archie's list." Kate nodded, smiled, swore it was no problem, but her heart ached. Ben hardly seemed to notice. When his own birthday came and she spoke to him about a party, he refused to give her any names for a list, covered his ears and shouted, "No. No party." He never invited a friend over to play, and the rare occasions when he was invited to someone's house – because another mum took pity on Kate – weren't successful, because Ben would monopolise his classmate's Xbox.

Now they live further away she drives Ben to school, but traffic snags up, so it still takes fifteen minutes. Guiltily she edges her car close to the school gates and pulls up in the no-go area marked out with yellow zigzag lines.

"Bye, darling," she says. "Don't forget we're off to Nana and Grandad's straight from school." She leans across to unfasten his seatbelt, but he bats her hand away and slams the door. Behind her, car horns hoot as they jostle for a parking space, but Kate waits stubbornly in the car, watching Ben trudge down the drive, head bent, greeting no one. Other children are arriving in pairs or groups; they dawdle outside to chat or run around in circles, tagging one another. High-pitched laughter rises in the air. As Ben reaches the door and scurries inside, Kate feels as if an invisible hand is squeezing her heart.

Back at home she packs a small rucksack to keep Ben occupied on the journey: books, Lego, travel games and his balding teddy bear – no batteries required. Her conscience nags. This isn't a day off. She finishes her *Life Offline* piece, saves it on a memory stick and puts it in a padded envelope to mail to Veronica.

If this was a normal Friday, if last Friday had never happened, they'd all be meeting up at Ceri and Dan's for supper tonight. Rotating around one another's houses to kick-start the weekend is a settled tradition. No one's been in touch with her since her outburst. She feels like an outcast. Ceri could have called to check she's okay. With a pang, she realises the others will probably meet up this evening as usual – with Nick – clustering around Ceri's white kitchen table, eating stir-fry and sipping wine, and no one even mentioning her name.

She locks the house, stuffs the bags in the boot and waits for a gap in the traffic. As she indicates to pull out, a van cuts in front of her and turns into the space outside number thirty-eight. That was close! Her heart pounds; a few more centimetres and he would have smashed into the side of her car. It's that blue transit again. What's his hurry?

She parks outside school and watches Ben dawdling along the drive, peering at something cupped in his hand.

"What's that?" she asks.

He uncurls his fingers and shows her an enormous spider cowering in his palm.

"You can't take him to Wales, Ben," she says gently. "He lives here in the school grounds."

Ben's face is flushed, and there's a hole in his school sweatshirt that wasn't there this morning. "Yes, I can."

"He'll miss his family," she begins, and then sighs. After all, what does it matter, as long as he doesn't drop the blasted spider down her neck while she's driving?

"Chocolate?" she offers, holding out a bar of Kit Kat. Ben shakes his head.

"Okay, I'll have it then." She takes a bite.

"No. Give it to me!" His mouth puckers into a scowl. She breaks off a stick and passes it to him.

"Some stuff for you to do in there." She points to the bag of travel games in the footwell. He rifles through, rejects the books and the Lego, prises open the Solitaire and upends it so pieces spill over the floor. But he takes his teddy, adjusts his own seat belt and settles the bear on his lap.

Ben's grumpy face travels with them as far as the Severn Bridge. Soon after, they stop for a short break, and he lets slip the first smile she's seen all week. Driving west they've been chasing the remains of the light, but now darkness has wrapped them in a private world. Ben's head lolls back and he dozes. Kate's thoughts hang heavy, and she turns the radio from music to speech, digging deep for the energy she needs for two more hours driving beyond Cardiff, past Carmarthen and on to Abercwmmer.

As she leaves the motorway, Ben is still asleep, breathing softly, fingers loosely gripping his anorak. She joins the country lanes that were the arteries of her childhood. The road dips and turns; high hedges and overhanging trees coalesce into a tunnel of blackness. Her headlights slice around bends, and she strains her eyes for the glow of an approaching car. As she approaches the final hairpin bend before the village, her head spins with memories and her stomach lurches. She eases her foot off the accelerator, watching the speedometer drop. Beads of sweat break out on her forehead, and she taps the brake to crawl around the blind bend at fifteen miles per hour. Ahead of her the road unfurls and straightens. She exhales, stamps down hard on the accelerator, and glides the final half mile to the farm.

Her father has remembered to leave the gate open. She turns in, and Ben wakes as the car bounces along the rutted track. She's glad it's too dark to see the empty fields where their cows used to graze. Her parents still have sheep – a broody flock that dwindles in winter and expands again in spring – but every year at lambing time her father swears it will be his last. Soon this could be a farm without livestock, and that would be a tragedy.

After the horrors of foot and mouth disease, the BSE years

and the economic downturn, debt tightened its grip on the community. Two farmers in the district took their own lives. Her parents were saved by the holiday lets: three cottages, painstakingly renovated from farm outbuildings. One summer, when she and Nick were newly-married and greedily hoarding every morsel of time they could spend together, they used their summer holiday to help with the renovation work.

"Are we nearly there?" Ben yawns.

"Better than that." She points the cottage out to Ben. "See Ben, that's the house Mummy and Daddy built."

The intricate brickwork is just visible under the orange glow of the single yard light. Her father had wanted to cover the bricks with render, but she and Nick persuaded him to preserve the original façade. Under the guidance of a local bricklayer, they repointed it using lime mortar. He took a craftsman's delight in teaching them the secrets of his trade. "See how them there bricks have crumbled away? That's laziness, that is. Folks used cement instead of lime mortar. Rain gets into the cracks and, when it freezes, it blows the brick faces clean off."

"I don't believe you," says Ben, rubbing his eyes and yawning. "Dad can't even build my Lego."

She smiles, remembering that rare scorching summer when the sun beat down from a cloudless sky and Nick stashed beers inside a newly-installed water tank to keep them cool. When they finished for the day they would perch on the wall opposite, bottles in hand, admiring their handiwork. Labouring together to build the holiday cottage from a slouched ruin felt like forging strong foundations for their own future. What happened to those dreams?

Her mother must have heard the car pulling into the yard, and runs out to greet them, wiping her hands on her apron. With her frizzy, grey-blonde hair and the broken veins that make her cheeks permanently rosy, she's hardly changed for decades and she's still wearing the apron Kate laboriously cross-stitched in primary school.

"Kate – and Ben! *A lanto bach; dewch i mewn...Croeso!*" Her mother slips seamlessly between Welsh and English, often mixing the two languages in a single sentence. Her parents are bilingual, but always spoke English at home because they thought it would be better for her and her brother Gareth.

Kate stoops to hug her mother, finding she has to bend a little lower; her mother has shrunk. She's not that old, having just stepped across the threshold of her seventies, but Kate feels a chill – her parents link her to her roots, to her childhood and to Wales. Home isn't just a house, it's about your community and connections, belonging. London doesn't yet feel like home.

"No Nick?"

"Too busy. These are for you." She hands her mother a bunch of travel-weary flowers.

"Thank you. I've saved supper for you."

"Kate!" Her father half-rises from his chair beside the Rayburn.

"Don't get up, Dad." She hurries across to kiss him. No one could accuse him of laziness; all day he's out toiling in the bite of the wind, but once he sits down of an evening, he and his chair meld into one body. He's younger than her mother, but decades of buffeting by westerlies that roll in from the Atlantic and drop their deluge over the farm have toughened his skin into leathery creases. His eyes, still blue as cornflowers, belong to a much younger man. He could be anywhere between fifty and eighty.

He up-ends his pipe and gives it a tap, and a shower of charred tobacco lands in the ashtray. The room smells of tar and lamb hotpot. Ben lifts the lid of the pan bubbling on top of the Rayburn. "Ugh!"

"Ben – stop it," says Kate.

"Don't you worry now." Her mother fusses around Ben. "I'll

fix him an omelette. Eggs from our own chickens, Ben. Do you want to see them?"

He shakes his head and yawns.

"Never mind. Maybe in the morning."

Kate gives her mother a grateful smile. She's never impatient with Ben, though he can be surly and monosyllabic.

Gripping his fork like a weapon, Ben shovels in mouthfuls of omelette and grunts occasional replies to his grandfather's questions about school and hobbies. When he's finished eating, he burrows his head inside the pages of the comic Kate brought for him. He keeps asking her for his phone or tablet. Without those crutches he's behaving like an amputee; part of him is missing.

"Glass of milk for you, Ben? From Hendy's down the road."

Kate glances at her mother, remembering the days when they had their own dairy herd.

"I'm not drinking that. It's yellow."

"That's real milk," Kate says. "The cream is good for you."

"Liar. Milk is white."

He's beyond infuriating, and Kate's patience is wearing thin. "Okay. You're tired. Time for bed." She leads Ben up to the room under the eaves where she slept as a girl. While he cleans his teeth in the bathroom, she glances around at the flowery pink curtains, the Nirvana and Oasis posters on the walls, and her riding hat on a high shelf. Everything is unchanged, as if seventeen-year-old Kate had stepped outside and would soon return. What happened to that girl?

Ben climbs into bed, rolls over onto his side and stares at the wall. "Nothing to do," he grumbles, but his breathing steadies and soon he's asleep.

She tiptoes down the stairs, remembering to avoid the creaky one: third from the top, but finds stairs seven and eight have developed the creaky disease too.

"We went on with our supper earlier," says her mother, putting a plate of hotpot and dumplings down on the scrubbed wooden table. "Your Dad can't eat late. Plays havoc with his digestion. We'll have our cocoa with you."

The Rayburn is throwing out heat, and her father shuffles over to join her at the table. There's a hole in the toe of his slipper, and she makes a mental note for her Christmas present list. With a stab of guilt, she realises she hasn't seen them since last Christmas. Her parents don't travel away from the farm. She and Nick were busy with the house move, but still found time to go to Greece with Ben in the summer. Nick never has time for long weekends, but there's nothing to stop her and Ben visiting. Her parents don't load her down with obligations or ask her to explain long absences. They are simply happy to see her.

While she eats, her father tells her about last spring's vicious weather and the impact on the farm. "I was glad we didn't have the cows to see to. Things were bad enough."

A bubble of froth from his cocoa sticks to his moustache as he describes how they got safely through the winter, and then a harsh spring slammed into the hillside bringing late deep snow. No one was prepared for such severity. "Sheep were buried under ten-foot drifts," he says. "We lost so many. We found one lamb with its tongue bitten out by a crow..." He links his fingers around his mug and grips it so hard his knuckles turn white. He seems to have slipped into a daze.

"You mean the lamb couldn't suckle?" she prompts.

He nods. "We had to destroy her."

Her mother reaches out a hand and pats his arm. He's not a sentimental man, but Kate can see this experience got right under his skin.

Her mother takes up the story. "Toll of ewes in childbirth was terrible," she says. "We had to remove the skins from dead lambs to drape over orphaned ones."

"To trick the bereaved ewes into caring for them?"

Her father swivels his head and stares at the wall. "Never had to try it before, but it worked. Every morning we dug out the ewes and it was a race against time to save the lambs. If it wasn't for our neighbours I don't know what we'd have done."

Her father is a proud man and would never ask for help, but every morning a posse of neighbours assembled with their pickaxes to help dig out the trapped sheep. "Kept their own lads off school until they finished helping us. To be honest, Kate, without them we'd be finished. There'd be nothing left for your brother."

The mattress in the guest bedroom is lumpy, but her mother would never think of changing it – only Kate and Nick ever sleep there. There's a sprigged flower design on the curtains, dried lavender in a vase in the fireplace, and a washstand with a jug and bowl: a reminder of the days when the farm had no running water upstairs. She drifts off to sleep and dreams of buried lambs, bleating pitifully while neighbours drag them from under the smothering blanket of snow. Her parents have neighbours they can turn to, while in London she and Nick bob along, marooned in a sea of houses where they know nobody. They cling to old friends like Ceri, Dan and Charlotte as a bulwark against the world. Ben can't link them to other families because Ben doesn't do friends. It's up to her to do it for him.

She rises at seven-thirty to find Ben already in the kitchen spooning cornflakes into his mouth, steeped in the same yellow milk he rejected the night before. She meets her mother's eyes and they exchange a smile. As Ben chats to his grandmother, his morose scowl fades and he looks almost cheerful. Gelis, the black and white collie who's normally out on manoeuvres alongside her dad, is curled up at Ben's feet.

"Look, Mum, he likes me." Ben bends to pat the dog, and Kate's eyes widen. This is a miracle. At home Ben takes no interest in Oscar the cat, and he's been oblivious to Gelis on previous visits. "Why's he called Gelis?"

"It's a nickname for Gelert," says her mother, taking a sip of tea. "Do you know that story?"

Kate remembers shedding tears the first time she heard the legend. She flicks the electric kettle off before it boils so she can listen to her mother tell it again.

"Once upon a time, as they say, actually it was back in the thirteenth century, Llewelyn, Prince of North Wales, called for his dog to go out hunting, but Gelert was nowhere to be seen."

Ben stops fidgeting and stays very still, eyes fixed on his grandmother's face.

"When the prince returned, Gelert ran to greet him and Llewelyn noticed he was smeared with blood. Alarmed, the prince rushed to check on his baby son, but found the cot empty, and the bedcovers and floor soaked in blood."

Kate watches to see how Ben will react to the story's harrowing ending.

Her mother clears her throat and continues. "Thinking Gelert had attacked and killed his son, Llewelyn flew into a rage, drew his sword and stabbed him."

"Oh no." Ben strokes the silky pelt of the dog by his feet. "Did he die?"

Her mother nods. "As Gelert let out his dying howl, Llewelyn heard a baby cry. He found his son unharmed in another room with the body of a wolf that Gelert had fought off to save the baby. The prince never got over his sadness. He buried his dog in that spot, and the town was called after it. Beddgelert means Gelert's grave."

"Huh," says Ben. "How stupid was he?" He looks at Kate. "Can we go and see the grave?"

"Maybe, yes. Why not – if we go to North Wales for a

holiday." But the story has brought a lump to Kate's throat and set her thoughts on another track.

"Poached egg?" asks her mother. "New-laid, this morning."

Kate shakes her head and drains her coffee. "D'you mind looking after Ben while I pop out for an hour?"

"Course not. He can help me with the chickens and take Gelis for a walk around the farm."

"Thanks Mum." She kisses her mother's cheek and runs upstairs to fetch her jacket. Opening the curtain, she notices a pool of condensation on the windowsill and wipes it with her hand. It'll be cold outside. Her thin city jacket won't be man enough for the trek she has planned.

"Can I borrow this?" she asks, lifting a green Barbour jacket off a peg in the porch. It's old and smells of dog, but it's still waxy.

"Go ahead."

She revs up her engine and waits for the windscreen to demist. It's her first chance in years to make this pilgrimage. When Nick's with her it doesn't feel right. She follows the route she and Ben took the night before, passing fields of contented sheep, a tableau perfect for an oil painting. She cranes her neck and squints into the distance, but she can't see cattle anywhere.

At the next crossroads, the signpost has been uprooted and dumped in the hedge. It's hard to be sure which way the arrows were pointing originally. Taking a wild guess, she follows the road uphill, changing down to a lower gear. Her guess proves right. As she approaches the brow of the hill, the grey stone tower of Eglwys Dewi Sant comes into view. The church is situated at the highest point, with panoramic views over the countryside and out to sea. Exposed to the elements, it seems to float on an ocean of fields. Winter sun, the colour of weak tea, brightens the remaining leaves on the trees encircling the churchyard. All the trees are bent over at the same angle; backs to the Atlantic, they bow their heads towards England, towards Mecca.

There's a sprinkling of cottages nearby, and scant traffic even at the busiest of times. Kate's mouth feels chalky, her lips are parched, and she runs her tongue across the roof of her mouth to stimulate saliva. She could keep driving straight on past, but she doesn't. She pulls in, hops out, runs up the worn steps under the lychgate and searches for Rhys's grave.

More than twenty years on, it's still the newest. At the time of his funeral the graveyard was already full, and closed to new admissions. Officials wanted Rhys to be slotted into a neat row in the vast municipal cemetery, but his distraught mother's agony ricocheted through the community. Rules were bent, an exception was made, and the funeral procession wound its way from his home to this remote resting place.

On the day of his funeral Kate had stood beside his grave, too tranquillised to feel anything. Grief engulfs her now, pricking at her eyes, gnawing at her throat, twisting and knotting her stomach. *Nobody made you come, nobody forced you.* Someone has woven a lawnmower in between the plots, but Rhys's unkempt grave shocks her. Wildflowers and weeds must have rampaged across it all through the summer but are now reduced to brown stalks, stringy and wizened. She grasps a handful of entwined stems and pulls. They come out easily, and in five minutes she's weeded the whole plot, uncovering fragments of pottery that were once a vase.

She understands why the grave looks so neglected. Rhys's mother couldn't get over his death and made repeated suicide attempts, leaving notes to say she wanted to be with her son. Eventually she was sectioned for her own protection, and soon after, Rhys's father and sister moved away. Kate heard they'd started a new life in France.

Now she must face Rhys and ask his forgiveness. There's

not a breath of wind rippling the trees, and the birds have fallen silent. She bows her head as she reads the inscription on the headstone, simple and dignified:

> *Rhys Ifor Williams*
> *4 March 1979 – 31 July 1996*
> *Our beloved son*
> *No words can say*

There's nothing about Rhys being in the arms of God, or asleep with the angels. Nothing to give comfort to the mangled souls he's left behind; only a soundless scream echoing down the years until all who loved and remember him fade away. With her forefinger, Kate traces the outline of the carved letters. The edges are rough, but the marble is cool to her touch. She's not religious, but she whispers a childhood prayer and angles her head to one side as if an answer might drop from the sky. Silence should hold some comfort, and this lofty spot, high above gentle sloping valleys, is steeped in tranquillity: a fitting place for an octogenarian to slumber after a busy life, but for the restless spirit of a seventeen-year-old, a place of eternal purgatory.

Kneeling, she grips the sides of the headstone with both hands, touching her forehead against the chill marble and letting tears slither down her cheeks. "I'm sorry, Rhys. So sorry."

A solitary bird breaks the silence with a chirrup. Has Rhys heard? Does he forgive her?

She stands up and brushes dried grass from her jeans. The knees are muddy: the stain of guilt. Has she done a single worthwhile thing with her life? Even as a mother she feels a failure. Why should Rhys forgive her? She can't forgive herself.

CHAPTER NINETEEN

The days Odeta works at the so-called Beauty Spa are a pinprick of light in a dark nightmare. Cassie is friendly, but the other girls are wary. Herded together for hours in a cramped sitting room makes her stir-crazy, but the others act as if life has been pummelled out of them. Elira's the worst of all; her moods are so changeable. Some days she sits in silence, morose and blank-eyed, peeling strips of flaking skin from her hands; other times she huddles with the fluffy blonde receptionist, chatting and emitting occasional screeches of mirth.

In the back of the transit, Odeta searches for a handhold to cling on to as they fly over a hump and she's jolted several centimetres in the air.

"Sleeping policeman got you. Hah, hah!" says Elira, keeping her voice low so Tomas doesn't hear them over the grumbling engine.

What does she mean? Did they hit a cop? There are no windows in the back of the van so she can't see out. Odeta shakes her head in confusion.

"It's a hump in the road to slow down traffic, idiot."

Odeta is baffled. 'Hump' is another word she's learnt in the beauty place, but how does it link to a policeman in the road?

"And remember to always use the bloody condom," Elira adds. Her conversation is always staccato, leaping from topic to topic.

Odeta nods, glad that Elira's in a chatty mood. "Elira, tell me about the keys. You said the rooms were locked because of another girl."

"That bitch. Everything is her fault."

"How do you mean?"

"Before her, we could go anywhere in the house, use bathroom, make our own food in the kitchen. Now they lock us up, day and night, like dogs." Elira holds up two fingers and spits on the floor of the van.

"But who?"

"Marije."

Odeta thinks of the passport, and feels an icy hand clamp around her heart. "Marije Kaleci?" she whispers.

Elira gives a single brisk nod. "Anyway, she's gone. You're Marije now."

"Tell me…"

But Elira pulls a scarf across her face and pretends to doze.

The blonde woman who runs the front desk is called Lou. Her face is caked with make-up that settles into the creases of her skin, like the paste Tomas used to fill the crack in the door. There are purple splodges on the backs of her hands, and empty folds of flesh dangle from her underarms – the girls call her 'Bingo Wings'. Lou guards the door ferociously, but in between busy times she likes to chat, and Elira is her favourite. Together, the two of them whisper and giggle like teenagers. Odeta notices that Lou only ever assigns a client to Elira when all the other girls are working. Even then, Lou vets the men and doesn't make Elira go with them unless they are clean and smartly-dressed.

Odeta is at the bottom of the heap; she gets the chefs in checked trousers and white jackets, smelling of cheap cooking oil; workmen with fluorescent jackets and brick dust on their meaty hands.

It's eleven o'clock in the morning and four girls are in. The TV is on, and Odeta watches for a while. The programme has numbers in it, and she understands numbers better than words. People are buying broken old houses, making them new and selling them for lots of money. Business is slack. Things normally hot up around lunchtime, when businessmen pop in. At those times the girls have to work fast; the men don't like waiting on the blue armchairs in Reception, darting their eyes around the walls or staring down at their shoes.

"I don't trust Elira," says Cassie. "Watch what you say to her. It'll get back to Lou."

"Why does Lou favour her?" asks Odeta.

"I think she's grooming her to go upmarket."

"What market?"

"Oh dear, Marije. You haven't learnt much. Posh hotels, smart nightclubs. Where rich people and foreigners hang out. They can make more money out of us there, but they have to be sure of us first. That we don't try to alert the authorities or run off."

Odeta shakes her head. It's all so confusing. "But what about Imani? Lou sends her out shopping. She could run off any time."

When business is slack, Lou opens her purse, counts out notes and coins and gives them to Imani, an African woman who wears her hair in corn rows, and sends her out to buy cakes and fizzy drinks. When she returns, Lou calls all the girls together. *Time for our little picnic.*

"Why does she let Imani go outside?" Odeta persists.

Cassie's painting her nails a shade of gold with sparkly bits. "She knows Imani won't run off."

"Why not?"

"She's an illegal."

"But you said we're all illegals. We have no papers."

"Yes, but Imani fled a war zone. She claimed political asylum here and was refused. She's terrified of being sent back."

"You mean she'd rather be here doing this?"

Cassie nods. "She's working here by choice. Not like us."

Odeta grapples with this information; it makes her head spin. Why would any woman choose to do this work?

Cassie seems to read her thoughts. "Imani has a child, a girl. She's afraid her daughter would be killed if she went back."

So it's not a real choice. Imani is shuffling a pack of cards where there are no winning hands. Everything is a fleeting illusion – like Lou's picnics. Russian Roulette might be preferable. Some days the idea of dying doesn't seem so bad; this life will kill her soon. The other girls tell her they pretend their bodies are machines, separate from themselves, going through a mechanical process. Odeta can't do that. Every time a man forces himself on her she experiences a violent rape; she refuses to mimic their pleasure or shout out swear words or encouragement, but lies rigid and waits for it to be over. Some of the men slap her to try to coax a response. She's low on repeat customers, but Lou feeds her to a string of new ones.

Cassie seems to read her mind. "Marije, you're the prettiest girl here, but you need to play along with them. Win their trust if you want to move on to a more comfortable place."

Conversations with Cassie are helping Odeta's English. Cassie never talks about a dog called Nip, or having tea with Mother, and she doesn't keep saying "Shut up, bitch," like Tomas and Stephan.

"Where are we, Cassie?"

"In London."

"No, I mean what part. The middle? The edge?"

"It's the place they call the West End. We're close to Soho but not in it. Lou says being on the edge is how this place managed to survive when police cleaned up the sex trade."

Lou sticks her head in through the doorway and holds out a white paper bag; Imani has returned with the cakes. Yesterday they had croissants; the pastry flaked off onto her clothes and dropped on the floor. Odeta bent down and picked up all the crumbs, licking every last morsel off her fingers. Today the bag contains chunks of brown sponge. Odeta hesitates – it smells good but looks like a flattened turd.

"It's a chocolate brownie, silly," says Cassie. "Eat it. It's good."

She nibbles one corner. Cassie's right – it is good. The flavour of chocolate explodes in her mouth, tasting of home. She's whisked back to her childhood, her grandmother's kitchen, helping make cakes for Sunday tea. Usually they had *baklava* from the shop, but sometimes her grandmother would lift down a heavy stone mixing bowl, pour in ingredients and stir them into a sticky mess. She always let Odeta scrape the side of the bowl and lick a great dollop of mixture off her finger.

Imani is sitting in Reception, chatting to Lou and knitting a child's sweater in a rainbow of orange and purple stripes. Cassie and Odeta are alone in the sitting room, and the taste of chocolate has loosened Cassie's tongue.

"I come to England to work as *au pair*," she says, a thin chocolate moustache coating her upper lip. "A friend of my aunt back home in Moldova gave me contact details for a family in Bayswater. I'm very excited. Very looking forward."

"When I arrive at Victoria Coach Station, a man is there to meet me. He looks young – about nineteen years. Seems too young to be father of ten-year-old girl I was to be looking after.

Still I did not suspect." Cassie's voice trails off and she puts her hands up to cover her face. When she removes them, Odeta notices she's rubbing away a tear.

"The man took me to a flat, tied me up and left me with water but no food. Then after two days he come back with three friends."

Odeta gulps. She doesn't need Cassie to tell her what happened next. She places her hand on Cassie's arm and squeezes it with gentle pressure. Her eyes feel misty; she thought she had no tears left to shed, but it turns out the well of despair is bottomless. Suddenly she wants to tell Cassie her own story.

"Kreshnik, my boyfriend, arranged for me a modelling contract," she says. "But the men he fixed it up with are bad. They tricked us both. That's why I am forced to be working here. Kreshnik doesn't know. He had to go away for business. When he finds out he will come help me."

Carrie stares at her with gimlet-sharp brown eyes, making Odeta squirm. She shakes her head. "Why do you look at me in that way?"

"You said this man, Kreshnik, is your boyfriend?"

"Yes, of course," she nods.

"And who did you say tricked you?"

"Tomas, Stephan – the men at the house where I stay."

"I see." But her eyes seem to drill inside Odeta's head, as if detecting more, much more, than she's saying.

"Here is my advice," says Cassie. "Maybe he will come for you; maybe not. You need to make your own plan. Can't keep living this life. Will kill you for sure."

"What do you mean?"

"Think what you can do to be stronger. Be curious about those men. When do they drink? When do they sleep? When do they forget to lock the doors? You need to get away from that place." She hands Odeta a magazine. "Stolen from the Reception. Take it, put in your bag," she hisses.

"Why?

"Stupid girl. You must practise your English. When you get away you need to tell your story, or police will lock you up."

Odeta shivers, folds the magazine and pushes it inside her bag.

"What if she searches me?"

"Has she ever done that?"

Odeta shakes her head.

"I won't be staying here much longer," says Cassie, tossing the mane of curly black hair she no longer bothers to straighten.

"What do you mean?"

"I make plan. Every day I watch Lou. I know how the door lock operates. Soon, when she goes to toilet, I will run away."

"Where will you go?"

Cassie shrugs her shoulders. "Who cares? I'll just go." She stuffs the last piece of chocolate brownie into her mouth and holds up her fingers. The golden nail polish sparkles in the light.

"Client, Marije," calls Lou from the Reception desk.

Odeta gets to her feet and trudges into the Reception. The sign fixed to the opaque glass door says: *Beauty and Grooming: Special Rates for Men*. She's never seen a woman enter the salon. Once, a man with thick black hair and an earring came in and asked about chest hair waxing. Lou had pulled her lips into a tight line and suppressed a laugh. "We can do a chest massage for you, my lovely. But not waxing. Not here."

Today's client is waiting, wearing spectacles, a grey suit and no tie. Perhaps he'll be short of time, anxious to get back to his office. Perhaps it will be over quickly. She doesn't smile, but beckons him to follow her along the corridor, past a warren of rooms with thin plasterboard walls and doorways covered only with a curtain. At peak times, you can hear the sound of swearing and panting from other cubicles above the noise of tinny piped music.

Lou calls the cubicles 'treatment rooms' and insists the girls keep them sparkling clean. On a cursory glance, the rooms could be a stage set for a beauty salon. Each cubicle has a shelf containing a row of skincare products and massage oils in bottles and jars. Behind these is an array of small white boxes with smart lettering: *Dead Sea Skin Scrub, Seaweed Face Mask, Detoxifying Body Oil*. But on investigation, Odeta found the boxes were empty. Beyond these props, the room has a bleak functionality and quasi-clinical trappings. Although one shelf is piled high with fluffy white towels, neatly folded, Odeta lifts down a roll of blue paper and spreads a length over the treatment couch, which is cranked down low, close to the floor. There's an antiseptic gel in a pump-action container. Lou tells the girls to use this on their hands before and after servicing each client. Odeta loves the strong medicinal tang. She daren't steal a whole bottle, but sometimes she squirts some into a plastic bag and takes it back to the house.

She offers the man a squirt of hand gel and he accepts. He looks shy, but she's learned that looks can be deceptive; she's endured some of her roughest encounters at the hands of pink-cheeked lads, scarcely old enough to shave. Why are they here paying for sex? Isn't there a girl in their office who would sleep with them for free?

Odeta points to a chair where he can leave his clothes. He strips down to his white boxers, looking shivery and anxious. She's the expert here – the one who knows the ropes. She hands him a foil packet containing a condom from the ration Lou doles out each day, leads him to the couch and waits for him to act out what he wants her to do. This one wants full intercourse and he wants to kiss her; she tries not to gag. He's gentle, and she doesn't have to fight to get him to use a condom. Afterwards he clings to her, shaking and emotional.

"Tell me about yourself," he asks.

She glances at the clock. Lou will be mad if he stays more than fifteen minutes during the busy lunchtime slot. "Nothing to tell."

Usually when clients want to talk, it's about themselves: how successful, how rich, how clever they are, and how their wives don't understand their needs.

"Are your working conditions okay, Marije?" he asks, reaching in his pocket for a pack of cigarettes.

"No smoking," she says, and nods her answer to his question. "Okay, yeah." *If people like you didn't come here*, she thinks, *places like this wouldn't exist and people like me wouldn't have to work in them.*

"And you get paid properly? Minimum wage?"

"Sorry, I do not understand."

"Where are you from?"

"Albania."

His eyes narrow and he begins to sweat. She realises he gets it now. He's not stupid, and he can't avoid knowing what he didn't want to know. He averts his eyes and starts to get dressed, his fingers twitching as he fumbles with his shirt buttons, not bothering to fasten the last three as he races to get away.

Perhaps this is the one who will listen. "Help me, please," she begs, locking her fingers together and holding her hands towards him like a prayer.

He angles his head away from her and mumbles. "Can't. Sorry. Must get back to work." He shoves his feet inside his brown shoes without tying the laces, and shuffles his feet across the tiled floor towards the exit. She steps in front of him, blocking his path. "Please."

Behind the thick glasses his eyelids are flickering. "Let me think." He passes the back of his hand across his shiny forehead, sidesteps around her, and he's gone, whipping up a draught that sends the curtains of each cubicle fluttering as he sweeps past. She hears the main door click shut behind him as she trudges back along the white corridor towards Reception, and Lou's shrill voice calling her. "Marije! Client."

CHAPTER TWENTY

Kate dawdles up the front path of number thirty-four, raps on the knocker and thinks about what to say. There's a pattering sound from inside: small feet crossing wooden floorboards. The door creaks open, and a woman wearing a headscarf, with startled dark eyes, pokes her face around. The slice of hallway visible over her shoulder is sunflower-yellow and smells of spices. When she sees Kate, she relaxes her grip on the door and lets it swing open to reveal a barefoot toddler, wearing a Real Madrid football shirt over his nappy and chewing on a muslin cloth. He potters forward and squashes up against his mother's leg. Taking the cloth out of his mouth, he grins up at Kate displaying four perfect front teeth.

"Hi, I'm Kate your neighbour from number thirty-six." She jabs a finger at her own house, next door. "We moved in two months ago."

The woman nods. "I know." She speaks good English, rolling her words with a rich, soft accent.

"I was hoping," says Kate, shuffling her feet – this is harder than she expected – "you might like to join us for a small get-together on December 29th."

The small boy isn't fazed. He pops his head out from behind his mother to peer at Kate. The woman's gaze is unwavering, a list of unspoken questions in her dark eyes.

Kate ploughs on. "There'll be soft drinks, nibbles. A chance to meet some neighbours."

The woman drops her eyes and stares at Kate's shoes. When she raises her head, it's already shaking in refusal. "Sorry, no. Not possible."

A pulse in Kate's forehead begins to throb. She should have planned her approach more carefully. She digs deep for another way to rephrase her invitation without causing offence, when a male voice booms from inside the house. "Fatima? Who is that?"

The woman twitches and turns her head towards the voice, easing the door closed as she does so. "It's no one," she says, and shuts the door in Kate's face.

What's wrong with the people around here? It's tempting to retreat home, but she stiffens her resolve and treks down the moss-seamed path of number thirty-two. The front garden is a tangle of brambles, and a solitary gnome lies on his back under a bush. She's often seen an elderly lady inside, staring out at the rain and the passers-by. Hers must be the last set of net curtains in the street; perhaps she thinks she's invisible behind them. The curtains look grey and frayed. In the old days this lady would have plunged her nets regularly into a sink of whitener; now they are a dust trap for the grime blown in through gaps in the rotting sash windows.

Kate gives a friendly wave in the direction of the bay window as she strolls up the path. Even before she lifts the door knocker there's the rattle of a chain being slid back, and the door opens to reveal a shrivelled woman, with bird-like bobbing movements and a pointy nose. The woman's eyes are blue with a piercing intelligence. Her left arm dangles by her side, the hand locked into a claw.

"What do you want?"

Kate clears her throat and introduces herself.

"And I'm Mrs Coleman," grunts the old lady.

Kate notices a single milk bottle standing on the step, bends down, picks it up and hands it to Mrs Coleman. Sliding her hand into her coat pocket she draws out a drinks party invitation. She's written *Thursday 29th December 2016* in her best italic script and drawn holly in the margins, colouring the berries deep red against the sketchy black ink of the leaves. Suddenly, her efforts at producing something homemade, in an age where anyone can pick a template from their computer and instantly become a graphic designer, seem tawdry.

Mrs Coleman raises her good hand, still holding the milk bottle and makes a gesture, as if waving the invitation away, but instead puts the bottle down on her inside windowsill and takes the card from Kate's outstretched hand.

"Christmas drinks," Kate explains. "On December 29th."

"I'll think about it."

"Oh, thank you." She wants to give her frosty neighbour a hug. "I expect you've lived here a long time? Who lives next door to you at number thirty?"

"Woman about your age. Hasn't been here long."

Kate feels a stir of interest. "With a husband?"

"Never seen him." Mrs Coleman spends all day staring out of her window, so if anyone knows, she will. "Has a child – girl, I think."

A child! Maybe close to Ben's age. Kate fingers the slim sheaf of invitations in her pocket as she says goodbye to Mrs Coleman, "Do you happen to know who lives at number thirty-eight?"

"Foreign-looking man with a blue transit van." Her voice bristles. "What would I know about them? They don't walk anywhere, that's for sure, but that van's always on the move. In and out, all day and night."

"I do hope you'll come on the 29th. I could ask my husband, Nick, to call and walk round with you?"

"Like I said, I'll think about it," Mrs Coleman says, but she's still gripping the invitation in her good hand as she clicks the door shut.

Outside on the pavement Kate hesitates. If the woman at number thirty is about her age, she's probably out working. Even if she's in, would she welcome a visit? Kate dreads meter readers knocking at her door and those newly-released young offenders who try to sell her dusters. She tries to fend them off by buying a tea towel, but they always insist on unwrapping a backpack of wares and displaying them on her doorstep, while her precious working minutes tick away.

Number thirty looks friendly, with soft lamp light filtering from behind slatted wooden shutters. On reaching the door she hears the plink-plink of notes being picked out on a piano – Beethoven's *Moonlight Sonata*. How she struggled with that piece as a child; she's never forgotten how it defeated her. She can't interrupt a pianist, so she turns to leave, when suddenly the music stops, rapid footsteps cross the hall, and the front door is yanked open.

"Thought I heard someone. You're early," exclaims a woman with a broad smile and curly brown hair, pulled back in a loose ponytail.

Kate holds out the invitation. "I didn't mean..." she begins, but the woman is beckoning her inside.

"Never mind. You're here now. Come in, take a seat." She points to an upholstered chair under the hall window. "Just finishing Lizzie's lesson. Be with you in a moment."

Kate perches on the seat and looks around. From the outside this house looks like her own, but the inside layout has been remodelled so that the hall is almost a room in its own right. There's a mahogany occasional table displaying photographs, and on the wall above framed music certificates in the name of Jessica Carberry. A picture in a silver frame shows a smiling Jessica in an emerald-green evening dress, cradling a gigantic bouquet and standing beside a famous conductor. Another photograph shows a younger Jessica graduating from the Royal Academy of Music.

The piano falls silent and Kate hears voices from inside the room. Minutes later Jessica emerges, followed by a willowy teenager clutching a sheaf of music. "Don't forget your theory," calls Jessica, closing the door as the girl departs.

She turns to Kate and smiles, "Come into my music room." The room is dominated by a grand piano in polished mahogany – a Steinway. Even with her scant musical knowledge, Kate knows this is a serious piano, a major investment – and she's here under false pretences.

"There – what do you think of that, Ruth?" Jessica asks, indicating the piano with a sweep of her arm.

"I didn't, err, I'm not..."

"That's right. You're early. I think we agreed three o'clock when we spoke on the phone."

"Listen. I'm really sorry to disturb you, but I'm not Ruth and I'm not here for a piano lesson." She offers her hand. "I'm Kate. Your neighbour from number thirty-six."

"Oh right. I was expecting..." As if unconvinced, she glances at a leather-bound diary lying open on top of the piano. "Ruth White."

"Look, I won't bother you now while you're teaching. I'll call back later."

"Nonsense. Ruth's not due for another hour. Now you're here, stay and have a cup of tea – Earl Grey? I'm Jess, by the way."

Kate follows her down the hall, all stripped floorboards and jade-green walls, and into a kitchen plucked straight from the 1970s, with sprigged Laura Ashley wallpaper, cream and green units and sludge-coloured tiles. Jess puckers her mouth. "Gross, isn't it? Still it'll have to do. Can't afford a new one yet." She runs water into the kettle.

"How long have you lived in this crazy street?"

"Almost a year." Jess smiles. "It is crazy, isn't it? Rat-run in the mornings, then calms right down once all the parking spaces have been nabbed. Tell me: where does everyone go in the day, and what are your neighbours up to at night?"

"You mean number thirty-eight, the detached house on the corner? I ought to know, but I don't," Kate admits, fiddling with her wedding ring. It seems strangely loose, as if it's trying to work its way off her finger. "I'm always busy working. I'm freelance. And I have Ben."

"Ben's your husband?"

Kate shakes her head. "My son. He's ten."

"A son. Lucky you!"

"Mrs Coleman next door said you had a daughter."

"Sadly, no. That old lady keeps an eye on everything. She's probably seen my pupils coming and going."

Kate covers her mouth with her hand. "Sorry. Didn't mean to pry."

Jess shook her head. "No worries. I don't have a child, but I do have a partner – Ian. He works in the States but he'll be back for Christmas."

Jess carries their tea into the sitting room, where an open fire blazes in the grate. Kate stands in front of it, letting the warmth lap at the back of her legs.

"Shouldn't really have a fire in here. Not good for the piano. But I compromise by keeping a window open." Jess points the end of her teaspoon towards the stained-glass half-lights above the sash windows. "So, what brings you to my door?"

"We're new in the road, so I'm planning a small Christmas drinks do for neighbours. Mince pies and mulled wine."

"Sounds good. When is it?"

"December 29th. Here's your invitation."

Jess uses a fountain pen to note the date in her desk diary.

"That's beautiful!" Kate runs her fingers over the smooth leather-bound diary and examines the elegant gold lettering on the cover. She feels a connection to Jess – here is someone who values elegance and craftsmanship in this throwaway society. Jess carries the invitation across to her mantelpiece and props it in front of a crystal vase containing twelve creamy roses. The fire hisses and sparks, and a log rolls out onto the grate. Swiftly Jess traps it with her foot and nudges it back onto the hearth, away from the rug. "Phew, that was close." She takes off her boot and shakes the ash off into the grate.

Kate glances out of the window and notices a woman in a belted white mac making her way up the path. "That must be your next pupil. I'll get going." She turns the handle to open the front door and steps outside. "See you on the 29th."

"Oh, you'll see me before that," promises Jess, greeting Ruth White and ushering her inside.

So there'll be at least one guest at her party. Emboldened, Kate strides on past her own house, determined to deliver her invitation to number thirty-eight, just as the blue transit streaks past her and pulls onto the parking space. This could be her chance to hand over the invitation in person. She hangs back, waiting for the van to come to a complete stop, and has a good view of a girl sitting in the passenger seat. She's in her late teens, with long dark hair and hollow eyes. As she catches sight of Kate she raises her hands, knits her fingers together and draws them across the van's side window. Demisting? Or – Kate thinks with a small shiver – trying to attract attention?

The driver's door slams and a man jumps out. She recognises the leering unshaven man with the bull neck, but he doesn't appear to notice her as he crosses in front of the van and opens the passenger door. The girl recoils, leaning away from him. As Kate watches, he reaches in, puts his arm around her and hauls her out of the van. She stumbles as he pulls her to the ground before ushering her up the steps to the front door. While he fiddles with the locks, the girl swivels round and fixes Kate with a stare so piercing that it makes her flinch. They go inside slamming the door behind them.

Perhaps they've had a row? If so, it won't be a good time to deliver a drinks invitation, but instinctively Kate makes her way up the steps. There's no doorbell, just a kind of keypad with numbers and a push button. She raps on the door with her bare knuckles but there's no response, so she presses the buzzer and listens to it echoing through the lobby. Could anyone ignore that racket?

Inside, a door slams, then there's silence.

CHAPTER TWENTY-ONE

When Odeta looks in the mirror, the face she sees isn't hers. Eyes red and puffy, skin stretched tight over the cheekbones Kreshnik once described as exotic. Her lips are cracked, and there's a crusty sore at one corner of her mouth. Herpes, Tomas called it. He gave her some ointment to rub on, but it doesn't seem to help.

Life is a place of chaos and horror. She can't focus on one day at a time. The days are too long, so she concentrates on each hour and wishes away each minute as she strives to wrest back some control from the depraved strangers who have taken over her life. She has to be subtle. If she makes any sign of protest Tomas will jab the needle into her arm, so she feigns compliance and stays out of the path of his anger. There are days when she wishes she could bury herself in heroin's oblivion, but Elira has trodden that road already and ended up monosyllabic, forgetful, and rattling her door at night screaming for a fix.

How long has she been here? Two months, maybe three. In the beginning she was too disorientated to notice, and one day leached into the next before she recorded its passing. They no longer keep her room in darkness; the soft pink light is on most of the time so she can never drown in the blackness of sleep. Her days are marked by comings and goings: nameless men arriving and departing like lurid shadows. Or a barked order to get moving may rouse her from sleep and she's packed into the van for the forty-five-minute drive to the other place, sometimes with Elira, sometimes alone.

For the last couple of days no punters have visited the house – business must be bad. She moves away from the mirror. Her face is unsightly, but her body feels almost rested. No doubt some swine-faced man will appear soon. She yawns and sits on the edge of her bed, tentatively stretching out first one leg then the other, tautening and relaxing the muscles. She stands up and lets muscle memory take over as she runs through her warm-up routine. She raises her arms above her head and lifts her chin so she's staring at the ceiling where a stain of brown damp has spawned tributaries. She doesn't notice the door edging open until a voice calls, "Oi, you."

Odeta flinches. It's not Tomas but Stephan, the skeletal guy who cooks her disgusting food.

"Come with me," he says, crooking his forefinger and beckoning. She freezes. What now? Weariness floods her body and she sinks down onto the edge of the bed. He walks over and puts his hands under her armpits. She shrinks away, bracing herself, but he simply pulls her up onto her feet. He's thin but wiry and strong. The high-octane threat of violence that hovers around him is absent, and so, she notices, is another of his tombstone teeth. He can't be much older than thirty, but already his face is collapsing.

"Follow," he orders. Mounting the basement stairs is usually a prelude to being bundled into the van, but today Stephan's in no hurry. She looks around and makes a mental map of her surroundings: kitchen along the corridor to the left, front door to the right, cloakroom straight ahead. She's often glimpsed the sitting room on the right of the front door but has never stepped inside. He pushes open the door.

"Eurgh!" The smell hits her; layered like a club sandwich: stale cigarette smoke sits on top, covering sour beer, but at the base is another smell, cheesy and rancid. There's no one else in the room, but rubbish clutters every surface: sandwiches curling at the edges, empty bottles, overflowing ashtrays and cigarette butts floating in mugs. Her family home is bursting with stuff too, but her mother packs it away and keeps the rooms clean and smelling of wax polish.

There's a gigantic television screen on one wall, and two sofas, covered in sludge-green fabric that might once have had a floral pattern. She touches the armrest; it feels sticky. Cushions are scattered everywhere – some plump, some flat, all either stained or torn – and there's a low table branded with interlocking rings made by mugs of hot drinks.

"There," he says, pointing into the far corner of the room. "Clean that up." She follows the direction of his finger and crosses to the far side of the sofa where the cheesy smell grows stronger. Down on the floor is a pile of vomit, stinking and fresh. She retches and clamps a hand over her mouth to control an urge to be sick.

She turns back to face him. "I need something. Water, a brush, paper..."

He nods and shuffles off along the hallway. To escape the stench, she follows him out into the corridor. Her eyes are drawn towards the front door, studded with locks and bolts, but on the wall is a small metal cupboard – that must be the box Elira mentioned where keys are kept. She hears Stephan turn off the kitchen tap and darts back into the sitting room, pulling the door closed behind her.

"Open the door, bitch." Before she can reach it, he kicks it open with his foot. He's holding a bucket, brimming with water and white bubbles. Balancing on top of it are a dustpan and a cloth, but no brush. Crooked inside the elbow of his other arm is a bottle of beer.

"Newspaper?" she asks.

He shakes his head. "Get on with it." The stench seems not to bother him. He takes a swig of beer. She kneels down and he stands close behind her; she feels his bony leg pressing up against her back. Using the flat edge of the dustpan she scrapes up the vomit. Soon the dustpan is full but she can't be bothered to speak to him. She stands up and gestures to it.

"Dustbin," he says, pointing with a forefinger along the hall. He lounges in the doorway whilst she walks to the kitchen, where open shelves are laden with pans, and in the sink a pile of unwashed pots with a frying pan thick with congealed fat balanced on the top. She opens the dustbin and recoils; it smells almost as bad as the sitting room. The lid is broken and drops off onto the floor with a clanking sound that makes her jump. In a cardboard box under the table she finds what she's looking for: a stash of old newspapers. She layers three sheets on the floor, scrapes the sick from the dustpan onto it, folds it into a pouch and puts it in the bin.

"Hurry," he calls.

She collects a wad of newspaper and carries it back to the sitting room where the task of scraping, depositing and parcelling up becomes simpler. Once she's removed most of the solid vomit, she dips the cloth into the warm soapy water, wrings it out and scrubs at the stain. Finally, the stench begins to fade.

"Good," he says and smiles. Those teeth again. She averts her eyes.

"Cigarette?" He proffers a squashed-looking packet.

She doesn't smoke, but why not? Smoking one cigarette

will buy her five more minutes outside her dungeon room. She takes one, and he lights it with a flourish using a purple disposable lighter. He sits down on the sofa and gestures to her to do the same. She perches on the sofa's threadbare arm and puffs on her cigarette like a bird pecking at a twig. The first drag makes her feel sick, but she persists, and as the smoke (or perhaps the nicotine) works its way into her bloodstream she feels light-headed and almost calm. She lets her shoulders drop.

"You are called Stephan?" she asks. That's the name she hears Tomas yelling out when he's in one of his better moods.

He nods. "Stephan, yeah."

"What was it – that mess?"

"That – pah! That was Christmas."

"Christmas!" She remembers now: the lit-up streets and decorated shops she's gazed down on from the windows of the salon. Christmas arrived and departed but nobody told her. It was the only day of the year her father closed his shop. She thinks of her family, clustered around the dinner table tucking in to their food; her father drinking plum brandy and smoking between courses. Tears sting her eyes. Would they be talking about her? Wondering how she's getting on in her new life in London? Have they even realised she's missing? Or do they just think she's swanned off abroad, leaving them behind and not bothering to phone or send a card? Hot tears spill over and slither down her cheeks. She sniffs, needing to blow her nose but has no tissue. Stephan is watching, his expression wary. He gets up and leaves the room, and she hears his footsteps padding along the corridor and the creak of a door.

"Here," he says, returning and pressing a bundle of tissue torn from a toilet roll into her hand.

It's almost the only kindness she's experienced since leaving home. She stares at him as she accepts the paper, blows her nose and dabs her eyes. "My parents," she says, with a shrug. "I miss them."

His face is solemn. "Family," he says. "I understand."

She sniffs again. "You have family?"

"Of course." He puffs out his chest and jabs his forefinger at the centre of his breastbone. "Very important family. Big family in Tirana."

"Stephan, do you know Kreshnik?" she asks. "Or his cousins?"

"Kreshnik? Yeah, we know him."

Hope flickers inside her as she recalls the days she and Kreshnik spent together in Albania; his hot insistent kisses, the pearl bracelet he gave her. Surely, he must have felt something? She leans towards Stephan, not even caring if she has to look at his teeth. "When will Kreshnik come here? I want to see him."

He gapes at her and takes a long swig from his beer before replying. "He won't come here."

"But why not?" She kicks her heels back against the sofa, trying to stop tears sliding down her face.

He wipes his mouth with the back of his hand. "Because of Marije: the one who was here before you."

An image of the passport comes into her mind. "Marije Kaleci?"

He nods, dangling his beer bottle between his thumb and forefinger.

There's no sound in the room, but inside her skull a clamour is building up and her thoughts are choked with noise. Every time she's asked about Marije she's been brushed off. Perhaps it would be better not to ask, not to know. She tugs at the hem of her t-shirt, pleating the fabric between her fingers and wishing she hadn't finished the cigarette.

Stephan cradles the base of the bottle inside his palm and

lifts it up close to his eyes, as if the answer to her question is printed on the label. He clears his throat.

"Marije was..." he begins.

"Yes?" She leans towards him, eyes fixed on his face.

He places the beer bottle down on the low table, precise as a chess player making a move. "Marije's gone," he says. "And Kreshnik owes us."

CHAPTER TWENTY-TWO

"Grab hold of this end of the lights for me." Kate passes the double twist of green wire down to Ben as she balances on the stepladder. Deftly she fastens one end to the stem of the wisteria, moves the ladder along and takes the loose end from Ben, draping the lights in an arc across the front of the house and fastening the flex to the drainpipe with a wire tag.

"We should have done this before Christmas," Kate exclaims, hopping off the stepladder. She's left it until the day of the drinks party, but Nick's gone back to the office and isn't here to help.

"I'll be home by five," he promised as he left that morning. The drinks party is due to start at six o'clock.

They'd survived their family Christmas, Kate staying resolutely upbeat and Nick retrieving forgotten board games from the attic and introducing Ben to *Scrabble*, *Monopoly* and *Cluedo*. For a Christmas gift, Kate bought Ben three Harry Potter novels. As soon as she'd put the turkey in the oven, she started reading *Harry Potter and the Philosopher's Stone* aloud to him, hoping he'd snatch it from her hands to read silently. By Christmas evening, in the gaps between cooking, eating and board games, she'd covered two hundred pages and her voice had shrivelled into a thin croak. Nick disappeared upstairs and returned with another gift, handing it to Ben, with a smug smile.

"A complete set of Harry Potter DVDs!" Ben exclaimed. "Thanks, Dad! Now I don't need you to read any more, Mum."

More excuses for screen time! Nick still doesn't get it, but it's Christmas so she won't pick a fight. She runs indoors to switch on the fairy lights. "Ta-dah!" The front garden sparkles red, blue and green to welcome her guests. The sitting room has the clean scent of a Norwegian pine that brushes up against the ceiling. "What d'you think, Ben? Does it look Christmassy?" She raises the sash window higher and pokes her head outside.

"When's Dad coming home?"

It's already five-thirty, so Kate shakes her head and admits, "I don't know."

If Nick doesn't turn up, this drinks party will be an embarrassing flop. She wanders into the kitchen and checks her preparations. Wine is mulling on the stove's front burner, with a non-alcoholic version in a smaller pan on the back; the fridge is fully-stocked with beer, orange juice and bottles of Pinot Grigio. On the table is a case of Merlot, courtesy of the supermarket's six-for-five offer. Not wanting to offend any Muslim neighbours, she's shunned buffet staples of pork products in favour of falafels, hummus and pitta bread. There are blinis with smoked salmon and cream cheese, and homemade vegetarian mince pies. She's handed out invitations to a dozen houses. If everyone comes there could be over twenty people.

Ben stumbles in with the box of glasses and almost lets it slip from his hands.

"Ben, be careful. But thanks for bringing them through."

"Can Woody come?"

Her heartbeat quickens. "Who's Woody? A school friend?" *Don't say too much, Kate. Stay cool.*

"He's a dog, silly. Lives at number twenty-eight."

"Lucy and John's?" A young couple she met when she delivered their invitation. How do they manage to look after a dog when they both leave the house before seven in the morning and don't get home until late? She visualises a dog bounding into her house and spreading chaos, but Ben's eager face convinces her. "If he's well-behaved and they want to bring him, why not?"

On the dot of six o'clock, Mr Chatterjee, owner of the corner shop, arrives looking festive in a dark red Nehru jacket. When she called at the shop with his invitation he smiled, stuck it up on his till and promised, "I will consult with Mrs Chatterjee. She will know."

A couple of days later, when Kate popped into the shop for milk, he informed her they would be delighted. "Uncle will take charge of shop."

Kate had turned and glanced at the ancient man with the long white beard perched on a high stool near the shop door. "Won't your uncle want to come too?"

Mr Chatterjee shook his head. "No indeed. To run shop with no annoying younger generation – such as myself and Sabrina – that is his dream."

"Well, if you're sure..."

"You need anything for the party, come to shop. Have a nice day."

Sabrina Chatterjee is standing a few paces behind her husband, holding a bunch of white and yellow chrysanthemums, still dripping from the bucket that sits on the pavement outside the shop.

"Thank you." Kate holds out her hand, and Sabrina allows her fingers to be pressed for two seconds. She hands the flowers to Ben, whispering, "Pop these in a bucket in the utility room for me."

Turning back to her guests, she asks, "What will you have to drink?"

Mr Chatterjee accepts a non-alcoholic punch and Sabrina has orange juice, adding two spoonfuls of sugar from the bowl on the coffee tray.

"How long have you had your shop?" asks Kate.

"My father had big shop on Fulham Road. Massive. Brother works with father but shop can only support two families. Me and younger brothers have to make own way so, in 2005, we come to this cheaper area." He wrinkles his nose and sighs as if the pilgrimage from Fulham had left him a broken man.

"You must have seen many changes."

He nods, but it seems it's the shop, not the area, that's at the front of his mind. "Newspaper business is going bad. Magazines don't sell. Papers, we make only few pence on a copy. I am sending back big bundle most days."

Kate joins in with his sigh. "That's a problem for me too. I'm a journalist, writing for magazines."

"I didn't mean to worry you, madam. I'm sure you will be writing for magazines for evermore."

Ben is hovering in the doorway, keeping his distance. Sabrina sips her juice and asks, "How old is your boy?"

Kate smiles. "He's ten. Your two?" She sometimes sees a serene young girl in a white dress flitting through the shop, and a lanky boy humping boxes of soft drinks out of his father's car.

"Halif is twenty. He is home for Christmas holidays from the university. Afterwards he will be an accountant. No shop work for him."

"And your daughter?"

"Pria is sixteen. She will go to the university too and then she will marry."

Kate smiles, hoping Pria has signed on to this plan. "You must know everyone who lives in the street?"

Mr Chatterjee makes a burbling noise in the back of his throat as if preparing to spit on the floor. He fumbles in his pocket for a handkerchief and discreetly blows his nose. "All foreigners," he announces. "Except you, of course, madam, and us."

"And Mrs Coleman, and Jess; and Lucy and John." But, come to think of it, aren't they from New Zealand?

Mr Chatterjee is into his stride now. "Those Polish people go only to Polish supermarkets and to Tesco. They don't come to buy from us. Croatians, Slovakians, Somalis come in to buy tobacco but they don't read newspaper."

"They can't read English," adds Sabrina in a soft voice. "We feel so sorry for them."

The doorbell buzzes, but Kate has left it on the latch. A moment later Jess strides into the hall and hands Kate a potted poinsettia.

"You shouldn't!"

"Nonsense. Ian sends his apologies. He's in bed with flu. Is this Ben?" She smiles, produces another wrapped gift from her bag and hands it to him.

He looks at her suspiciously, then slots a finger under the Sellotape and tears off the wrapping.

"It's chocolate. Hope you don't mind, Kate. Now, tell me what I can do to help."

A short queue has formed, and Kate is drawn into handshaking and air-kissing duties. Still no sign of Nick. She smiles gratefully at Jess. "Well, if you wouldn't mind pouring some drinks. Get one for yourself first. Ben, give Jess a hand."

Some of the neighbours she knows and others she's meeting for the first time. "Lucy, John – welcome. And you've brought Woody."

"Hope you don't mind. Your son said it would be okay." It seems Ben knows Lucy, John and Woody better than she does.

"Here, Woody. Here, boy," Ben calls, slapping his hands on the front of his thighs while the Springer spaniel strains at his leash, tail quivering like a branch in a hurricane.

"Take him out in the garden for a bit, Ben," she hisses. "Keep hold of his lead." She turns back to her guests. "You know Mr and Mrs Chatterjee?"

"Sure. Hi, Rahul." They shake hands, and Mr Chatterjee grins, displaying a startling gold tooth.

Mrs Coleman totters in, leaning on her stick and breathing heavily. Kate guides her to an upright chair in the sitting room and she settles into it, bones creaking. "I'll keep my coat on for now, dear. I'll have some of that punch. And a mince pie."

The Chatterjees wait for her to settle then take their places on either side in honour of Joplin Street's oldest resident.

Three young men and a girl arrive bringing chocolates. "From number twenty-four. From Poland. Thank you for your kind hospitality." They all ask for beers and set off to do their own introductions, shaking hands and repeating their hard-to-pronounce names. Kate seizes the chance to pour herself a drink. Standing in the kitchen, chatting to Jess and Lucy, she feels the warmth of belonging wrapping round her. Ben has brought Woody back inside, and the two of them crouch on the floor playing. Ben's eyes are bright with laughter.

"Where is your husband?" a couple of people ask.

"He'll be here soon," she promises, but she has no idea if Nick's even remembered. Suddenly she wants him here, to see that her drinks party idea was a success and not another hare-brained scheme. "Give Dad a call," she whispers to Ben. "Ask him when he'll be home."

"Can't. You took away my mobile, remember," says Ben, glaring at her with such savagery that she backs away.

Lucy is chatting to Mrs Coleman, who has, it seems, visited New Zealand. Mr Chatterjee is deep in conversation with

Hanna, the Polish girl. Fatima, the nervous woman in the headscarf, arrives with her husband, toddler, and another son who looks about six.

"Welcome."

"This is Zayd," says the woman, pointing to her older son, "and the small one is Samir."

"Does Zayd go to Morton Road Primary?" Kate asks, beckoning Ben over to meet him. It seems he does, but Zayd won't leave his father's side. Politely refusing offers of food and drink, the family enter the sitting room; the husband shakes hands with everyone and exchanges a few words. Fatima is more reticent; cradling her younger son in her arms like a bullet-proof vest, she lets his smiley face do the socialising for her. After a while she takes the chair next to Mrs Chatterjee and sets Samir down on his sturdy legs, watching over him as he bumbles around the room.

Lucy holds Woody next to her on a short lead and Ben turns his attention to the toddler, soon deciding he's less interesting than a dog, so he starts collecting empty beer cans and builds a pyramid in the hall.

"See – a social triumph," exclaims Jess, waving an arm towards the assorted groups of neighbours chatting comfortably in the sitting room. She takes a sip of mulled wine. "I bet most of those people have never even passed the time of day. Now they're nattering away like old friends."

"No sign of our neighbours from number thirty-eight," says Kate. "Thickset guy with a nervous young wife. Drives his transit like a maniac."

Jess wrinkles her bow. "The ones who have late night visitors? Perhaps they're having a party tonight that clashes with yours?"

"You don't think there's anything odd about them, do you? So many people calling?"

"Drug-dealing, you mean?"

"It's possible, isn't it?"

Together they wander to the kitchen, where Jess has been manning the bar for most of the evening.

A clattering sound from the hallway makes everyone look round. A shoal of empty beer cans from Ben's pyramid is rolling across the floorboards. Conversation stutters, and the room falls silent as all eyes turn and focus on the door to the hall, where Nick is recovering his footing. In his work suit, laptop case over one shoulder, he looks stiff and formal.

"Dad!" Ben scampers to greet him, tugging Woody on his lead. "Say Hello to Woody!"

It's obvious from Nick's dropped jaw and darting eyes that he's forgotten all about the party. He bends down and pats the dog absentmindedly. Woody licks his hand.

Kate links her arm through Nick's and draws him into the gathering. People cluster round to meet him. For once he doesn't push her away, but she can feel tension knotted through his muscles. He must want to slink away upstairs, but she won't give him that option.

"I'll get you a drink." But Jess is already standing in the doorway holding a can of beer out towards him.

"Nick, meet Jess," says Kate. "She's been brilliant. Manning the bar for me all evening."

"Thanks." Nick accepts the beer, takes a swig and gives her a faint grin.

"You're welcome. I've been enjoying your hospitality."

"Not mine." Nick grimaces.

"Well, the party's been great fun," Jess continues, meeting his eyes with a look of cool appraisal.

John and Lucy hover, waiting to leave. "See you around, mate." John slaps Nick on the back, while Lucy holds out her hand for Woody's lead and loops it around her hand.

"Aw. Does Woody have to go?" asks Ben.

Lucy smiles. "Come and see him any time. And walk him."

"I will. Yes." Kate and Nick say their farewells on the doorstep and Ben follows them out to the gate and trots along the street chatting almost as far as their door.

"See," says Kate, pointing down the road after them. "I told you Ben's getting interested in animals. You should have seen him in Wales, playing with Gelis."

Taking their lead from the first departure, other guests start collecting their coats and sloping away. Nick nods and exchanges a few words as they leave, but the party atmosphere cooled with his arrival. Soon only Jess is left. She brings a tray from the kitchen and collects up glasses and empty food platters.

"One left," she says, offering Nick a silver foil dish containing a lone falafel.

"No thanks."

Jess puts the tray down on the coffee table. "I must be off too." She loops her scarf around her neck and ties it in a loose knot.

Please don't leave, thinks Kate, glancing at the purple-stained glasses and the tumbleweed of scrunched-up paper napkins. The guests have taken away the cinnamon-scented magic that temporarily cloaked the sadness that has seeped into her home. Will she and Nick ever resolve their rift?

"Thanks so much for your help, Jess."

"Don't mention it." She gives Kate a quick hug. "You two must come round to us for a meal."

"We will," promises Kate, but a glance at Nick's face tells her that's unlikely to happen.

CHAPTER TWENTY-THREE

Odeta knows when Tomas is out, because Stephan comes skittering down the basement steps, unlocks her door and beckons her to follow him up the stairs. In the sitting room, he smiles his gappy grin and presents her with a plate of food, setting it on the low table in front of her with a flourish. It's not the lumpy porridge or cabbage soup he fed her in the early days; he's making an effort. Today the plate contains some floury lumps of potato, beans in a lurid orange sauce, and thin rectangles of white fish covered with what looks like toast crumbs.

"Fish fingers," he says.

She laughs. Fish don't have fingers, and this squidgy mess looks nothing like fish.

"Are you having some?"

"I have eaten already."

She shovels up forkfuls of food, pressing any overspill rapidly into her mouth with her left hand before the plate can be snatched away. Her senses have been dulled by a cocktail of pain, terror and hunger. Now the hunger is easing, leaving space for curiosity.

"How did you and Tomas come to this house?" she asks, feigning innocence. At the Beauty Spa, while the other girls stare into space or idly turn the pages of fashion magazines, Odeta watches television. She's seen programmes showing people buying houses for vast sums of money. The girls have told her that rent in London is very high, so how could two Albanian men afford to live in a big house like this one?

Stephan is puffing on a vile-smelling cigarette and dragging smoke into his lungs, but her question makes him laugh. The laugh sets him coughing; he hawks and spits into a grubby handkerchief. He picks up the remote control, flicks the television onto silent and leans toward her. "You seen the idiot?"

Idiot? Well, Stephan himself seems like an idiot to her, so she widens her eyes and asks, "What idiot?"

"Geoffrey. Guy with the big head."

Now she remembers. The shadow hovering behind Tomas in the basement doorway, the childlike man who looked so terrified when Tomas manhandled him into her room – his name was Geoffrey. She nods.

"Yah. Him. It's his house."

His house. How can that be? Odeta shovels the last forkful of finger fish into her mouth; the taste isn't that bad once you get used to it. Some fruit would be nice. She's not had fruit since the meal on the plane, apart from a banana that a client left behind. How Lou had laughed when she'd spotted it on a chair. She held it up in front of the girls and dangled it from a limp wrist. "Some punter must've brought this in case he couldn't get it up." She offered the banana around, but only Odeta and Imani were interested. Lou split it in two and gave Odeta the smaller piece.

Stephan has found his voice now, and he won't stop talking. "Tomas found this place. Was when we first came over here. Five, six years ago."

"Isn't it very expensive?"

"Tomas answered a job advert. Live-in carer to look after disabled man in his own home."

"And Geoffrey's that man?"

Stephan nods and grins, giving her a front-row view of his sparse teeth. "Yep. Twenty-nine years old. Born brain-damaged. Parents died and left him this house and a trust fund."

"So, Geoffrey still lives here?" She shoots an anxious glance around the room as if Geoffrey might pop up from behind the sofa.

"Why not?" he laughs. "Guy with a trust fund, soft in the head. Doesn't speak much. At first Tomas was thinking to get rid of him, but why bother? Much safer for us if he's still here. Geoffrey can write – signs his name on cheques, pays all the bills. He doesn't know it, but his trust fund is paying for our food too. Hah!"

He pauses and gives her an accusing look. "And yours."

"But doesn't he have other family?" she asks. She feels a twinge of sadness for poor Geoffrey, but it doesn't last long.

"Nah. Every year the bank sends Geoffrey a letter to ask if he's still alive. All he has to do is sign it and send it back. Bank puts money into his account every month. Simple. Perfect for our business."

"So, where does Geoffrey live?"

"His room's upstairs in the attic. Sometimes Tomas lets him out to go and walk around the park, but he always comes back. Where else would he go?" He shrugs and curls his lips up on one side.

Lucky Geoffrey. If only she could go outside and walk in a park. "Doesn't he tell anyone about you?"

Stephan bristles. "What would he tell? We look after him. Tomas is his carer. I make his food and take it up to him. Sometimes give him beer."

What a strange country. In Albania, families are poor but

they look after their disabled relatives; neighbours help one another out. Tomas should be caring for Geoffrey, not taking over his home and stealing his money.

"You said he has a trust fund? What is that?"

"Yeah – hilarious, ain't it?" His laugh cackles around the room. "Geoffrey's a rich man with money in the bank, but who can he trust?"

Me, thinks Odeta. *He can trust me.* What was it Cassie told her? *Don't wait around for Kreshnik – make your own plan for escape.* She feels a rush of adrenalin. She will work on these men – first Stephan, then Geoffrey – and she will find a way to escape.

CHAPTER TWENTY-FOUR

The January sky is heavy with the promise of snow. Although it's Saturday, Kate drags her eyes away from the window and tries to concentrate on work, but the phone keeps ringing. First it was her mother, then her neighbour Fatima asking for advice on something to do with Zayd's school. It sounded complicated, so Kate agreed to go and see her on Monday. The phone in the study shrills again. She considers leaving it to ring, but habit is ingrained.

"Ceri!" How long since she heard from her one-time friend? Two months? More like three? At least Charlotte and Lisa bothered to send a Christmas card.

"Kate," Ceri's voice sounds breathless, "I've been trying to contact you for ages."

"I've been here," she says stiffly. "Haven't noticed any answerphone messages."

"Duh! That's why I'm phoning your landline now. I've been texting, sending WhatsApps, leaving voicemails... It was only today when I read your *Women First* article I realised you'd probably cancelled your mobile contract."

"What article?"

"Don't be dense, Kate. *Life Offline* – the one called *Cutting the Cord* or something."

"But that hasn't been published." It takes at least three months for an article to appear in a monthly magazine. Veronica hasn't even told her it's been accepted.

"It's in the *Women First* online magazine. I picked it up on Twitter, but it must have been up on their website at least a week. There are loads of comments – your experiment's created quite a stir. We women really don't know what we want, do we?"

What does Ceri want after all this time? Kate pushes her hair out of her eyes, gropes behind her for a chair and sits down. Her eyes wander to a framed print by Norwegian artist, Harriet Backer, hanging above her desk. At its centre a young Edwardian woman leans back in her chair, sewing. She's wearing a long skirt but her legs are thrust confidently out in front of her. Shades of blue permeate the picture: the woman's clothes, two chairs, greenish-blue walls; but her desk is the colour of an autumn leaf. Kate chose this picture for her study because it evokes timeless calm and intense purposefulness, far removed from the frantic scramble and clamour of modern life.

"I can see what you're aiming for now," Ceri continues. "It's all a set-up, isn't it? Using shock tactics to get a reaction from Nick. Like reality TV?"

Ouch. Ceri's infuriating, but they've known each other since they were tiny. At primary school in Abercwmmer they used to tell everyone they were sisters.

"Can we meet?" Kate asks, tentatively.

The line goes silent as Ceri considers. "The thing is, Kate – and Dan and I have discussed this – we don't want to take sides."

"I see." A feeling of bleakness grips her as she replaces the receiver. She's kept loneliness at bay by taking on more work, but now the morning's over with no writing done. Ceri's news about *Cutting the Cord* being on the *Women First* website intrigues her, but with no Wi-Fi she can't view it, and she can't contact Veronica on a Saturday. She'll ring first thing on Monday. She pops a pizza in the oven for Ben and sets the timer. She's not hungry; she'll eat his leftovers.

"Go and change out of your football kit, Ben. Lunch'll be ready soon."

"Anything for me?" Nick asks, opening the fridge door and scrutinising the meagre food supplies.

"Sorry. I've had no time to shop. You can share Ben's pizza."

"Missing online shopping yet?" Nick cracks open a beer. "Think of all the time you'd save."

She stiffens. "The Internet, social media – they're the time-stealers."

He sighs and mooches around the kitchen cradling his beer. "Well, I've got work to do. I'm getting sick of calling up friends to ask if I can use their Wi-Fi. Makes me feel like a lowlife."

"Is it time yet?" asks Ben.

"We'll go round straight after lunch," she promises. Since the drinks party, she and Ben have become Woody's unofficial dog-walkers. On weekdays, Lucy pays a firm called Puppy Love to walk him, and sometimes Ben and Kate give him an extra walk after school. Today is John's birthday, and Lucy's arranged a theatre trip and dinner, so Kate has agreed that Ben can be paid because Puppy Love doesn't come on Saturday.

"What are you going to spend it on, Ben?" Lucy had asked yesterday, handing him a crisp fiver.

"I'm saving up for a new mobile."

"Good for you."

"Yes. Mum stole my last one."

Lucy looks puzzled, but Kate has no intention of explaining their family arrangements. Other people wouldn't understand.

After lunch Kate lifts Lucy's key from the hook in the kitchen and puts on her coat, stuffing a notebook and pen in the pocket. It's sure to be freezing in the park, but Ben will be running round so he won't notice. This morning Nick took him to football training, and his cheeks are still glowing. Fizzing with energy, he runs on ahead to Lucy and John's door.

He still nags her with, "When can we get our own dog?" But Woody has partly filled that void for the time being.

Kate uses her glove to wipe the damp park bench before sitting down. She scribbles ideas for her next article, keeping an eye on Ben putting Woody through his paces. He thinks his dog-walker job description includes dog trainer, though Woody's behaviour is immaculate. Families traipse past her to the children's playground where dogs are not allowed. A new *Do Not* has been added to the long list of prohibitions. This one says: *The use of metal detectors is forbidden in this playground.* An elderly couple hobbles along the path, arm-in-arm, the woman pointing out a snowdrop pushing up through the sodden earth. Their closeness brings a lump to Kate's throat.

On the opposite side of the park, beyond the field marked out with goalposts, is a strip of trees and wilder parkland where dogs can be let off their leads. Ben is playing over there with Woody, still holding the lead, but appears to be deep in conversation with a teenage lad. Kate screws up her eyes against the watery winter sun to watch them more closely – it's not a lad, it's a short plump man. Fear rocks her to her feet; she jogs straight across the football pitch towards Ben and this stranger.

"Who's that you're talking to, Ben?" she calls as she draws level, her voice oddly high-pitched.

"It's Geoffrey. He's my friend."

Kate takes in the man's large head and moon face. He's not wearing a coat, but he has a long checked shirt over a too-small t-shirt, exposing a girdle of mottled flesh in the gap between his t-shirt and jogging pants. She stifles her earlier sense of alarm; surely he must be harmless?

"Hello, Geoffrey." She holds out her hand and Geoffrey places his lumpy fingers in her palm and submits to a feeble shake. "Do you live nearby?"

Geoffrey points out through the park gate and across the road towards Joplin Street. She follows the direction of his finger and realises, with a hint of shock, he's pointing at the house next door, with the blue transit van.

"Number thirty-eight?"

He nods, licking his lower lip with his protruding tongue.

"So you're our neighbour." Ben skips in a gleeful circle, pulling the barking dog with him.

"Ruff! Ruff!" parrots Geoffrey, stamping his feet on the ground and making doggy sniffing noises.

Ben erupts into giggles. The sight of her son larking about with this oddball man makes Kate uneasy. Ben needs friends of his own age; he shouldn't have to go to the park with his mum. Come September he'll be starting secondary school; she can hardly follow him there and back like a stalker. Most of his classmates already walk to school on their own or in groups. Perhaps if she let Ben do the same he'd mix with others more informally. She's over-protected him. It's time he had more freedom. Starting from next Monday, he can walk to school on his own.

The park is full of families: young children laughing in high-pitched musical voices and spattering bark chippings as they chase around the adjacent playground. In the wooded copse, Ben plays with Geoffrey and Woody. He fits right in.

January twilight descends without warning and blankets the park in grey chill. "Time to say goodbye to Geoffrey."

"See you here tomorrow?" asks Ben. Geoffrey alternately nods and shakes his head, setting Ben off on another round of giggles as Geoffrey slopes off ahead of them towards the park gate.

"That was the best time ever," says Ben, grinning. "When can we get a dog?"

They let themselves into Lucy's house, hang Woody's lead up on the hook inside the backdoor and check his water.

"Can I feed him?" Ben eyes up an enormous tub of dried dog food.

"No, Ben. Lucy said they'd do that when they get home from the theatre. He mustn't have too much."

"Aww."

She locks up and tucks the key in her pocket before walking the short distance home. Mr Chatterjee's uncle nods to them as they pass the shop. Igor, one of the Polish lads, is getting out of his car and gives a wave. Already, Joplin Street is taking on something of a village atmosphere. A few neighbours have remained aloof, but now that Ben has met Geoffrey from number thirty-eight, perhaps even that stronghold will be penetrated. The house, with its hi-tech entry phone and bars at the windows, must be divided up into flats and bedsits. The stream of visitors is just multiple residents coming home after shift work.

As soon as they open the door to their own house, the comfortable afterglow of their walk evaporates. Ben spots the letter on the kitchen table before she does, and reaches out to pick it up. She shoots out her hand slams it down, covering the envelope before he can get to it.

Ben puckers up his mouth and slaps the back of her hand. "Mine!"

"Ouch, Ben, that hurt." The envelope is in Nick's handwriting and addressed to her. She folds the letter in half, then folds it again until it's small enough to secrete inside her left fist. With her other hand, she levers the lid off a tin of chocolate biscuits and shunts it across the table towards Ben. "Here, have one of these."

"No." When Ben's in a rage, the first person he hurts is himself. "Mine! I saw it first."

She shakes her head. "Sorry, Ben. It's addressed to me."

He storms upstairs, bangs his bedroom door and plays music, very loud.

With a deep sigh, Kate fills the kettle and waits for it to boil, still gripping the folded envelope inside her fist. But not opening it won't make it disappear. This must be it: the stormcloud she's been expecting to break over her head. Why is Nick such a coward? If he wants to deliver bad news, he should tell it to her face.

She takes her mug of tea across to the table, opens the letter, and reads:

Kate – Sorry, but I can't go on living like this. We need a break. I'm moving in with Dan and Ceri for a while.

Ceri!

Didn't she say "Dan and I have discussed this – we don't want to take sides"? She's my oldest friend, but it seems she doesn't understand. I've lost her.

With a wrench, Kate looks again at the note. He's signed it "*Nick*" but with no kisses. No mention of Ben.

It's true, then. Nick is leaving her.

CHAPTER TWENTY-FIVE

Stephan is banging about in the kitchen, clanking pans, and the aroma of caramelising onions wafts into the sitting room where Odeta and Elira sit, surrounded by empty mugs and stubbed-out roll-ups. Nothing has been said, but Stephan seems to be in charge and he's allowing them unfettered access to the ground floor.

"Keep an eye on Stephan." Elira lights another roll-up. "Soon he'll get sloppy. Forget locking up."

"But the front door is always locked and windows have those cages."

Elira yawns. "I'll figure it out." She reaches for a glass of Stephan's leftover wine and swallows the dregs. As she raises it to her mouth, her hand is unusually steady. She's abandoned the skimpy tops she wore before Christmas in favour of a baggy sweater of pale blue wool. In this innocent colour her face looks younger, her expression less taut; even her empty eyes have a soft glow.

"Where's Tomas?" Odeta keeps her voice low, but starts to cough as the caramelising smell turns to singeing. There's more clattering from the kitchen, then a sizzling sound of tap water pouring into a hot pan. Stephan's trainers slap unevenly along the hallway and he bangs two plates – one china, one plastic – down on the coffee table. Each plate contains one pink sausage and a clump of charred onion. Odeta eyes it cautiously.

"Here. Eat." Stephan takes two forks from his jeans pocket and hands her one. The slippery sausage rolls across the plate as she tries to carve off a segment with the side of the fork, so she stabs it in the centre and nibbles one end.

"Where's Tomas?" asks Elira, ignoring the plate of food. Stephan drops the second fork on the table, reaches for his beer and takes a long swig. "None of your business."

Elira shrugs. "Me – couldn't give a shit. This one – Marije – was asking."

"Missing him, are you?" He leers at her, and the rash on his cheeks and chin glows pink.

Odeta bows her head over her plate, letting her dark hair swing forward to curtain her face. Why won't Elira stop baiting Stephan?

"Thought you might be missing him," Elira continues. "Not much action for you when he's not around, skinny boy." She picks up the pallid sausage and waggles it suggestively.

Stephan's acne scars darken to scarlet. "Bitch," he snarls, flexing his fingers. "I go only with women. Any woman I want, I have." His fingers encircle Odeta's wrist and grip hard, jerking her up onto her feet and reeling her in towards him. "This one – I can have her right now."

Odeta twists her head away, but he stretches his hand to its full span and places it on her throat, lifting her chin and turning her face back towards him. Odeta winces. His grip is firm. His fetid breath stifles her, and as he clamps his mouth over hers she tastes stale beer and feels his tongue – moist, slimy and probing.

"Leave her alone!" Elira is tugging at Stephan's t-shirt and he lets her pull him away. Suddenly, Odeta can breathe again.

She wipes her mouth with the back of her hand and gags. He glowers at her, at both of them, then picks up his mug and leaves the room.

Odeta sits upright on the sofa and tucks her legs up under her. She curls her body into a ball and rocks, gripping each elbow with the opposite hand. Why does she feel so violated? Stephan's no worse, and no better, than dozens of other men who force themselves on her.

"You'll live," says Elira, flopping down beside her. "At least you've escaped this. Feel here." She takes hold of Odeta's hand and rubs the palm across her own stomach: solid, curved, almost bouncy. She's put on weight. Odeta's grown so used to Elira's pinched drawn face and scrawny arms that she hasn't noticed her belly expanding into this smooth mound.

"Baby in here," says Elira, grimacing and pulling up her sloppy sweater to display skin stretched tight across her belly.

Odeta's mouth drops open as she stares from Elira's face to her belly. She reaches out her hand and touches it again. "How long you know this?"

"About two months. But Lou say it probably six months gone."

"You never said..."

"Nah. Thought it would die, but Lou says no."

Everything begins to make sense. The favoured treatment Lou gives Elira; the times she's in the salon, being called to client after client, while Elira relaxes in Reception, chatting to Lou.

"And the father?"

"Who can say? Maybe is Stephan, maybe not."

"Stephan?" The revulsion Odeta feels is physical – a crawling sensation below the surface of her skin. Her hand moves automatically to scratch her arm, leaving a criss-cross pattern of white marks.

"Yeah. Always use condom with client, don't you? But Stephan – that bastard –" She spits into the purple-stained wine glass. "He wants it skin to skin."

The shrivelled sausage left on Odeta's plate is pink with burnt edges like a nicotine-stained finger. Elira has one foot on the coffee table as she leans forward to tap cigarette ash onto the plate and knocks over a bottle. Beer foams and dribbles out onto the coffee table. She moves her foot out of the way and watches the liquid drip on the floor.

Odeta takes her hand and squeezes it. "You can't stay here, Elira. Not with a baby. I will find a way."

CHAPTER TWENTY-SIX

The crocuses came early this year. Cowering beneath dustings of frost to avoid the snow that threatened but never showed, their endurance was rewarded. Waiting by her front gate for Jess to join her for their walk, Kate notices the park is alive with splashes of purple and yellow flowers. Since Nick moved out three weeks ago, work has been her saviour.

"Kate – why didn't you get back to me sooner?" Veronica had asked when she called. "I emailed you a contract and a proposed fee. When I didn't hear back, we decided to test out *Cutting the Cord* in the e-magazine."

"I don't do email, Veronica. That's the point of *Life Offline*."

"Well, never mind. Terrie can send it in the mail. Reader response has been phenomenal. I'm commissioning you to write a *Life Offline* article every week."

Regular work – and well-paid! What a thrill. Some good news to share with Nick. But it's too late. She's driven him away.

Jess hurries along the road and thrusts a cake tin into Kate's hands. "Sorry I'm late!"

The tin is still warm. Kate lifts the lid and sniffs an intense, chocolatey aroma. "Jess, you shouldn't. Ben will be thrilled." Since Nick left, Jess has been her mainstay, dropping in to check she's all right, listening, telling funny stories about her younger piano students. But she's had no word from Ceri or Lisa.

"I'll take this inside. Come in for a coffee before we set out. House is a bit of a mess, sorry."

Reaching the kitchen ahead of her friend, Kate nudges the overflowing laundry back inside the utility room with her foot and closes the door. A pile of unread newspapers has grown into a small leaning tower. She and Nick used to read their newspapers online, but since she switched back to print versions they've invaded her space like an occupying army.

Strewn over the kitchen table are sheets of A3 paper with headings in thick black felt pen and scrawled notes underneath.

"You've been busy here!"

Kate smiles. "Advance planning for my *Life Offline* pieces. Thought I'd run out of ideas, but it hasn't happened so far."

"What's this one about?" Jess picks up a sheet headed *Exclusive or Excluded*.

Kate peers at it over her shoulder. "That piece is inspired by the problems Fatima's having with Zayn's school. They've stopped sending letters home with the kids, only communicate by email, and expect parents to log on and pay for school trips online. Fatima can't afford a smartphone and they don't have Internet."

"Doesn't Ben go to Morton Road, too? How do you manage?"

"It's an opt-out/opt-in thing. School assumes you'll do everything online unless you opt out. But Fatima didn't understand, so I sorted it out for her."

"Well done, you!"

Kate smiles. "It's great being able to help a neighbour."

Joplin Street is beginning to feel like Abercwmmer – her community.

"Any word from Nick?" asks Jess.

"He comes every Saturday to take Ben out, but otherwise, no. I miss him, Jess. D'you think we'll ever get past this?"

"You need to decide what you want." Jess sets down her empty coffee mug. "Come on, let's walk while it's still sunny."

Energised from the walk and Jess's company, Kate is settling back to work when the phone rings. "Drat."

The number flashing in the display looks familiar. She snatches it up just before it goes to answerphone. "Lisa!"

"Hi Kate." Lisa's tone is hesitant, apologetic. Her familiar voice sparks an ache inside Kate's ribcage.

"How are you? I've missed you," Kate says, dropping her voice to a whisper. Perhaps Lisa didn't hear.

"Sorry Kate. I should have tried harder, but it's been difficult..."

"Don't worry. You've rung me now." Her heart skips with joy.

"Listen. There's something I need to tell you." She pauses, as if gathering the right words of condolence. "I know Nick's moved out, and I feel awful about it."

Why couldn't she have said this sooner? Perhaps she or Josh could have talked to Nick, helped him understand...

"Yes. He's moved in with Dan and Ceri."

"Dan's away, Kate. In Dubai." She clears her throat and continues, "According to Ceri, he's 'running the Middle East'. I thought you should know."

CHAPTER TWENTY-SEVEN

Odeta hears Elira's laugh floating from the kitchen, and tiptoes into the hall to see what's going on. As usual Stephan is standing at the stove, labouring over a pan. Elira is sitting perched on the draining board, drumming her feet against the cupboard and puffing on a cigarette.

Odeta returns to the sitting room and sneaks behind the sofa to examine the bay window alcove. She presses her hand up and under the strut of the sash window, and pushes it with all her strength. The window frame has two tiny, metal-lined holes drilled into it – some kind of lock – but even if she could open the window to reach out, her slim hand would get stuck between metal bars fixed to the outside.

"Oi, stop that!"

Heart hammering, she spins round as Stephan and Elira enter the room. He thumps across the floor, grabs her arm and roughly pulls her out of the window bay, her shins banging against the sofa.

"Ouch. Let me go," she yells, struggling to shake free of his grip.

"Back to room," he commands, tugging at her arm.

"Oh, leave her," Elira chimes, settling herself on the sofa.

Stephan hesitates, looking from Elira to Odeta and back. Elira has a way of neutralising Stephan; he seems mesmerised by her. He must know about the baby, but has she told him it could be his?

Odeta edges away from them to the furthest corner of the room, and sinks down on the floor in the space beside the sofa where once she cleaned a pile of vomit from the carpet. She leans against the wall and closes her eyes, soon achieving the invisibility she's praying for. Elira and Stephan turn away and continue their conversation.

It's easy to block out their voices as exhaustion descends, and she dozes, dreaming she's back at home at a wedding – Ariana is marrying Sami. Her friend is centre-stage, sparkling in a dress so white that everyone around her blends together into a sepia backdrop.

Holding her bouquet stiffly in front of her, Ariana strides along the lines of assembled guests, peering into anonymous faces. "Where are you, Odeta?" Ariana is asking. "Why didn't you come to my wedding?" Tears are running down Ariana's cheeks and falling like raindrops on her bouquet. Suddenly the tableau moves, and the frozen faces of guests blink into life and begin to weep. There is her mother and her dad, with Afrim and Leon.

"Odeta, come home," they wail in a chorus. Her dad lights up a cigarette, his presence so palpable she can smell the smoke tickling her nostrils.

She opens her eyes, and the room is full of smoke. Elira and Stephan are sharing a spliff and talking quietly. Odeta keeps her eyes closed and listens to their conversation.

"So, where's he gone?" Elira is asking, coughing as the smoke tickles her lungs.

Stephan shrugs. "Doesn't tell me."

"He's been gone weeks."

"Maybe Albania."

Tomas's van has been absent from the parking space for some time. That must be why the pattern of their days has altered. There have been few clients, and she and Elira have spent most of their time on the ground floor of the house, with Stephan seeking out their company.

"You didn't want to go with him?"

"I have to stay here take care of you, yeah? Otherwise, you'd starve." He puffs out his chest. Beer cans and empty vodka bottles are stacking up in the room like a lost weekend. No one has emptied the ashtray for days; cigarette butts float in wine glasses, and Stephan stamps out his cigarettes on the rug.

Slowly, Odeta opens her eyes.

"Bitch is awake," says Stephan.

"Here, have this." Elira shunts a mug along the low table towards her. The aroma of coffee is tantalising, and even though the mug has a smudge of Elira's scarlet lipstick on its rim, Odeta wraps her fingers around it and raises it to her mouth. The taste is thick and gritty; it coats her palate, sparking a vision of the battered old coffeemaker in her parents' kitchen.

"The coffee – it's from Albania?" she asks, tapping her forefinger against the side of the grimy mug. No one replies, but the warmth of the liquid emboldens her to ask another question. "Why did you leave Albania to come here?"

Stephan won't meet her eyes, but he scratches one of the pimples on his face until it starts to bleed.

Elira nudges him. "Tell her."

Stephan moves his hand away from his face and inspects his grimy fingernails. "We came here to make money, of course. To work. Build better life. Then it went wrong."

"What?"

"That thing with Marije – it finished Tomas."

Odeta's pulse is racing as she waits for him to continue, but Elira highjacks the conversation. "You got anything stronger? Crack or something?"

"No! You mustn't." Odeta reaches out her hand, thinking of that tiny new heart beating inside Elira's body.

"Shush." Elira shoots her a warning, eyes snapping with anger – and Odeta realises he doesn't know! She hasn't told him she's pregnant, and he's too naïve to notice.

"Think I'd give it to you?" Stephan's lips say no, but his eyes travel lustfully over Elira's figure, seeming to contemplate another possibility.

"Come on, babe." Elira puts on a wheedling voice and leans in close to Stephan, sliding her hand up to trace the V-neck of his t-shirt where wisps of hair are visible. "Get me some and we'll go to your room."

Nausea wells in Odeta's stomach, and acid reflux burns her throat. She swallows and chokes on the thick coffee grounds still lodged under her tongue. Elira runs her palm the length of Stephan's torso and threads her fingers into the belt of his jeans.

Stephan straightens up, stretches his neck and scans the room with meerkat precision, then relaxes. He strokes Elira's hair with his filthy hands that stink of cooking oil. "Might have something upstairs," he mumbles.

"Elira, no." Odeta pleads, sensing her intervention is futile. Elira laughs and drapes herself around Stephan, clinging to his side.

"Can't trust you," says Stephan, producing a key from the pocket of his jeans and dangling it in front of her face. "You'll have to stay in here."

Odeta jumps to her feet and springs at him. "Give me that!" As she makes a grab for the key, Elira releases her hold on Stephan and stumbles sideways. There's a clunk as the key falls to the floor. Odeta can move faster than Stephan. Heart hammering, she swoops, her hand touches the cold metal and scrabbles to pick it up. "Ow!" Stephan stamps down hard on her hand. The pain is sudden, sharp, unbearable. The key drops from her fingers as she clutches her injured hand and holds it against her chest.

Cursing in Albanian, Stephan stomps out of the room. Elira follows, fluttering her hand in a farewell gesture but not looking back. Stephan slams the door and locks it. Odeta flings herself on the sofa, dry-eyed, and stares at the ceiling as she massages the aching bones in her hand. So close, but not quick enough. The key was in her hand! She should have been the one turning it, locking Stephan and Elira inside the room.

CHAPTER TWENTY-EIGHT

Ben's hunched shoulders have lifted and he's grown taller. His eyes sparkle, and he's almost chatty as he and Kate set out for their afternoon dog-walking shift. As soon as they've crossed the road to the park, she lets him take charge of Woody's lead. He seldom mentions his banished iPad and Xbox, or even his absent father.

When Geoffrey's in the park, he comes lumbering over to greet Ben and Woody, twisting his fretful expression into a smile. Kate parks herself on her usual bench, pretending to work but watching them tramping through the copse, following the dog. Soon the season will fast-forward, and the daffodils will be uprooted to make way for bedding plants. When summer comes, will she and Nick still be married? She shrugs the thought away.

Kate always puts chocolate bars in her pocket before setting out. Geoffrey's always famished. She wonders who looks after him and cooks his meals, but Geoffrey won't meet her eyes or answer any of her questions. He seems to regret pointing out that he lives at number thirty-eight, but Ben won't let it go.

"We're neighbours, Geoffrey. You can come to mine for tea. He can, can't he, Mum?"

"Well, um," Kate begins, but Geoffrey shakes his head, eyes flaring with anxiety. Today, instead of his usual shrunken attire, he's wearing an over-sized duffle coat, his hands invisible inside the sleeves. He looks like a cornered deer.

Ben doesn't appear to pick up on Geoffrey's mood. He prattles on like a child half his age. "And I can come to your house, can't I, Geoffrey?"

"No," shouts Geoffrey, shaking his head and twisting away from Ben. Two young mothers, sitting on the adjacent bench, turn and stare as Geoffrey grinds his heel into the gravel, turns his back and trudges towards the park exit.

"Where's he going?" wails Ben, watching the unfastened duffle coat billowing behind Geoffrey's departing back. "Why can't I go to his house?" He chases after Geoffrey, with Kate sprinting to catch up.

"Geoffrey's my friend." He glares at her as she grabs hold of his arm. "How would you like it if someone stopped you seeing your friends?"

With a sharp intake of breath, Kate hands him the dog's lead. "Here, take Woody. It's time we went home."

"Why?"

"It's your induction evening at Bankside Academy."

Ben takes charge of the dog but scuffs his feet along the gravel path, stirring up grey dust. "Do I have to?"

"Sure. It'll be interesting. Dad's coming." Her voice falters. Getting through the evening will be tough. Ben quickens his step and trots beside her to the park gate. The traffic is juddering towards a rush-hour climax. Kate takes the dog's lead back from Ben and winds it around her hand as they wait to cross the road.

"Why can't I walk Woody on my own?"

"It's a big responsibility, Ben, looking after someone else's dog. What if he ran away? Or got hurt on the road?"

"So, when will I be old enough?" He waits while Kate unlocks Lucy's back door, almost tripping her up as he blocks the doorway, bending down to pat Woody.

"See, his water needs filling," she says as Woody bounds inside, panting, and heads for his basket. "You can do that."

Ben fills the bowl from the utility room tap and carries it across to the dog without spilling a drop. "Goodnight, Woody."

Kate smiles and strokes Ben's hair. For once, he doesn't dodge her affection. Woody the dog is teaching him how to be more tactile.

At home, the light on the answerphone is blinking. Kate jabs the button and listens to the recording. "Ring me, Kate. Ring me whatever time you get this."

Kate's lips pucker into a wry smile as she thinks of all the years she's been chasing Veronica, practically begging for work. Now that *Life Offline* has become a surprise hit with readers, Veronica's pursuing her. Ignoring the plates waiting to be stacked in the dishwasher and Ben's shirt that needs ironing before he meets his new form tutor, she presses *Call-Back*.

"Wonderful news, Kate," Veronica purrs. "I've had a call from Carl B – you know him?"

"Can't say I do."

"Independent television producer. Does lots of work for Channel Four. He wants to turn your *Life Offline* experiment into a film. Err, I mean a documentary."

Kate shudders. She's a journalist, not a fantasy novelist. Everything she's written in her articles is true – except that she's muddied the timeline and not yet revealed to her readers that experimenting with Internet-free living has driven her husband away. Documentary – what a euphemism! Does this Carl character want to turn her frayed life into reality TV? In her mind, she already hears the presenter's nasal voice intoning:

"*The Davison family have set out on a bold journey. They have vowed to live their lives free from the Internet. How will their experiment unfold?*"

"Think about it, Kate. A huge opportunity for you – and for *Women First*."

Kate glances at the kitchen wall clock. "Sorry, Veronica, I have to go now. I'll think about it."

Kate and Ben enter the portals of the refurbished Academy, now scrubbed clean of graffiti and bursting with primary colours. Once branded as a failing school and populated by student gangs who rampaged through the local shopping centre terrorising pensioners, it now has a corporate look. At a shiny beech reception desk, a smiling administrator ticks their names off a list and hands over a stern-looking navy-blue folder, emblazoned with the Academy's logo. They wait in a queue, like tourists in a theme park, until a young student, proudly wearing her striped blazer, gathers them up and takes them along for the ride. She ushers them along a polished corridor to the school auditorium, vaster than some commercial theatres. Kate scans the rows of solemn parents and offspring, and spots Nick. He's seated himself in the centre of a row that's already full, leaving no space for her or Ben to join him, so they find a seat a few rows behind.

The headteacher struts in, wearing a grey skirt suit and red shoes. Even with those staggeringly high heels, adolescents tower over her. She begins her welcome speech, and her voice booms out into the furthest corners of the auditorium, leaving no hiding place, no chance for a student to nod off.

Kate sits quietly, hands folded in her lap, while details of homework, uniform, and codes of conduct trickle over her. Should she tell Nick about the producer who wants to make a documentary? He'd have plenty to say about the evils of reality TV. But then, it wouldn't affect him, would it? He's already packed up his life and taken it elsewhere.

The speeches finish, and they're herded into groups for a tour of the school. Footsteps shuffle along corridors, parents cough and whisper to their offspring. Ben hangs back at his father's side, but the pompous thirteen-year-old lad who is leading their group spots him and ushers him into his peloton, treating him to an insider's view of cool and uncool teachers. Ben's a soft target for a struggling first-time leader needing someone to impress, but Kate smiles to see him interacting with someone closer to his own age. Perhaps Ben's obsession with Geoffrey will start to cool.

They enter a science lab – "Well cool," according to their guide. Certainly, it's nothing like the souk of strange smells, grubby workbenches and high wooden stools Kate recalls from her own schooldays. Her chemistry master, who had lost three fingers in some youthful experiment that misfired, delighted in running his stumps through the female students' hair. These days he would probably be denounced as a paedophile, but she and her friends knew he was just a harmless sadist.

Bankside Academy's lab is white and clinical, with not a whiff of sulphurous egg smells. Ben and the other students are summoned to watch an experiment. A student in safety goggles and a white lab coat is heating up a coke can and waiting for it to implode. *A metaphor for my life*, thinks Kate, as Nick takes hold of her arm and draws her away from the craning necks of the children towards a quieter place at the back of the lab.

"How's Ceri?" she asks, balling her right hand and digging her fingernails into the palm.

A shadow passes across his face and he angles his head away towards Ben. When he turns back he meets her eyes. "Kate, we need to talk."

"Well, I know that, but we can't do it here!"

He pulls out his mobile and scrolls through his online calendar. "Can't make tomorrow, and Wednesday's a work do. I'll come Thursday evening. About eight."

"Fine." Kate writes the date and time on the back of her hand. "But if we're talking about serious stuff it might be better away from home. Jess will babysit. How about the White Horse, or the Oak Tree?"

He shakes his head, grim-faced. "No. It's my house, and I want to meet there."

"You mean you want to pick up more of your things?" She juts out her chin, trying to be brave. Nick's clothes are rumpled. Isn't there an iron he can use at Ceri's? His right eye is pink and sore. "You should get something for that conjunctivitis." Or is it an eye infection at all? Perhaps he's been punched?

"Okay, I'll drop by the pharmacy." His voice is flat, and there's not a flicker of an expression on his face.

"Nick, how did we get into this tangle?" She blinks back tears pricking her eyes. This isn't the time to show her feelings – too much of her life is unravelling. As they stroll towards Ben, Nick's hand brushes hers. She snatches it away, and they stand on either side of their son and watch the embers of the coke can experiment.

CHAPTER TWENTY-NINE

Odeta hears tyres squeal on concrete, a roaring engine fades to a stutter and a loose exhaust clanks. Tomas is back. What will he say when he finds them out of their rooms? She gathers up a cushion and hugs it to her chest, keeping her eyes fixed on the door, and waits.

The script plays out just as she's imagined it. He stops in the doorway and yells, "Stephan. What the fuck are these bitches doing in here?"

Elira yawns, eyes veiled beneath half-closed eyelids. Does Tomas know about her pregnancy?

"And where's my fucking money?"

Calmly Stephan produces a wallet from his pocket and counts out a pile of brown and purple notes with his greasy fingers. It's quite a small pile, and Tomas's black pinprick eyes spit fury. "Where's the rest?" He turns his thick creased neck and glares at Stephan, who shrugs.

"Quiet time. Not many calls."

Tomas balls his fists and aims a cuff at Stephan, who sees it coming and dodges. "Imbecile. Lazy dog. Letting these bitches lounge around while my business loses money and clients." Stephan has left an opened bottle of Heineken on the table, and Tomas swoops on it and pours it down his throat without appearing to swallow. He wipes his mouth with the back of his hand. The beer calms him. He yawns and blinks, looking down at the mud-spattered rucksack he dropped near the door. "Bushed," he announces, swinging the bag over one shoulder.

"How was visit in Tirana?" asks Stephan. "Did you see my mother?

Tomas ignores the question. "Lock up these bitches," he says, and stomps out of the room.

Odeta exhales.

"Two years he's been crazy like this," says Stephan, tapping on his forehead with his index finger. "Once he was normal. Never recovered from what that bitch did to him."

"What bitch?"

"Marije Kaleci. His fiancée. Promised by their families when they were very small."

"I don't believe you."

He shrugs. "Suit yourself. It's true."

What was it Stephan said to her a long time ago? Something like *Marije's gone and Kreshnik owes us.*

She shivers. What has Kreshnik to do with this?

Tomas's visit home did nothing to improve his temper. Early next morning he rattles Odeta's door and wakes her from sleep. He bursts in and bellows at her, "Complaints, always complaints about you, bitch."

She won't listen. She untethers her conscious mind and lets her thoughts float away from this room, from Tomas. She's heard it all before. "These men are paying good money for you, Marije, bitch. If they wanna talk, you talk to them. If they wanna kiss, you kiss."

He's taken everything from her and still he wants more. Why doesn't he put a bag over her head and finish it? She feels like the runt of a stampeding herd, left behind for lions to feast on. Strangers come and go and gorge on her entrails; they try to entice her to join their sick fantasies, but she stays expressionless and unflinching. She won't kiss the men or talk to them.

Now he's ranting on about something else, as if he's forgotten she's there. "Trouble, always trouble," he mutters, banging his fist down on the flimsy bedside table and knocking a glass of water onto the floor. She turns her back and stares at the wall.

"Bored, is it? You telling me you're bored?" He leans over, grabs her arm and pulls off the thin blanket and sheet. It's so cold in the room that she sleeps fully-dressed, but she's not wearing shoes. As he drags her up the basements stairs, the floor feels damp and sticky beneath her bare feet.

She must have slept for a long time, because Elira is already sitting in the lounge, smoking a bitter-smelling cigarette and gawping at the television. Or perhaps she didn't spend the night in her basement room but stayed up with Stephan, letting him grope her with his mucky hands.

"Bitch is bored. Talk to her," Tomas commands.

Elira's eyes are glassy and expressionless. Her arms are the spindliest tree branches, and even her baby bump seems deflated. Surely she hasn't...

Elira stretches her mouth in the shape of a word, but no sound comes; her head looks too heavy for her thin neck to support. She slumps back against the cushion, turning her face to one side.

Crack!

Tomas's palm slaps Elira's cheek, and her head bounces forward and recoils like whiplash. She puts a hand up to her face and whimpers but doesn't shout out, though the pain must be terrible; Odeta's own head is pounding with referred pain. She takes a step towards Elira, but Tomas pushes her away. He glares down at Elira, his crimson face contorted with fury. No one moves. Finally he shrugs and stamps out to the kitchen. Odeta hears him muttering curses and smells burning bread: that thing they call toast.

Elira taps her forefinger on the opposite side of her face from where Tomas hit her. "Last night, after you'd gone, he came back downstairs. He'd been drinking vodka straight from the bottle. He asked me why I was still there. Without waiting for an answer, he smacked me here: my ear – it went pop." She circles her hands in the air, and flings them wide apart, mimicking an explosion. "Pain is dreadful. Only this stuff helps." She reaches out with her fingers and picks up a crinkled strip of silver foil from the coffee table. Nestling in its folds is a pea-sized black substance. Elira wraps it up carefully and drops it back into the ashtray, next to two disposable lighters. She picks up the purple one, ignites it, and holds the golden flame close to her wrist. Before Odeta can restrain her, she runs it up and down, singeing the fine hairs that coat her forearm.

As if nothing had happened, as if what just passed was a normal social interaction, Tomas returns carrying two plates: toasted buns, smeared with butter. Wordlessly he hands one plate to Odeta, who stares down at it.

"Here. See!" Tomas flicks one of the pieces over and points out a pattern of a cross, pale and raised against the brown crust. "Something of Easter in this country."

The bun is speckled with pieces of hard black grit; if it's the same as the stuff in the silver foil, she won't touch it. Cautiously she scrapes out one of the black dots with her fingernail and tests it on her tongue. It's sweet, like a dried plum, flooding her mind with memories of home. She glances at Elira, who is almost no longer a person, and vows she won't follow her to that dark place. She'll stay strong and cunning. Even if Kreshnik doesn't find her, she will survive.

Later, in the bleak pink light of her room, she summons an image of her grandmother's crucifix and prays there will be no clients tonight. She begins her exercise routine, but even a simple warm-up drains her energy; a ten-minute workout leaves her exhausted. For the thousandth time, she studies the crack of window high up her wall. It must once have been a full-sized window, but over many years the level of the front garden has been raised up so three-quarters of the window is now buried beneath the ground. She drags the chair across the room, stands on tiptoe and stretches every vertebra in her spine, but it's too high even to catch a glimpse of the park.

Odeta jumps down from the chair, blinking back tears, and sits on the floor leaning her back against the side of the bed. She wraps her arms around her knees and rocks. *Where are you, Kreshnik? Why are you taking so long? How could you abandon me?* Her thoughts form a mantra, round and round in her head, driving her insane. She has to hold on to that thought. If a gap appears, a new chorus will force its way in. Cassie's words: *"Who did you say tricked you?"*

The ceiling above her head rumbles and vibrates. Doors slam, footsteps pound along the hall, and above the clatter she hears Tomas yelling at Stephan. The door leading down to the basement crashes open, Tomas's boots on the stairs and the metallic thud of a kick against the door opposite. "Where the fuck is she?"

And Stephan yells back, "It was you who left the bloody front door open."

Odeta's heart canters. She swallows, and the taste in her mouth is like mothballs. So many months waiting for something to happen, and now it has: a seismic shift and a personal betrayal. Elira's gone, and she's been left behind.

CHAPTER THIRTY

As soon as Jess arrives to babysit, Kate catches the bus to Clapham South and walks briskly along Cavendish Road. It's six-thirty on a Wednesday evening, but the bars and restaurants are buzzing as she makes her way through Abbeville Village to the leafy street where Ceri and Dan – and now Nick – live. Except that she's banking on Nick being out at a work function. Dan, as far as she knows, is still working in Dubai, but Ceri should be home. She's never been one to put in long hours at her office.

Since her last visit, the front door of Ceri's Edwardian villa has been painted primrose yellow. Its cheerfulness mocks Kate as she rings the bell and waits.

"Kate!" Blue eyes widening, Ceri gapes at her visitor and takes a step back, holding on to the door.

"Can I come in?"

"Nick's not here." Ceri's lips twist in a lop-sided smile. She's not wearing her usual nail polish, and Kate notices the tips of her fingers turning yellowy-white as her grip on the door tightens. Finally, she edges it open, just wide enough for Kate to enter.

Ceri's kitchen, scene of so many lively gatherings with friends, brings a lump to her throat. Work surfaces still polished to a high gloss; a third shelf added for Ceri's vast collection of cookery books, and pots of fresh parsley, mint and basil growing on the windowsill.

"Drink?"

"Just water, please." Without waiting to be invited, Kate pulls out a chair and sits down. Ceri pours herself a glass of Sancerre and hands Kate a small bottle of sparkling mineral water.

"So, what's this about?" Ceri remains standing as she waits for Kate's reply. As silence extends, Ceri twirls her wine glass and teases her hair with her fingers, rearranging strands to cover darker roots.

"Can't I call on my oldest friend without it being about anything? Or is there something you want to tell me?"

Ceri sips her wine. "I don't think so." Outside, the sky darkens and the first drops of rain spatter on the patio.

Kate sighs and prompts. "About you and Nick?"

Ceri's hand trembles and a few drops of wine spill on to the table, but she doesn't deny it. "Who told you?"

"Does it matter? Not Nick. I'm seeing him tomorrow. I guess he'll tell me then."

Rain is lashing against the kitchen window. Ceri turns her back on Kate and walks across to the sink, setting down her wine glass as she closes the blind. "It's not what you think," she says, spinning round to face Kate. "Besides – you threw him out."

"That's not true!"

"Made it impossible for him to stay, then. With your stupid no-Internet experiment. Look – Dan's away. I was lonely. Nick was depressed. It means nothing."

"Ceri," Kate fights against a choking sensation in her throat.

She half-rises from her seat, reaches out her arms and clutches at thin air. "I loved you. We were best friends."

"So we were. But don't forget about Rhys."

Kate's legs tremble and she holds the edge of the table for support. "What's Rhys got to do with this?"

When she closes her eyes, Kate can almost smell the salty tang of the sea and feel the wind lapping across the rugged Welsh coastline. At seventeen, she was the first of her friends to pass her driving test. Months before, her father had bought an old Ford Fiesta and started teaching her to drive on the farm. By the school summer holidays Leighton James had passed too, and one Saturday night he suggested driving down to the coast ...

Kate drove Ceri in her Fiesta, while Leighton took three lads, including Rhys Williams.

"Open the window, Ceri," Kate said, as the car filled with cigarette smoke.

"I tried. It's stuck."

"It's not electric, you know. You have to wind that handle."

"Oh, yeah. I see."

Ceri blew smoke out of the window and finally Kate could breathe again, but as soon as Ceri chucked away her fag end, she took a pot of nail vanish from her bag and started painting her nails lime-green. Now the smell in the car was pear drops.

When they reached the coast, the guys had gathered dry fallen branches from trees fringing the beach and built a bonfire. They cooked sausages, laughing when the bonfire claimed its burnt offerings. As dusk fell, Leighton rolled a joint and passed it round, the tip glowing against the inky sky. Smoke burned the back of Kate's throat. She inhaled more deeply, holding it in her lungs, until her head began to swim. They smoked and giggled until their insides ached, their laughter floating out across the silent sea.

Around midnight, Kate's euphoria ebbed and she felt light-headed and nauseous. "I think I'm going to throw up." She stumbled towards a rock pool, apologising to any limpets and crabs for wrecking their home. Rhys followed, draping his sweater around her shoulders and supporting her as she staggered back towards her parked car.

"What about Ceri?"

"Leighton'll take her home. Don't worry. Here, give me your keys."

"No, honestly, I'm fine."

"No arguing."

Relief flooded through her as she handed Rhys the car keys and let him take charge. She settled in the passenger seat and he leaned across and fastened her seatbelt. She lay back, closed her eyes and dozed. On the final bend in the road leading to the farm, a squeal of brakes jolted her awake. She heard a sickening thud and flew forward, but her seatbelt pinned her back. Her body lurched to the right as the Fiesta flipped over onto its side.

Everything happened in slow motion. The sky was moonless; her brain shut down. She came round, dangling sideways from her seatbelt, blinking at shattered safety glass and disorientated by the car's reconfigured layout. In the blackness she could make out Rhys's shape, huddled beneath her, his head lodged between the steering wheel and the side window. The driver's side of the car was now its floor.

"Rhys?" Her voice was a hoarse whisper. He didn't answer. She called louder, with more urgency, gently prodding his back. In the inky sky, a single star shone down on the rear of the vehicle that had hit them, spun across the road and lodged in a hedge. As she tried to wriggle free of her seat belt, the car rocked, ready to complete a full somersault.

Oh my God. "Rhys, don't move, I'm coming to help you." She rebalanced her weight and uncurled her legs, one at a time. The car bobbed like a fishing boat on a rough sea. The only way out was to kick the last shards of glass from the windscreen and crawl through. Rhys's head was resting on an arm; he seemed to be asleep. Sobbing, she took aim at the glass with her foot.

There was a shout of, "Hey, you okay?" as the driver of the other car, a man in his forties, stumbled into view, blood pouring from a gash on his forehead. He approached on unsteady feet, walked around the front of the Fiesta and braced his trembling body against it. Taking off his jacket, he wrapped it around his lower arm and fist and punched out the last of the safety glass. Kate smelt alcohol on his breath as the man leaned in through the windscreen and helped her clamber out.

"In a bad way, is he?" he asked, jabbing a finger at Rhys.

"I think he's unconscious."

Kate crouched on the grass verge, keeping her eyes fixed on the back of Rhys's head while the stranger rocked the car, testing it was solid on its side panels. He slid his arm through the windscreen, hooked it beneath Rhys and lifted his head.

She couldn't speak, she couldn't scream. She could only keep on staring into the bloodied pulp that had once been Rhys's face...

"I've tried not to hold it against you, Kate." Ceri's voice cuts through her memories. "You were ill. Rhys drove you home. What happened was an accident."

Kate bows her head and sobs, covering her face with her hands. Why shouldn't Ceri blame her? She blames herself, and she's carried the guilt with her ever since that day. She peers through her damp fingers at Ceri, who has a red shiny nose and smudges of black mascara on her cheeks. She lowers her eyes and waits until Ceri stirs, reaching into a drawer for a box of tissues and placing it on the table between them. Kate takes a tissue, dabs her eyes and crumples it in her hand. They sit in solemn silence, wrapped in their separate thoughts.

Finally, Ceri speaks.

"Rhys shouldn't have been in that car, Kate. He noticed you were stoned and unwell that night, and did his best to take care of you. But he wasn't *your* boyfriend. He was mine."

CHAPTER THIRTY-ONE

There's a tap on the door of Odeta's room. She stares at it, more puzzled than startled; since when did anyone knock? Stephan opens the door a fraction and leans in, beckoning to her to follow him. At the top of the stairs, he waits and hands her a cigarette. "Take this. Maybe you need it." He lights it for her and she takes a long drag, pulling the smoke deep into her lungs.

She hasn't been out of her room since the day Elira disappeared, nor has she seen Tomas. She lingers in the hallway, resting her back against the wall and puffing on the cigarette. She runs her free hand over the embossed Grecian urn wallpaper; its furry texture feels strangely comforting. The patch of wall by the basement door feels damp. She scratches it with her fingernail and peels off a strip of soggy wallpaper, kneading it into a ball inside her palm with the fingers of her left hand.

From behind the closed sitting room door floats the sound of muffled male voices. She can't make out what they're saying, or even what language, until Tomas raises his voice and spews out a stream of English swear words.

"Have you found Elira?" she asks Stephan, her heart hammering. *Please say Elira has got away.*

Stephan puts a finger up to his lips and shushes her. "You should know not to mention her name." He jabs his thumb at the closed door. "Don't make him angry." He rests his hand on the brass doorknob and waits. The pause seems to last for ever, as if he's holding his breath or waiting for the temperature inside the room to change. Odeta's cigarette burns down to the filter; she squeezes the smouldering end between her left thumb and forefinger, feeling a sharp cleansing pain as it burns her.

The voices inside the room fall silent. Stephan turns the knob, pushes the door and stands aside, waiting for her to enter.

Tomas is standing between the sofa and the bay window. It must have been a squeeze to manoeuvre his bulky torso into such a confined space, almost as if he wanted to place a barricade between himself and his visitor. A tall man with a shaven head, wearing a well-cut grey suit, is standing with his back to the door, examining the fireplace. On the crown of his head is a raised scar, the length of her little finger and the colour of uncooked pork. It's raining outside, and the room has a damp chill, as if a late slice of winter has dropped down the chimney. There's a gas fire in the grate, but she's never seen it working. The stranger bends down and fiddles with a switch, holding his finger on the ignition for thirty seconds. The fire makes a popping sound and erupts into life. Blue and yellow flames dance in a basket of fake coal.

The grey-suited man must be a new client, but what were he and Tomas arguing about? Tomas is always picking fights, so it was probably nothing. The stranger straightens his back and stands up. As he turns around, Odeta's throat goes dry. Thoughts tumble inside her head. She moves her lips in the shape of his name, but her voice won't respond. Her knees tremble and she struggles to keep her balance.

Kreshnik stares straight through her. Yet he's the one who has changed, she thinks angrily. Baldness really doesn't suit him; the smooth dome of his head throws his hooked nose into relief. Even when he had a full head of dark hair, his narrow lips sometimes curled into a sneer.

Something inside him snaps into gear. His eyes widen, and he gazes at her as if he's seen a ghost. She tries to smile and takes a step towards him extending her hand, but he turns away from her and addresses Tomas. "You bastard. What have you done to her?"

Odeta feels a sob welling up inside her. *Never mind Tomas, speak to me. Can't you see I need help?* Does he think she's an inconvenient piece of rubbish from his past? The trembling returns, travelling through her body to the tips of her fingers. She perches on the arm of a sofa and braces her feet on the floor.

Tomas glares back, his eyes narrowing to slits. "What have I done to her? Marije the Second? She's nothing. Pah." He spits in the direction of Kreshnik's face, but his aim falls short and the glob of spittle lands on the sofa back. Kreshnik raises his hand as if to strike him, while Tomas squeezes out from behind the barricade of the sofa to face him.

"That girl, she was a jewel," hisses Kreshnik, pointing at Odeta but not looking at her. "Only just a little more than a virgin. Couldn't you see that?"

"These girls are all the same."

"How much are you getting for her?"

Tomas scratches his head. "About three hundred."

"Each client?"

"Three hundred a day."

So Kreshnik knew! He was always part of this horror and betrayal.

Her face and hands are clammy, but her feelings have turned to ice, and bile rises in her throat. So that's what they pay. Three hundred lek? Or three hundred pounds? How much is that anyway? It sounds a lot. In the salon, she sees money changing hands: clients count out bank notes on the desk and Lou stashes them away in the safe. Once she overheard a client asking to pay by credit card, and Lou laughed. "Everyone pays cash here, love. There's a machine three doors along, outside the deli."

"Three hundred? That's madness." Kreshnik lowers his voice, and she strains to catch his words. "You told me you were moving upmarket. Into hotels, dancing clubs. Odeta is a gymnast, a champion. She could make more money from pole dancing."

"She's a lazy, disobedient bitch. If anyone ruined her, it was you. Just as you ruined my fiancée, Marije."

Odeta stops trembling and her whole body turns rigid. She leans forward, struggling to catch her breath. So what Stephan told her was true: Marije Kaleci was Tomas's fiancée.

The men aren't talking any more. They're prowling round one another like animals squaring up for a fight. Kreshnik balls his fists and raises them in front of him, sparring. Tomas, the shorter of the two by some margin, dips forward and headbutts Kreshnik in the diaphragm.

Kreshnik springs back, winded, and glares at Tomas.

"Guys, guys!" Stephan injects a temporary truce. She didn't notice him leaving the room, but he's been out to the kitchen and returned with a bottle of Scotch and two tumblers, smeared with fingerprints. "Sit," he orders.

Kreshnik, rubbing his stomach, looks from Stephan to Tomas, glances at the bottle and nods. In that moment, his eyes had travelled the length and breadth of the room without alighting on her even for a second. Stephan pours out two tumblers of amber liquid and hands one to Kreshnik, who takes it and walks across to where Odeta is perching on the threadbare arm of the sofa. He takes hold of her hand and pulls her down onto the seat next to him.

It's a simple gesture, but his touch holds such memories that tears sting her eyes. He turns towards her and examines her face, stroking a lock of hair back behind her ear. She knows her face is altered; her eyes are hollow, and her skin flares up in an angry rash. She doesn't want him seeing her like this, so she leans her head against his neck and inhales his clean pine-forest smell. So good, so familiar.

Tomas gulps his Scotch and pours another slug into his glass. Stephan is drinking beer. Neither of them speak, but they keep their eyes fixed on Kreshnik with a look of contempt.

He keeps hold of her hand, but he doesn't caress or squeeze it. There are so many things she wants to ask him, like *Why did you make me go with this man? Did you know how he would treat me?*

Eventually she asks, "Have you been in Albania? Are my parents looking for me?"

To her surprise, he nods. He wets his lips with the tip of his tongue. "They are looking. Your picture was in the newspaper some weeks back."

Joy surges through Odeta. She thought she might be dead to them, that they'd think she's turned her back on her home as she moved on to a new life. But they haven't forgotten her. She is brimming with love for her parents and brothers and longing to see them again. She half rises, smoothing down her mini-skirt to hide the tracery of blue veins visible on her bare ivory legs. "I must go home."

Kreshnik rubs his forehead. His hand glides on over his temples into the unfamiliar geography of his shorn scalp, where he pats down an illusion of hair. "I'm afraid that's not easy, Odeta."

"What do you mean?" She's angry now, and her dull eyes

come alive and flash at him. "They are searching. Of course they will find."

"But Odeta Lazami never entered the UK, did she? Think about it: the passport – the girl who arrived here was called Marije Kaleci." His tone is light, but the words are heavy and loaded.

She furrows her brow. "But you've come here to take me away, back to them?"

Tomas puts his glass down with a clatter so her eyes swivel to look at him. "Forget your parents. They won't want to know you now. Look at you – slut. You're dead to them." And with a spiteful glance in Kreshnik's direction, he adds, "Just like your filthy slut of a sister."

Kreshnik utters a curse in Albanian. Swinging his fists he gets to his feet, but Odeta holds on to his arm and drags him back, her face wet with tears. "Explain to me," she screams. "You have to tell me. Who is Marije Kaleci to you?"

"You heard him. She's my sister."

"Oh my God!" She pummels his chest. "Your sister! What did you do to her?"

Kreshnik fends off her flailing hands and sits back, crossing his arms over his chest. He's barely touched his whisky, yet his face is frozen and vacant, and his chin sinks down and rests on his chest. She plucks at his sleeve, but he's unresponsive like someone in a trance. Tomas, too, is brooding into his glass of whisky; the name Marije Kaleci has stirred bitterness and anger.

With a heavy grunt, Tomas pushes Stephan out of his way, stumps across to Odeta and yells in her face. "His sister. My fiancée. He brought her to London. Not telling me. They were living an immoral life sharing a flat with other men. Our women are spotless."

He blunders around the room, bumping into furniture,

kicking over Stephan's beer bottle. Six paces bring him to the door. He pummels it with his fists and howls like a dog.

"Bastard. You destroyed my life," he yells, springing away from the door back to where Kreshnik is slumped beside Odeta, lost in thought. Grabbing his collar, he yanks him up. Kreshnik rocks unsteadily on his feet.

What's happened to Kreshnik? He seems almost submissive, but it must be an act.

Thwack – Kreshnik lands the first punch on the left side of Tomas's head. Odeta restrains a whoop and a cheer; a small payback for beatings she's received at Tomas's hands.

Tomas retaliates, snarling. Kreshnik sidesteps the fist as it slashes through thin air. Tomas's face is the colour of tomatoes, his eyes sinking under fleshy lids. He grabs Kreshnik in an armlock, but being so much shorter, he can't twist his arm high enough up his back. And then Kreshnik laughs.

Tomas draws energy from his fury and brings his bull-shaped head back into play, ramming into Kreshnik's stomach just below the ribs. Odeta can almost hear the whistle of air leaving Kreshnik's lungs as he stumbles, falls back against the sofa and slithers to the floor.

Before he has time to recover, Tomas is crouching over him, punching and pummelling his head. Kreshnik cries out in pain and raises both arms to protect his face.

Dredging energy from somewhere, Odeta grabs Tomas and tries to pull him away, but he's solid as a stone pillar. He won't budge. She owes Kreshnik nothing, but some instinct drives her to stretch out her arms to shield his body from the tempest of blows. Dealing with pain comes easy to her, and she buffers the punches, giving Kreshnik time to suck in oxygen. He whispers "Thanks" as he rolls sideways and curls into a foetal position.

"Get this bitch out of here," shouts Tomas, and Stephan swoops, grabs her and pulls her to her feet.

"Come on. Get moving." He drags Odeta towards the door. She digs her feet into the carpet and holds onto the doorframe. Turning her head, she notices Kreshnik has got back up onto his feet. He'll be all right.

Then she notices the flash of silver. Tomas has pulled a knife from his pocket, and is pointing it at the centre of Kreshnik's chest.

CHAPTER THIRTY-TWO

After her talk with Ceri, Kate can't sleep. Her marriage was already hanging by a thread, but that was because she and Nick couldn't reconcile differing views on how to help their son. How could Ceri, her oldest friend, choose this time to exploit their vulnerability? When she offered no support back in October, Kate felt as if a lump of stone had lodged in her heart. But an affair! How had Ceri described it – *a casual fling?* That was betrayal on a seismic scale.

But Ceri didn't leave it there. She didn't give Kate the opportunity to yell at her, or accuse her of taking all the friendship Kate had so freely given over almost four decades and flinging it back in her face. No. She summoned up the ghost of Rhys Williams.

Kate can't sleep because she's terrified of the nightmares lying in wait if she slips beneath the surface of consciousness. She snaps on her lamp and sits up in bed, leafing through an old copy of *Women First*.

Next morning, she swallows two strong painkillers, waves Ben off to school and goes back to bed. Exhaustion claims her and she drifts into a heavy dreamless state, waking befuddled late in the day. She stumbles downstairs and surveys the chaos in her kitchen. She can't let Nick see the house in this state when he comes round tonight. Most evenings she gives Ben supper after they return from walking Woody, but it's often nine before she makes something for herself. Sitting down to eat is too much faff, so she stands by the stove and scoops her supper straight out of the saucepan into her mouth. Much as she dislikes her austere black granite kitchen, it's where she lives now – where she works, cooks and watches television. She hasn't opened the sitting room door in weeks.

Nick's due at eight o'clock, but she won't prepare supper for him. Why drag out the agony? Let him come round, say what he wants to say, then go. But Ben will need supper, so she finds a pack of lasagne sheets, chops up vegetables and makes the sauce. She grates in some nutmeg and sprinkles cheese on top then glances at her watch. Four-thirty – Ben should be home by now. She strolls to the front door and walks to her gate, her steps quickening as she reaches the pavement. She looks right and left – the street is empty.

She turns right, pads to the end of the street and peers along Boundary Road, still wearing her furry slippers. A gaggle of older teenagers returning from college drifts round the corner, but no mums with younger children. Turning back towards her house she breaks into a run; her left slipper slides off her foot and lands in the gutter. Feeling ridiculous, she hops forward and puts it on. As she straightens up, pinpricks of light at the back of her eyes disturb her field of vision and giddiness grips her. She waits, standing stock-still, but there's no ache around her eye or in her temple. *Don't let it be a migraine.*

Her front door is gaping wide open, just as she left it, handbag on the hall floor in full view of any passer-by. In her bag, she finds a blister pack of painkillers and walks to the kitchen to swallow a couple with a glass of water. She picks up the house phone, but the days when she could just tap a screen to make a call are a distant memory. Her address book is in a drawer by the phone. She flicks through to find the phone number of Ben's school. Breathing rapidly, she dials and waits for an answer. *"The office is now closed and will reopen at eight o'clock in the morning,"* says the machine. *"Please ring back then."*

She knows damn well the school isn't closed. After-school clubs run until five, not that Ben will ever agree to go. Her throat is tight, and giddiness is blurring her vision. Perhaps Ben decided to go to a club today? Isn't that just the sort of random thing he'd do?

She dials the school's number again and waits. This time it's picked up by an actual person. "Ullo? Morton Road Primary."

"It's Mrs Davison. My son, Ben – he's not home from school yet. Has he been kept in?"

"Dunno, love. I'm the cleaner. Just popped into the office to hoover when I heard the phone."

"But can you see any children waiting in Reception?"

"I'll ask the site manager."

Jacob the caretaker comes to the phone: polite, condescending and defensive all at once. "Clubs finished twenty minutes ago. I've been round and locked up. There's no one left."

"Could you check again?" She drums her fingernails on the side of the phone.

Jacob's sigh echoes down the line, encompassing all the weariness of the world. "Leave your number. I'll let you know if he turns up."

She puts the phone down and flops into a chair, straightening her back and trying to think logically. First, retrace his route. She grabs her car keys, but hesitates. Perhaps she should walk – there's more chance of spotting him if he's wandered off along a side road. If only she could ring him. Whose idea was it to separate him from his mobile? She rummages through the drawer where she hid it when she called time on technology, wondering if he might have stolen it back. But no, the phone is lying there obediently waiting to be released at the end of its sentence.

She can't wait any longer so she thrusts her feet into her boots, without zipping them up, and flies out of the door. She drives at snail-pace along Joplin Street, turns right into Boundary Road and cuts through the Orenstein Estate, just in case.

The school gates are still open. She drives in, parks in the headteacher's space next to the main entrance and runs up the steps. The door is locked. She rings the bell and shouts for attention.

Footsteps tramp towards the door and Jacob opens it, laden down with three bulging rubbish sacks. "Look, he's not here. I told you."

"Please let me come in and check his classroom: Room 6B."

Muttering, Jacob leads her inside. His jangling keys set off her headache as they walk along the echoing corridor. She can see through the glass pane in the door that the classroom is empty, but Jacob solemnly unlocks it and stands back to let her enter.

The classroom is like a cross between the Royal Academy Summer Exhibition and an industrious beehive: paintings are framed on blue or black card; charts, maps and posters shriek knowledge from every wall. Kate crosses to the place where Ben normally sits and runs her hand over it, but there are no names carved into the wood by generations of pupils; the surface is smooth and eerily pristine. There are no drawers in the tables; each child has a filing tray stacked in a shelf unit to hold their work-in-progress. She lifts out the tray with Ben's name on it.

Inside is a plastic-covered library book, Maths and English exercise books, and a drawing of a dog that looks a bit like Woody. When Jacob isn't watching, she folds up the sketch and slips it into her bag.

"Might as well check the toilets," says Jacob. "You won't find 'im though."

The toilets are on the far side of the cloakroom: a forest of abandoned coats and shoebags dangle from hooks. The stench alone is enough to draw her in the direction of the boys' toilets. "Urgh!"

"Disgusting, isn't it," agrees Jacob, happily. "Cleaners won't touch 'em. Worst job. I leave it till last then go home and have a shower." There's no one at the urinals. She pushes open the turquoise door of each cubicle, but all are empty.

Kate's tongue is sticking to the roof of her dry mouth. She breaks into a run. Leaving startled Jacob behind, she squints through the glass panel of every classroom, calling out Ben's name. Finally she reaches the Head's office, sinks down on the naughty chair outside the door and buries her face in her hands.

"Don't worry now, Mrs D," says Jacob, patting her shoulder with his large meaty hand. "He probably stopped off with one of his mates and forgot to ring you. Those Year Six lads have their own agenda."

"Of course," she nods, moving her head mechanically like a marionette. This man doesn't know Ben, but he's offering her a straw and she grasps it. Surely Ben will be home by now. She must get back.

As soon as she spots the blank windows of her house she knows he's not there. Ben has his own key and he doesn't like the dark. If he came in at dusk to an empty house, he would walk around switching on a light in every room. She fumbles her key into the lock, hurries inside to the phone and dials Nick. It's six o'clock now, but he's bound to be still at his office. Perhaps he decided to pick up Ben and take him out for a couple of hours before coming on to see her? Nick's phone is on voicemail, of course. She stutters out a message: "Nick, Ben's not with you, is he? It's nearly six and he's not home from school yet. Ring me when you get this." She adds, as an afterthought, "...On the landline."

A sense of helplessness forces her to confront the irony of her situation. Nick has all the technology that modern life can offer, but she still can't reach him; her son is uncontactable because she's taken away his mobile phone. Why, oh why, did she do that? No wonder he hates her; he's probably done this disappearing act on purpose to punish her. She rings Lucy and John. Their answering machine butts in, neither of them will be home for at least an hour. She tries Jess – again, no reply.

She remembers a boy Ben once went to tea with – a Felix. What was his family name? She flicks through her address book but can't find it. Of course, that was back in the days when she saved numbers in her smartphone, before she ended her mobile phone contract. She scours her memory and recalls where Felix's family lived: those new houses – Elm Tree Close. When she went to collect Ben, Felix was sitting sulking on the stairs because Ben had taken over his Xbox and played on his own all evening, not letting Felix come near. "Sorry," whispered Felix's mum, bundling Ben out of the door. "They seem to have had a little tiff." What was the woman's name? Mrs Vardy – that's it. Kate opens the phone directory – the last before BT put everything online and stopped issuing them – and runs her finger down the list of Vardys until she finds one in Elm Tree Close.

If Mrs Vardy is surprised to hear from her, she doesn't show it. She's polite and expresses her concern, but no, she hasn't seen Ben since that ill-fated play date.

The painkillers Kate took to stave off the headache are

making her woozy and seem to be blocking rational thoughts. There are other people she can try. She must get out there and search. She glances at her watch. If Nick arrives he'll have to let himself in. She scribbles him a note and leaves it propped up against the fruit bowl that contains one black-splodged banana and a bar of chocolate.

Locking the door behind her, she crosses the road and hurries along to the Chatterjees' corner shop. As she steps through the doorway a faraway bell pings, and Uncle struggles down from his stool and bows.

"Mrs Davison, so wonderful to see you," says Mr Chatterjee, coming from behind his counter to shake her hand.

"How are you, and how is Sabrina?" she blurts out in a rush.

He is all smiles. "We are very well. You must come out the back and have some tea, Sabrina will be happy to see you."

Kate's smile quivers and fades, she chews the inside of her lower lip. Mr Chatterjee seems to pick up on her mood, and his tone of voice changes.

"Something is wrong?"

She nods. "It's Ben. He's not home from school yet. Has he popped into the shop this evening?"

Mr Chatterjee shakes his head, his expression grave. "He has not been in today." He cocks his head towards the old man with the white beard. "Is that right, Uncle? We did not see young Ben today?"

In a melange of languages and head-shaking, Uncle confirms that, indeed, he has not seen the boy. There's a quiet rustling as Sabrina parts the heavy brocade curtains that separate the Chatterjees' living quarters from the shop and bustles in. She must have overheard their conversation; she weaves her hands together and raises them to the sky, and her own eyes are moist with tears as she looks at Kate, sharing another mother's worry.

A queue of customers is building, but Mr Chatterjee ignores them. "We will close up shop. We will come and help you search."

"You are so kind. But really don't worry. I'm going to call on a few more neighbours. If I don't find him, I'll go home and ring the police."

Sabrina lays a hand on Kate's arm. Her touch is light, but her fingers transmit strength. "Go and search. Do not let us detain you. We will ask our customers to look out for him too."

Kate shuffles out into the street, blinking back tears, suddenly unsure which way to turn. Passing traffic belches dust and fumes into her face, making her head throb. She glances back along the street at her house – still no lights on. Through a gap in the traffic she sees the blue van in its parking space. Number thirty-eight! Where Ben's strange friend, Geoffrey lives. She thinks of how Ben is always pestering Geoffrey to let him visit. Could he have bumped into him on his way home from school and gone to his house? There's only one way to find out.

CHAPTER THIRTY-THREE

"No.......!" Odeta's scream echoes around the room and bounces off the walls. With hands outstretched, she darts forward, but Stephan grabs her from behind. His arm presses on her windpipe as he drags her towards the door. Tomas brandishes his knife in the air, plunges it into Kreshnik's chest and twists it.

She sinks her teeth into Stephan's arm, kicks back at his shin and breaks free just as Kreshnik collapses to the floor, clutching his chest. The knife is still twitching in Tomas's fingers.

"That bastard. It's his fault." He flings the knife down onto the floor and heads for the door, kicking the writhing body as he passes.

"Murderer!" Odeta screams.

Tomas turns in the doorway and holds up two fingers.

She kneels down beside Kreshnik, whose body is buckled and sagging sideways with one leg bent beneath him. His head is wedged against the coffee table, and he's struggling for air.

Sobbing, she pulls a cushion from the sofa, puts her arms beneath his neck and gently lowers his head onto it. She places her ear against his chest and listens to his breathing: a bubbling sound. Scary.

"Help him," she yells to Stephan. "Get a doctor."

Stephan gawps and shuffles his feet. "Not my business."

Fighting her own terror, Odeta whispers, "You will be all right." But soothing words won't mend Kreshnik's damaged body. Blood is soaking through his shirt and stains her hands. She fumbles to undo his buttons, ripping off the last two in her haste. The size of the wound makes her gasp: a jagged tear ripping through flesh, exposing muscle and greenish-grey fat.

Her heart jumps with fear as she looks for something to staunch the bleeding. The cushion cover has a zip fastening; she takes it off, folds the material into a pad and presses it against his chest. Kreshnik's eyelids flicker, and a crackling noise rises in his throat but fades without turning into words.

"Oh God. No. Help him, someone." Odeta presses down harder with the cushion pad, but the damp stickiness is creeping through and a pool of blood is forming on the carpet.

The sound of the door buzzer rips through the room. Usually it signals a client. Odeta raises her head – maybe there's someone outside who could help. Stephan hurries across to the bay window and closes the heavy curtains while Odeta gets to her feet and edges towards the door. Too late – Tomas pounds along the hall and reaches the door first.

"Piss off," he shouts to whoever's out there. "We're closed."

He doesn't even bother to peer through the spyhole but leans his back against the door, leveraging his full weight against it like a barricade. For a short time the visitor seems to accept the order to piss off, but then buzzes again. Tomas stamps back into the room. "Gotta get rid of that." He points his forefinger at Kreshnik, who is prone on the carpet, making gurgling sounds.

"Yeah," agrees Stephan, scratching his chin and inflaming the acne scars.

"He needs a doctor," yells Odeta.

Tomas smirks. "Sure. And we're gonna get him one." He nods at Stephan. "Let's get this mess out of sight first." Stephan disappears out of the door while Tomas kneels down, grasps Kreshnik's bent leg and straightens it roughly. Kreshnik's lips curve in a grimace and he groans. Stephan returns with a bucket of water and a cloth, setting it down on the carpet and starting to scrub at the bloodstain.

"Not that, imbecile." Tomas kicks out at the bucket so soapy water slops onto the floor. "Here – grab his other leg and arm." Shunting Odeta aside, they bend either side of Kreshnik, each wrapping an arm under his back, then lift his legs and hoist him up, letting his head loll.

"Be careful, you're hurting him. Where are you taking him? To the hospital?"

"Shut up, bitch, and help us."

Odeta follows them along the hall where the door leading down to the basement is swinging open. "Oh no, my God, no. You can't—"

"You wanna look after him while we fetch the doctor? Then get the fuck down those stairs."

Kreshnik's eyes stretch open and gaze at her. If his face has any expression at all, it's bewilderment. Her heart contracts. His bearers shuffle down the steps and disappear from view while Odeta clasps the bloodied cushion pad between her hands. The front door, just seven paces away, pulls her with magnetic force; the key safe is open, rows of keys on hooks and a few loose on the lower shelf. With plunging heart, she turns her back to it. Kreshnik needs her; she can't abandon him now.

"About fucking time," says Tomas, when she appears. They've manhandled Kreshnik down the stairs and dumped him on the floor. "See to him till we get back."

She nods dumbly. She squats by Kreshnik's side on the

threadbare rug, feeling the rough floor beneath pressing into her knees. She doesn't notice Tomas and Stephan leaving the room, until the door slams and she hears the metallic scrape of the key turning.

"Kreshnik, wake up and speak to me," she pleads, with a sob. And then the miracle she's been praying for happens: his eyes open and he blinks. His eyes have a milky stare, but seem focused. He struggles to raise his head but it flops back.

"Let me help you." She lowers his head to the ground while he flaps one hand and concentrates on breathing. She takes two flat pillows from the bed and stuffs them under his neck. Feeling his body tremble, she drapes the blanket over him.

"Water?" she asks, and he nods. She fills a plastic tumbler at the grimy sink and carries it to him. Grunting, he levers himself up onto his elbow and takes two tiny sips, but his hand is shaking and water spills on the blanket. Turning his head, he looks slowly around the room, taking in the basin with its cracked mirror, the metal bedstead, the lumpy mattress and the single dangling pink lightbulb.

"This is how they've been keeping you?"

She nods, unable to hold back her tears. She thought she'd never hear his voice again. Kreshnik's face creases with pain, and he takes the blood-soaked pad from her and presses it against his wound.

"I didn't know, Odeta. I thought you would be modelling, or perhaps dancing." But he doesn't meet her eyes.

"You're lying. I know it now. You kidnapped me and sold me." It's a relief to say it out loud. She didn't need Cassie to spell it out. She knew the truth all along, but she needed to believe in him so she could hope. "Just like you sold your sister, Marije."

He takes his hand off the makeshift compress and his fingers encircle her wrist. His effort to speak sets off a hacking cough;

he sips from the tumbler and gulps in more air. "I did not sell you and I didn't sell my sister. They stole her. It's the truth, Odeta. I will tell you everything."

He tenses his body and furrows his brow as if to control the pain. "Some of what they said is true. My sister was engaged to Tomas, but she did not love him."

"How could she?"

"His parents wanted it. His family is powerful in Tirana. My parents are educated, but they're not wealthy, not an important family at all. I think they were too afraid of Tomas's family to refuse." His cough grates, rusty and metallic.

Odeta bends to check his wound. As she lifts the pad, it sticks. Not gushing, but weeping and forming brown crusty patches. The torn flesh is raw and angry.

"When Marije finished her nursing training in Tirana, I suggested she come with me to London. Just a holiday." He clears his throat. "Through an Albanian man we found a flat in Earl's Court. Others living there were all men, Croatians and Slovakians. Marije was the only woman."

His supporting elbow slips, and he slumps back down on the pillow. Under the dome of his bald head his face puckers like a baby. She's so close to him she can smell his vinegary breath. He meets her eyes, struggles to lift his head, and kisses her. The taste is metallic, but his lips brushing hers bring back memories of happier times. As she pulls away, she notices a stain of blood at one corner of his mouth.

He coughs. "Sorry."

"Tell me what happened."

"Marije grew close to one of the Croatian men. They started a relationship."

"Isn't that wrong if she had a fiancé?"

He nods. "She should have told Tomas first. But he found out anyway."

"How?"

Cough, cough, wheeze. Kreshnik spits into the plastic beaker, and a brown viscous stain swirls in the liquid. "The Albanian man who helped us find the flat was a cousin of Stephan. One day, when I was out, they came to the flat. Told Marije they were taking her to visit Tomas. She went willingly. Later, I learned she told him she was breaking off their engagement."

Odeta pictures Marije, young and innocent, away from home for the first time, enjoying the easy-going freedom of London. She must think she has control over her life. Arriving at this house, attempting to break off her engagement, she could never have imagined the maelstrom of violence that would break over her head. One thing Odeta has learned: Tomas hates women. To him they are possessions: objects to torture and destroy.

Kreshnik's head slumps forward and he groans. "She never returned, Odeta. No one would give me news of her. It took months for me to trace her." He reaches for her hand, but she snatches it away. "By the time I found Marije – here, in this house – I didn't recognise her. She looked worse than you..."

Odeta flinches.

"They'd cut off her beautiful long hair and dyed it purple. Her face was covered in sores; she'd been starved, drugged, abused." He covers his face with his hands and howls. "But Tomas won't let her leave with me. Hearing her cry, scream and beg is his only happiness. That – and all the money she's making for them."

"We make a deal. I promise him anything. I don't have money but I will try to get it." *Cough, whoop, croak.* "And then Tomas says to me: this bitch, Marije, is all washed up. Bring me another one: a new Marije who can make us as much money as she did. Then I will let your sister go."

Odeta is falling, spinning out of control, fighting waves of nausea. Her head feels as if it might explode. Everything – from his first visit to her father's shop, the seduction and courtship ritual, the promise of modelling work – was a plan to trap her.

She gets to her feet, hands on hips and glares down at him. "You bastard. You picked me as a human sacrifice. You knew I'd be destroyed just like your sister."

"No." He's shaking his head, his eyes are red and he's coughing, coughing, coughing. "I meant only to set my sister free. Then I was coming back for you."

"Liar. Swine. I hate you." But it's as hard to hate him as to feel anything at all. With his shaved head, his injuries and his cold words, he's withered away in front of her eyes. "So you got Marije back in exchange for me, at least."

He shakes his head, solemnly. "No, Odeta. They don't keep their word. Remember I told you, at the airport, I had business to see to before I could come back for you?"

She nods. He did say that, yes. Those exact words were imprinted on her mind, and she has cradled them for months.

"Tomas gave me documents and an address where he said I would find Marije. I went there. She wasn't there, but other thugs were. They beat me up." With his forefinger, he taps the angry scar on his head. "I spent two months in hospital, first here and then in Tirana. But I still don't know where my sister is."

Pieces of memory fall into a pattern like leaves dropping on a forest floor. What was it Elira told her? That they used not to be locked up in the basement but could use all the rooms in the house, until something happened. Something Marije did.

"I think she escaped," she says slowly. It can only be that.

Kreshnik knits his fingers together and lifts his hands. "Praise God that's true." He sucks in another deep breath, his head twitches and his face contracts in pain. Closing his eyes, he moans while she kneels beside him and listens to the air bubbling inside his chest cavity. She turns his head to one side; his mouth hangs open, blood slithers out and dribbles on his chin: *drip, drip, drip.*

A shiver grips her. She's not safe with her feelings towards this man. She slides his right eyelid up; his eye is opaque and milky. Blood trickles faster from his mouth. She slips her hand beneath his jaw, fumbling for a pulse. She finds it, but it's fluttering and unsteady.

Where is Tomas with the doctor? He must realise Kreshnik is mortally wounded. A new terror slices through her tense body: what would a man like Tomas, a bully and a coward, do in such circumstances? He would run away. And if he and Stephan have fled, she'll be locked in here for ever. She'll never see her family, never step inside the park to see the trees or smell the blossom. Kreshnik will die first, and then she'll starve and wither alongside his corpse in this basement prison.

CHAPTER THIRTY-FOUR

"Piss off, we're closed."

Hurled from behind a locked door, the words make Kate jump back. But what if, as she suspects, Ben is in there? She stabs her finger on the buzzer again, and pounds on the door with her other fist. Nothing.

Who are the crazy inhabitants of number thirty-eight – Geoffrey with his odd behaviour, and the man who yelled at her to piss off? Could it be some kind of community hostel? The thought that Ben could be inside triggers a fit of trembling. At moments like these she wishes she could smoke a cigarette or something stronger.

She retreats down the front steps and notices a light on in the front room, visible through the gap where the heavy curtains don't meet. A dark silhouette passes the gap, temporarily blocking out the light. She can't make out if the shape is Geoffrey, and it's impossible to imagine him shouting at anyone to piss off. She waits, shivering in the cold damp air, pacing the pavement and glancing at her watch: seven-thirty. Soon Nick will arrive next door for the conversation she's been dreading, but how can she go home without Ben?

The bleary sky grows darker. The light in number thirty-eight goes off; the front door opens and two men emerge: one is the stocky swarthy one who drives the van, the other a skinny man she's never seen before. Startled, she presses her body into a space between two overhanging bushes, watching the men climb into the transit and start up the engine. Its headlights paint a yellow arc across the front of the house as it reverses out onto Joplin Street. The van passes the end of the street, smoke belching from its exhaust. When the engine noise fades, she shakes the twigs off her coat and steps out of her hiding place.

The man who yelled at her must have been one of the two who just drove off, and Geoffrey definitely wasn't with them. Nervously she approaches the dark doorway. A pink glow spills out onto the tarmac from a tiny gap in a blocked-up basement window and lights her way. Once again she mounts the front steps, presses the intercom and waits. Nothing. She punches it harder. This time she senses, rather than hears, a faint tapping, but it could be her own heartbeat.

"Geoffrey," she shouts into the unresponsive intercom, "It's Kate. Ben's mum. Answer the door, please."

This time there is a definite sound: a sort of shuffling. She calls out Geoffrey's name again, pounding on the door and stamping her foot in frustration. Traipsing back down the steps she crosses the front of the house to the side passage, her flesh slithering as she imagines Geoffrey or someone else watching her from indoors. The external wall of the house has bulged out into the passage and she has to squeeze along it, her coat gathering green moss and brick dust as it brushes against the wall. The wooden gate at the far end of the passage has coils of wire on top, but a pool of rainwater has collected and the wooden slats have sucked it up, turning spongy and weak. As she prods it with her foot, the rotten slats give way and the gate creaks open.

"Phew." That was almost too easy. She's standing in a back yard. Any lawn that might once have lain here has been buried beneath concrete and junk: a rusty wheelbarrow, bulging rubbish bags split open and ransacked by urban foxes, a soggy mattress. The high wall that abuts the road, and the fence that separates number thirty-eight from her own house, are both topped with coils of wire.

The back door has been reinforced with a metal grille, but at the far end of the wall is a window with no bars. "Hello," Kate calls. "Geoffrey? Are you there?"

Silence. The sill is a little above her chest height, and by standing on tiptoe she can see inside to a kitchen. Close to the fence are two gassy-smelling wheelie bins. She drags both of them across the uneven patio and turns one over on its side. She leaves the other upright, rammed against the wall, and using the first as a step clambers up onto the closed lid of the second bin. As she explores the edge of the frame with her fingertips, the window swings inwards. It wasn't latched.

Grasping hold of the window frame, she levers her knee onto the sill and wriggles through the window onto an enamel draining board. This must count as breaking and entering. Standing in the centre of the kitchen, she looks around to get her bearings.

The kitchen is dark, but moonlight illuminates a stove piled with pans, and the air is filled with the sweet greasiness of cheap cooking oil. If this is Geoffrey's home no wonder it's a shambles. But what about the van driver, and that young girl who was with him? And wasn't there another man – how do they fit into the picture? Her pulse is racing and her stomach feels queasy.

There's that scuttling sound again, coming from somewhere beyond the kitchen. She walks slowly along the hall rehearsing what she'll say. "*Hello; I'm your neighbour and I've just broken into your house to look for my son*" somehow doesn't seem to cut it.

At the end of the hallway she pushes open a door and enters. A shadow tries to streak past, bending low to duck under her arm.

"Geoffrey!"

He cringes, holding his forearms crossed in front of his face as if warding off a blow. His breathing rasps and he twists his head repetitively from side to side. Reaching out, she peels one of his arms away from his face. "Geoffrey, it's me, Kate," she says, forcing him to meet her gaze. "I'm not going to hurt you."

Beyond him the room is cheerless and functional, smelling of cigarette smoke, with worn green sofas, a gas fire and a monster television screen.

"Go away," Geoffrey hisses, his head still bobbing up and down. There's something feral about him.

She puts her hand on his arm and steers him to the sofa. "Sit down."

Geoffrey sits, but he's still twitching.

"You know who I am, don't you?"

He nods.

"Ben's disappeared, Geoffrey," she says. "Has he come here to visit you?"

Geoffrey's pink tongue protrudes from a corner of his mouth, and he shakes his head. "Ben not come here. Only bad people here."

He's speaking in riddles. She doesn't have the patience to deal with his existential crisis. "Listen," she says, injecting a note of steel into her voice. "You're not in trouble. I just need to find him. Tell me the truth – is he here?"

Geoffrey shakes his head so fast his hair sticks out and his features blur. "No," he insists. "Go away."

"Look, Geoffrey. Ben's been pestering you for weeks to invite him to see your house. And I know you told him straight that wasn't possible. But perhaps he called round anyway and someone else let him in? One of your housemates? Perhaps he's hiding?" Her patience is thinner than tracing paper. She gets to her feet and walks to the door. "Remember that time you and Ben were playing in the park, and when I called it was time to go home, he crept away to hide because he was having so much fun?"

"Yes," Geoffrey nods. "Ben is my best friend."

"Well if you won't help me, I'm going to have to search the house."

She heads towards the stairs. Geoffrey follows, pigeon-toed and trembling. The centre of the stairs is carpeted, after a fashion – the carpet is held in place with stair rods, some of which are loose or missing. She misses a step and grabs the banister for support. If there's anyone else in the house they will have heard her clumping around, so why bother staying silent?

"Ben," she calls. "Where are you?"

There's a turn in the stairs before the first-floor landing with three rooms leading off. Ahead of her is the kind of stripped-pine door, fashionable in the seventies, with a round brass handle. Someone once loved this house, and spent hours painting layers of Nitromors on the door, waiting for the paint beneath to bubble and crack so they could scrape it off. Inside the room are bare scuffed floorboards, a shaggy grey rug that might once have been a fluffy white bath mat, a metal bedstead and a clump of bedlinen. Men's t-shirts and jeans are strewn in piles; empty beer and whisky bottles line the walls. She opens a wardrobe and peers under the bed. Everywhere smells of mildew.

Geoffrey stands on the landing watching her. She opens the door to the next room and it's eerily similar, right down to the pile of crumpled jeans. In one corner is a stash of magazines; she picks one up and a cloud of dust flies up, making her sneeze. It's a hardcore porn magazine, with images of extreme sexual violence. She drops it as if she's been stung.

Everything about this house spooks her. "Ben," she calls, dashing into the bathroom opposite where the walls are speckled with tiny black spots – more mildew. She flings opens the airing cupboard door. "Come out if you're hiding. You're not in trouble, I promise."

"What's up there?" she asks Geoffrey, pointing towards a narrow flight of uncarpeted stairs leading up into the eaves. He opens and shuts his mouth wordlessly, cringing; he reminds her of Uriah Heep, only more humble. She sprints up the narrow winding stairs with Geoffrey trundling behind. It leads to a single room with a low ceiling and a skylight window. She bends her head to duck beneath the beams.

This room is the antithesis of the Spartan spaces below. It's like a junk shop, crammed with furniture: two chairs upended on a chest of drawers, bookcases spilling their contents on the floor, old paintings propped up against the wall. In one corner is a portable TV, and in the centre of the room a single bed covered with a duvet, an eiderdown and a patchwork quilt, but beneath these layers she can see the stained black and white ticking of a mattress. There's no sheet. On a side table is a week's supply of used mugs, some with teabags inside, and on the floor, just visible under the bed, plates of half-eaten meals with the knives and forks crossed neatly on top. The room smells of old socks and tomato ketchup.

"This is your room, Geoffrey?"

Geoffrey hovers in the doorway. His mouth turns down at the corners as he mumbles a reply that could be yes, could be no.

Kate sighs. It's hopeless. Clearly Ben isn't here. She casts a final glance around the room, noticing that the window is locked but not barred. The room could do with an airing. "Where's the window key, Geoffrey?" she asks, and is almost surprised when he produces it from a drawer beside his bed.

She unlocks it and peers down to the yard below where the two wheelie bins mark the incriminating evidence of the spot where she clambered in. Two rusty cast-iron drainpipes zigzag from the gutter down past Geoffrey's window to the drain below. She stares across the fence into her own back garden; so close and yet so far away from this dismal place.

She turns back to Geoffrey. "Leave the window open for a while, Geoffrey. Get some fresh air inside your room."

She was so certain she'd find Ben here, but she was wrong. She rakes her fingers through her tangled hair, kneading her temples to dull the headache. There's one last place left to try. "Look, Geoffrey, I know you and Ben love to play hide and seek in the park. Is he hiding in the basement? I won't be angry, but you must tell me."

"No! No, no, noooo." Geoffrey's wail echoes around the room, infecting her with his sorrow. Kate sets off down the stairs, two at a time.

The door to the basement has a lift-up latch and a simple bolt on the outside. As she goes to open it, Geoffrey rematerializes beside her, plucking at her sleeve and wriggles his body into the space between her and the door, breathing heavily. She's about to shove him aside when they hear the grinding wheels of the transit reversing into its parking space. Kate's heart lurches. The Piss-Off man is back, and he won't be pleased to see her.

Geoffrey starts to tremble. "Go," he shouts. "In there." He points towards the gloomy sitting room and pulls her along the corridor, motioning with the flat of his palm to hide behind the sofa. Some instinct drives her to do as he suggests. She squeezes into the cramped space of the bay window and ducks down behind the sofa. Geoffrey goes back out into the hall just as the front door opens.

From her hiding place, she hears someone yelling at him in a foreign language, then breaking into a string of curses in English. There's a scuffle, and the voice tells Geoffrey to get the fuck back upstairs, followed by a slap, a whimper and Geoffrey's scuttling footsteps. No wonder he's terrified; someone in this house is abusing him. A switch snaps on, the room floods with light, and someone enters.

Kate holds her breath and freezes. The man switches the television on, and she recognises the commentator's voice: football. Damn. Is he about to watch a whole game? How long will she have to crouch here, and what possible excuse can she make when he spots her?

Again, the front door slams and there's a new voice in the hall: the Piss-Off voice this time, shouting at the man watching football. Craning her neck, she can just see his bulky outline framed in the doorway; he's carrying some sort of bag made of white spun plastic and shaking it at the other man. The bag is vast, like those sacks used for delivering sand and cement to building sites. She catches a side view of the man's face. It's the leering van driver, and his expression is grim.

The other man gets to his feet, grumbling, and leaves the football turned on. At least it should cover any sound she makes. They leave the sitting room door open and she hears their footsteps fading along the hall. Another door opens, signalled by the draught wafting into the room, and footsteps clatter down into the basement.

Fidgeting in her cramped hiding place, Kate moves her legs and catches sight of a brown stain on her shoe. Brick dust from the side passage? She rubs it, raises her hand to her nose and sniffs: something faintly biological. Earlier on when she stood in this room with Geoffrey it was in darkness. Now the light is on, she peers around the sofa at a large rust-brown stain on the carpet, the same shade as the mark on her shoe. With a jolt of horror, she realises what she's trodden in.

CHAPTER THIRTY-FIVE

Odeta clings to Kreshnik's motionless body and weeps. She places her hand under his nostrils, but can no longer detect his breathing. Remembering what she was taught long ago, by her gymnastics coach, she pumps the centre of his chest: *One-two-three-four, pause, repeat.* She searches for a pulse on his wrist and prods beneath his jaw. Nothing – yet when she touches his cheek it's warm.

She hardly notices the door opening until Tomas sidles in with Stephan close behind.

"Help him," she begs, not caring if they see her tears. "Where is the doctor?"

Tomas grunts and slings a huge white sack onto the floor. Stooping down he lifts Kreshnik's wrist and feels for a pulse. "He's gone," he pronounces, letting the arm drop.

"No!" whispers Odeta. Her heart somersaults. She sniffs and wipes her nose with the back of her hand, leaving a brown streak across her cheek; Kreshnik's blood is caked under her fingernails and dried in clumps on the ends of her hair. His eyes stare up at her, glassy as a fish on a slab, and his mouth sags open from his last gasp to draw breath.

Tears well in her eyes as she stares at the man she once loved. The creases of pain between his eyebrows have relaxed, and his face is smoother. Kreshnik has left pain behind, but her own feelings are in turmoil. A single tear falls onto his face as she leans close, whispers "Goodbye" and closes his eyelids with her index finger and thumb; there's nothing more she can do for him. Trembling, she holds onto the bed and drags herself up. Her legs could fold at any moment.

Stephan unwraps the massive sack, which has four sides, handles and a rigid base. She watches as he places one side down on the floor, squats down, lifts Kreshnik's head and slides the sack underneath him. One side of the bag has words stamped on it: *SAND, CEMENT*, and one she's never seen before: *AGGREGATES*.

"What are you doing?" Odeta's jaw drops. She stretches out her hands and tries to push Stephan away. "That bag is for building materials. Not for people. You must show respect!"

Stephan steps between her and Kreshnik's prone body and blocks her. She clenches her fists and thumps him in the centre of his chest, but he swats her hand away like a troublesome fly.

"Enough," says Tomas. "Work to do." Furrowing his brow, he looks from the body to the sack. Kreshnik's long body won't fit, however they fold it.

Tomas takes out his knife and runs the flat of the blade across his palm, transporting Odeta back to her father's shop. She remembers how he would sharpen his knife before dismembering an animal carcass. Nausea collects in her mouth. She pictures Tomas carving Kreshnik's body into joints.

She remembers, too, overhearing her parents whispering that blood feuds still take place in northern Albania, in the shadow of the Accursed Mountains. Once her grandfather told her how, under Kanun law, any threat to a family's honour must always be avenged. Vengeance could mean wiping out every male in the family that caused the harm. Seeing her frightened face, her grandfather quickly back-tracked. "We do not believe in such things, Odeta. Our family is modern, we look to the future." Adding, "Your grandmother was once a Catholic," as if this solved everything.

Anyway, Kreshnik and Tomas are not from the north. They are from Tirana. But who knows what might happen when someone interferes with another family's interests – or insults their pride?

Tomas runs his knife along one seam of the sack, slitting it to widen the opening. Odeta exhales as he and Stephan work in tandem to prop the body upright. Stephan anchors it against his legs while keeping one hand on the shoulder to prevent it toppling sideways, while Tomas eases the sack over Kreshnik's head and upper torso.

That's it, then, thinks Odeta, as she watches the sack swallow Kreshnik's head. Her stomach is churning but empty. She runs to the sink and vomits up clear gastric fluids. Listlessly she runs water over her hands, watching it turn from brown to red to pink. She'll never be free of this filth; she'll never be clean again.

Tomas tips the bag backwards with Kreshnik's torso and one leg inside it, and tries to bend his other knee. Stephan grunts, twists and pushes. She waits, expecting to hear a bone snap, but the body can't be stiff yet. It's too soon.

Tomas watches, stroking his chin. "Leave it," he commands. Stephan drops the leg to the floor, Tomas yanks the sheet off Odeta's bed and aims a karate-chop at the back of the protruding knee, and it bends like a branch cracking in the wind. He ties one end of the sheet to the bag handle, swaddles the leg then pulls the remaining sheet through the second handle, tucking the ends inside the bag. The trussed-up sack brings fresh tears to Odeta's eyes. Kreshnik deserved to be punished – he should have been arrested and charged – but not to lose his life. Not like that.

"Filthy murderer, swine," she yells at Tomas. "Why did you do this to him?"

Tomas stares at her, his black eyes spitting venom. "You want to know?" He aims a kick at the sack. "He was scum."

"Liar. Scum, it's you."

Tomas takes two steps towards her and lifts her chin with his hand. Flecks of spittle land on her cheek as he yells, "I'll tell you." He shoves her away. "You think he cared about you? He didn't even care about his sister."

Odeta rubs her chin. Why didn't he just throttle her? He's abused her physically in every possible way, but she hasn't let him mess with her mind; she's kept the heroin at bay, and she no longer fears death. Tomas is muttering in Albanian spattered with English and shuffling his feet. "You tell her," he says to Stephan.

"Me?" Stephan acts surprised at being appointed spokesman. Scratching his greasy forehead, he begins: "Kreshnik's family in Tirana is all up themselves but have no power. Pah!" He spits on the floor. "Our family could shred his mother's skin with a grater, or follow his father into an alley and shoot him in back of head. Or order our people to snatch his wife."

"His wife?" All the air leaves Odeta's body. She covers her face with her hands, but rose-tinted light seeps past her fingers. Everything she sees is red.

"Of course, he has a wife." Tomas wrings out every drop of Odeta's anguish, savaging her with words in places where the flat of his hand, the buckle of his belt and even his disgusting penis can't penetrate.

"Taking a leak," he announces, and lumbers along the narrow corridor to the stinky toilet which clients sometimes use.

Through the thin walls she can hear clanking and splashing. When she lifts her head from her hands, Stephan is watching her.

"What happened to Marije? She escaped, didn't she? Elira said so."

Stephan glares at her, a caricature of flaring nostrils and terrible teeth. He lights a cigarette and fills the air with smoke. "Don't believe what you hear," he says, tapping ash onto the floor. "In England, they have a saying that gossip is like dirty linen. We don't wash ours in public."

Tomas returns, zipping himself up as he enters. "And when we have rubbish, we get rid of it."

He bends down, takes one handle of the sack and tugs, but it scarcely moves. "Put that down," he orders, knocking the lighted cigarette out of Stephan's hand to smoulder on the thin carpet. He watches it briefly then stamps on it, grinding it beneath his boot. Between them, they heave and drag the sack towards the basement stairs and start bumping it up one step at a time. Halfway up they stop, and Tomas shouts, "Help us, bitch." Kreshnik's protruding foot has got stuck through one of the uprights. As Odeta pushes it back through the slats, his shoe drops off. She picks it up and cradles it. Tomas pulls, Stephan pushes, and they puff to the top of the stairs, with Odeta trailing behind.

They swing and drag the sack through the cellar door into the main hallway, Stephan's breath whistling as he drops his end and it thuds to the floor. Abandoning it, he strolls into the kitchen and runs water into a glass. "Bloody window's open in here," he calls.

"Well, fucking shut it and make sure it's locked," replies Tomas. Odeta hears the sound of the television through the open door of the front room, and edges towards it. A slight movement catches her eye – did she imagine it, or is there a shadow behind the sofa? Just near to the place where Kreshnik fell. She shivers.

"Hurry," calls Tomas. "Gimme that key."

Stephan hands him the window key and drains the last of his water. Tomas pockets the key and picks up one end of the sack, waiting while Stephan puts his empty glass down on the floor. They drag the bag towards the front door, flattening the carpet pile like sled tracks on snow. Odeta tries to memorise the pattern of unlocking as Tomas opens the key safe, removes two keys from the top row and undoes the top and bottom locks of the front door. He slips them into his pocket and opens the final lock using a key from a bunch he always carries with him. Outside, the van waits, with its engine still running, backed right up to the steps. Its rear doors are flung wide as an eagle's wings, shielding them from view as they swing the body bag into the van.

Odeta has traded weeping for frozen stillness. Still cradling Kreshnik's shoe, she watches Tomas slam the rear doors with a metallic clunk. Tomas hasn't noticed the shoe, but Stephan has. He tries to wrest it from her, but she holds on. Finally, his strength proves superior. He tugs it from her hands, starts walking towards the van, then appears to change his mind. He turns, and pushing Odeta in front of him walks back inside the house to the top of the basement stairs.

"Please," she whispers. Is he planning to push her down head-first? "Don't."

He grunts, raises the hand carrying Kreshnik's shoe, and tosses it down the basement steps. Tomas yells his name, telling him to hurry. He rushes off, slamming the front door.

She holds her breath, listening to the familiar pattern of locking-up from outside. She's alone in the house and not locked inside her basement room.

As the van drives away, she grasps the door handle and

rattles it. Of course, it doesn't budge. She'd watched Tomas locking the key safe and knows some of the front door keys are on the bunch he carries with him everywhere, but perhaps there are duplicates? She opens the drawer in the hall table and scrabbles through the contents: unopened brown envelopes, a knife, batteries, and more keys in all shapes and sizes. She gathers up all the keys and ranks them by size on the table top. Most are small and flimsy, like suitcase keys, but she picks out a selection of larger ones and tests them in the door locks, working a system, so as not to use the same key twice. After five combinations, she's used up all the large keys. Panic and nausea coalesce in her stomach, and she flings her body up against the unyielding door.

A noise in the hallway behind her makes her spin round. Just six paces away stands a woman with short brown hair and skin that shimmers with health. They stare at each other.

Odeta speaks. First in Albanian, then in English: "Who are you?"

CHAPTER THIRTY-SIX

Kate takes a step towards the girl with porcelain skin, the haunted eyes and the foreign accent, and recognises the young woman she once glimpsed in the transit van, clasping her hands up against the glass.

"I'm Kate. From next door." She pauses as if expecting the girl to acknowledge her, but no sign of recognition comes. "I'm ... looking for my son."

"Uh?" Still the girl gapes at her. Perhaps she doesn't understand.

"Blond hair – ten years old."

The girl presses her back against the front door, tossing her head like a wild pony. Her eyes, darting with suspicion, remind Kate of poor Geoffrey, who tried to flee approaching footsteps but was slapped. Fear contaminates this house, spreading like a virus, and she's caught it too.

The hall light glares harshly from a single bulb. Kate studies the girl's face, noticing a sore on her lip, and her dark hair, unravelling from a backcombed style. Her eyes fall on the rust and white t-shirt, and she realises it's not tie-dyed, as she'd first thought. The girl's arms, like the sitting-room carpet, are streaked with dried blood. What's been going on in this place?

She steps forward and takes hold of the girl's wrist. "What have they done to you?"

Tears well up in the girl's eyes and slide down her face; she wipes them away. In heavily-accented English, she whispers, "Not to me. They killed Kreshnik."

What did she say? Kate feels breathless, dizzy. Did she say someone's been killed in this house? And Ben is still missing. She tightens her grip on the young woman's wrist. "Who's been killed? Where's my son?"

The girl recoils and moves away from her, petrified, her eyes watchful, her face hardening into a mask.

"Let go!" she shouts, striking out at Kate with her fists.

"I'm sorry. Really. I didn't mean... But my son..." How could she forget Ben, even for a moment? She turns away and darts towards the slatted basement door, unbolting it and tugging it open. A layer of polystyrene is stuck to the inside of the door: draught-proofing – or soundproofing? "What's down here?"

The girl doesn't answer.

"Ben," she shouts, gripping the edge of the door and digging her fingernails into the polystyrene.

The door bounces against the wall, tapping out a staccato beat, while Kate pauses and listens to silence. She places one foot on the top step.

"Stop." This time it's the young woman's turn to grab hold of her. Her face is ashen, and her wild eyes shift around like a frightened animal's. "Don't go down there. We must find a way to leave now." Her words are thickened by her accent, but the terror in her voice is clear.

"Well, of course, we'll leave. As soon as I'm certain my son's not here." She pauses. What did the girl mean by *find a way to leave*? She feels a stab of fear. Gripping the flimsy handrail, she sets off down the stairs. Two steps from the bottom, her foot spins on something loose, her ankle twists and she falls.

"Ouch." She rubs her sprained ankle, noticing the thing that tripped her was a shoe. Ahead of her is a room with the door ajar and a pinkish glow from inside. She hobbles towards it. On the threshold she stops, her lower jaw dropping open. A blood bath has taken place in this room. Bedsheets stained crimson, a brown puddle, spattered mirror and sink, the grisly scene illuminated by a single rose-tinted light bulb. The assault on her senses is as disorientating as if she's travelled back in time to a Dickensian hovel.

She panics. This room holds many secrets but few hiding places: no cupboards and no corners. It's obvious Ben isn't here, yet she forces herself to peer underneath the bed at sandals from different pairs and a half-full chamber pot reeking of asparagus. One more minute in this room and she'll throw up.

"Hello?" calls Kate, into the echoing silence of the passage. She tries the door opposite. It's locked, but she hammers on it, calling Ben's name and listening. The next door swings open to reveal a primitive toilet, stinking of piss. "Ben," she shouts, limping back along the corridor to bash her knuckles against the locked door. Whatever's happened in this house, whatever Geoffrey's role in it, it's not about Ben. It's time to go home and call the police. As she hobbles back up the stairs, leaning on the rail for support, noises erupt in the hall. The front door slams, and she hears a crack of laughter and heavy footsteps.

CHAPTER THIRTY-SEVEN

Tomas strides along the hall towards Odeta, his face crumpling into a scowl. "What you doin' up here, bitch?"

His fists are clenched by his sides and he's muttering under his breath. Odeta pulls the basement door shut and stands with her back against it. Where has that crazy woman gone? Why didn't she listen? What will they say when they see her? Tomas raises a fist and shakes it close to her face, but Stephan steps in and catches his arm, easing it back down. "Lay off, man. We're all stressed out."

"Get me a beer, then." Stephan heads for the kitchen, and Tomas plants his feet so close to Odeta that she can smell his fishy breath. Specks of dried blood mark his t-shirt, but he's not coated in it – not like her. "Where's that fucking beer?"

"Here, man." Stephan twists off the cap and spins it Frisbee-style along the hall. He presses the green bottle into Tomas's hand.

Where have they taken Kreshnik's body? A thousand pinpricks of light pirouette in Odeta's field of vision, but she stays silent.

From behind the basement door, a shuffling sound. Odeta

freezes, but Tomas barks, "What the...?" Shoving Odeta aside, he whips the door open with one hand, lifting his beer bottle above his head with the other.

Odeta follows his gaze. Framed in the doorway is the mad woman who appeared from nowhere and said she was looking for her son. What's she really doing here? No one in their right mind would stay in this house for ten seconds.

The woman blinks. She notices Tomas's beer bottle poised to strike, and her hands fly up to guard her face. Tomas grasps her arm and drags her up the last three steps. She seems to be limping. His face is a mask of fury, but he doesn't look at the woman. He turns to Odeta and gabbles in Albanian, "Who the hell is she?"

Odeta shrugs. "How should I know? Says she's looking for her son."

Still gripping her arm, Tomas puts his face up close to the woman's. "What the fuck are you doing here?"

She must have smelt his sour breath because she flinches. "Get your hands off me and I'll tell you." Her voice has the stern authority of a schoolteacher. Tomas removes his hand but still looms over the woman, who has a loose hank of hair over one eye. She smooths it back with her hand. "I'm Kate Davison, from next door. I'm looking for my son, Ben. He's missing."

"What the ..." Tomas booms. His forehead creases as he shouts, "He's not here."

The woman, who said her name was Kate, shuffles from foot to foot as if her left leg can't take any weight. "There's a man, Geoffrey, who lives here. Ben, my son, made friends with him in the park."

Odeta tries to follow the conversation but the woman is speaking too fast. Something about her son being friends with weird Geoffrey?

"Now you're having a laugh," says Stephan, unclamping his

mouth from his bottle so beer fizzes up and slops white froth down his front. "Geoffrey don't have friends. Don't know no one."

Tomas silences him with a glance.

Kate fixes her eyes on Tomas as if she's trying to bend him to her will. Odeta could tell her that's hopeless. He could erupt at any moment. Besides, Kate isn't as brave as she pretends. Odeta can hear the sound of her breathing.

"I'll be on my way, then," says Kate, wriggling out from the place where Tomas had her pinioned against the wall. He lets her go and watches her limp towards the front door, a callous smile on his lips. She turns the door handle; it doesn't budge. She examines the lock, twiddles the latch up and down. Still nothing. She twists her neck and looks back at them, fear flickering in her eyes. "If you'd kindly open it."

Tomas reaches the door in five loping paces. "Not so fast." As he clamps his hand on Kate's shoulder and steers her away, she winces. Her limp seems to have worsened. Odeta's used to accidents occurring around these men: slaps, kicks, casual punches. Has he laid a hand on Kate?

"What ya gonna do with her?" asks Stephan, dragging on a roll-up. There's not a mark on his denim shirt; the afternoon's exertions have left no blood on his hands.

Tomas leaks sweat from every pore, his cheeks are puce and his hair is slick on his forehead.

"I'll bloody show you, nosy cow." Tomas twists Kate's arm behind her back and kicks open the basement door. "Get back down those stairs."

"Take your hands off me." But her posh schoolteacher voice isn't working anymore. With her free arm, she hits out at Tomas but her balled fist bounces off his barrel chest. Stiffening her middle three fingers, she jabs at the indent in the fleshy centre of Tomas's throat.

"Ouch," he yells, bringing his chin down and trapping her fingers between his chin and neck. "Fucking bitch." He swings at her and slaps her face.

"Oh." Kate staggers. If Tomas wasn't holding her up she'd crumple.

"Stop it," Odeta finds her voice. "She did nothing to you. She's only looking for son."

"You too." Tomas's fist slams into her face. Pain shoots through her jaw and she feels a second tooth loosen. Stephan fixes her with his gappy grin. Soon her own teeth will look like his, but what does it matter? She'll never smile again.

"Okay I go," she croaks. She touches Kate's sleeve and links an arm through hers. "Come," she says. "Is best."

"Hey!" Stephan jabs his elbow into Tomas's ribs. "Perhaps she could work?"

"Too old." Tomas's laugh bounces along the hall and seems to echo back. But the echo is a scream. Kate has found her voice, but no words; her scream could slice through metal or penetrate walls. Anyone passing by on the street outside would be sure to hear it.

Odeta understands. She's lived that feeling. Kate is screaming for her life.

CHAPTER THIRTY-EIGHT

Kate opens her eyes onto dense grey fog. Her body aches all over. She's lying on a hard mattress, her hair is stuck to her face and she can smell vomit. She puts a hand up to touch her head and recoils: the vomit is in her hair. A spasm passes through her body.

"You okay?" A slim figure is leaning over her. It's the young woman with the guttural accent.

Kate nods, but the pain throbs and she has to hold her head still. "Who are you?"

The girl shrugs. "Sometimes they call me 'bitch', sometimes, Marije. But my name is Odeta."

"Swan Lake?" Kate remembers a childhood trip to the ballet in Cardiff.

"What?"

"Never mind. Can you put the light on?"

Odeta shakes her head. "Switch is outside. They decide when I have light and when not."

Unbelievable. Kate gets it now. This place is a prison and the girl is a prisoner. What goes on in this house? Drug dealing?

Outside the narrow sliver of window, cloud cover is

thinning and grey light seeps in. Her arm itches like crazy. She rubs it. "Did they," she asks, grimacing, "inject me with something?"

Odeta nods.

Oh God. Dirty needles, hepatitis, HIV. Panic. She struggles upright, wrestling with dizziness and a pounding head. "What was it? Heroin?" She pinches Odeta's hand.

Odeta shakes her head. "Something for sleeping, maybe?"

"How long have I been asleep?"

"Not long. Maybe seven hours."

"Seven hours!" A memory knocks at the back of Kate's mind, something to do with why she's here. Ben! She swings her feet to the floor. Pain shifts from her head and jolts through her injured ankle.

"My son." Her eyes are hot and stinging. She clears her throat and sniffs.

Odeta nods. "Yes. Ben. You said."

Kate stumbles towards the door. Memories clamour for her attention. This must be the room she saw yesterday, when she was searching for Ben in the basement. Wasn't there blood on the floor and in the sink, or was that part of a nightmare? She rattles the door handle. It's locked. She groans. "How do I get out?"

Odeta's laugh is grim.

"We're prisoners here. Is that it?"

Still Odeta doesn't reply. Kate walks the couple of paces towards her and touches her arm.

Odeta flinches as if stirring from a trance. "I see his body here. Everywhere."

"Whose body? Ben's?" Kate's fingers tug and twist a strand of her own hair. Her stomach lurches like a plummeting elevator.

"Kreshnik's."

Kate's tongue feels raw as sandpaper. She swallows.

"Tell me everything." She perches on the edge of the filthy mattress. "What are you doing here? Who is Kreshnik? Who are those men?"

"I will tell, but you will not believe me." Odeta lifts her thin arms and hugs them across her chest.

As the sky outside brightens, Kate listens. The line of cigarette burns dotting Odeta's inner arm add force to her words. She reaches the part of her story about arriving in England with Kreshnik and meeting Tomas at the airport, and her eyes cloud over. Even now she can't seem to stop making excuses for him. "Kreshnik had first to go and rescue his sister, you see. They tricked and beat him. He was in the hospital so could not come back for me."

Kate listens to Odeta's account of rape, violence and exploitation at the hands of Tomas and strangers, and it chokes her. Odeta is mourning the death of a man who cloaked his inhumanity in the guise of a lover.

Kate reaches out to stroke Odeta's arm. The girl's wrist is as thin as a child's.

"You were trafficked," says Kate.

Why hadn't she realised? She held all the pieces of the jigsaw – the blue transit on the move at all hours, the bars on the front windows, visitors to the house day and night – and still she's been blind. This is her street, where she had a notion of raising her son to rely on neighbours and their community. Behind an ordinary front door so much rot and rubbish is piled up she can't slam it shut. Her terror for Ben mounts.

"How long have you been in this place?"

"What is the season now?"

"It's the end of March."

"Maybe six months. I think October."

Six months of hell. The room is chillier than the frozen food aisle of a supermarket. What must it have been like in winter?

Odeta breaks the silence. "Your son. Where can he be?"

Kate's shoulders droop as she shakes her head. If she knew Ben was safe she could bear anything.

Odeta answers her own question. "He is ten, yes? So, he is with friends, playing football." Her face glows as she pronounces her conclusion. "I have young brothers, Afrim and Leon. Always they are playing football."

Kate shakes her head. "Ben doesn't find it easy to make friends. That's why he was drawn to Geoffrey when we met him in the park." A terrible shudder streaks along her spine. What if Geoffrey is part of it too? Maybe he works for those men, enticing young boys to the house?

"Geoffrey. He is...not always all there." Odeta taps a forefinger on her forehead.

"So why is he living here in a household of Albanians?"

"This is his house. He owns it."

"Geoffrey's house?"

"Yes, why not? You think Albanians could afford this house?"

Kate's brain is spinning; her synapses can't make connections. Does she mean Geoffrey is the Mr Big, the man in charge? Where, oh where, is her son? She forces herself to think logically. Nick will read the note she left him, and if Ben's still not turned up he'll call the police. But will he realise that she is missing too? Or think she's fled to avoid the 'talk' he planned – so she wouldn't have to listen to him pronouncing the death sentence on their marriage?

"Odeta, did you hear any sirens outside last night? Or see any flashing blue lights?"

Odeta shrugs. "Sirens? I hear them often. Sometimes I think they are inside my dream. But lights, no."

Outside the narrow cell window, Joplin Street rumbles into life. Intermittent car engines blend together into a symphony of traffic noise, the familiar sound that rouses her from sleep each morning. Next door is her home, but she's never been further away. Kate closes her eyes, imagining she's in her own bed where this collage of street sounds belongs to her, but a hand on her arm jolts her back. It's Odeta, probably checking she's still alive.

"We need a plan," Kate mumbles, her head still woozy. "Tell me everything you know. How often do they leave the house?"

"I only know when buzzer rings and a client comes."

"What about doors, windows?"

"All windows have bars or locks. At first I try many times to escape – push past Stephan, run upstairs; ask client for help, but they beat me and bring me back. Front door is always locked and keys with Tomas or in key safe."

"But not the kitchen window I climbed in through."

"No. I saw them lock it. But maybe..." A hopeful expression flits across Odeta's face. She pushes her hair back behind her ears. "We try something else. Kate you have phone, right? You call for help."

Kate's no stranger to bad days: days when hope deserts her and she flounders in a pit of despair – but always a chink of light illuminates a way forward. Now, in this chasm of hell, she has severed her own lifeline.

"I don't have a mobile phone," she confesses.

"What!" Odeta's eyebrows dart up and her forehead creases. She paws at Kate's wrist. "Are you crazy? You lose your son, you break into house. And you don't have phone!" Sliding her hand between the mattress and the bedsprings, she pulls out her charger and shakes it in front of Kate. "What is wrong with you?" she yells.

CHAPTER THIRTY-NINE

Time has no rhythm. In Albania, the days dawdle but night always arrives to blot them out. Here, night and day blend into one, punctuated only by the buzzer and clients stomping down the stairs.

Odeta senses today will be different. Perhaps there will be no food and no clients. She's scrubbed the basin clean, but there's nothing she can do about the bloodstain on the floor. Yesterday it seemed as if every last drop of blood was spilling out of Kreshnik; this morning the colour has faded to brown and merged with the pattern in the rug. Still, she calculates, they wouldn't risk sending a client into this room. Blood on the carpet is bad for business.

After she yelled at Kate about the mobile phone, they drifted into moody silence. They drink water from the tap, Kate finds some mints in her pocket and shares them. She has a watch and keeps looking at it but Odeta doesn't ask the time, it only marks more hours of imprisonment. The sky looks inky. Has another day passed, or is a storm brewing?

"Look, we have to get out," says Kate, her eyes travelling

around the room again. "You know this place. Think of something."

"But your family will search for you, yes? Police will come." Odeta screws up her eyes and looks at Kate intently.

Kate glances away. "Perhaps. If Nick realises I'm missing." She gets to her feet, places her hand on the end rail of the heavy iron bedstead and gives it a tug. It budges, but only just.

"Help me with this, Odeta." Together they shunt the bed up to the wall just beneath the window. Kate kicks off her shoes, ignoring her painful ankle, stands on the mattress and climbs onto the slippery metal end rail. She hauls herself up, stretching her arms above her head so she can just reach the blocked-up lower half of the window.

"Have you checked this?"

"Yes. Many times. It's blocked."

"Not all of it," Kate taps on the glass. "This part up to here is concrete or tarmac on the outside." She indicates a spot on the window about twenty centimetres above the original sill. "Above here is just a build-up of earth and stones."

Odeta shakes her head. Countless times, she's examined the window, standing on a chair and craning her neck. She's measured the gap with her hands, holding them apart in the air and measuring the space between them against her own hips and shoulders. Not even a child could wriggle through. From her higher vantage point balanced on the bed rail, Kate has a different view.

"So if we smash window and shovel earth away ..."

"Exactly."

"I could do it. Once I was gymnast."

"How much time do we have?"

Odeta spreads her hands apart and shrugs. "Elira is gone. If client comes I must work."

But they won't want to risk bringing a client into this room, Kate thinks.

"Don't they feed you?"

"Once a day. Stephan brings food."

"Then we start on the window. But if Stephan turns up, we must overpower him."

"Overpower?"

"Hit him. Tie him up."

"If it goes wrong they'll hurt us real bad. Maybe kill us."

"Odeta. I can't wait here any longer. Ben might be in danger."

"We, too."

"We need to take care breaking the window. It'll be tricky reaching above our heads to smash the glass."

"There's nothing sharp."

"Something blunt and heavy, then?" Kate seizes the cheap modern chair and upends it; surprised to find it's made of wood. The legs are stuck on, not moulded into the frame. "Here, help me break this off." Kate places her foot on the upturned chairback and waggles one of the legs.

Odeta joins in and rocks it. "Like dentist taking out tooth." The chair creaks and the leg splits away from the frame. It's not a clean break; the broken end is rough with splinters.

"Good. With this we can smash the window and use it on Stephan."

"You mean hit him?"

Kate nods. "Grab another one." With a little levering, the chair's second leg breaks off in Odeta's hand. Instinctively, they square up to one another, brandishing their spindly clubs in a play-fight.

Kate lowers hers first. "Once Stephan sees the broken window there's no going back. We have to be ready."

"What shall I do?" Goosebumps appear between the burn marks on her bare arms.

"We'll take turns waiting behind the door while one of us works on the window."

Odeta moves into position behind the door.

"You know you have to hit him hard, right here?" Kate raises her own makeshift club and points to a spot on her head. "And we'll need something to tie his hands and feet."

"They took away sheet to cover Kreshnik's body."

Kate unfastens her leather belt and hooks it over the bedstead. "What about that phone charger lead?" Odeta pulls it out from under the mattress and drapes it next to the belt.

Kate climbs back up on the rail and taps her stick along the lower edge of the window pane, scraping away putty until a few chunks drop out. She thumps harder, and a section of glass shatters into a spider's web. She leans down and picks up a pillow, ignoring the bloodstains, and holds it in front of her like a shield. She bangs on the pane and pushes the glass splinters outwards. Cold air streams into the room with its heady cocktail of freshness and pollution.

Odeta leaves her post and walks across to inspect the broken window.

"Get back." Kate's tone is harsh. Odeta flinches and slopes back to her station behind the door. Grim-faced, Kate prods at the banked-up soil outside the window. Shovelling with such a narrow implement is painfully slow, but gradually the gap enlarges and the swatch of daylight broadens. "Odeta, if you get away and I don't, run straight to my house, okay? It's next door. Number thirty-six."

Odeta nods but her face holds a question.

"You can't miss it. The door is white and there's a privet hedge around the front garden."

"Hedge?"

"Yes. Nick should be there. Tell him not to come here himself. Tell him to send the police to number thirty-eight Joplin Street."

"Joplin Street. I can read the sign." She can tell Kate doesn't trust her. Kate probably thinks as soon as she gets outside she'll keep on running and disappear.

Through the broken window pane traffic noise thickens, and although the room is small they have to shout to hear each other. An engine splutters closer and stops outside. Through the opening she's created, Kate can see the wheels of Tomas's transit van. Does that mean he'll see the hole they've made in the window?

Odeta glances at the window. Kate still hasn't cleared a wide enough opening. She'll need to hoist herself up before she can crawl out. It won't work. This plan is rubbish. Outside, rain begins to fall, pattering on the ground and tapping on the metal roof of the van. Now it sounds like a gushing tap; the wind picks up and flings rain inside, staining the white brickwork the colour of weak coffee. Kate ignores it and works on.

Odeta is clutching her chair-leg weapon so tight it makes a groove in her hand. She circles her shoulders, shifts from foot to foot and yawns. Outside, the rain slackens to a pitter-pat, traffic whooshes along the sodden street, sounds mesh into a regular pattern. And then the pattern breaks. A door crashes open – it can only be the door to the basement.

They exchange glances; Kate jumps down and winces as she forces her swollen foot back inside her shoe. She picks up her weapon and takes up position on the opposite side of the door, flattening her back against the wall. As long as Stephan steps inside the room, without pausing in the doorway, he won't spot them; they can both pounce and strike him from behind.

Her heartbeat pounds in her ears as she listens for footsteps approaching the door. Neither of them breathe. Outside the door, a clinking sound suggests he's dropped the key, followed by a curse and a clatter.

Odeta raises the stick high above her head as Stephan enters. He takes a pace forward and she's on him, smashing her weapon down heavily on the back of his head. He cries out as he loses his balance and lurches forward, but he doesn't fall to the ground. He turns his head, flailing, hits out at her and tries to grab her stick. She tweaks it away and hits him again.

"Shit." His hand flies up to pat his injured skull, and he snarls. Kate springs forward from behind the door. Crouching, she smacks her stick across the back of his knees. This time he topples, putting out his hands to break his fall. Odeta whacks him across the back, landing blows faster than he can fend them off. He's growling, groaning, cursing and hitting out, he curls up on the floor clutching his head.

"Now," yells Kate, gripping Odeta's wrist and tugging her towards the door. An abandoned tray with two bowls of soup stands between them and the bottom of the stairs. Odeta dodges round, but Kate notices too late. Her foot catches one of the bowls, slimy green liquid slops onto the floor and she skids. "Damn!"

Back inside the room, Stephan is slowly raising himself onto all fours and turns his head to look at them. Kate picks up the second bowl of hot soup and flings it into his eyes. Her aim is on target. He roars with pain and gropes towards the sink, running the tap and splashing water onto his face.

"Come on," hisses Odeta from the top of the stairs.

Kate limps up behind her. From below, Stephan is shouting, already stomping towards the stairs.

"Oh shit. We meant to tie him up. And I didn't lock the door."

"Lock this one." Odeta points with her index finger to the

large bolt on the hall side of the cellar door, and Kate slides it into position. It won't hold for ever, but it will give them a head start – if they can find a way out of the house.

They flatten their backs against the wall. Where is Tomas? Her stomach gripes with cramp and she badly needs the loo, but now is not the time.

Behind them Stephan's voice bellows, "Open the bloody door." He's hammering on the wood; the planks vibrate, but the bolt is holding. How can Tomas not hear it? Another sound – just as loud – is coming from beyond the locked front door. Rock music! Kate tiptoes along the hall and enters the sitting room. When she peers out from behind the curtains, she sees the transit van, backed up close to the steps, with the rear doors flung wide. Heavy metal music blasts from the cab radio, cloaking other sounds. Inside the van, the m-shaped curve of Tomas's podgy backside rises above his trousers directly into her line of vision. He's on his hands and knees, scrubbing bloodstains from the van floor and head-banging in time with the music. Her stomach lurches. She watches the manic jolting of his head, wondering if he's about to turn around, or if he'd see her hidden behind the curtain.

"Quick." She hobbles down the hall, grabbing Odeta's hand as she passes, pulling her towards the kitchen. Stephan's shouts are muffled by the door, but he's rattling the handle. If Tomas comes inside it's all over.

Kate pushes the kitchen door but it doesn't move. "It's locked!"

"And so is the window – I told you," echoes Odeta.

Kate's injured ankle is throbbing and her legs feel shaky. "I have an idea. Follow me." She hobbles to the main staircase, trying not to put weight on her injured ankle.

Odeta hesitates. She's watched Elira go upstairs with Stephan but has never been up herself. By the time she reaches the first landing and three closed doors, Kate has disappeared. Another staircase lies ahead. It disappears around a bend and leads on upwards to a second floor.

"Come on!" Kate calls down to her. Odeta follows her up under the sloping ceiling, arriving just as Kate opens a door onto what looks like a furniture storeroom. In the centre of the room is a bed and on that bed is a crumpled mound of bedcovers. As she watches, the mound begins to move.

"Aargh. Go away." Geoffrey sits bolt upright, rubbing his eyes and blinking at them.

So this is where Geoffrey lives.

"Don't hurt me." He shrinks back pulling the covers up and over his face.

Kate reaches under the duvet for his hand and strokes it. "Geoffrey, it's me, Kate. Don't be scared."

"Ben's not here. No one's here." He sits bolt upright and drums his balled fists against the bedcovers.

"I know." Kate passes him a smeared glass of what looks like water from the small cupboard beside his bed, and he gulps it greedily.

Odeta's eyes complete their circuit of the room, noticing something unusual, something she hasn't seen for a while. "The window – it's open."

Kate nods. "Yes. I opened it yesterday. I didn't think Geoffrey would have locked it. Look outside – see those drainpipes?"

Odeta leans out across the sill and looks. It's a long way down to the ground, a concrete yard with moss and grass poking through cracks. This is the back of the house, on the other side from where Tomas is working on his van. She senses what Kate is about to ask her, and feels giddy.

"You said you were a gymnast, right?"

"It's true. But it was a long time ago."

"Odeta – you're very slim and light. If I tie Geoffrey's blankets together to make a rope, do you think you could climb down, holding onto the drainpipe?" Kate's eyes gleam as she tugs the top bedcover off a startled Geoffrey, twists it diagonally between her hands and knots both ends. "Geoffrey, this thick cover is hard to work with. Are you sure you don't have any sheets?"

Odeta stares out at the drainpipe that plies its course down the wall from the gutter and runs alongside Geoffrey's window. She leans out and rattles the pipe with her hand, trying to tug it away from the wall. It feels solid enough. Her dizziness fades, and a strange calm descends. All those months locked inside her basement cell, forcing herself to follow exercise routines to stay fit and sane, must have been leading to this moment.

Geoffrey is joining in as if it's a game. He pulls open drawers, seemingly at random, and locates towels and sheets: pink, slippery and thin. Kate nods her thanks as she continues knotting, offering the end of her makeshift rope to Geoffrey. "Tug of war."

"What?"

Kate demonstrates by pulling hard on each joined section of the rope. She hands one end to Geoffrey and he leans back and pulls on it, tugging until his morose expression fades away and he starts to giggle.

"Shh." Kate puts a finger to her lips. "Time to get going before Tomas hears Stephan's knocking."

She stoops down and knots one end of the rope around the leg of Geoffrey's iron bedstead. "Odeta, help me." She tugs the single mattress off his bed, and with Odeta's help manages to fold it lengthwise so they can lift and slide it out through the window. "Sorry, Geoffrey."

"Crash pad," she remarks, as it tumbles to the ground and lands flat and close to the wall.

Geoffrey flaps his hand and grumbles. Kate pats his hand. "Sorry again. Time to go. Odeta – you first." She puts the rope of tied-together bedding in Odeta's hand and nudges her towards the window.

"You're climbing down, too?" She looks at Kate doubtfully.

Kate nods. "The only way."

Odeta scrambles up to sit on the narrow sill, feeding the rope through her hands and letting the free end drop out of the window. It stops about two metres above the ground, but from there it will be an easy drop onto Geoffrey's mattress.

Cautiously she leans across to grip the drainpipe with one hand, holding the improvised rope with the other.

"Pull the rope back up and tie it round your waist, Odeta," Kate urges, but Odeta shakes her head. She braces her legs against the wall and kicks off with her feet. It takes just moments for her to shimmy down the wall, swinging with elegant, gymnastic moves from hand to hand, from drainpipe to rope. Adrenalin fuels her body, her heart lifts and she tastes freedom. In a short final leap, she drops onto the mattress, landing in a squatting position. She gets to her feet and shuffles along the wall to the edge of the kitchen window, standing on tiptoe to peep inside. It's empty.

She looks up at the window where Kate is hauling the sheet-rope back up and signals the all-clear.

When Kate clambers onto the sill, Odeta notices she's tied one end around her waist. Won't that make the rope too short? From below she makes an untying motion with her hands, but dares not shout. She looks on anxiously as Kate descends in a clumsy abseiling movement, not leaning back far enough to brace her feet because she's hugging the drainpipe. Slowly, centimetre by centimetre, she progresses. Odeta watches, heart in mouth. Halfway down, Kate loses her grip on the drainpipe and swings away from the wall, dangling from the flimsy rope, legs flailing.

Odeta watches with rising panic, until Kate secures her handhold. She sees the problem. Kate has run out of rope. She's struggling to untie the knot around her waist with one hand while clinging to the drainpipe with the other. Even if she succeeds, she's too high above the ground to jump onto the mattress.

"Wait," Odeta mouths. Gripping hold of the drainpipe she shimmies back up until her head is level with Kate's waist. The pipe creaks under the combined weight of the two women, and she can feel Kate's body trembling. Holding on with her left hand, Odeta teases the knot apart with the fingers of her right. At last it comes free, baling out the extra metre of rope that should bring Kate close enough to jump to the ground.

Odeta lets go of the drainpipe. Muscle memory carries her to the mattress, where she rolls a somersault and springs to her feet, arms flung wide, as if facing an imaginary judging panel.

As Odeta clears the mattress, Kate jumps, trembling and gasping as she lands awkwardly on her damaged ankle. "We mustn't stop," she whispers, staggering to her feet. "We'll go out the way I came in." She leads Odeta around to the side passage through the rotting gate she'd forced open the day before. Reaching the end of this narrow passage, Kate flattens herself against the wall and peers round to check the front of the house. Heavy metal is still blaring from the van, and she leans forward as far as she dares. It's impossible to tell whether Tomas is still working on the van or has gone back indoors.

"Follow me," hisses Kate. "Stay quiet. Duck down and tiptoe past the van. When you reach the pavement, turn right, and next door is my house."

Kate goes first, wriggling alongside the parked van, keeping her head bent down so it's lower than the van's windows. Odeta nods and waits. It's her turn.

She advances slowly towards the van, every step leading her

closer to safety. She lifts her eyes and sees the park, across the road ahead of her. Forgetting Kate's instructions and her example of crouching down to pass the transit, she stretches out her arms and runs full pelt towards the longed-for trees, greenery and freedom.

"Hey!" The rough voice stops her; she freezes in her tracks. This is it. The end of her brief bid for freedom. Kate is nowhere in view, and like everything else she's dreamt or imagined for the past six months, the park was just a mirage: fate playing a trick on her.

Blinking back tears, she turns and meets Tomas's eyes. He glares at her through the van's front windscreen. The man's a murderer. He knows no pity, and won't hesitate to kill again. Those small, mean eyes strike terror into her soul, draining her energy and will. Above the discordant banging of his music, he shakes his fist and shouts something that sounds like, "I'll get you, bitch!"

He's still in the back of the van. To catch her he'll need to climb out of the rear doors, but her trance-like state persists; she watches as he straightens up from his crouched working position, then hears a dull clanking sound, followed by "Shit!" Tomas has banged his head on the van's roof.

His setback galvanises her. As he clambers out of his van, she sprints towards the pavement and turns right. Tomas gives chase, he's just behind her, an arm's reach away, his yells echoing in her ears, his breathing laboured and creaky.

Odeta runs on towards the house next door, throwing glances behind her, keeping an eye on Tomas. Suddenly, he stops. Puzzled, she looks ahead to where Kate is beckoning her from the front gate next door. A car with a white roof and acid-yellow and blue squares painted on the doors is parked outside. A thicket of overhanging bushes blocks the view of the vehicle from number thirty-eight, but Tomas must have seen it too. He turns and sprints back the way he came.

"That's my house," says Kate, her voice croaking as Odeta catches her up. She points at the police car parked outside. "Something's happened to Ben!"

CHAPTER FORTY

O deta watches Tomas sprint back to his van, climb into the driver's seat and start the engine. He drives off, without stopping to close the rear doors. The van doors rattle and clang, fading gradually as the van turns into Church Road. She follows Kate slowly through a gate edged by a green bush: that must be hedge. Kate limps ahead up to the front door, lifts a brass knocker and hammers on it, shouting, "Come on, come on. Open it." *Doesn't she have a buzzer? Or a key?*

Odeta hovers by the gate, trying to make herself invisible. A man opens the door. He must be Kate's husband, Nick. He's dark-haired, with handsome features, but frowning, and he doesn't seem pleased to see her. He's saying something Odeta can't quite understand – it sounds like *Where the hell...* – and something about Kate playing a trick on him. But he doesn't know about Tomas and what's been going on at number thirty-eight. Until Kate tells them, no one will know.

Odeta hesitates, focusing on the wilting yellow flowers in the tub outside the door. Should she wait here or follow Kate down the path?

Kate is talking now and weeping. "Ben? Where's Ben?"

she's repeating over and again, lifting her hands to claw at the man's shirt.

What's wrong with her? Why doesn't she tell him they've just fought their way out from number thirty-eight? Odeta shudders, casting a glance at the house next door, and edges further into the shelter of the front garden. She heard Tomas drive off, but she can't quite believe he won't return and snatch her. And what about Stephan? Is he still in the basement? Someone should go and catch him, right now, but Kate has forgotten everything. It's Ben, only Ben, everything's Ben.

The handsome man sighs, and Odeta sees that he's not cross at all, he's tired and sad. Words slide out of his mouth. "Ben's here," he says. "Where else would he be?"

"Thank God!" As Odeta looks on, Kate seems to crumple. She staggers and collapses against the wall and the man puts out his arms to catch her. Now he's helping her inside and closing the door.

That's it, then. Kate's back home, Ben's returned from wherever he got to – probably out playing football, just like Leon and Afrim. Everyone has slotted back into their places. But where is her place? She has no one to welcome her and nowhere to go.

Rain begins to fall again: fine drops, cool and refreshing. She turns her face up to the sky, parts her lips and lets it dribble into her parched mouth. Pitter-pat, pitter-pat turns to tump-tamp; the drops are huge. She puts a hand up to feel her hair, it's drenched. Rain dribbles down her neck and soaks into her blood-stained t-shirt. She closes her eyes, but the sight of Kreshnik's body lying in a pool of blood is seared onto the inside of her eyelids. She leans against the gatepost, trembling.

One sodden minute bleeds into the next. Odeta waits. Magnetised by the police car and a promise of drama, passers-by dawdle, safe under their umbrellas, and stare at her bare arms.

The rain has washed the blood off her skin, but not off her t-shirt. An elderly lady raises her walking stick and points it at her. She cringes.

And then, the door of the house flies open. "Odeta. Forgive me," calls Kate, extending her hand as she limps back down the path towards her. "Ben's home. Safe. I had to see him." As if that explained everything.

"Is good? Goodbye."

"No, you must come inside. There's so much we have to explain."

Turning her back on the gaggle of spectators, Odeta follows Kate inside. This house is warm. Passing through the front door doesn't spark a sense of dread; instead, there's a feeling of comfort seeped into the fabric of the building. On the hall windowsill are more wilting flowers in a blue vase. In number thirty-eight, just inside the door, Tomas kept his jailer's key safe – and here there are flowers.

Kate strides ahead and opens a door at the end of the hall, waiting while Odeta dawdles, touching a radiator, glancing at a picture. A sound like gunfire rattles from behind the doorway where Kate is standing. Odeta flinches. Did Tomas and Stephan storm in through the back with guns?

Kate beckons her into the kitchen where Nick and another man are watching a blond boy about Leon's age, shooting up baddies on a screen. The other man wears a dark uniform; he must belong to the car with the blue light parked outside: Police. He seems to be watching Ben playing a computer game.

Kate drops to her knees on the floor beside her son, hugging him so tight he almost topples over. "Where were you, Ben?" she's asking. "I looked for you everywhere."

He shrugs his shoulders and wriggles away from her embrace. "Where were YOU, Mother?" He keeps one eye on the screen.

The police officer gets to his feet. "Are you Mrs Kate Davison?"

She nods.

"I'll need to speak to you in a moment." He picks up his chair and moves it to a corner of the kitchen, a discreet distance away.

"Honestly, Kate," says Nick. "I don't get why you were so hysterical. I got your voicemail but Ben was here when I arrived. Scared and upset because there was no sign of you."

"I don't understand. He never came home from school."

"Then I find a note from you saying he's missing," Nick continues.

Odeta can't follow. They're both talking over the top of each other: Kate is saying Ben had gone missing; Nick is saying no, he was at home all the time. Perhaps Kate isn't quite right in the head?

Kate clambers to her feet, white-faced, and puts her hands on her hips, some splinters of glass still visible in her tangled hair.

"Stop twisting everything. I was frantic. Certain he'd gone to see Geoffrey. He was obsessed with visiting his house – talked about it for weeks."

Nick draws his lips into a tight line and gives Kate an odd look. Perhaps he also thinks she's not right in the head. "He went to visit the dog."

"Woody?"

Nick nods. "He said you'd told him there wouldn't be time to walk the dog because I was coming round. So he took the key from the hook in the morning, and went straight there after school."

"Are you telling me he stayed in John and Lucy's house for four hours? I don't get it – I rang them three times. There was no answer."

Nick nods. "He was pretending to be Woody's owner. Fed him so much dried food, the dog shat all over their kitchen floor. John told me the crap was like a stinking coil of Cumberland sausage."

"Oh."

"Yeah. Ben got scared and tried to clean it up. Terrified he'd made the dog ill. Thought Woody would die if he left him alone."

He looks up and seems to notice Odeta for the first time. "Who's she? And where were you last night?"

Three sets of eyes swivel towards her. Only Ben keeps his eyes fixed on the computer screen.

"This is Odeta." Kate walks across and puts her arm around Odeta's shoulders. "You're soaked through," she exclaims. "Chuck me that towel, Nick."

Nick takes a towel off a hook by the sink and passes it to her. Odeta pats her arms and chest. The towel is red and white check. If there's still any blood, it won't show.

Kate takes a deep breath. "It's a long story," she says. "Odeta's been held captive in a basement next door by two men. Last night they kidnapped me, too."

Odeta feels the weight of their stares. They're repeating her name, but talking so fast she can't unpick their meaning. She tries to fasten on to a word or phrase, any phrase, that will tell her what is happening.

"How d'you mean, kidnapped?" A spot of colour appears in Nick's pale cheeks, his eyes are hard with disbelief.

"Look," says Kate, raking her fingers through her tangled hair and speaking in a low voice – perhaps she's hoping Ben won't hear. "Next door, at number thirty-eight, two men have been running a brothel with trafficked women. I went in there, searching for Ben, and they locked me up too."

The police officer snaps to attention and scrambles to his

feet, tripping over the trailing lead. Ben, seemingly oblivious to the drama, whines, "Aw, Dad. Why don't you get a wireless controller?"

"What's this about a kidnap?" asks the police officer.

Kate's face clouds over. "Look, I don't want to talk about this in front of..." she jabs an elbow towards Ben. Dropping her voice to a whisper, she continues. "There are two violent men in that house. And yesterday they killed someone."

Nick parrots the police officer's words. "Will someone please tell me what this is about?" He stares from Kate to Odeta, and his eyes light on her bloodied t-shirt. "Is that what I think it is?"

Odeta drops her eyes to stare at the floor. Shame burns her face; she can't pretend to be the innocent who left Albania six months ago. That girl is gone for ever.

"Sorry," Nick mumbles. "Look, let's get Ben out of here, yeah?" He takes hold of his son's arm and pulls him up onto his feet.

"Aww, Dad."

"We'll take the Xbox into the study, okay. Mum needs to talk to PC Blunt."

"Thanks." The officer nods as Nick unplugs the machine and they leave the kitchen. "Mrs Davison, if this is an emergency I'll need to call for backup. But you'll have to give me more information."

"Look," says Kate, holding up Odeta's arm to reveal a snaking line of cigarette burn scars. "How d'you think she got these?"

Shamefaced, Odeta tugs her arm free and pins it to her side so the scars can't be seen. "Kate – don't."

"One at a time. I need to know what's going on." PC Blunt clears his throat. Beneath the disguise of his uniform he's very young, with dark curly hair and a shaving rash on his chin. "Who's in the house? Did you say they were armed?"

"Tomas has gone already," says Odeta. "I saw him drive off in the van."

"Did you get the registration number?"

Kate and Odeta exchange a glance. Kate shakes her head. "It was a blue transit. Quite old, rusty. Looked like an old gas van. Resprayed."

The officer clears his throat and speaks into his radio. "Charlie One. From PC Blunt. Number 79368. I'm at number thirty-six Joplin Street following up on a concern for safety report. I've been made aware of armed men at number thirty-eight. Basement brothel. Possible fatality." He feeds more details to the Control Room. "Two female victims. Can you run checks on the address, make the Inspector aware? Consider armed response."

Kate crosses the kitchen and runs water into the kettle as Nick returns and stands beside her. "Ben's in the study. He's all right. I've set up *Minecraft* for him."

"How long did you wait before calling the police to report me missing?" Kate gestures with the kettle in the direction of PC Blunt, who holds up a hand to signal for quiet.

In the pause that follows, Nick pushes up his shirt cuff and scratches his arm. "I didn't call him, Kate," he confesses. "After Ceri told me about you turning up at her house, I assumed – wrongly – you'd gone away on purpose. To avoid seeing me."

Kate gapes at him, too shocked to speak.

"It was Mr Chatterjee from the shop who called the police. He was worried about you and Ben. A patrol came to the house last night, but Ben was home and I was here with him. They took a brief report. PC Blunt has come back today to follow up."

"Because?"

"To rule out the possibility of child neglect."

The kettle jolts in Kate's hand: the hand that's spent hours smashing a stick against glass, scraping away dirt, bashing Stephan over the head, and abseiling down a wall. She blinks away a tear as water spills from the spout onto the kitchen floor.

Odeta looks around for a cloth to mop it up – clearing up mess is her job – but the rapid movement makes her head whirl. Her legs are no longer able to support her own weight. She stumbles, slumps down onto a chair and battles against the tug of unconsciousness.

CHAPTER FORTY-ONE

"You're going to have to let her sleep," says Kate to PC Blunt. "She's shattered."

She's helped Odeta upstairs and put her to bed in her spare room. She nibbles on a biscuit but it does little to quell her hunger pangs. The cup of tea helped; she'll make another one in a minute.

She and PC Blunt are sitting in her dining room. He's facing the window, keeping his eyes trained on the house next door.

"It won't be me doing the interview," PC Blunt says. "They'll send a specialist unit."

"She'll need a translator, you know," says Kate. "Her English is surprisingly good, but her vocabulary..." She grimaces. "Well – it's limited to things she's experienced. Do you want to hear what happened to me?"

"No. We'll take your statement later. Back-up should be here soon. I have to keep an eye on next door."

The last time Kate sat in this room to eat a meal was when Ceri, Dan and the gang came round for supper last October. Now the dining table is a wasteland, covered with piles of papers and boxes. The papers are hers – invoices, receipts for

283

expenses, stuff she's been assembling to get a head start on her year-end accounts and tax return – but the boxes are new. They contain Nick's collection of CDs and vinyl, and they weren't here two days ago. Her stomach clenches. While she was locked in that basement, fighting for her life, Nick's been boxing up the remnants of their life together.

"Why's it taking so long?" she asks.

"An investigator will come here first. The rest of the team will be putting plans in place for number thirty-eight. You said the men were armed?"

Kate feels a giggle bubbling below the surface of her hysteria. She shrugs.

"Tomas and Stephan will be miles away by the time the back-up team arrive." It's impossible to believe Stephan won't by now have found a way to smash down the basement door and get away, even if Tomas didn't wait for him.

PC Blunt fidgets and scratches his chin as if remembering something. "You said your son has a friend who lives at number thirty-eight?"

She nods. "Geoffrey. Not a friend exactly. Someone we met in the park."

"And had he visited Geoffrey's house before?

"No."

"So, your theory that Ben was there seems a little far-fetched."

"Look. I was frantic, okay? Perhaps I wasn't thinking straight, but it seemed logical to me at the time."

"This Geoffrey chap," asks PC Blunt. "He was part of the gang?"

Kate hesitates. With so much to explain, this important thing has slipped her mind. She shakes her head. "No. He's vulnerable. I'd say he was a victim, too."

"Why didn't you tell me sooner?" His face reddens and he

fumbles with his radio. "I'll need to file a vulnerable adult report. Give me some more details."

She tries to recall everything about Geoffrey: what she and Ben know of him, what Odeta has told her, and what she saw of his living conditions inside the house. "I've been told that Geoffrey owns the house," she begins. "But he can't look after himself. Maybe those other men moved in with him to exploit him?"

"Cuckooing," says PC Blunt briskly.

"Pardon?"

"Criminal gangs befriending vulnerable adults, then taking over their homes – usually to deal drugs."

Kate shudders.

There's a tap at the dining room door. It edges open and Ben races in, his socks skidding on the polished floorboards. When he reaches Kate, he presses up close and stretches out his arms, wrapping them around her in a hug. "Where were you last night, Mum? I was worried."

Her heart swells. She pulls him closer and breathes in his smell of unwashed boy, his thick hair tickling her face. Ben wriggles out of her embrace and moves just out of reach of her arm as if daring her to try to hug him again. She smiles at him. He lifts his head and grins back, and for the first time in so very long he lets his eyes meet hers and holds her gaze.

Kate's heart skips and the beat quickens. In that moment, she knows that whatever happens to her and Nick, Ben will be all right.

CHAPTER FORTY-TWO

Sirens wail and blue lights paint patterns across the ceiling, visible to Odeta through her closed eyelids. She struggles awake, fearful of what lies ahead.

The room smells different. What's happened to musty damp and the stench of body odours? This room is warm, with an everyday smell of soap and dust. She opens her eyes to see she's not in the basement but lying on a soft bed in an unfamiliar room. Someone has covered her with a duvet, and her heart flips at this small kindness. The blue light flickering in the room is from the street outside. She slides out from under the duvet and pads across to the window. She pulls back the curtain, and the first thing she sees is the hedge. Of course: Kate's hedge, Kate's house. She's escaped.

She pulls a coverlet from the bed and wraps it round her shoulders. Beyond the hedge, she can see activity out in the street. She counts three police cars with their lights flashing, and officers in high-visibility jackets shooing bystanders away. She tiptoes out of the bedroom onto the landing. Kate and her family are standing in the hall below. The police officer is leaving through the front door.

"Stay inside," he tells them. "Keep the door closed."

They nod, shut the door behind him, and wait a few seconds. As Odeta looks on, Kate and Nick whisper to one another above Ben's head, open the front door again and go outside.

Odeta doesn't want to be left alone; not even in this comfortable house. Padding downstairs on bare feet (the carpet feels like silky sand between her toes), she passes through the open door and hovers on the doorstep.

Ben turns around and spots her. "It's that woman, Mum." He grins at her, and she notices his teeth are perfect: white and even, top and bottom. Seeing them makes her feel happy.

Kate smiles and comes back up the path. Inside the porch is a row of coats on pegs and a low shelf piled with shoes and green plastic boots. Kate hands her a green wax jacket and picks out a pair of blue clogs with holes punched in them. "Slip your feet into these Crocs."

Odeta wriggles her feet inside, and Kate takes her arm. Together they walk down the path to the gate. More kindness. Odeta no longer thinks Kate is crazy or old-looking, though she has frown lines on her forehead and her hair is a mess.

"See, Odeta," Kate says. "The police are about to enter number thirty-eight." An officer in a yellow reflective jacket is unfurling a roll of blue and white tape, marking out a boundary which extends to their gatepost. A female officer is shepherding people away from the cordoned-off area.

"Van is not there," says Odeta with a shrug. "Tomas gone."

"But what about Stephan? Do you think Tomas drove off leaving him locked in the cellar?"

"Perhaps he crawl out through window we broke? Was thin enough."

"Look," Kate points across the road. "That's Mr Chatterjee,

who owns the corner shop. The lady is his wife Sabrina, and the old man's his uncle."

Mr Chatterjee disappears back inside his shop and comes out carrying a shallow cardboard tray of cans and bottled water. Holding it in front of him like a cinema usher, he crosses the road and hands out drinks to the watching neighbours.

"Thank you, Mr Chatterjee. This is my friend, Odeta."

Hearing Kate call her a friend gives her a warm feeling. And seeing this man coming out of his shop at this tense time, quietly making sure his neighbours have something to drink. Odeta accepts a Coke, cradling it in her hands like a precious treasure, before breaking the seal and taking a long swig.

The police have fixed up a floodlight on a stand, with the beam directed onto number thirty-eight's front door. An officer with a megaphone calls out instructions and yells at the small crowd of onlookers, "Move away."

"Do you know all these people?" Odeta asks.

"Most of them. This is my community."

Police officers slam car doors and shout to one another. The noise level is ratcheting up.

"Surprise can't be part of their plan," says Nick, as an officer strides towards their gate. They've retreated into their front garden, but are craning their necks to see out past their hedge.

"Sorry, sir, I'm going to have to ask you to go back indoors. For your own safety."

"We have a personal interest in this, officer," says Nick, planting his feet firmly across the boundary between his own path and the pavement.

The officer is unmoved. "If you don't go inside, we may need to evacuate your house." He lifts the blue and white tape and starts to extend it as if to include their house inside the cordon.

Nick scowls and grinds his heel into the pavement as he

turns towards the house. "Come on." He beckons them to follow. "We can watch from the upstairs window."

They hasten indoors and up the stairs to take their places at the window of the room where Odeta was recently sleeping. Nick opens the sash window and slides it up, and the four of them bunch together – Ben and Odeta in front, Nick and Kate looking over their heads – and lean out across the sill.

Two officers are climbing the steps leading to the front door of thirty-eight; three others squeeze past the overhanging bushes and approach the side passage. The officers on the step press the buzzer. They wait one minute, then rap on the door and call out, "Open up – police."

"Is that a truncheon they're using?" asks Kate.

Nick shakes his head. "They use Asps now."

"Asps?"

"A spring-loaded telescopic baton made of steel," Nick explains.

"Yeah, Dad, I've seen them on TV. Tiny to carry round and mahoosive when it expands."

"Will they break down the door?" Odeta asks.

Nick nods. "Eventually. If no one answers. They'll give plenty of warnings first." It's the first words Nick has spoken to her directly. It makes her feel less of a ghost. Perhaps one day she will exist again and re-join the world.

"Hey look at that – cool!" says Ben. Another police van has drawn up and an officer clambers out, lugging a massive red steel pole with handles.

"They call that the Big Red Key," says Nick. "It's a kind of battering ram."

The warning call goes up, and an officer begins bashing the red steel implement against the door. It takes only a few minutes before the door gives. All those locks that held her and Elira captive for so long surrender their strength, and the door cracks in several places. As it swings open, several officers disappear inside.

"Where's all the traffic gone?" asks Ben. Under the floodlight, the buzz of activity outside number thirty-eight resembles a film set – but the street itself is like a deserted car park, with stationary vehicles parked up nose to tail, but nothing on the move.

"They've closed the street at both ends while the police operation is in progress."

Further along the street a dog barks. "It's Woody." Ben leans out across the windowsill and waves frantically in the direction of the barking dog. Nick puts a restraining hand on his shoulder and pulls him back to safety.

For ages it seems as if nothing is happening. Down below, groups of neighbours mill around at the edge of the cordon, mesmerised. And then there's a shout of "They've got him!"

Odeta leans out of the window as far as she dares. Ben is beside her clinging on to her arm. Nick and Kate are craning their necks to look over Odeta's head. Two burly police officers are escorting someone down the steps: a stout man, not very tall. She's confused. Tomas?

It's Ben who identifies the man, as the police conduct him to the police car and propel him into the back seat. "That's Geoffrey. My friend."

Kate lifts her hands and frowns. "But I told PC Blunt he was vulnerable..."

"Then I'm sure they'll treat him sensitively." Nick puts his arm around Kate.

"I suppose they'll need his statement?"

"Exactly."

The doorbell rings, long and shrill. They stare at one another, locked in fight-or-flight mode. Nick reacts first, hurrying down the stairs to answer the door. "Detective's here with the Albanian interpreter to take Odeta's statement," he calls up to them.

"Then tell them they'll have to wait," says Kate, taking a fluffy turquoise bath towel out of a drawer and placing it in Odeta's hands.

"I've put some clean clothes of mine in the bathroom. They might be a bit big for you but they'll do for now. Have a shower, take your time. I'll go down and talk to them until you're ready."

<hr>

PC Blunt has morphed into Detective Constable Robson, and Kate finds him sitting in the kitchen stirring sugar into a mug of instant coffee. He stirs in a second spoonful, taps his spoon on the rim of the mug, and gazes thoughtfully around the room. The interpreter, a sallow-skinned, balding man, paces the kitchen looking at his watch. From what she can make out from his mutterings, he has an irrational fear of anywhere south of the River and a fixation with the time of the last tube to Stanmore. Too bad.

Ben comes and leans against her chair, and she slides across to make room for him on the seat next to her. He slips his hand into hers and squeezes: two shows of affection in one day. He strokes her arm with his forefinger, and she feels all the tiny hairs standing up.

"What did your guys find in the house next door?" Kate asks, dropping her protective act towards Ben. How can she hope to keep him sheltered from goings-on next door?

DC Robson's expression is guarded.

"Come on, we saw them leading Geoffrey away. He's harmless, you know. Not part of the gang."

He stiffens "That's for our team to find out."

"Geoffrey won't be able to cope with your questions. He'll need someone to support him – an advocate."

DC Robson refuses to be drawn.

She shifts tack. "What will happen to Odeta now?"

"If it turns out she's a victim of trafficking, we'll find her a place of safety to stay. There are hostels with front-line specialists in caring for women in her situation."

"Will she be deported?"

"Not right away. It'll depend on what comes out of our interview. I'll file a report, and if she agrees, she'll have a period of leave to remain, initially, while there's an investigation into her case."

"Let her stay here tonight." Kate glances at Nick and searches his face for assent. He inclines his head, ever so slightly. Why is she asking him when he doesn't even live here? Her sprained ankle throbs with pain, but there's no one she can turn to for comfort. If only Nick would stay just for tonight. But she can't bring herself to ask him.

CHAPTER FORTY-THREE

Odeta badly wants a cigarette. Smoking with Stephan bought her more minutes outside the basement, and she's developed a craving. Do Kate or Nick smoke? Here in Kate's kitchen, the morning is bright with watery sunshine. Yesterday's storms have rolled on out over the Channel. Joplin Street is still blocked at both ends and closed to traffic, and the silence is surreal. The blue and white barrier tape flaps in the breeze, and a lone police officer stands outside the door of number thirty-eight, yawning.

It's going to drag on. "Explain me, Kate, what will happen now."

"Did the interpreter not explain to you last night?"

"Bah – him. He wanted only to get to his Stanmore home before the end of the train. He spoke such short summaries. I know he did not tell me everything."

"A liaison worker is coming to fetch you this afternoon," explains Kate. "They've found a place for you in a hostel in Ealing."

"I can't stay here?" Odeta's eager expression wilts.

"You need help, Odeta. From someone experienced. What you've been through needs to mend before you go home."

"But I can never go home, Kate." With the fingernail of her right index finger, Odeta picks at the cuticle on her left thumb, scratching it until she draws blood. "You know what happened to me. Many men raped me. My parents will never forgive."

Exhaustion makes Odeta's brain fuzzy. She tries to take in what Kate is saying about the hostel. "They'll organise medical checks, counselling, and legal advice."

"Why I need legal advice?"

"Trafficking is a crime, Odeta."

"You mean I am criminal?"

Kate looks distracted, unhappy, her face is pale with exhaustion. And where is Nick? It's midday. Surely, he can't still be sleeping?

Kate yawns and looks embarrassed. "No, you're the victim, definitely."

While they wait for the liaison worker, Kate takes Odeta upstairs to her bedroom. The lightly-perfumed air reminds her of a rose garden in summer. The walls are white, and there's a velvet-soft bedcover in midnight blue.

"Sorry it's a bit austere," says Kate. "I painted it white when we moved in. Haven't decided on the final colour yet."

"I've never seen a more beautiful room."

Kate smiles and slides back a mirrored door to reveal a hidden wardrobe, containing neatly-folded sweaters, skirts, trousers, and dresses on hangers. "Try this." She hands Odeta a blue sweater, soft as a kitten's fur. "This will look great on you."

"And these." Black stretch jeans.

"I can't."

"Nonsense. These are too small for me anyway." While Odeta tries on the sweater over her t-shirt, Kate takes a carrier bag and fills it with more tops, socks and freshly-laundered underwear, which has another flower smell – lavender. She opens a drawer and takes out three small bottles in a plastic pouch.

"Shampoo and shower gel. Travel sizes to keep you going."

Odeta unscrews one of the bottles and sniffs an exotic scent – something like jasmine. She can't find words, so she nods her thanks and blinks away a tear.

The liaison officer has kind eyes and a bushy beard. It's a relief not to see a chin covered with black stubble like Tomas's, but the beard hides his mouth, and she wonders what his teeth are like.

"Goodbye." Hugging the bag of clothes and goodies to her chest, Odeta turns to follow the man out to his car.

"Wait, Odeta." Kate hands her a piece of paper. "Look, here's my number. Ring me. I'll visit you."

"I have no phone."

Bushy Beard turns, taking a card from his pocket. "Here's the hostel phone number. Speak to Dave, the manager."

"No address?"

"No, we don't publish the addresses of our hostels. If you ring him he'll take you through the formalities, clear it with Odeta, and tell you where to come."

Ben is waiting in the hall. He's been to John and Lucy's to fetch Woody, and is holding tightly onto the dog's lead.

"Is she going now, Mum?" He nods in Odeta's direction.

Kate gives him a frosty look. "Say goodbye properly, Ben."

"Bye!" he says, swinging the lead in front of him. "Come on, Mum. You said we could walk him now."

Odeta reaches down and pats Woody's wiry fur, holding on tightly to the bag Kate gave her. She straightens up and follows the bearded man outside to his car, taking a last look back at the house but not waving. What's the point? Kate won't come to visit. She'll never see her again.

CHAPTER FORTY-FOUR

"Good morning."

Morning? It can't be.

Odeta groans. She's still striving to empty her mind so she can sleep. She opens her eyes and sees a young woman with straight brown hair and a heavy fringe standing over her. She turns over to face the wall, waiting for her brain fog to lift.

"I've brought you tea."

Tea again. She's sick of it. Does no one drink coffee in this country?

"Come on, Odeta, wake up. Your case worker will be here to meet you soon. Can you be ready in half an hour?"

"Why not?" Odeta takes the mug. It burns her hand, and she places it down on the cabinet beside her bed. The room is tiny and cramped, but has clean white walls, a bed, a beech cabinet, and a line of clothes hooks nailed to the wall, where she's hung the clothes Kate gave her. Today she'll wear the skinny jeans and the soft blue sweater. As she pulls it over her head she catches the lingering scent of Kate's perfume, and feels warm for the first time in months. Even her feet are thawing out in the narrow ballerina slippers Kate gave her. Her body feels prickly. Is it the wool of the sweater? No, her nerve endings are reawakening. She's coming back to life.

The case worker is waiting for her in the manager's office, just off the main lobby. It has no windows on the outside, but two glass walls let in light from the entrance hall. It's like sitting inside a giant fish tank. Odeta keeps her eyes fixed on the door to make sure no one comes and locks it.

"I'm Gemma," says the woman, offering her hand. She's very young, but her grey eyes are serious, and she has a calming smile. "I'm here to help you through all the next steps. It sounds as if you were a victim of human trafficking. If that's the case, you'll have a period of forty-five days for recovery and to think about what's next. I'll help you with that, don't worry. Let me tell you about the procedures first, and then I'll ask you a few questions. We'll fill in this paperwork together." She points to a printed form on the table in front of her.

Odeta nods and listens, but Gemma doesn't speak slowly like Kate. She's romped ahead, leaving Odeta lost in a jungle of meaningless words. Finally, she hears Gemma say "doctor." Something about making an appointment for a health check?

She leans forward, furrowing her brow and holding on to every word. This is real. She's never going back to that room. Tomas, Stephan, even Kreshnik, are all in the past. Some sort of life can begin again.

Kate drives to Ealing to visit Odeta in her hostel. The atmosphere reminds her of a transit lounge: brisk and efficient, but with hard-backed chairs, a scattering of Bibles and prayer leaflets, and a sign saying other holy books are available.

When Odeta enters, she's flicking through the leaflets and turns round to greet her with a smile.

"Those leaflets!" says Odeta. "They thought I would be a Muslim and offered me a Koran. For years my family in Albania must pretend they have no religion. I think my grandparents were Catholics. Or maybe Orthodox? But they couldn't explain to me what that means."

"Do you think of yourself as a Catholic now?"

"When I was in that basement, I looked everywhere for God. But could I find him? I could not."

"That's a long speech, Odeta. Your English is better every day."

"I did learn some English at school," she admits. "I thought I had forgotten, but when I needed, some came back to me. Only they did not teach us words like *bitch* and *fuck*." She laughs again; a surprisingly bright smile, with one blackened tooth interrupting the row of good white ones. She claps a hand over her mouth.

"Loose tooth is where Stephan hit me, almost on first day. I think it will soon fall out." She wrinkles her mouth.

"A dentist can sort that for you, Odeta. I'll come with you if you like."

Kate glances round the cheerless room, with its hard upright chairs and red plastic coffee table, and wonders who chose the décor. "Come on, let's go out and get a coffee."

They stroll around the corner to a Turkish café, where real coffee is served. April is defying its showery reputation and the sky is cornflower-blue. Although it's chilly, they sit at one of the green metal tables arranged under a striped awning outside the café. Kate tries to move her chair closer, but it's bolted to the pavement. She and Odeta exchange a glance and smile. They have an unspoken understanding never to sit anywhere they can't see outside.

Odeta stirs a third spoonful of sugar into her treacly coffee. "Police took me in a car to an area near to Soho." She taps the spoon briskly on the rim of the cup. "Wanted me to point out Beauty Spa. I say I never saw place from front. Always, we entered through rear yard, up fire escape."

Steam curls from her cup, but she sips without seeming to notice. "Then I see Golden Dragon restaurant with parrot in cage."

"Did the police go in?"

Odeta shakes her head, her disappointment clear. "No, not then. They ask me what are busiest times. Say they will go back with vice squad."

"Tell me more about your family," Kate prompts, wondering if this will nudge Odeta to share her thoughts about the future.

Kate has done her own research, and spoken to experts so she can understand how to support Odeta. An investigation has concluded Odeta is a potential victim of trafficking, so she's been granted time for recovery and reflection, but the clock is ticking and there's a risk of deportation at the end of that period. The alternative is to claim asylum, but there's no guarantee it will be granted. The thought of Odeta being put in a detention centre after everything she's been though makes Kate shudder.

Odeta shrugs. "I have a father, mother, two brothers – what else you want to know?"

"Did your parents treat you the same as your brothers?"

"Sure. Except they want Leon and Afrim to have good education. For me, their plan was only working in the shop, then marriage, babies, then back to working in shop. Huh!"

"They probably thought marriage would bring you security." The sun emerges from behind a cloud, and Kate reaches into her bag for her sunglasses and swings them in her hand. "Have you thought any more about going home?"

"In our country shame is everywhere. Albanian women must be pure. Parents could never forgive me for what has happened."

"But it's not your fault, Odeta! You were a victim of human trafficking. That's not the same as prostitution. I'm sure your parents love you and would want you to come home."

Odeta squints and raises her hand to shield her eyes from the sun. Kate hands her the sunglasses, and she puts them on.

"Those days when I was gymnast, winning all the competitions, they were so proud," says Odeta. "I think they learned to love me then."

Odeta is alone in the hostel sitting room, randomly pressing buttons on the TV controller. She's been here for three weeks, and is growing tired of her room with its narrow bed and slippery white sheets smelling of disinfectant. Her channel-surfing lands on a football game, and she watches for a moment, thinking of Afrim and Leon endlessly kicking their ball against the side wall of the shop.

She's wearing knitted socks pulled up over her knees and her favourite blue sweater from Kate. She wears it most days, even though it has a tomato ketchup stain on the front, but she worries it will shrink if she trusts it to the washing machine. These days she keeps her face scrubbed clean of make-up and wears her hair scraped back from her face and tied with an elastic band, so her expression looks drawn and stern. She's built a sort of nest around her out of her meagre possessions, carried down from her room in a carrier bag, marking her territory and spreading scarves, magazines and pairs of rainbow-coloured socks over adjacent chairs. She's propped the sitting room door open so she can see Dave, the duty manager, in his glass-fronted office in the reception hall. If she can see him or anyone in authority, she feels safe. Next time she looks, he's not there. Alarmed, she rams her feet into sandals and pads out into the hall to find him. There he is, standing by the front door. She has the briefest glimpse of a woman outside on the step as Dave closes the door on her.

He turns and notices her, seeming startled, as if he's the one with a guilty conscience. "A woman called. Asking for you, Odeta."

"Was it Kate?"

"Don't know. But I can't admit unauthorised visitors."

What value is freedom and a place in a hostel if your friends are turned away? It must have been Kate. Odeta has no other friends, only officials, interviewers, and case workers who come and ask questions, nod, smile, fill in forms, and disappear never to return. Odeta stabs at the red button to release the door and wrenches it open. Dave watches, making no attempt to stop her rushing outside. A slim young woman with orange hair, and wearing high shiny boots, is retreating along the street. Something about the woman's shape is oddly familiar. Curiosity drives her on. She breaks into a run and catches up with her close to the Turkish café. The woman turns.

"Elira! How did you find me?"

"You'd be surprised. We know everything."

"Who is we? Tomas?"

Elira shrugs. "Him! No idea."

"Stephan, then?"

"I heard he left for Albania. It was Lou who told me you were here. She has spies."

Odeta shivers. How far must she run to escape the past?

Elira sits down at one of the tables outside the café. Odeta remains standing. A waiter emerges and walks across to them. "Coffee?"

"Espresso," says Elira.

"Nothing." Odeta waves him away.

"So how is that place where you live now?" asks Elira. "Different from our last house, yeah?"

Odeta nods, tight-lipped. Unpacking the memory is making her feel nauseous.

"Me – I graduated," continues Elira. "Sharing apartment with five girls now. We decide when we work, when not."

Odeta looks Elira up and down. Her leopard-skin top clings to her body. The baby bump has gone, but the rest of her has filled out. The orange hair suits her. Even her skin looks healthy.

"You had your baby?"

"Yes. Was a girl."

"But the drugs, Elira? Was the baby okay"

"Who knows? Baby was born too early – all floppy, looked like a slippery blue fish and yowled all the time. Disgusting. Lou sorted it out."

"What did the doctor say?"

Elira shrugs. "Lou knew a man who was looking for a baby for a couple from Russia. Was so easy. I gave that Russian woman's name when baby was born in the hospital. They took papers and registered baby as their own."

A sly smile lights Elira's face. "Lou even shared the money with me."

Odeta's tongue lies thick in her mouth so she can't speak. But Elira's not finished. She rambles on. "One day I will have my own man and then we have baby. But not yet."

Odeta presses her palms over her eyes then lets her hands drop to her sides. "Elira, please go. Don't come here again."

Elira's smile slips, and her glassy china-doll eyes turn fierce. "Bitch." Her eyes fall on Odeta's stained sweater, taut face and unwashed hair. "You don't look so good yourself."

Odeta turns and runs back towards the hostel without looking round.

The television in the sitting room is on, entertaining an empty room. She jabs at the remote control, turning the volume louder and louder, until the tribal chanting of football fans drowns everything and banishes unquiet thoughts from her mind. The football ends and the News comes on: conflicts and bombings, devastated cities, crying children, residents fleeing the next bombardment. Odeta yawns. She's not interested in disasters afflicting other people. She just wants to be safe.

The national News glides seamlessly into local headlines for London. Municipal workers have found a body concealed in a woven bag. The bag was about to be loaded onto a barge at the refuse tip. The reporter holds up a similar bag – off-white, woven plastic – to demonstrate. It looks oddly familiar.

"This type of bag is used to deliver sand to building sites," intones the reporter. "It holds a volume of up to one tonne. But this bag held a deadly secret – the body of a man, thought to be in his late twenties."

The presenter turns to a man in a blue boilersuit, standing beside him, and shoves the microphone towards his face. The refuse worker blinks at the camera and describes how he lifted the bag, disturbing vermin, and saw the body. "His face was almost eaten off," he says, taking a handkerchief from his pocket and dabbing his sweaty brow.

Two grainy photographs flash up onto the screen. They show the back and side views of a shaven head. A man's ear is just visible, but his head is turned away so it doesn't show a face. The dead man is wearing a grey jacket.

Odeta's hand flies up to cover her mouth. She rocks forward in the chair and up onto her feet, screaming, "Noooo."

Odeta rushes into the lobby. Dave is in his glass cubicle flicking through paperwork. When she beckons to him, he doesn't respond immediately, so she yanks the door and bursts in.

"Dave, come. Now." She grabs his sleeve and drags him past the jacket (some sort of uniform) hanging on a hook, knocking his trombone case to the ground.

"Careful!"

"Hurry."

He follows her into the sitting room and she points at the television screen, wringing her hands. "Translate," she commands.

The News report is wrapping up. "Who is the mystery man?" the reporter is asking. "And how did he come to make his final journey in such terrible circumstances?"

The screen fills with a long-distance shot of a refuse collection centre. In the distance, sun shimmers over the Thames. The scene captured by the camera is almost pastoral.

"Body of some poor guy dumped at the tip," says Dave, reading from illiterate sub-titles scrolling across the screen, two sentences behind what the reporter is saying. "Man's face unrecognisable. No ID on him. Police are appealing to the public for information."

Odeta crumples, her sobs come in waves. She grips onto Dave's arm, her face bleary with tears.

He's young with a fluffy growth of hair on his chin. His soft skin turns pink when Odeta touches him, and his mouth opens slightly, revealing buck teeth from all that trombone practising.

"Don't let it upset you," he says, patting Odeta's arm, and helps her into a chair. "Hang on – I'll get you some water." He dashes out and returns with a box of tissues and a yellow plastic beaker. He puts the water on the table and holds the box out to her.

"Thank you," she sniffs, tugging out a handful of tissues and blowing her nose with a trumpeting sound.

"Here, have a clean one." With delicate fingers, Dave plucks a single tissue from the box and hands it to her like a precious rose. He hovers beside her chair, shifting from foot to foot.

"I know him," she says in a flat voice. "The dead one. Kreshnik. He was my man, my boyfriend."

Dave knits his fingers together, holding them level with his chest, and brings his chin down to rest on them. Surely, he's not going to start praying for guidance?

"I have to tell someone," Odeta prompts.

"Of course. Yes." Youthful Dave must be at least ten years older than her, yet she is weighted down with years.

"I'll call the police," he says, his head bobbing manically.

"Wait – I have card." She hurries up to her room and finds the card with DC Robson's contact details in the drawer of the bedside cabinet.

"Here." She clatters back down the stairs and thrusts it at Dave, who's still bending forward with his head bowed. He jolts to attention (perhaps he really was praying), takes the card and retreats to his fish-tank office. Odeta paces the tiled lobby while he makes the call. What is he saying to DC Robson? Doesn't he believe her?

But the police believe her. Two officers arrive within thirty minutes, but DC Robson isn't with them. Reluctantly, Dave vacates his office for the officers. Even with the door shut, it's noisy. It's the time of day when bored residents congregate in the hallway and lounge waiting to be called to supper. They mooch around, rarely making eye contact with one another. Kate said to her, "It's important to talk to girls of your own age. Find someone you trust – help each other." But Odeta can't do it. She doesn't want to hear about horrors they've been through; her own burden is too heavy to carry. She talks to Kate and to the counsellor who comes to see her, but she never wants to talk to other girls. It's in the past.

"I'll be out here if you need me," says Dave, with a hopeful smile, as he carries an armful of files from his office and parks himself on a wooden chair where visitors usually wait. "Anything I can get you?"

"Water please, sir," says the younger officer, who's female with flame-red hair that Odeta can't take her eyes off.

Dave nods, and fetches a glass jug of water and three plastic beakers.

"Thank you, sir." She holds the door open and ushers him out of his own office.

The male police officer is on the phone. "Where's the interpreter?" He looks across at his colleague. "Bloody useless. Asked them half an hour ago."

Odeta hopes it won't be the man from Stanmore. Maybe Kate could come? She doesn't speak Albanian but she seems to understand what Odeta's trying to say. But Kate lives far away and has her own family problems.

"I can try without," she suggests.

The male officer looks dubious, but flips open his notebook and clears his throat. "Okay, let's make a start. See how we get on. We can always get one on the phone."

They have copies of the statement she made previously to DC Robson, but they don't seem to have read it. "Just take it slowly and tell us everything in your own words."

For the umpteenth time, Odeta searches for words to tell them what she witnessed on the night of Kreshnik's murder: how she tried to save him, and how Tomas put his body in the bag and slung it into the van. "They treat him worse than animal."

The two officers nod solemnly, and the red-haired female gives her a sympathetic smile.

"You got those photos?" asks her colleague.

She nods, reaches into her bag and produces a tablet computer. After tapping in a few characters, she angles the screen towards Odeta. A couple of swipes bring up the two shots of the back and side of Kreshnik's head, the same ones she saw on television. The officer stretches the screen to give her a close-up view of the clothes he was wearing.

"He was wearing only one shoe," says the male police officer.

"I know." She nods, remembering how she cradled his shoe until Stephan snatched it away.

He looks at her sharply, as if he doesn't believe her, leans across his colleague and taps the screen.

"Oh!" The female officer gasps, clamps a hand over her mouth and turns her head away. "Sorry." Too late. She slams the cover closed, but Odeta's already glimpsed the picture they didn't want her to see: nibbled flesh, bone, and an eye socket, black and empty.

"Excuse." She leaps up, runs out to the cloakroom and throws up in the toilet bowl.

When she returns, still trembling, the interpreter has arrived. It's a woman called Anna, not the man from Stanmore.

Anna shakes her hand. "I understand you've had a shock. Have some water."

Odeta nods, and takes a sip from the yellow beaker.

"They want you to confirm this man's identity, if you are able."

"It's Kreshnik. Kreshnik Kaleci."

The officer makes a note and says something to the interpreter.

"They want to know how you can be certain."

She is certain: that bag, those clothes – who else could it be? "Let me look at photo again. One with clothes."

They flip up the photo showing the view of Kreshnik's torso, up to the neck. He's wearing an open-necked shirt and no tie, but nestling in the hollow of his throat is a silver pendant. She jabs at it with her finger and says to Anna. "See that?"

Anna peers at the grainy photo. "Is that a St Christopher?"

Odeta nods. "Was mine – gift from my friend, Ariana, when I left home." She pauses as a shiver runs along her spine to her neck. Her hands tremble. Soon her whole body is shaking. Anna takes her hand and holds it loosely. "Take your time, Odeta."

"St Christopher did not help me at all. Before Kreshnik died, I put it on him. Perhaps it help him in place he is going to."

"We need to contact his family in Albania," the officer says to Anna. "Ask her if she has an address?"

"Odeta, do you have his family's address?"

"No. I never went there." What, after all, does she know of Kreshnik or his family? Did he really have a wife, as Tomas had said? She shudders, but she doesn't believe that he was married. Tomas was lying. She and Kreshnik were together, and happy, for three months in Albania – and she has paid for that happiness with six months of her own life.

"Okay." The officer sighs and puts down his pen. "We'll get on to the Missing Persons Unit to see if he's been reported. With his full name it shouldn't be too difficult to track the family down. Now we need to ask you more questions about the man you said stabbed this Kreshnik." He glances at his notebook. "Thomas."

"Tomas."

And so it goes on, and on, round and round. Questions she's answered many times before. "Where did he go each day? Who did he see? What were the names of his associates or acquaintances other than Stephan?"

Ten minutes, twenty, half an hour. Her head is spinning. She turns to Anna. "I have told everything. Everything I know."

"Okay. We'll wrap it up there. But there's some other stuff we need to go through. Do you need a short break?"

Outside in the hall, Dave gets to his feet and peers hopefully in through the glass wall of his office. Odeta grimaces, lifts her hands and turns to Anna, who says, "A coffee?"

Odeta shakes her head. "Let them go on until they finish. Then I will have coffee."

The officer signals to his female colleague. "DC Young, do you have that other file?"

"Yes, sir." She taps more commands onto the tablet and pulls up a page with some sort of checklist. She runs her finger down the list, clears her throat and speaks to Anna. "This wasn't the first body that's been found dumped there." She points at a line in the list. "On May 31st last year, the body of a young woman was found at the same tip."

"Did you understand?" asks Anna.

Odeta nods, and braces herself for more horror as DC Young pulls up a photo on the screen and slides the tablet across the table towards her. She and Anna bend forward to look at it, their heads so close that Anna's blonde hair brushes Odeta's cheek. Odeta blinks. It's a picture of a statue, marble-white, with blank staring eyes. A dead fish on a slab would have more expression. The stone-blind eyes freak her out.

She straightens her back. "That is not a woman. That is sculpture from museum."

"Yeah," agrees the officer. "Not much left of her when she was found. Had to use computer imaging to reconstruct what she might have looked like from the skull. Reckon she was a looker."

DC Young grimaces.

Odeta's head reels. Is there no end to these horrors? "That's me," she says, gasping for breath. Everything is clear; bright as the noon sun. She's up in the sky, looking down on an aerial view of her own death. This is where she was heading.

"You mean that could have been you if you hadn't escaped?" says DC Young, pouring more water into Odeta's glass.

"Sorry, I do not understand," says Anna, looking from Odeta to the officers.

They fill her in on brief details of Odeta's story from the earlier part of the interview she missed. Anna turns to Odeta with a smile of encouragement.

"They are asking if you know this woman?"

Of course she knows who this woman is: it's her alter ego, Marije Kaleci. But she doesn't have to say – she can make it stop.

She tells the truth. "I don't know her," she says. "I have never seen her before."

The novelty clock on Dave's office wall signals seven o'clock in the evening with a burst of nightingale song. The police officers exchange a glance.

"Okay." DC Young looks disappointed, but she nods and snaps the cover over her tablet. The officers gather up their papers, express thanks, and exit in a whirlwind of brisk efficiency.

Anna lingers. Trains to Stanmore – or anywhere else – seem not to be a problem for her. "I'll come again and visit you, Odeta. Next week," she promises, smoothing her skirt down over her knees before getting to her feet. She gives Odeta a quick hug and heads for the door, her high heels tapping on the black and white floor tiles.

Odeta's missed supper, but she's not hungry. Images of Kreshnik and Marije loop endlessly in her head. The police are not interested in Kreshnik or Marije; it's Tomas they want. He should be brought to justice, but after he's gone, there will be other men just like him. Men who see women as rubbish to be used and discarded on a refuse tip. But she has the power to scrub him out. With every passing day, Tomas is fading from her memory. She scarcely recalls what he looked like.

But she can't blank out Kreshnik. His face haunts her still.

CHAPTER FORTY-SIX

It's Saturday, and Ben is out with his father. Nick has moved out of Ceri's and is staying in an attic flat belonging to a work colleague. While she waits for her son to return, Kate thinks how traditions run deep in families. Odeta's parents plan to educate their sons and marry off their daughter. But her own family is traditional, too. She's always accepted that her brother Gareth would inherit the farm; he's slaved on it most of his life while she escaped to the city. What if she wanted to go back to the village and start over again so Ben could have a simpler life, within a close-knit community?

She puts the final touch to her *Life Offline* article – she's already decided this will be her last – and glances out of the window as Nick's car pulls up outside.

"Hi, Mum!" Ben races in, dropping his anorak on the floor.

She smiles as she bends to pick it up. "Did you have a good day?"

"Yeah. But you said Dad and I could have an hour on the Xbox when I came home."

"Sure. I'll make you a snack." Kate's bowed to an unspoken agreement with Nick that she won't stop Ben from using technology any longer. After a six-month break, he seems less fixated with all things Xbox and Internet, and no longer flies into a rage if she tries to unplug him. Playing alongside his dad soothes him. She watches them chatting, discussing tactics. Ben is fluent and animated, no longer scared of making eye contact.

Before the hour is up Ben scrambles to his feet and high-fives her on his way to watch *The X Factor* in the sitting room. She moves Ben's plate from the floor to the table. "Drink?" she asks Nick, opening the fridge door and offering a beer.

He hesitates, shuffling his feet, pulling his fleece off the back of the chair and starting to put it on.

"Don't go." She puts the bottle down on the table, unopened, and touches his arm. He turns to look at her, his eyebrows lifting in a question.

"Nick, I admit I was wrong." She scans his face for some wavelength to connect to. "Experiment's over, okay? I've just completed my final article and told Veronica this is the last."

Veronica's enthusiasm for *Life Offline* began to dwindle when Kate turned down the approach from Carl, the television producer. Kate never told Nick about the offer. She's glad she didn't have to.

"I was rash to take Ben's mobile away. It affected his safety. But you have to admit banning computer games for six months has helped him to come out of his shell. That, and, of course, Woody."

Nick picks up a fork and pushes Ben's leftovers around his plate. "So, tell me, Kate – what d'you think is wrong with him? You go on about it all the time, yet you refuse to have him tested. He seems fine to me. Bit geeky, slow to make friends, but that will come."

"I don't want him labelled."

"If it is Asperger's – so what? It's not the end of the world."

"I just wanted us both to help him be the rounded person

he's meant to be." She lowers her eyes and stares at the kitchen worktop. Silvery specks in the black granite seem to be winking at her. She grips the cool edge of the butler sink to steady herself while she fills a glass with water, hand trembling as she lifts it to her mouth, and turns to face him. "Are you going to come back home?"

There, she's done it – woken the elephant in the room. Her heart lurches as she waits for him to reply.

Perhaps he noticed her tears, because he slips his arms out of his fleece, leans back in his chair and says, "I'll have that beer now."

CHAPTER FORTY-SEVEN

Odeta's case worker arranges for her to enrol at a gym, and her days fall into a pattern. Working out on sleek treadmills, watching buff guys lifting weights, and feeling the floor of the fitness centre vibrate under pounding background music, the fog that has held her in limbo slowly lifts. She recreates familiar exercises from her gymnast days and tries out a floor routine in the cramped warm-up area. Her leg muscles strengthen, and her lungs expand as oxygen replaces choking dread.

Her fitness instructor pushes her to achieve more. "You've got talent, Odeta. If you get permission to stay in the country, you could take a course to become a personal trainer."

Her brain is swimming with new possibilities, but it's hard to think of the future when she's still shackled by the past.

Some instinct tugs her back towards the fringes of Soho to look for the place she pointed out to the police when they drove her round in their patrol car. She won't travel by Tube. She won't go underground. Not ever. The thought of speeding through a dark tunnel beneath the city sparks palpitations. She takes the bus and alights near Leicester Square, then strides north, weaving through streets of restaurants and tacky shops, until she finds the Chinese restaurant. She stares into the window pretending to be admiring the parrot's green feathers, postponing the moment when she'll look across the road at the sign on the wall that says *Beauty Spa.*

She takes a deep breath and turns round. The sign is still there, but the pink neon light is switched off and the first-floor windows are blacked out. She crosses the road and works out which entrance leads up to the salon, but the door has been boarded up and padlocked.

Below the salon, at street level, is a bookshop. The books displayed in its window look old and used, with faded covers like the textbook and dictionary she left behind when she and Kate fled. She misses that book. Dick, his mother and Nip were familiar friends in those dark times.

It starts to rain. It's always raining in this country. One moment the sun is shining, the next huge grey clouds come barrelling across the sky. Raindrops splosh on the pavement all around her. Today she's left the blue sweater for washing, and is wearing a blouse with a lace collar and a linen jacket. She's put on some make-up and washed her hair, but she doesn't have an umbrella. She noticed a café, tucked away in a side street, so she pulls her jacket over her head and runs towards it.

Entering a café on her own robs her of all the progress she's made in spoken English. Although the café has table service, she queues at the counter, points to what she wants and pays in advance.

As always, she chooses a window table, close to the door, and watches passers-by dodging puddles and weaving in and out of doorways to avoid the rain. A fly is buzzing against the inside of the window, flinging its body against the pane. The thought that she can get up and walk out of this café whenever she wants makes her feel giddy. She pulls out a small mirror and checks her face. Her skin is improving: there's a hint of colour in her cheeks and her eyes are clear. She doesn't notice a man in a greasy leather jacket enter the café until he pulls up the chair opposite her. "Mind if I sit here?"

There are plenty of empty tables, and, yes, she does mind – but she shrugs and focuses on her coffee, swirling it round in the cup and sipping slowly to make it last.

The man keeps staring at her. He has a young face, but his hair, pulled back into a pony tail, is already turning grey. His coffee arrives and he strikes up a conversation. "Where are you from?"

She glances at him but she doesn't smile. Maybe she'll never smile again; her missing tooth, even though it's quite far round to the side, makes her look like an old crone. Kate has promised to take her to the dentist to have it fixed, but for now it reminds her every day that she's damaged.

"Albania," she replies, wishing she'd lied and said Greece.

"Cool. Have you ever thought of a career in modelling?"

There's a scream that lives inside Odeta's head, crouching out of sight. Now the scream struggles to escape. She fumbles with the straps of her bag and leaps up from her seat so rapidly that the table tilts and sends the man's hot coffee sliding into his lap. He might even think she did it accidentally.

Without looking behind, she flees the café. Her body is trembling, but not with fear – with laughter. She feels confident and strong, but she doesn't want that man to follow her. A few doors along is a boutique. Normally she wouldn't dare cross such a smart threshold, but today she strides inside and rifles through a rack of summer frocks.

A shop assistant approaches her, slim and brisk with a painted-on smile. "Can I help you?"

Odeta stands very still, holding a green and black cotton dress on its hanger.

"You wanna try that on?" asks the assistant, checking the label inside the dress. "It's a ten." She measures Odeta with an expert eye. "Should fit you just fine."

Odeta nods. The dress fabric has a slight sheen, and feels soft when she strokes it. Anyone would look beautiful in that dress. Even her.

"Follow me." The blonde assistant takes the dress from her and Odeta traipses behind her to a small room, with a curtain over the entrance: a cubicle. For a second Odeta freezes, but when she slides the curtain back it's nothing like the one in the Beauty Spa. It has carpet, a full-length mirror, soft lighting and a comfortable chair. The assistant hangs the dress on a hook and hands her a pair of stilettos. "Use these to check the length is right."

She withdraws, swishing the curtain shut behind her. "Ring the bell if you need another size."

The armchair is upholstered in soft pink velvet. Odeta's feet are aching and she sits down, thinking she could curl up in here and stay for ever, comfortable and safe. She feels inside her bag for her other lifeline, Kate's latest gift: a Pay-As-You-Go mobile phone. Kate's topped it up with plenty of credit, and Odeta charges it every night. She never wants to be without a phone again, but apart from Kate and her counsellor, she has no one to call.

She remembers how desperate Kate felt when she thought she'd lost Ben. How would her parents feel if Leon or Afrim went missing? *But I'm their child too. Perhaps, even after all this time, they are still worrying?* The changing room mirror illuminates her face; in the warm glow of the lighting her skin looks flawless, but her eyes have the sorrowful look of an ancient soul.

"How are you getting on in there?" asks the shop assistant from the other side of the curtain.

"Good, yes, good," she replies. The silky green dress waits on its hanger, and she continues cradling her phone.

On autopilot, she punches in the dialling code for Albania and the number of the shop. There's a long silence, followed by a fractured beep that seems to go on forever. Her stomach churns. She's on the edge of panic, about to cancel the call. Then someone picks up the phone and she hears his voice.

Do her parents love her, despite everything, as Kate suggested? There's only one way to find out.

"Dad?" she whispers, hoarsely. "Dad. Is that you?"

The line isn't crackly at all. It's crystal clear. She can hear his rattling smoker's breathing perfectly.

"Eh? Who is that?" His voice creaks like a door when the hinges need oiling.

"Dad – it's Odeta."

THE END

ACKNOWLEDGEMENTS

Huge thanks to Bloodhound Books for publishing this new edition of Girl Out of Sight. Originally published in 2017 under the title After Leaving the Village, it won first prize in the opening pages of a novel category at Winchester Writers' Festival. A lightly revised second edition with the current title Girl Out of Sight was published by Darkstroke Books in 2022.

I'm grateful to everyone in the Bloodhound Books team especially Betsy Reavley, Tara Lyons and Hannah Deuce.

Thanks also to my brilliant author friends in Oxford Narrative Writers and Ark Writers, and my talented critique buddies, Katharine Johnson and Jane Risdon for unwavering support.

This is a crime novel and entirely fictional but it was endorsed by the anti-slavery charity Unseen UK for raising awareness of the hideous crime of human trafficking. I'm proud that Unseen has appointed me as an Ambassador to support their mission of working towards a world without slavery. I donate a percentage of my royalties, and fees I receive for author talks, to the charity. If your book club would like to read my novel and learn more about modern slavery, please get in touch.

When I visited Albania to fact check my research for this book, I was privileged to spend time with a local family. I'm acutely aware that much about that fascinating country is unknowable to an outsider so any remaining errors in the book are mine.

Thanks to my family for their unstinting support: my husband, Alan; my children, Alex, Bronwen and their partners, and my sister, Fran.

ABOUT THE AUTHOR

Helen Matthews writes page-turning psychological suspense novels and is fascinated by the darker side of human nature and how a life can change in an instant. Three novels, shortly to be re-released by Bloodhound Books, include *The Girl in the Van*, suspense and thriller genre winner in the 2022 Pageturner Book Award, *Girl Out of Sight* and *Façade* (family noir). She was previously published by Darkstroke Books. Her domestic suspense novel *Lies Behind the Ruin,* set in France, and a collection of short stories *Brief Encounters* are available from Amazon.

Born in Cardiff, Helen read English at the University of Liverpool and worked in international development, consultancy, human resources and pensions management. She fled corporate life to work freelance while studying for a Creative Writing MA. Her stories and flash fiction have been shortlisted and published by Flash 500, 1000K Story, Reflex Press, Artificium and Love Sunday magazine.

She is a keen cyclist, covering long distances if there aren't any hills, sings in a choir and once appeared on stage at Carnegie Hall, New York in a multi-choir performance. She loves spending time in France. Helen is an Ambassador for the charity, Unseen, which works towards a world without slavery and donates all of her author talk fees, and a percentage of royalties, to the charity.

Find out more at:

https://www.helenmatthewswriter.com
https://www.twitter.com/HelenMK7
https://www.Instagram.com/helen.matthews7
https://Facebook.com/HelenMK7Writer

A NOTE FROM THE PUBLISHER

Thank you for reading this book. If you enjoyed it please do consider leaving a review on Amazon to help others find it too.

We hate typos. All of our books have been rigorously edited and proofread, but sometimes mistakes do slip through. If you have spotted a typo, please do let us know and we can get it amended within hours.

info@bloodhoundbooks.com